Child Ellen

PRENTICE-

Child Ellen

by

FRANK TRIPPETT

HALL, INC. *Englewood Cliffs, New Jersey*

Child Ellen by Frank Trippett
Copyright © 1975 by Frank Trippett

Prentice-Hall International, Inc., London
Prentice-Hall of Australia, Pty. Ltd., Sydney
Prentice-Hall of Canada, Ltd., Toronto
Prentice-Hall of India Private Ltd., New Delhi
Prentice-Hall of Japan, Inc., Tokyo

10 9 8 7 6 5 4 3 2 1

Library of Congress Cataloging in Publication Data

Trippett, Frank.
Child Ellen.

I. Title.
PZ4.T839Ch   [PS3570.R55]   813'.5'4   74–30088
ISBN 0–13–130757–6

Designed by Carl A. Koenig and Janet Anderson

For John, Bess, Bob, Nan

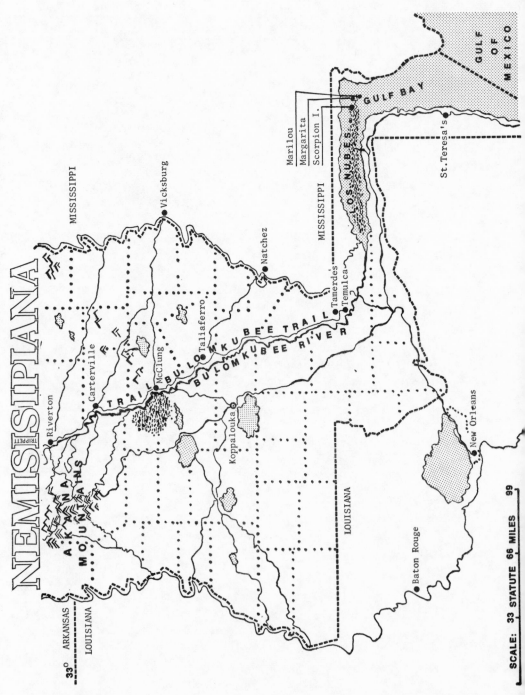

NEMISSIPIANA

MISSISSIPPI

ARKANSAS
LOUISIANA
33°

TRIPPETT

Riverton

Carterville

A K T A N A S
M O U N T A I N S

McClung

T R A I L   B U L O   M K U B E E   T R A I L

B U L O M K U B E E   R I V E R

Vicksburg

Natchez

Taliaferro

Koppalouka

LOUISIANA

Baton Rouge

New Orleans

Tamerdes
Temulca

MISSISSIPPI

L O S   N U B E S

Marilou
Margarita
Scorpion I.

GULF BAY

St. Teresa's

GULF
OF
MEXICO

SCALE: 33 STATUTE 66 MILES

99

FORENOTE

Unfortunately our mapmakers have left us—some of us—in darkness about the primary locale of the following story. I do not intend to waste time cursing that darkness. I prefer to light a candle: hence the map opposite.

There sprawls the pertinent region. Its primordial tenants, the Lomkubee Indians, called it AMAOMANTA. The white man who appropriated and corrupted the land appropriated and corrupted its ancient name as well. Nemisisipiana is what he came to call the place.

Not even the conquering white man could change its location. It is of course situated between Mississippi on the east and, on the west, Louisiana and Arkansas. The map, even though it fully documents this elementary fact, is intended to be not definitive but sufficient.

It indicates the state's main political jurisdictions and the outstanding geographic features. There in the northwest are the Akana Mountains. Waters flowing out of them form the Bulomkubee River. It runs the length of Nemisisipiana, spilling at last into the estuary of the southeast. There the mingled waters of the Gulf and several rivers wash among the innumerable islands that form the distinct locale known as Los Nubes. Further south is the bay, and on its west bank is the sunny and airy city of St. Teresa's along with a stretch of beaches and other smaller communities omitted from the map in the interest of clarity.

In these and many other places are to be found Ellen and the other people of this account. Most of them were born and grew up in or about McClung. It is situated there by the Bulomkubee in the very heartland of the state. The map, naturally, does not show these people. To see them one must go to the place itself.

FRANK TRIPPETT
Doubloon's Inn
St. Teresa's

LISTEN WITH REVERENCE TO THE

SILENT SINGING OF THE STARS.

THEY SAY THAT WE ARE

NOTHING AND EVERYTHING.

From the Credo of the Lomkubees

BOOK I

1940-41
Winter

——I——

In the end, she had decided that, yes, she would go, but once there, she still wondered why. She sat wondering as the little world that surrounded her struggled against disintegration, or seemed to.

Familiar forms were segmented, vivisected by the whirling, racing, darting, multicolored lightspots. Frantic sound filled the cavernous armory—babble and clank and tinkle and hooting and hungry laughter and brassy, thumping music. All together it seemed to fill the vast room as breath fills a toy balloon to some critical tension beyond which it must burst.

It seemed an ocean of sound in which they were submerged. The patternless commotion of bodies jostling and dancing and milling was like the flick, flash, and float of exotic marine life on the floor of the sea, the lightspots an exploded spectrum come down from an unseen sun.

At their table in the inner circle of hundreds that formed a crude horseshoe about the dance floor, she felt distinct, insular,

3

bewildered by the inchoate hubbub. At the same time she felt expectant, enlivened by some obscure unreasoned prescience or premonition. She was puzzled. Why was she there? She thought, *It must be for something.*

At moments she had felt very tiny, walled off from the crowd, alien to these people, most of whom she knew well, old and young. She who would soon be sixteen, and who was one of only a few so young in the room, had oddly felt older than all of them at one point. And then she had grown almost dizzy in her walled-off place, had felt as though she were plummeting, or about to. She had felt an eerie loss of volition, had felt not lost but as though she were about to become lost, as though she might, in the dissolving moment at hand, cease to be who she was.

And at that moment, as though it might slip away, as though retrieving it, she had actually summoned her name to mind and murmured it to herself: Ellen Emily Worth.

Then, as though at a great joke, she had burst out laughing, at herself, and to herself—and finally, by chance, to the puzzlement and pleasure of her companions Horris and Claudette, who at that instant returned to the table from the dance floor it abutted. T.C. and Claudette Horris were both twenty-seven.

"Ellen, what on earth is so funny?" said Claudette in an accent that betrayed and even celebrated her French nativity.

"Nothing much," said Ellen, letting her laugh gasp out. "Or maybe everything. I don't know."

"Anyway, are you glad I bullied you into coming?" said Horris. He mopped a patina of sweat from his hairless, globular head, taking the chair to her right while Claudette, sheathed in lavender, sat facing them both from Ellen's left.

"I'm glad you asked me," said Ellen. "It was worth coming just to see you in a shirt with a collar."

"That begs my question," said Horris.

"Nonsense!" said Claudette. "It is answer enough. And now, champagne, *s'il vous plait*. M. Hawrees, pour!" Claudette took up a silver cardboard hat from an assortment on the table and fixed it on her head, tilted just above the forehead.

"Maybe I ought to wait," Ellen said, as Horris poured. "I can still taste the wine I had for supper."

"Drown the old wine with the new," Claudette said.

"And the new with the old," said Horris.

"Papa asked me if we were going to celebrate the year just past or the one we don't know anything about yet," Ellen said.

"And you said—?" Horris asked.

"I said, 'Papa, please pass the fish.' Horris, you know coherent conversations are against the law at Papa's table." Ellen raised the glass that Horris had just filled. "Anyway," she said, beginning to laugh again, "happy something or the other!"

"Bon voyage!" said Claudette.

"Pass the fish!" said Horris, drily. He sipped, leaned back and extended a paternal arm around the back of Ellen's chair, and with his glass pointed toward the bandstand, where, amidst the musicians of the band that had been imported for the dance, a tall, lean, dark-haired schoolmate named Henry Rust was sitting curved intently over his guitar, Horris said: "What do you think of Henry being up there with the pros?"

"I'm impressed," said Ellen. "I only wish we could hear him."

"What did you say?" said Horris, turning toward her and cupping an ear.

"I said I only wish we could hear him," Ellen shouted, and again collapsed in a laugh that she quickly controlled, and took another sip of champagne.

"Horris, tell me," said Claudette, "don't you think it's surprising Henry is playing tonight after what happened?"

Horris flicked a peeved look toward his wife as though wishing to censor her question, grunting some inaudible response as he looked back toward the bandstand, toward Henry Rust.

Ellen, perplexed, glanced from Horris to Claudette to Horris. "So what happened?" she said to Horris, and to Claudette, "What do you mean?"

Horris put his arm about her chair again and leaned close to avoid the need to talk loud. He said: "They just got word last night that Henry's old man died."

"Ooooooooooh!" Ellen said, her face gathering in a somber knit. "Oh, that's awful! How did it happen? I mean, was it—"

"Well, I don't think they know for sure. Pneumonia, maybe, but—when I called the house, Portia, Mrs. Rust—well, she was about as vague as usual."

"Mr. Rust never came here, did he?" Ellen asked.

"Not much. Now and then. Not recently," Horris said.

"Was he old? Was pneumonia—" Ellen said.

"Forty-three, I believe," Horris said.

"Oh, that's just awful," Ellen said. "Claudette, I feel like you. I wonder how he could feel like being up there playing. If it happened to me, I—I—"

"Well, Ellen, who knows? Maybe it makes more sense to—" Horris abruptly dropped his sentence when Claudette broke in.

"Come now, you two," Claudette said, "I shouldn't have mentioned it. Let's talk about other things."

"It's all right," Ellen said. She smiled, but barely.

And now Horris popped to his feet and invited Ellen to hers. "Let's go, Dumpling," he said, and, bowing to Claudette, went on: "I hope you won't grieve in our absence, *mon cheri.*"

As Ellen stood by, Horris grabbed from the table a cardboard hat of shiny blue with silver stars and centered it on his hairless head, drawing the elastic string under his chin. "I can be as depraved as the next fellow," he said, and took up another hat that he handed to Ellen—a squat, cylindrical pillbox with vertical stripes of red, green, and blue. "Pop it on, Dumpling," he ordered.

"You don't mean it," said Ellen, regarding the hat with a wry smile.

"Ellen, now you heard our President say we've got to be the great arsenal for democracy, and what that means, in translation, is get in the uniform of the day. Pop it on, or else the enemy may overrun us."

Horris led her deftly, holding her at talking distance. He, at five-seven, was only an inch taller than she.

"Ellen, you don't know Henry except in passing, do you?"

"I guess so. I know him, but—no, I don't guess real well."

"Let's don't assume he's not grieving just because he's sitting up there. Okay?"

"Oh, no, I won't. I know."

"He sure has started to take that music seriously, hasn't he?"

"Fanatic. He takes Carol Burcell pretty seriously, too. At school you see 'em together every day. And Matt and Mark—" Ellen trailed off from an intent to quote her older twin brothers.

"Matt and Mark what?" Horris said.

"Oh, nothing," Ellen said, but smiled a tilted smile at what she had remembered.

"There they are. Now, by God, they're in the spirit of things!"

"Aren't they always?" Ellen said. "Or more than in the spirit of things. Horris, they've got everything but a sense of proportion."

"Well said," Horris said.

Matt and Mark were sitting at a crowded interior table not far from where they were dancing by. They were conspicuously tall when standing and were conspicuous now even while sitting asprawl, highly visible with their almost indistinguishable long, mobile faces and tousled heads of brown hair. Each sprawled in his chair with an arm draped about the shoulders of his date. They looked exuberant, were no doubt already tight, and doubtless growing loud.

Spotting Ellen, Matt and Mark let their faces explode into maniacal grins. They waved preposterously as though seeing her for the first time, even though they had swarmed all around her when she had first showed up, and they yelled something that got lost in the general uproar. Ellen laughed, brimming with a warm, pulsing bloodreach.

"Now I know you're glad you came," Horris said.

"Yeah, I'm glad." Suddenly she laughed and added: "Strangely enough."

Only with great reluctance had Ellen decided to go. She had turned down the invitations of two not steady but dependable boy-friends. She had stubbornly held out against her brothers' insistence that she come along with their party, either alone or with an escort they would enlist according to her specifications. And only the day before, finally, she had squirmed away from a downright plea from their neighbor Percy Ensley that she go along as the date of his cousin who had unexpectedly come over from Louisiana.

Ordinarily, she would have done anything to help out Percy Ensley, a friend of hers as well as a crony of her brothers. But not this time. She had retreated from Percy's plea with a reference to other plans.

"What other plans?" Mark had demanded of her that afternoon.

"My plans," Ellen had said.

"Ellen, what the hell's the matter?" Matt had demanded.

"With my plans?" she had said.

"Now, Dumpling, don't bullshit us. We want to know what's happening to you," Mark had said.

They had found her sitting on the front steps at home, an immense and historic frame house offering continuous porches or galleries on all four sides at both the first floor and the second. They had found her on the front steps but, at her evasiveness, had taken her prisoner in their way. Older than Ellen by fifteen months and, at their father's height of six-three, taller than she by nine full inches, they had lifted her between them, and had carried her kicking to the southside porch where a swing hung suspended from the uncommonly high ceiling.

"Let's swing," they had said, as one, and had wedged her in the seat between them.

"Goddamit, let me go," she had said, as they set the swing flying with thrusts of their feet.

They took it higher and higher as they confronted her with their concern, and no doubt exasperation, too, over the mood into which she had seemed bogged down in recent days, or weeks, or even months, since it had begun in October after she had found Mr. Sorrel's lifeless body.

Soon Matt and Mark were almost kicking the ceiling as the swing flew forward, and at the apex of its backward sweep it seemed that all three of their heads of wildly blowing dark curly hair would smash into the planking above.

In years past the twins had many times fetched her out of some sour mood with what they called The Swing Treatment. But now, as they gained altitude, Ellen protested the indignity with fire.

"You can't do this to me," she yelled. "I'm not a goddam child any more."

"We want to know what's wrong," said Matt.

"You haven't been like yourself," said Mark.

"For weeks," said Matt.

"For months," said Mark.

"Years!" yelled Ellen, clinging to their arms as the swing flew higher and higher, gasping each time it plummeted into a new oscillation. "Years!—I haven't been—like myself—for years!—Don't you remember?—What the hell—am I like—anyway?—Do I have—a goddam label—with ingredients—and directions—and all that?—That you can see—but I can't?—Come on, Dr. Freud—and Dr. Jung—stop the goddam swing—and tell me—what I'm like—Come on—read my label—smartasses!"

"You're fun," yelled Matt at the rocketing top of the back flight.

"You're funny," yelled Mark as the swing plunged toward the floor.

"Oh, shit, stop it!" yelled Ellen.

"You're beautiful," yelled Matt as they gaped precipitately down toward the deck.

"You're witty," yelled Mark as they hurtled upward toward the ceiling.

"Vivacious," said Matt.

"Friendly," said Mark.

"Helpful."

"Courteous."

"Kind."

"Et cetera."

"You sit your horse well."
"You're sexy."
"You have a shirt full of goodies."
"You turn a neat phrase."
"You paint a neat picture."
"You swat a mean tennis ball."
"You swim like a fish."
"You dance like a moonbeam."
"You smile like a sunbeam."
"Your abundant curls are gorgeous."
"Your blue eyes are the envy of all womankind."
"You seethe with the milk of human kindness."
"And have the eye of an eagle."
"With the heart of a lion."
"The leg of a doe."
"The grace of a dove."
"And the charm of Helen."
"And the freshness of Eve."
"Ellen, you raise songs in the hearts of men."
"And mad yearning in their loins."
"Also, you're cute," said Matt.
"And bring home good grades," said Mark.

Now she was laughing and gasping, and they were letting the swing die down.

"You're the dumpling of your father's eye," said Matt.
"The first hope and pride of the family," said Mark.
"If I weren't your brother I would take you as my bride."
"But only over my dead body."
"Goddamit, you're our sister."
"Goddamit, you're Ellen."
"Only you haven't been acting like Ellen for weeks."
"Months."
"Years!" said Ellen. "Remember? Years, years, years!"
"You've been too quiet," said Matt.
"Too much alone," said Mark.
"Too sorrowful."
"At Christmas you seemed almost sad."
"And now at New Year's you're withdrawing."
"You're acting like someone in mourning."
"Mourning!?" Ellen shouted. She took a sliding leap out of the swing that had now slowed toward stopping. She had leaped and whirled about to confront them, a furious figure crouching as for an

attack, legs sheathed in beige jeans and her torso and chest lost in an oversized yellow pullover. "I'm not in mourning!" she shouted. "Just because I'm thinking about things you think I'm in mourning? Don't you two ever think about anything?"

"Think?" said Mark.

"Sure, we think all the time," said Matt.

"Yeah, but what do you ever think about? All you ever think about is getting in some girl's britches."

"Not so," said Mark.

"In fact, just awhile ago we were thinking about getting drunk tomorrow night," said Matt.

"Oh, shit," said Ellen.

"Now, wait a minute, Dumpling," said Mark. "If you stop to think right now, for just a second, you'll remember that what we're thinking about right now is you."

"Oh, shit, I know it," she had said. And had burst into tears.

And they had gotten up from the swing and hugged her, and one of them had issued her a soft command to take a walk before supper.

She had walked away from the house and toward the river in the greengold light of the late afternoon. The winter had been mild and the holidays particularly so, almost like early spring except for the sharper smoke-bitten fragrances.

She ambled across the back grounds, going away from the house in which she and Matt and Mark had been born, in which their aging Papa Sam Worth still presided with earthy insouciance, and in which her Mama, Emily Boisseau Worth, had died on a greengold day in December five years before, had died at age thirty-four of the ravaging disease that had first shown itself in China when they had stopped there on the last stage of their trip around the world. She had walked toward the river half a mile west of the house, thinking: *Mourning?*

Ellen passed by a helter-skelter woodpile, a chicken yard, a fenced vegetable garden with a hothouse in one corner and a weathered old privy in another. She passed amidst numerous prowling cats and others that were dozing, went by an arbor of muscadine vines, a wire pen within which seven hunting dogs were already sniffing impatiently for their feeding. She entered and exited a barn with a wing of stables adjoining, and passed among immense oaks and gums festooned with pendant graygreen moss. From two of the trees hung thick weathered ropes with rag-filled crocus sacks attached at the bottom.

She vaulted a low tilting fence enclosing a pasture in which four horses and five tan and white cows browsed. Through her teeth, she issued three shrill whistles. The horses started toward her. She raised a negating hand. The horses stopped, looking puzzled.

At the pasture's other side, she bent and climbed between loose strands of rusty barbed wire, and entered onto a worn path that snaked amidst brush and mixed hardwoods and pines and cedars, ascending gradually to the edge of the eighteen-foot bluff from which she had dived a million times into the river below, the old Bulomku-bee, and her brothers, too, who when they were young would impulsively drop off their overalls and send their naked bodies outward into the summer sun and the bluebrown waters below.

Downriver some several hundred feet was the mock Lomkubee village toward which she had peered for a moment, though it was out of sight, the circles of lean-to shelters that had been constructed as the set of the movie that Mr. Sorrel had finished last summer, that had excited the whole town and that she had watched him make for a year, almost, and that he who would never say anything for the public had called a masterpiece before leaving McClung, going he wouldn't say where while his wife went to Reno, going away to come back without a word to a soul, coming back in October a few days after the company had announced it was killing the film, coming back and leaving his brand new car at the road, locking the doors as if it mattered, locking it up as maybe he always locked up himself, and walking through those woods that were like nothing he had seen as a boy in the city and that he said he had come to love as though he were a Lomkubee himself, walking through the woods in those shoes he had had hand-customed in London, and that he wore with the khakis Horris got him at J.C. Penney's downtown, walking through the trees and then out into the village that he had had built but that had come to seem so real at moments with the Lomkubees he had brought up from the preserve in Temulca, walking alone among the lean-tos with the notes in his pocket, thinking . . . *What?*

Ellen had found him in the village center, had heard, in a season when gunshots were common, a particular *kapow* with a strangely particular sound, had heard it from a direction where none such was likely, had gone running, impelled by the strangest prescience. He lay askew with the top of his skull gaping. How had she *known* she would find him? Ben Ezra Sorrel: that intense, moody man some called a genius, who was so caustic and biting when he talked to others and so gentle and hesitant when he talked to her, who for some reason liked to talk to her even when he was refusing to talk to anybody else, who in his inscrutable way had paid her obscure compliments that at once puzzled and pleased and disturbed her, who had put the note to her in with the one to Horris, as though he wanted it delivered secretly by the only man he had left to respect: Horris, who had written or at least found and translated the story that had turned Mr. Sorrel's life inside out, and maybe ended it, down the river in that real unreal village.

Abruptly she had turned upriver, now briskly walking the roller-coaster riverside path toward the house where Horris lived, Horris and Claudette, the house half a mile distant that was the next north of theirs.

It was a breezy house with big screened porches that had been built by Horris's father on land that had been a gift of Ellen's Papa Sam Worth. Her Papa had reared the elder Horris from early boyhood, from the day in 1887 when Thomas Horris had simply wandered up to the plain farmhouse east of McClung, where Sam Worth was then still living with the first of three wives who in turn gave him children and then left him widowed.

Except in name, Thomas Horris had been like one of Sam Worth's own. He had grown up to make his living as a drummer, traveling about four states to sell encyclopedias of which he could, and sometimes would, recite immense chunks of text verbatim, a feat made possible by a phenomenal memory that he had passed on to his only offspring, Thomas Churchill Horris, whose mother Beth Churchill Horris had died at his birth. Sixteen years later, the elder Horris had died, bequeathing to T.C. Horris, not only his memory but the house on the river, $719.27 in debts, and 837 collarless shirts, size 15½–32, mixed patterns—all but a few of six gross shirts that Thomas Horris had once accepted from a textile manufacturer in payment for six sets of encyclopedias. He, the elder Horris, of whom Ellen owned only a shadowy recollection, had been the one who introduced her Papa to young Emily Boisseau, whom he had "discovered" in a library in New Orleans.

T.C. Horris was more than a close family friend, he was more like a kinsman. Within a year after her mother had died, Horris had come home from two Rhodes years in London and Paris with his French bride Claudette, had set up housekeeping, and, with Sam Worth's help, had bought the weekly McClung *Mirror*. Ellen, on her own, but without ever thinking of it that way, had gradually adopted them as ancillary parents. When her first menses had alarmed her, she had turned to Claudette, and any matter she couldn't take to her Papa or brothers, she freely carried to Horris.

She had found him with his hairless head, as usual, bent over the rapidly turning pages of a book, the fingers of one hand mindlessly searching about the neckline of his collarless striped shirt. Claudette, as usual, was slouching in jeans and a roomy pullover, a style Ellen was scarcely aware of directly emulating, and, as usual, was chattering away in French as Horris read, or tried to. For a while, they had talked about nothing much, but then finally the floodgates of her distress had come open.

"Why does everybody want me to go to the goddam dance?" she had blurted out. "Why would they say I'm in mourning? Am I in mourning if I just think about what's happening? Don't they pay any attention to what's happening in the world? Don't they know Paris is full of soldiers and London is burning down and the whole world is going to blow up? With the President and everybody talking about war and making the country an arsenal and everybody getting drafted and people even killing themselves and dying all the time and—"

And she had burst into tears again, and they had decided she should stay for supper and had called her house, and had then talked for a long time into the night. And Horris, to her surprise, had finally said that, yes, he also thought it would be a good idea for her to go to the dance. And that, in fact, he would expect her to go with Claudette and him as their guest, which would give her an excuse for not going with those she had turned down. And she had said, well, maybe.

And next morning, before she had actually said yes, Claudette had come by with the box, the present, the beautiful, pale yellow, calf-length gown and the matching satin pumps.

Funny thing, a fist fight was going on just as they had arrived at the armory, a moil of shouting, hooting youths encircling two or maybe more combatants just at the edge of the recently completed structure.

"What a bore!" said Claudette, sweeping into the door without a second glance at the rhubarb.

"Happy new year," said Ellen drily.

They had made their way along, nodding in response to greetings from friendly and familiar faces, and a few unfamiliar ones, and found their table, and Ellen, as she sat down, had felt overwhelmed by the hubbub, had wondered at the noise and reek of the place, the reverberant air shot through with a mingling of flowery perfumes and the soursweet reek of liquor and the acrid drift of smoke and the coarse fragrances of the lotions of men. She sat watching, too, the ubiquitous fleshquake, the mingled bodies, the fleshreach working in secret pelvic touches, the fleeting passage of hands across the peripheries of flexing haunches, some of it brazen but most of it sly, clandestine, as though it were evil instead of a hunger as natural as that for food. Watching, she became aware that Horris was watching her watching, and so turned to him with a satirical smile, holding silent when she saw that he was about to say something.

"Ladies," said Horris, glancing from her to Claudette to her, "did you know that during the Dark Ages when the plague swept Europe the revels of life went on amidst mountains of corpses?"

The old mothergone pang, as Horris called it, had come back, waned and come again and then receded once more as she had become submerged in the hubbub and the darting multicolored light-spots. Right away Matt and Mark had spotted her, had barged through the crowd towing their dates, had swarmed briefly about her, showering her with compliments and jibes, then had receded in a confused stir into the dancing couples, Matt quickly getting cut out and coming back to get her and launch her in the dancing. Percy Ensley had then cut in, and then that obnoxious college boy who thought his ass weighed a ton, drunk and aroused and trying to press his hard against her until she had abruptly extricated herself and gone back to the table, sweating and disconcerted, and had a moment alone to sip ginger ale and examine the crowd of friends and familiar strangers, their faces gaping or grinning or looking hungry or lost or cheery or angry under the absurd cardboard hats, faces and figures constantly whipped and fragmented by the darting, spiraling light-spots, coming and going among the dancers, table-hopping or tilting drinks.

She had seen Claude Atwell the dentist who habitually whistled but only with an insuck, Shorty Haines the mailman who collected everybody's foreign stamps, Annie Buckleman who in her husband's absence had gotten drunk and painted their bedroom, linens and all, George Appleman the electrician whose father had been tried and acquitted for his mother's death by shotgun, Doug Lenoir who would leave a customer waiting in his shoe store while he strolled down the street for a drink, Sidney Carter Fletcher who had been a preacher until his congregation fired him for claiming to have seen a vision, Connie Singleton whose skinny daughter Dora was said to read comic books while letting groups of boys fuck her, Nub Cachet who spent most nights in his woodwork shop, Frances Whitcomb the seamstress who at three had seen her drunk father tumble backwards down the stairs to his death, Maynard McComb the lawyer who could sometimes be seen sitting unperturbed under his banyan tree during fantastic thunderstorms, Bill Turnbull the hardware man who had committed his father to the asylum and banned his younger brother from their house, John Edgar Heever who at nineteen had grown chubby eating Post Toasties so he could get Junior G-Man stuff with the boxtops, Dr. Amos McCall the medical examiner who Horris said could autopsy a gnat while drunk and flub a tonsillectomy while sober, Stephen Cromwell, Jr., whose father had killed his wife with a 7 iron and himself with a .22 and who played dominoes all day long at the pool hall, and, among others, Tom Pickett who at six foot seven was the tallest boy in school, who had read practically everything in the world, who hauled scrap iron in his horse-drawn wagon, and who would say, when somebody asked him, "How's the weather up there?"—would say, "Why don't you crawl up my ass and see for yourself?"

She had scrutinized the band that had come up from New Orleans where her mother had been born and where the mornings smelled like hemp and where her older half-brother Cliff had first gone to sea, and noticed Henry, Henry Rust, who was in her brothers' grade, the eleventh, and who was their friend but not a close one, who was a good friend of Percy's, but who lately spent all of his time practicing and going around with Carol Burcell whose older sister Dixie had gone off to Hollywood with one of Mr. Sorrel's technicians and whose brothers ran a honky-tonk east of town and strapped revolvers to their steering wheel posts. Henry Rust was clutching his guitar almost as a mother might clutch an infant, working fanatically at the thing, his face scowling and seeming oblivious to all else, maybe the way she could get oblivious while painting or sketching.

Just below Henry, close by the bandstand, his girl Carol Burcell was cutting up with a succession of schoolmates as well as older college boys, including that one who thought his ass weighed a ton, who was even sitting down beside her, no doubt to give her a treat of charm.

"Henry's either gonna keep on til he gets it or keep on getting it, I don't know which," Matt had said about Carol Burcell at the start of school when they all sat gossiping. *"Man, any boy who'd put his thing in her would be violating the pure food act,"* Mark had said. *"Don't you two ever think about anything else?"* she had said. *"Sure,"* came the expected answer, *"sometimes we think about whisky."*

She had been, as she sat alone, a world within the maelstrom world about her, awakening at moments to the hysterical spirit of things and at others wistfully yearning for the quietude that she thought of as pinehum and windcool and birdsong. At home it would be quiet now except for the wind and the barkings of dogs and the yowls of cats or maybe Aunt Margaret's crepitant nocturnal meanderings or perhaps one of those terse soliloquies that her half-brother Cliff yielded up sometimes as he walked down the hallway. *"Stranger than a goddam dream,"* Ellen had heard him say the night before.

Aunt Margaret: *Cliff, why do you talk to yourself?*

Cliff: *Because I'm a good listener.*

Clifton Worth had gone off to sea at sixteen and come home for the first time twenty-six years later, in January, 1925, on the day that his Papa's third wife Emily had gone into labor in the southeast corner room upstairs, had come in lugging two sea bags containing a shipmaster's license, books, mementoes, and ledgers recording deposits that totaled almost a quarter of a million dollars in banks scattered all over the world, and, as soon as Emily Boisseau Worth had given birth to a daughter, had approached his Papa with a strange proposition.

Cliff: You picked out a name?

Papa: Thought I'd name her after her mother.

Cliff: Name her Ellen too and I'll make her a rich woman.

Her Papa had taken up the bargain, not out of avarice but intrigue, and the next day Cliff went to the bank that his Papa owned and deposited fifty thousand dollars, with interest to compound, in the name of Ellen Emily Worth.

Papa: Cliff, how'd you save so much money?

Cliff: By putting it in banks.

Papa: Well, then, at least tell me this—what does the name Ellen happen to mean to you?

Cliff: Papa, that comes under the heading of personal.

Ellen early in childhood had learned from Cliff that he had made her the namesake of an English woman he had loved, and, so she supposed, probably loved still. Quitting the sea at forty-one, Cliff had enrolled in the state university at Riverton, had taken a degree in law, and had opened an office where, as Horris had once put it, anybody was welcomed for conversation but paying clients were ruthlessly screened out.

Earlier tonight, just after supper, smelling as always of the bay rum he used after shaving, Cliff had headed out for Carterville "to sit up with a sick friend," as he usually put it when he was going to see his current womanfriend, had headed out amidst the usual jibes from Matt and Mark.

They: Old Cliff's gonna get some tonight!

Cliff: Yeah, son of a bitch, old Cliff's gonna get some tonight —some boiled peanuts, if he's lucky.

Aunt Margaret: Sam, why are all of your children so foul-mouthed?

Papa: Son of a bitch if I know.

He would be asleep by now, her Papa, probably, and in the morning would pretend to be astonished that anybody thought the day special. Ellen thought, *Eighty-two. Eighty-two years old. And Aunt Margaret older.*

Her Papa at sixteen, in 1874, had run up to the courthouse in McClung just in time to see his own father, her grandfather, shot dead by the militia—his father Aaron Worth along with a number of other scratch-hard farmers, farmers who had come to be called Rooters, who, in what the books later called the Rooters Rebellion, had occupied the courthouse, crowding into the corridor to protest starvation conditions, protesting specifically the wave of foreclosures that, on top of hard times, was costing many of them their farms.

Margaret had sent Sam Worth running into McClung to tell their Papa that their Mama had suddenly been taken with a bad spell of the sickness that had lately been cutting her down, their Mama, her grandmother never-to-be seen, a brave, soft-spoken woman with some Lomkubee blood and lovely black hair, dead by the time her Papa had hauled back the body of his Papa in the mule-drawn wagon that Aaron Worth had driven to town, to the courthouse, to protest against the bankers and the courts that did their bidding.

Her Papa and Margaret had gone on to raise their three younger siblings, had saved their own farm from foreclosure only after Margaret had come into possession of some gold in some odd way that even today she was tight-lipped about.

Papa: Ellen, she won't tell you, because it was stolen gold. Hell, I know because I was supposed to be in on the robbery with the man who stole it.

Margaret: Sam, you don't know any such thing, because you were unconscious and delirious from two snakebites when I found that gold. Which I do know because I was the one who was awake for forty-eight hours taking care of you.

Papa: Well, don't you know what I would have been doing if those goddam moccasins hadn't hit me that morning when I got the trots and ran out barefoot into the bushes? Don't you know that?

Margaret: Sam, I know what you say you would have been doing, but I don't know what you would have been doing, and you don't either, and I doubt you would have been robbing that bank wagon.

Papa: Well, it was all arranged, and you know that's the truth.

Margaret: I know that's what you tell me as truth, but I also know you didn't go out robbing, thank God.

Sam: Well, you and I know who did, and you and I know that when he got shot he came by and dumped that gold in your lap and then somehow got back to his house and died.

Margaret: Sam, how can you pretend to know all that when while all that was supposed to be happening you didn't know whether it was noon or midnight.

Sam: Well, all I can say is if those snakes hadn't hit me I'd probably have been dead too before that day was out. I'll tell you, though—Ellen—it's hard to recognize a snakebite as a blessing when you get it. Especially when you get two at once.

Her Papa, with Margaret at hand ever since, had worked furiously, had prospered as better times came back, had bought land when he could, had branched into timbering, and finally, in the late 1880s when a huge bauxite deposit had turned up on his property east of McClung, had become more than well-off. He had dealt cannily with agents from the industrial north, holding rights for himself and demanding controlling interest in the mining operations, and had, backed by that bonanza, capitalized a bank in spite of or maybe because of his loathing for bankers. His had undercut all the others in dealings with the small farmers, catering to their erratic needs and dealing with them leniently, meanwhile handling the funds of the miscellany of clients brought in by his timber trade and the bauxite operations. Before many years her Papa had absorbed both the bank that had indirectly destroyed his father and its like-minded competitor. And in 1890, three years widowed and two years newly married, he had bought the big house where they lived today, the house erected in the eighteenth century by the French-born woman who was the very earliest settler in the state, and had moved in with his first brood of seven children and his second wife and Aunt Margaret and Thomas Horris—Tom Horris who in 1922 when her Papa's second wife had died had invited up from New Orleans the Emily Boisseau who, at twenty-one, had become her Papa's third wife and her mother.

Her Mama, who had given Ellen the abundant shock of dark

feathery curls and the figure that had now burgeoned to awaken in men the looks that Ellen had first noticed her mother getting when they were in Paris before she understood why. Against whose bosom she had leaned in some large silent room in Mexico where they were standing before the murals of Mayan women naked from the waist, and she, staring, shaped like a spindle and pressing her head back on her mother, had silently prayed she would grow up with breasts like that, and had made the horrible error of confiding the wish to Matt and Mark later, to be tormented with derisive laughter that their mother had finally silenced, almost laughing herself and hugging them all, saying: *"Que sera, sera."* Who had always repeated words and phrases they asked about as when Ellen one rainy day in London got that eerie feeling that she had been there long before. "It's called déjà vu," her mother had said. "Déjà vu, déjà vu, déjà vu. Say it now." Who had never actually seemed old or young to Ellen, but only— what? Who had seemed only as she was, as she had always been, would always be, only suddenly they got back from the trip and suddenly she wasn't.

Matt and Mark bounding down the stairs with wide terrified eyes. "Ellen, Ellen, Mama died! Mama's dead!" And she fleeing, feeling blown, hearing them cry out behind her: "Papa, Ellen's running away! Papa! Papa! Ellen! Ellen!" And she fleeing out of the house, flying across the grounds, through the pines, fleeing and flying and dying through the pines, and to the icy spring, and diving in, diving in and hoping never to come up, and going down to meet that fierce, implacable cold that sent her shooting back to the surface, screaming, as Cliff in his good suit leaped out into the water and took her in his arms, and out, and up, back to the house where she couldn't bear to open her eyes, couldn't bear not to see what she no longer could see and would never see again.

Strange, stranger than a goddam dream, Ellen thought. Strange to think of it here amidst the revelry. Bombs in London, jubilation here, and at home they sleep. Her Papa. Eighty-two. "You folks gonna celebrate the year just past or the one you don't know anything about yet?" Strange, too, that she had never been aware of the vast difference in her parents' ages when her mother was alive. Only later. And only later had felt uneasy about it, as though thinking about it was some kind of betrayal. Not long ago Matt and Mark laughed and passed on some remark overheard downtown about their Papa's protracted virility. But what was so funny? They managed somehow to reduce it all to mockery and ribaldry.

Matt: *Ellen, tell us, what's the best way to get in a girl's britches?*

She: *Well, I guess the best way is to be invited in.*
Mark: *Ellen, are you going to stay a virgin until you're married?*
She: *I guess I would if my husband asked me to.*

Lately they loved to bait and regale her with vexing questions and real or invented stories of passionate adventure, they who after their mother died had taken her in hand and practically turned her into a boy, teaching her to shoot, trap, fish, and poach, encouraging her to ride like a maniac, taking her camping in the Akana Mountains where she had slipped off a ledge and almost got killed, taking her along the summer they had drifted down the river on the raft made of washtubs and planks, they whom she had declared at eleven she intended to marry.

They: *But, Ellen, you're our sister!*
She: *I don't care, what difference does that make?*

To whom, her brothers, she had decided at some recent but uncertain point that it was hazardous to disclose her actual thoughts about certain things like love and passion.

They: *You never really tell us how you feel about it.*
She: *You might be shocked.*

Sitting alone at the table, she had felt expectant, beset by that ineffable sense of prescience, and then again had suffered the mother-gone pang, and again had imagined that afternoon in October, the gunshot and running and discovering the lifeless body of that strange and intense man whose note had filled her with disturbing wonder. The hubbub had begun to sound like hysteria rising at an intimation of some pending calamity. *"During the Dark Ages when the plague swept Europe the revels of life went on amidst mountains of corpses."* Horris seemed to remember everything he had ever read or seen or heard or done or touched or tasted.

She had thought, *Memory is so strange, so real but so private.* And had got that walled off feeling, that dizzy sensation, the feeling of plummeting or becoming lost, no, of losing herself, so that she had actually called her name to mind, and laughed. And then they had come back to the table, Horris and Claudette.

Now, dancing with Horris, she thought, *Maybe they were right, maybe I was mourning. Am. But, no, was.* Now she was feeling different, better, and now she was also becoming aware of the keen response she had felt, was feeling, at the news of Henry's father, at the thought of whatever it was that made it better for him to play at a time like this. And as well was becoming aware that she was irresistibly staring at Henry each time she faced the bandstand. She knew him, as she said, not well, but some, knew him as a person who spoke in a friendly way but seldom tarried to pass the time, knew him from the corridors and grounds of school, where he had run as a miler last year and been praised by the coach as having Olympic promise, but who had surprised everybody this year by giving up all athletics to concentrate on his guitar. She knew him as a person not much given to smiling: his face of concavities and jutting bones beneath the shock of dark hair was set characteristically in a seeming scowl overlined by heavy brows that only accentuated the pale blue eyes that Ellen now remembered some girl once calling scary. She wondered now why he smiled so little, wondered if it was because of his father having gone away. Suddenly she realized she was wondering about something she had never wondered about before.

Back at their table, after the band with a brass flourish had signaled an intermission, she watched the dance floor clear, the crowd disintegrating into myriad crisscrossings. The musicians got up stretching, hopping off the stage into the crowd. And now Percy Ensley was vaulting up onto the stage and exchanging words with Henry Rust, a tall figure whose tux had pants too short. And now both jumped down, Percy veering back toward her brothers' table where he was parked with his cousin Florence Ensley, and Henry, to Ellen's ill-defined surprise, striding swiftly past the lively, close-by table where his girl Carol Burcell sat exhibiting some mirth with an exaggerated flinging of her head.

Henry strode past with neither a glance nor a nod at Carol or anyone else at the table, Carol taking note of his passing with only the fleetest of glances. He zigzagged among the thinning celebrants, and now, approaching, noticed Horris waving him over. Horris got up quickly and stepped out to put a hand on Henry's shoulder, speaking to him quietly and quietly receiving some very few words spoken in return by a mouth that then tenuously smiled.

Henry glanced at her with a brief nod and then on to Claudette, who was speaking up to be heard over the babble.

"We're all proud of you, Henry," Claudette said, pronouncing his name almost in the French way, "but we wish we could hear you!"

Henry nodded, again with the tentative smile. "Maybe you'll hear me after the break. For better or worse, they're gonna let me do a special."

"Bravo!" Claudette said. "What are you going to do?"

He paused, as though reluctant, then spoke, still looking at Claudette. "Something I wrote. I'll probably be sorry."

"No, no!" Claudette protested. "You'll be *magnifique!*"

Horris, back at his chair, asked Henry to join them for intermission, but he shook his head. "Thanks, but—" he said, jerking his head toward the front door. "I need some air." Henry's glance passed from Horris to her, but before she could say any of the somethings she felt impelled to say, he had shifted as though to go.

But he didn't. Henry Rust suddenly arrested his movement and looked at her. He was not glancing but looking, scrutinizing as though actually seeing her for the first time. He was steadily looking with no change whatever in his earnest expression.

Ellen felt herself reddening, growing warmer, felt an uprush within, an impulse to squirm, felt as though she were about to be accused of something. And, in his steady scrutiny of her, discovered something wordlessly reminiscent of the intense look that Mr. Sorrel had sometimes directed at her.

Now he was leaning his hands on the outer edge of their table and staring directly into her eyes, and her eyes felt suddenly incised, penetrated, disconcerted to the point of panic, they wanted to turn away but couldn't. Earnestly and almost with gravity, and yet with some amazement in his voice, he was saying something that set her careening.

"Ellen—you are absolutely beautiful," Henry Rust said.

And while she was careening and before she had even managed to think to say thank you, he straightened and half-raised a hand by way of so-long and walked briskly off, not toward Carol Burcell's table but toward the front of the armory.

"Well—" Claudette said, and, after a silence that seemed an age, called for more champagne.

Ellen, feeling no longer tiny and obscure but highly visible and vulnerable, gulped down her glassful and slid the glass toward Horris for a refill.

"Dumpling, you're as depraved as I am," he said, and poured.

Soon Henry had come back into view and traversed the dance floor, ignoring Carol Burcell's table as he hopped up onto the bandstand among the ghostly forms of the other musicians.

Another brass flourish had signaled the end of intermission, and the band leader had announced the special number, and now Henry was in a spot, standing with his foot propped on a chair, and was picking a moody melody not with a pick but his fingers, and then the blonde girl singer came into the spot and up to the mike and, while he played a fast suspenseful cadenza, said she was honored to introduce a song called "No More Time" that had been written by young Henry Rust there beside her.

"It's a very blue song," she said, and added in a down-and-dirty voice, "—and that's my kind of song."

Then with the drums and bass backing in the darkness behind, they were into it after a forceful introduction of powerful plangent runs that seemed to clean the air, and Ellen at their table was moved to blurt out.

"Claudette, that's marvelous!" she said.

"Very good," Claudette whispered.

"I didn't know he could write things like this. He always—"

"Shhh," said Claudette.

. . . *When your dreeeeams commence to cry, no more tiiime, on your miiiind, no more time* . . .

By the end of the first stanza the crowd was silenced, and it was rapt during the second, and on.

When the last long shadows fall, when the big man comes to call, no more tiiime, on your miiind, no more time . . .

It was a long number, after which the crowd roared as though purged of melancholy and grateful for it, yelled and clapped as Henry receded, leaving the spot to the leader, who instantly stomped off the beat for a fast and frenzied semi-Dixieland number.

The song had made her shiver, and for awhile some of its words, along with the words he had uttered to her, ran through her mind again and again. Ellen was lost in elation or perhaps confusion or some kind of a daze at the unsettling uprush that was going on inside her at this person who had so unexpectedly and emphatically smashed into her feelings and consciousness from the time they had gotten there almost. She was scarcely aware of what was going on about her until suddenly Mark materialized at their table—his hair unruly, his eyes glazed, a wide and maniacal and joyous grin on his face—and hoisted her like a large toy out of her chair just as she was taking the last gulp of her champagne, which now dribbled down onto the snug bodice of her pale yellow gown.

"My dance, Dumpling," Mark said, as she whooped and was raised aloft. As he backed into the thick of the dancers he yelled toward Horris and Claudette: "You folks having a good time?"

"It's obvious you two are," Ellen said as they were swept into the currents of the crowd.

"Are what?" said Mark, towering above.

"Having a time! Having a time!"

"Dumpling, are we having a time! And we gonna get some tonight!"

"Some what?" said Ellen, shouting.

"Well, I'm not talking about boiled peanuts," said Mark.

"Then don't make it sound like boiled peanuts," Ellen said.

"Ellen, we gonna steal you away from those old folks and get you a boy," said Mark in a confidential shout.

Mark yielded her to Percy Ensley, to whom he issued a command: "Percy, when you're done you bring her little tail over to our table, you hear?"

Percy was slight, wiry, deft, bouncy, not so tall, only a couple of inches taller than she.

"When did Henry start writing songs?" Ellen asked.

"Told me he just worked that thing out last night."

"Didn't you think it was terrific?" Ellen said, and, as Percy nodded, went on: "I noticed he's been walking right by Carol without even speaking—or even looking."

"So?"

"Well, I just wondered. Aren't they, well—"

"They're on the outs tonight."

"What happened?"

"When did you get so interested in them?"

"Hey, who said I was so interested? I just wondered, that's all."

"Well, what happened is, Carol didn't want him to play, because she just wanted him to be with her, and—well, when he told her it was too good a chance to pass up, she blew a gasket and told him to go to hell. And promptly snookered herself an invitation from that college guy at the end of her table there. You know him?"

"She's with him? He is such a nerd," Ellen said.

"I wouldn't want any of him to rub off on me either," said Percy.

"I guess you heard about his father."

"Who's father?"

"Henry's."

"What about him?"

"He died yesterday, or at least they heard yesterday."

"Died? Where'd you hear that?"

"Horris told me."

"Goddam! Henry didn't tell me that!"

"Listen, Percy, he will, so you let him tell you when he's ready, okay? Probably he hasn't told anybody himself."

"He didn't tell Horris?"

"You know Horris hears everything. I'll bet you'd be the first person Henry would talk to."

"If he talks to anybody," Percy said. "Come on, let's go over to the table."

"Percy, don't let this get you in a mood," Ellen said.

"You're really somebody to preach about moods."

"*Touché,*" said Ellen, and Matt cut in to josh and tease and badger her about the floor until they were approached by the almost staggering collegian who thought his ass weighed a ton.

"You want him?" Matt asked as the hand tapped on his shoulder.

"He's just what I don't want," Ellen whispered.

"You want me to deck him?" Matt said.

"Oh, hush," said Ellen, "let's go to the table. I want to see Florence and Clara and Lucy."

Matt turned to the collegian, who was still tapping at his shoulder, and said, "Go 'way, boy, there ain't nobody at home, can't you see that?"

Then he gripped her to his side, an arm about her shoulders, and bulled them through the dancers toward his table.

"You don't like that dude?" he said.

"He's a nerd," Ellen said, "Percy says he's with Carol tonight."

"So I hear," said Matt. "Well, I guess she can satisfy him and six more like him."

"You're awful," said Ellen.

"You're beautiful," said Matt. He bounced her against his side like a giant rag doll.

"Hey, I'm your sister!"

"That's my tough luck."

"What do you mean by that?"

"Think it over."

They squeezed her in amongst them into a chair stolen from a nearby table, and then they were a tight circle of seven around a table for four. Percy was to her left and then his girlfriend/cousin Florence Ensley, and then Mark and his girl, red-haired Clara Collins, and then blonde Lucy McDonald, who was with Matt, who was now reclaiming his seat at Lucy's left and Ellen's right.

"Ain't she scrumptious tonight!" said Matt with one of his maniacal grins.

"Ain't it a shame she's our sister," said Mark to Clara.

"What do you mean?" Clara said.

"I mean," said Mark, raising his eyebrows grandiloquently, "that this morsel of a girl is right there living in our house, but—"

"You're horrible," said Clara, hiding hysterical giggles with her hands.

"He's worse than that," Ellen chimed in.

"Fix Ellen a drink," said Matt.

"I've already had some," said Ellen.

"Champagne doesn't count," said Mark.

"Thanks to you," said Ellen, pointing to her damp bodice, "most of mine didn't."

"Fix scrumptious Ellen a scrumptious drink," Mark said.

"No, really," Ellen said. "I'll just sniff Matt's breath from time to time—or Percy's. Percy, are you sober?"

"I may be the only sober man in the whole damn place."

"Percy's very crafty," said Mark. "He gets Florence plastered, and then just before she passes out—" Mark issued a shrill descending whistle.

"Hey, I've only had two drinks all evening," said Florence, reddening.

"Besides," Percy said, "I can't whistle through my teeth."

Everybody burst out laughing. And then, for no reason at all, Mark led them all into a brief parochial rouser vaguely addressed to the people of states to the west and the east of theirs:

Oh, here's to Louisiana and to Mississippi too! We're the bastards in the middle, so to hell with both of you!

Now Ellen was all but lofted by the upseethe within her. It was growing with the din of the night, and she felt enlivened, elated, almost dazed, distinctly stirred and warmed by the animated flesh-quake around this table. Her sense of expectancy seemed now more sharply defined.

She felt painfully in suspense and oddly conspicuous when, during one break, Henry Rust materialized at the table and privately exchanged some words with Percy, then, with a nod at her and everyone else, departed.

Time passed in a palpitant swirl of motion, noise, nonsense, as the music resumed. Once she started to get up, saying she had to go back to see Horris and Claudette, but her brothers promptly clamped her back in her seat.

"You can't go until it's 1941," Matt said.

And then for no clear reason he and Mark began singing the thing about drink-and-be-merry-for-tomorrow-we-die. A shiver ran through her.

"Why sing that?" Ellen said when they had stopped.

"Well, we're going to war, aren't we?" Mark said.

"Don't talk like that," Ellen said.

"Well, you believe Cliff, don't you. Cliff's been all over the world, and he says we're going to war," Matt said.

"If Cliff says we're going to war, we're going to war," said Mark. "So goddamit, drink and be merry."

"Well, I've been all over the world and just maybe we won't," Ellen said.

"Ellen, why do you suppose they're drafting everybody?" Mark said.

"And building an air corps place up the road?" Matt said.

"Percy," Ellen said, "get them to shut up, will you?"

Percy began singing, *Oh, here's to Louisiana and to Mississippi, too,* and the subject of war passed into the hubbub and revelry. And then suddenly—

Pow! At the sharp report like a gunshot the image of Mr. Sorrel flew up into view, but only for a flick. It was instantly banished in the immediate *pow-pow-pow* uproar of popping balloons and shouts and singing, and everybody was standing and hugging and kissing, and Ellen was wedged into the very middle of the tight delirious huddle of them while they sang in the new year seemingly forever amidst the blasts of tinny horns and under showers of serpentine that was unfurling weirdly in the garish swirling and darting of the lightspots.

Extricated at last, she struggled through the crowd to greet Horris and Claudette, but found them gone from the table, and decided to sit down anyway alone, flushed and sweating, to catch her breath. And just then, although the band was still playing the ump-teenth chorus of "Auld Lang Syne," he materialized out of the moil of bodies on the dance floor, solemn-faced as before.

He leaned on the table, as before, and looked at her, as before.

"Happy New Year," he said, not loud and not quite smiling.

Ellen almost gasped, startled. She negotiated a deep intake of breath.

"Oh, happy New Year," she said.

He was going to sit down in Claudette's chair, was sitting down sideways in that temporary kind of posture. "They're trapped over by the band if you were wondering where they are."

"I was wondering."

"Are you only with them?"

"Well, I'm with them, but I wouldn't say only," she said, and laughed nervously. "But if you mean—"

"Well—I didn't mean—what I meant was, do you think I could see you home?"

"Oh—well—I—aren't you—I mean, I don't think we—I don't think Horris and Claudette are going to stay til the very end, but—"

"Well, I could leave any time."

"But don't you have to—" She tilted her head toward the band.

"Naw, I don't have to go all the way. I'm just playing for myself, anyway. I mean, they're just doing me a favor, I'm not obligated."

"But what about—I mean, aren't you—" Ellen glanced toward the vicinity of Carol Burcell's table.

"What about what?" he said, only he made it sound like a statement instead of a question and went on: "Listen, if you don't feel like it, just say so, and—well, my feelings won't be hurt."

"No—listen—no, I do feel like it. It's just—I mean, I really would like it. So—so I accept, okay? And, listen, Horris'll give us a ride whenever, I'm sure, so—"

"Well—okay—good. Listen, I'll play one more set with them and then come over here and maybe we can dance a couple of numbers and then go. That be okay?"

"Sure, that's okay. That's fine," Ellen said.

Henry Rust fleetingly extended his hand and barely grazed it over the back of hers and then was gone. She watched him jostle back toward the stage.

Ellen thought, *Maybe this is why.*

He said he would only sit for a little while, had obviously not wanted to go in, had said it was so mild out that it would be nice to sit on the porch.

And so she had led him around to the south side, and they sat in the swing, and had talked about the dance some more, and about the song he had written and gotten to play, and he about the band leader who had told him that maybe they could use him next summer down in New Orleans.

They had talked low, with a lot of long silences during which she felt the warmth pounding in her even more than it had when he had come up and asked to see her home, pounding as it had when he had come back to take her on the floor for their first dance when he had held her not firmly but so lightly she could scarcely feel his hand behind her at all.

They had danced and sat talking with Horris and Claudette and then danced a lot more, with her dreading every cut, and then had sat and talked for awhile more before Horris had driven them home, and all with no mention whatever of the subject she had decided once that she simply couldn't mention but that at last she had felt absolutely compelled to talk about while they sat in the swing, and so had.

"Listen, I heard about your father, and—I was so sorry to hear it—I know—I know how you must feel," she had said.

And he had sat silent for a long, long moment during which she could hear her heart and the rush in her ears and his breathing and the creaking of the swing chains. And then he had finally spoken, had spoken so softly he seemed remote, had spoken not with bitterness but only with a strained and resigned matter-of-factness.

"Yeah—well—actually, I guess I don't give a good goddam."

And she had felt as though she were plummeting again after he had said that, and had sat in shocked silence, groping for something to say, groping until suddenly her eyes had filled up and she was crying profusely without a sound at all, without moving a muscle or making a twitch, simply sitting very still and absolutely quiet while tears poured down her face until she began to taste them at the corners of her motionless mouth that she didn't dare move or else she would let go. And had become aware that he was surreptitiously studying her for a long moment before, for the first time since they had sat down, his hand had come over and taken hers in a firm bony clasp with fingers whose callouses she could feel. And then he had spoken again.

"Listen, Ellen, you've got to remember he's been gone a long time. You know something? Until my sister and I got the wire, we didn't even know he had another wife. I didn't mean I was glad."

"I know that," she said, amazed that her voice didn't break, because her face was still dripping with tears.

"I didn't mean that—or that I didn't love him—or that—"

"I understand," she said, and he went on.

"—or that I don't care—but—goddam, Ellen, what can I say? I guess I don't know what I meant. Or how I feel. It's like he's been in some other world. I guess you know he drank himself to death. He was always drunk. He was drunk the last time he came here two years ago—or maybe it was three. Drunk and talking about the war that was coming even then, and got me upset as hell, I remember. And, sure, I loved him, but—what can I say?—You know, I was nine when they broke up and—well, I'm almost seventeen now. I think it's going to go harder on Polly because she's older and got to know him better."

"I was ten when Mama died," she said.

And he had fallen silent and finally said: "Ellen?"

"I'm okay," she had said.

"You know something? Even when you're crying, you're absolutely beautiful."

And just then Matt and Mark had come roaring up the graveled drive in their bizarre old limousine that they had sawed the roof off of, and had piled out boisterously drunk, towing Clara and Lucy to the front steps, singing loudly as they went, singing "Happy New Year to You" to the tune of the childhood birthday song—

   . . . *Happy one nine four one . . . happy new year to yooooooou.*

"Happy New Year to you!" Ellen had suddenly yelled out, and they had stampeded around the porch and surrounded the swing and sung the stupid song again all through—

   . . . *happy one nine four wuh-unn . . . happy new year to yooooou!*

—and, calling Henry, "the Maestro," had demanded that they come in with them to the kitchen where Clara and Lucy were going to cook up a supper or a breakfast or whatever-the-hell there was to cook up. And had gone.

And he had at first said, well, no, he would sort of be crashing, and she had said, well, heck, how could he be crashing when he was with her, and so they had gone in, too, and eaten, and Matt and Mark had kept on drinking and gotten Henry to get out his guitar, and he had played a lot of songs, and they had sung, and finally Matt and Lucy and Mark and Clara had drifted out into the parlor and gotten quiet, and then he had said he had best go, and she had offered to get the keys and drive him, and he had said, no, it would be good to walk, and so, with him in his tux with the pants too short and she having pulled on one of the twins' coat-style letter-sweaters over her yellow calf-length gown, had walked first down the steps, and then across the yard to the drive, and then, after he had reached out again and taken her hand, all the way down the quarter-mile drive to the Trail.

And now he squeezed her hand and let it go and stood and stared at her again as if he were examining some fascinating curiosity for the first time. And now, no, he wasn't going to try to kiss her, he raised his right hand and touched the back of it very gently to her left cheek, and now his eyes were incising hers, which were threatening to water over again for different reasons, there at the top of the impossible upsurge within her. And now he was saying something.

"Goddam, Ellen, I think I love you."

And she felt as though she had to say something but absolutely couldn't, but her head was nodding, *yes, yes, yes.*

And now he turned and was walking away, guitar case in his right hand, and now he was looking back, and raising a hand, and stopping, a ghost in the first light of the new day, and was yelling back to her.

"Can I come see you tomorrow?"

And again her mouth didn't speak but she could feel her hair shaking as her head vigorously nodded, *yes, yes, yes, yes, yes, yes.*

Then he was gone, and she whirled and sprinted down the drive toward the house, her yellow pumps scattering pea gravel as she went, flying, exploding with the strangest impulse to leap and shout and laugh and maybe cry, exploding and flying up the front steps three at a time, and down the front hall past the parlor, and then skidding, and going back to the parlor door, and sticking her head in to issue, in a loud stage whisper, goodnight, and happy new year, and getting back groans from the forms sprawled on two separate couches, and then flying up the stairs two and three at a time, and down the hall, and into the southeast corner room in which she had been born, and thence, after flinging off the coat-sweater but carefully hanging the yellow gown, into bed where she lay marveling at the dawn light that pressed through the windows while she remembered and remembered and remembered until everything that had happened that night and in her whole life seemed strange as a dream, stranger.

THOMAS CHURCHILL (T.C.) HORRIS:

He had dropped them off at 2:40, and, as they walked with linked hands but without haste toward her front steps, had backed, turned, and driven out the quarter-mile drive and up the Bulomkubee Trail half a mile, and had turned left onto the dirt lane to his house, riding along in comfortable silence all the way, silence not broken by a word from either him or Claudette as they parked and went in, nor while she mixed an iced toddy as a nightcap for him and poured a tall glass of cold buttermilk for herself, but when they had sunk down in big chairs in the living room, he began to talk.
He said:

Well, by God, she's out of mourning even if she may be going into something slightly worse. But at least she's out of mourning, and I only wonder how soon she'll see that that's what it was, what it has been, that her brothers hit the nail on the head even if they didn't understand what it was they were driving it into.
It sure wasn't just the old mothergone pang this time, and it wasn't just Ben Sorrel either, and it wasn't even both of them put together. It was a great deal more that I would guess she hasn't quite seen yet, but that she will, of course, sooner or later, because sooner or later she sees everything. Sooner, I suspect she'll lay it all to Ben Sorrel's death and only much later come to see that was only the proximate cause, which isn't to diminish proximate causes generally

or a young man's suicide in particular, but which is only to point to a certain order of anguish. There is focused anguish and unfocused anguish, and I'm speaking of unfocused anguish, which is the kind we don't tend to recognize and deal with and that thus persists longer and pervades us more deeply and that can actually kill us or get us killed.

Now, Ellen had both kinds, and it was the latter that lingered. Her grief for Ben Sorrel, or what she preferred to call her "thinking" about him, would have passed much more quickly because it was clearly recognizable. But the grief we've been witnessing, and which is only abated now, and not dispelled, because it won't be dispelled except by wisdom, was from something much deeper, and at the moment I suspect it was for the very thing that Sorrel himself could finally bear no longer.

You know, I got to thinking about Sorrel while I was watching her tonight, and for the first time I began to see that he didn't kill himself at all because of what they did to his film, and certainly not over the breakup of that marriage, which I have never thought anyway. That fellow killed himself over the very thing that impelled him to make the film in the first place and to make it the way he did in the second. What I'm saying is that the film itself was his real suicide note, and his note to me was only an addendum, a postscript. As he dramatized it, after all, *Journey to Amaomanta* was a celebration of all that he had inchoately yearned for and at the same time was a devastating repudiation of all that assured that his yearning would remain unrequited, his vision unfulfilled.

On reflection I'd say—and this may sound odd—I'd say that in the profoundest sense the very venture of making that movie was an act of mourning for Ben Sorrel, although he, with all his brilliance, would have rejected this notion much as Ellen resisted her brothers' proposition that she was in mourning. Still, I think I could make a case, and I say this even though I never saw the finally edited film, and presumably never will now that the money boys have decided to bury it for the safety of the public, bury it or burn it or do whatever they do with dangerous celluloid out there in Hollywood. But I don't have to see it to know what was on Sorrel's mind, because I began to see that the first time he called me just after he had stumbled across the book quite by chance. It was clear to me that his thoughts were just like mine after I, also quite by chance, stumbled onto that old wrapped manuscript in the medieval stacks at Oxford, or after I had read it, rather, and found myself compelled to translate it and get it published. Ben Sorrel was suffering the same sort of excitement that first time he called me. He absolutely had to make the movie.

So I wouldn't even have had to spend all that time down the river watching him make it to know something of what was on his mind. Actually, any sensitive person who reads the book is likely to get much the same feeling, though, of course, it won't take root as a mania in every case, only in a mind already properly tilled for raising manias.

But who could fail to weep for mankind, or maybe howl, along with laughing at the immense ironies in the thing, after reading about Jose Caldas, that devout little Spaniard and his companions among the gentle and innocent Lomkubees? Who in hell could read about the destiny of Jose Caldas, his fate at the hands of both his blood brother and his brothers in the church, and not howl with anguish at least privately?

Who, that is, but the state legislators who were ready to destroy the University Press up in Riverton to prevent them from publishing it, and the prosecutor who helped them form the charges against me and the staff and even the printer? And who, that is, besides their kinsmen, the company men in Hollywood, who buried the film as thoroughly as the Inquisition buried Jose Caldas?

Well, in fairness, we'd have to admit that none of that ilk has ever truly read the book. They couldn't read it even though their eyes might take in the words. They couldn't comprehend it, couldn't admit it to their minds, simply because they are in fact possessed of the very condition of mind that the book and Jose's destiny implicitly condemns. The same condition of mind that keeps them from comprehending the book obliges them to condemn it. And, of course, that's the same condition of mind that impelled the Inquisition four hundred years earlier to order it burned long after Jose Caldas had handed it as a confession to his brother the priest and had wound up in the dungeon as the cost of his honesty.

Hell, the ire of the Inquisition is separated only by time from the ire of those state legislators after they heard some rumors about this thing that the boy bookworm Horris had dug up at Oxford, and can only on the scale of style and manners be distinguished from the motives of the bosses of Penultimate Films. The Inquisition burned it, the state legislators wanted to censor it, and the film company dropped it like a hot turd. No, I retract that. A hot turd they would have distributed and gotten richer off of. They dropped it like a stick of lit dynamite.

So what was Ben Sorrel mourning? He cried out when he read

the book and he raged at the fate to which Jose Caldas's immensely innocent honesty led him, true. But what he truly mourned, without quite knowing it, was the goddam pervasive and persisting and probably irreversible condition of quote civilized unquote mankind that made the whole story not merely poignant but tragically inevitable. What discloses the perfection of Sorrel's mourning is the fact that he so made the film as to insure the result that he was doomed to face, and that we can now see was just as inevitable as the sentence that sent Caldas to the dungeon for being truthful.

It must sound presumptuous for me to say that Sorrel didn't quite know his deeper mind. Yet, what did he think his film was about? Well, he thought it was about the *loss* of innocence, he fashioned it in some ways as an analogy to the Eden story. On reflection, however, we see that neither the book nor the film is or could be about the *loss* of innocence, even though this theme glimmers at the surface. Actually, the story reeks with innocence not lost but possessed, innocence retained, innocence not abandoned but cherished. The Lomkubees, for Christ's sake, were the very embodiment of innocence when Jose Caldas and his four companions happened among them back when this whole region was still called the *amaomanta*.

And of course, it was Sorrel's determination to be faithful to this innocence that got him into hot water right off, as you remember, when the stories leaked out about the nude scenes and the depiction of quote primitive unquote love-making. Hell, if he hadn't had what they called the egomaniac clause in his contract, the company would have jerked the rug from under him way back then. But the point is, what did he expect to happen later? Could he really have believed his efforts to keep the shooting secret would be successful? Of course not. He had to know that would only stimulate the gossip industry. Well, he did know he retained absolute control during the making of the thing, but he also knew that when it got into the hands of the company it was their piece of property. And what could he have expected to be their state of mind in a country where the word "damn" was the big sensation in the movie of the century?

I'm suggesting that he was already in grief when he made the film and that, consciously or not, he also created the events that provided him with a proper or plausible setting to act out his ultimate grief. Which wasn't, in the end, over the loss of innocence at all. That film expressed grief not over the loss of innocence but over the actuality of innocence confronted by civilized man's incapacity to accept it. That's what the book is about, too, although Jose Caldas never intended it that way. Jose, after all, was begging his companions, imploring them, to leave the gentle but sinful Lomkubees and go back with him to Spain, to civilization, he was exhorting them to do their duty to civilization. And what does he hear from his erstwhile sergeant who has now almost taken on the appearance of a Lomkubee? His sergeant says: "They can take civilization and shove it up a pig's ass."

And that, for God's sake, summarizes both the book and the film, or at least encapsulates the impact of them. The outcry you want to make when you confront the story isn't about lost innocence but is at civilized man's incapacity to accept innocence, to admit it, to acknowledge it even.

And there, by God, is something to mourn, and there, by God, is what Sorrel was actually mourning, and to the mourning of which he created his film and finally extinguished his own life, which perhaps—just perhaps—he might not have done if he had not missed his own point, if what he was mourning had ever come into focus in his own mind. Because if he had seen it, it would have been only a short step to seeing that the proper gesture to make before the bastards of the world is not to end life dramatically but to live it joyfully in spite of them.

But what was on his mind at the end, the day he drove back into McClung and parked and locked his shiny new car and walked across the fields in those hundred-dollar shoes? Well, we know he had put his whole mind in the film, and then we have his note to me. And we know that, consciously or not, he appropriated almost the very words that the sergeant had uttered to Jose Caldas. "They can take Hollywood and shove it up a pig's ass." So from this we know that Ben Ezra Sorrel must have thought that he was acting primarily in the name of artistic integrity, or plain old honesty, protesting the unacceptable assassination of his artistic truthchild. Still, it had to be more. It had to be the larger thing that he couldn't bear.

And I think that's what Ellen has been mourning along with Sorrel's death, and with the old mothergone pang sharpening and in a strange way dissembling her anguish. I wouldn't minimize the impact Sorrel's life and death had on her, of course. In him, after all, she witnessed for the first time a vital being so possessed by a vision that he would and did commit every ounce of his brain and body to the making of a single expression of his vision. She saw and sensed what he was doing, saw it with such innocence and perfect clarity that she didn't even have to put it into words, didn't need to articulate it any more than she would need to articulate the fact that she had just seen a tree or a bird or the sky.

Nor did she have to say anything to Ben Sorrel—to Mr. Sorrel, as she would have him in spite of his plea for informality—for him to see or sense that she understood perfectly. Her natural wordless perception—and where does it come from? from her grandmother's Lomkubee blood perhaps?—wherever, it must have been evident to Sorrel just as soon as he got to know her. Because it was almost immediately that he was able or willing to talk to her when he was walled off from everybody else. He could always talk to Ellen.

Whence, of course, the supposition, by his colleagues and entourage, that he was infatuated, whence, of course, the cheap gossip that even got printed out west that the young genius had fallen for some nameless quote country girl unquote, as they put it, probably without realizing that the country girl had been all over the world by ten and could speak four languages by age twelve and had published a monograph on the Lomkubees and had an art show in New Orleans by age fifteen.

Well, maybe the gossip was fair, considering the nature of gossip, because, in fact, to the unknowing who witnessed it all, it no doubt looked as though he was infatuated. And maybe he was. But what a story the truth more fully told, the truth that far from merely falling in love, he was a man of thirty-three years who had in fact for the first time in his life come to *feel* love for another individual human being.

Hell, Ben Sorrel had loved mankind abstractly, and had *fallen* in love dozens of times, with a dozen young actresses, among other exotic creatures, had done all that before he finally fell in love and married that chuckle-head who didn't have enough sense not to call him Benny. Who didn't have enough sense to stop calling him Benny even after he had told her he always wound up hating anybody who did. Who didn't have enough sense or sensibility or taste even not to call him Benny on the day she breezed in from Reno to watch us commit his ashes to the river. God, I'll never forget the look on Ellen's face when that woman walked up to her, all furs and frills and hairdo, with her press agent at hand presumably telling her what to say, and saying: "I do so want to thank you for all your family did for *Benny* while he was working here. He wrote me et cetera et cetera." She actually flinched, Ellen did, when she heard Mrs. Sorrel call her husband Benny. I think it was at that instant I realized that her feelings so far hadn't even begun to surface and disclose their depths, not even in the hysteria after she found the body.

But was she mourning only Mr. Sorrel? Only this strange man who wrote her that note that she says she has thought of a million times? "Dear, dear Ellen: I have felt for you a love that I have never felt for any other person on earth." Well, a young girl who is handed a note like that is given something to mourn, true, and a great deal to be perplexed about. Yet, I'm convinced that it took a great deal more to hold a vital soul like Ellen in gloom for two whole months. And I'm convinced she was mourning the exact thing he was, not the loss of innocence but mankind's incapacity to embrace it. It's the only thing that explains why she got so profoundly aware—so incredibly aware for a fifteen-year-old who has a million other things to think about—of the holocaust in Europe. Which is, of course, the awareness we could hear when she came by last night.

But, anyway, I think she's out of it. I think she sees, even if she doesn't yet quite see what she sees. I hope so. Of course, as I say, and as you could see as well as I tonight, she may have come out of it only to fall, willy-nilly, into something else. Which may soon teach her to grieve not the dead and gone but the presently living. But which, let's remember, is about the only thing there is to teach her how goddam sweet it is to be alive even amidst the holocaust and even when the holocaust comes home as it must.

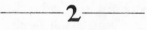

2

She had dreaded seeing her. Ever since it had happened, had dreaded an encounter, feeling absolutely sure that with that spitfire temper she would insist on saying something and would likely make it nasty, she who was now approaching through the scampering crowd of students pouring out of classrooms into the corridor for the lunch hour: Carol Burcell.

Ellen recoiled from the encounter not only out of distaste for a sour scene but even, she admitted, out of some feeling of guilt, a feeling that now resurged even though Claudette had laughed it out of her for awhile. She had felt almost reluctant to go to school when it had resumed after the holidays a week ago, sheerly out of fear of what evidently was about to happen now, with Carol coming on wearing a fixed sweet smile and swinging nearer and nearer through and against the tide of outpouring students.

When Carol hadn't shown up at school the whole first week back, Ellen's dread had gradually waned, and then just last weekend it had been mixed with another feeling, maybe sympathy or pity or something, when Matt and Mark told her they had heard Carol had been hanging around and drinking a lot at the seedy roadhouse called Jack & Jim's east of town, the place named for and run by two of her older brothers who had accumulated pungent reputations, being well-known for selling liquor after hours and on Sundays, and for running a dice table in their backroom, and though it had never been proved, for running the local numbers game that was called *bolita*. And everybody knew they often if not always kept revolvers holstered to the steering posts of their cars.

Ellen sighed as Carol approached, still wearing the sweet smile and now raising a hand to signal her to wait, and now Carol suddenly looked older than she ever had, older or maybe only tired.

"Well, hi," Ellen said, barely audible, when the smile was at last before her, by which time the corridor had almost cleared, said that, and waited, but only waited a few seconds before Carol spoke in a voice as sweet and controlled as the smile.

"Looky," said Carol, her hands folded about a book held over her stomach, "I was wondering—I haven't been able to get hold of him, so I was wondering if you would give Henry a message for me?"

"Well—I don't know—I guess I could—if I see him." Ellen quaked inside as she strained to sound casual.

"Well, from what I hear, you'll surely be seeing him—right? —so I wondered if you would tell him that I have a very big problem, and that if I can't talk to him about it, I'll just have to talk to my brothers."

"Problem?" Ellen said, grappling with dawning horror. "Tell him what? To talk to your brothers?"

"No, you tell him just what I said. That I'll have to talk to my brothers. He'll understand." Carol's smile was still there as though it had been sculpted into her face.

"Listen," Ellen said, with some urgency, "wait a minute. I can't tell him anything like that."

"Like what? It's just a simple little message."

"But what are you saying?"

"Ellen, honey, if you don't know what I'm saying, you've sure led a protected life in that great big house out there."

"Well, anyway, Carol, I'm not going to give anybody a message like that." Ellen started to walk around her, but Carol with a sidestep held her in place, and now her smile was collapsing and reconstructing itself.

"Honey, you make it light on yourself—you hear? But if Henry Rust doesn't get the message, you just remember—my brothers will. And they're not much for talking."

Ellen bristled, clenched her teeth, speared Carol Burcell with blazing eyes that were already threatening to water over. Her voice snapped and lashed: "Goddam you! Why don't you have the decency to say what you mean? You either say it or get out of my way!"

"My, my! She turns into a wildcat, doesn't she. Okay, Ellen, goddam you, too, and you just listen to me if you want it so a child can understand. I'm pregnant!" Carol whacked the book against her stomach, her smile vanished into a gathering of venomous twitching lines. "I'm pregnant! And I want you to know! And I want you to tell Mr. Rust! And I want him to tell me what he's going to do about it! And if he doesn't do something about it, I'm going to have my brothers do something about him! Now do you understand that, little girl?"

After a paralyzed moment Ellen broke away at a run down the now virtually empty second-floor corridor, bounded down the stairs to the basement, her eyes filling as she ran, her heart pounding. Outside, at a stacked tangle of bikes, she furiously extricated her own and flung her books in the basket. She left pedaling at a stand, got to the main street and cut westward toward the Trail, and soon was on the winding dirt drive to Horris's house. She let the bike drop and bounded through the front screen door and was across the porch before it slammed behind her, thence into the living room, calling out for Claudette, but getting only silence for an answer, an abandoned stillness in which she could hear a wild rushing sound like surf in her ears and could feel her chest thumping and pounding as though it would explode.

On the phone in the kitchen she held the receiver to an ear that was still roaring, and waited with leashed exasperation for the operator to come in so she could give the number of the *Mirror*, waiting and beginning to believe that the operator had closed down shop and gone out for lunch. She was clenching the receiver and impatiently jiggling the hook, squirming with agitation on the little stool by the phone table. Then suddenly behind her came a loud, abrupt explosion of incomprehensible human speech.

Ellen screamed, popped the receiver onto its hook, leaped up, overturning the stool. She whirled about, mouth agape, to see the source of her fright standing with immense unconcern in the doorway of the kitchen: a small, short, frail-looking man whose limbs and body were lost in the folds of an enormous World War I army overcoat, a frazzled relic with bulging pockets and its hem dragging the floor. His eyes peered at her out of a wrinkled and wizened face that was of an exceedingly dark purplish black except for the lips, which were showing bright, wet pink as they continued to issue the explosive rattle of human speech that could be comprehended only by the experienced paying very close attention.

"Dickey-devil, goddamit, you almost scared me to death!" Ellen blurted, springing toward him and giving him a hug of relief, dropping her head on his shoulder as she broke into a spate of hysterical half-laughing, half-crying. "Can't you let somebody know when you're coming up on them?" she said at last, during a brief pause in his jabbering.

He had been in and about McClung longer than even her father remembered, and had been called Dickey-devil so long that he would sometimes claim he had never had any other name, although the truth was he had been born Richard Devers and had been called since childhood by the corruption of Dickie Devers. He worked, when cornered or inveigled by someone he approved of, at a variety of odd jobs, executing them with a skill and strength that belied his mysterious but extraordinary age, and slept in perhaps a dozen different places around town, including sometimes a storeroom in the Worth's carriage house, and sometimes a room over the Ensley's garage, and at different times, with permission, in various nooks and crannies down at the Ensley Lumber & Heading Mill. He went about by foot and always with a shoulder-slung crocus sack in which he carried all of his worldly possessions save those that caused the enormous bulges in his overcoat pockets.

Dickey-devil claimed to know everything, and, in Horris's view, came close. Such was his way of speech, however—the compulsive eruption of torrents of sibilance and resonance wherein entire sentences were ellided into single words of myriad syllables—that it was not invariably possible to refute or embrace much of what he claimed as ultimate knowledge of the goings-on around McClung. Yet, Horris had once concluded: "If you recorded everything he says, and if you then played back the record at, say, one-tenth the normal speed, you would soon possess enough intimate scandal about the population of McClung to make a fortune in blackmail and piece together a dozen unpublishable novels besides."

Dickey-devil could slow himself down even if he didn't do it often. He did now, to fuss at Ellen because he had come here to fix a screen but didn't know which one to fix, since he had been round outside and found three that needed fixing.

"Oh, hell, Dickey-devil, can't you just fix all of them?" said Ellen, yearning to get back to the phone.

"One is all old Horris mentioned to old Dickey-devil," he said, only it came out: "Wunsallolorrismenchedtadickeydevil." Said as his scrawny body shifted about not quite visible within the enormous overcoat.

"Well, listen," Ellen said, hysteria gone but urgency remaining, "I was just going to call 'em, so let me go ahead, and I'll ask Claudette."

This time she got the operator, while Dickey-devil softly muttered interminably behind her, got the operator and then the *Mirror*, and Horris said, yes, Claudette was there and they were just about to head down to the drugstore to get a sandwich, and what the hell was she doing at their house this time of day, and she said she had hoped to find Claudette and could she talk to her now, and Claudette came on, and Ellen told her about the encounter with Carol Burcell, and Claudette told her not to take it too seriously and said they could talk after school, and Ellen said she didn't feel like going back to school this afternoon, and Claudette told her, nonsense, it was out of the question for her to stay out of school, she couldn't run, to eat a sandwich there and get her tail back to school, and just before they hung up Ellen heard Dickey-devil muttering about screens behind her, and so remembered to ask about that, and Claudette said, exasperated, that if it wouldn't seriously inconvenience him they would in fact like for Dickey-devil to fix not one but all of them, bye-bye.

"WellenIllfixemallifaysayso," he said when she had delivered the message, and then looked at her with solicitous, suspicious scrutiny and went on: "Elnworthyoumesseduppitdemburcells?" Which was to say: Was she messed up with them Burcells?

"Well, I had a run-in with Carol Burcell, is all. Dickey-devil, don't you know it's not nice to eavesdrop?"

"I know it's not nice to mix up with them Burcells," he said, enormous authority in the voice that he began slowing down for her benefit, slowing it down though he continued to reduce her name to a single word: Elnworth. "They bad medicine, Elnworth, and you mess with one you mess with 'em all. Those boys got no conscience. You know *bolita?* Just a way to steal a nigger's money all it is. You know they get black boys to push that thing, black boys to do their stealing from other black boys. Then when the black boys want to stop—*they* get messed up. Bad medicine, Elnworth, you stay away, you hear what Dickey-devil tells you. You don't I'll tell your Papa. He knows 'em. I'll tell Cliff too. He knows 'em. Yes mam your brother Cliff he tells me they amongst the ones getting this Klan thing cranked up again. 'Fraid cause seven little ole niggers showed up wantin' to vote come last November. You stay away you hear me."

"But Dickey-devil, I—"

"Now jusaminute, Elnworth, you listen to Dickey-devil. Don't know 'bout that girl Carol Burcell but she sho swishes around and I know her sister, she ran away out to Hollywood, so she couldn't be *much* good. Now you tell Dickey-devil, Elnworth, what got you mixed up with folks like that? Bet it's you taking that Henruss away from that girl Carol. Ain't that so?"

"Dickey-devil, I didn't *take* him away, but how on earth would you know anything about that?"

"So I's right, huh? Listen, ole Dickey-devil knows all, sees all, and you pay 'tention, you hear? You take bad medicine you gonna get sick sure." With that, shaking a disproportionately long and bony finger in a final admonishment, he turned away, went out across the back porch, muttering: "*Three* screens, *three* screens. They say *a* screen turns out to be *three* screens. No rest for the weary, no rest atall . . ."

She found the note rolled and stuck in her dry inkwell in study hall. It said: "PS If I don't hear by tonight it's out of my hands."

So the afternoon passed as an eternity of distraction and indecision, of rising terror and welling sorrow. Ellen thought, *The best thing that ever happened to me is over.*

She saw no more of Carol Burcell. But in the corridor, during the class change before the last period, she encountered Henry, and stopped for a couple of seconds, and could tell from his face that hers, in spite of her best efforts, was showing something was wrong.

"I didn't see you at lunch," he said.

"Well, I had to go somewhere," she said.

"I'll ride home with you when we get out."

"Well—okay."

"Is everything all right?" he said, his head tilting and his brows drawing in to form a deep V-shaped furrow between his eyes.

"Well—I'm not sure." She raised a hand. "I'll talk to you later." She thought, *God, I could never tell him.*

Knowing now that she would see him later for sure only intensified the almost sickening anguish that was coiling up inside her in a writhing knot. Ellen felt almost dazed or stupefied: it was hard or even impossible to believe how far she had plunged since the morning, when she had felt so good, as good as she had every day and maybe even every minute since the night of the dance. Ever since, she had felt elated and animated, at times almost soaring, rich and warm inside, full of sweet imaginings and excited plans, sharing his recent sorrow, yes, but somehow drawing strange strength from that instead of plunging.

Since New Year's Day, she had seen him every day but two. He had taken her twice to the movies. He had come to her house on the seventh for her birthday dinner, the usual family celebration of teasing and joshing, with the cake-cutting and the candle-blowing and the present-opening afterward, when the table was cleared. He had himself given her what she had promptly framed and hung in her room: a manuscript of his song "No More Time," with the hand-notated music on one page and the hand-scripted words on the page facing, with "For Ellen" written in the ear of the first page across from his by-line.

His gift had moved and filled her even more than the certificate in the envelope that her papa had casually slipped her and that entitled her to go to the local Ford dealer and pick out a new car, one that she had now ordered, but even before ordering it, she had imagined them driving in it to the Akana Mountains in the spring and to St. Teresa's in the summer, or maybe, she had imagined, this summer, if he were going to work with that band, she could drive him to New Orleans and drop him before going back to their beach house in St. Teresa's, where of course he would be coming on his days off and at the end of the summer.

It had been just so goddam good, everything, everything, even and maybe particularly his mother Portia that day Ellen had ridden home with him, and Mrs. Rust had, without quite saying it, intimated that she was so happy to see him with Ellen instead of you-know-who, as she had put it. And Henry, he had been nothing less than just right, not trying to push things at all, not trying to rush, not at all the guy to "look out for," as Matt and Mark had inevitably warned her when they realized she might be smitten. He hadn't even tried to take her hand again, except by the finger, in his way, until she walked him out to the yard the night of her birthday, and hadn't tried at all to kiss her until that night either, and then had only given her a quick brushing kiss, and that look, which was maybe even more powerful than a kiss could be. And only last weekend, after the

Saturday night show, had kissed her goodnight in a way that caused them both to let go and draw themselves together and melt for a minute before she extricated herself, breathless, and went inside and to bed to remember and remember until she got dizzy again the way she had the night after the dance.

Such was his way that at last she had been unable to believe that he had been the way Matt and Mark in the past had intimated he was with Carol Burcell. Sure, maybe something had happened with them, and what if it had, what was wrong with that if they loved each other when it happened. But maybe it hadn't, too, and from the way he was, maybe even probably it hadn't happened, but if in fact it had, well, she didn't want to know anyway, and couldn't know, actually, because her mind could not even admit the image of him making love with Carol Burcell, who couldn't have cared for him deeply anyway or she never would have treated him the way she did the night of the dance, breaking off because he wanted to play, doing that and then right under his nose throwing herself at one boy after the other and rubbing it all over that farthead college guy.

"Now that I know him, I mean know what he's like, I can't even imagine him taking up with a girl like Carol," she had said to Claudette.

"Maybe he needed a girl like that," Claudette had said. "He may have needed a girl who would betray him."

"What!"

"Ellen, some men are like that, some women too. Something has somehow and somewhere taught them that life is like that, that those they love must betray them. And so they go through life reconfirming what they already believe over and over again. What lesson would Henry have learned when his father moved out of his life?"

"You think he's like that?"

"No, no, no, I do not say *is*. But perhaps he *was*. And perhaps he doesn't need that any more. Perhaps, underneath it all, that's why he noticed you that night and asked you to let him see you home. I don't know, of course, but I can imagine. All of a sudden, with what's-her-name throwing it around, as you say, right under his nose, he realizes that he doesn't need that any more. Who knows?"

So Ellen had felt that, yes, it was going to be perfect all the way, because it was a new beginning for him, and a new one for her, too, in a way, coming out of that deep dark mood that had been nothing but unrecognized mourning, coming out of that and turning sixteen, and finally thinking about what she was going to do with her life, and deciding that she was going to be an artist, and they would live back and forth between McClung and New Orleans, and when the Nazis got beaten, as Horris said they would be, they could go to Paris and London and walk where she had walked with her mother and the others when she was nine, and to Mexico to see the Mayan murals if they could find them, and to China where the waterfront was like a hive of zillions and the countryside as calm and droning as the country around here in the deep heat of summer.

And, yes, had felt the yearning for him, the fleshhunger, the passion that wasn't brand new to her, that she had felt before simply with smoochy boyfriends, but that was different now, because it was fleshhunger with something else, fleshhunger with a deep yearning for a sharing of tenderness and mindstuff and carings and thinkings. And had known it would come, sometimes, but no hurry, just whenever it came, whenever it had to come, whenever it was time for it to be, which would be when things were right and not rushed or crowded or frantic or ridiculous like in the back seat of some goddam car. It had all, every bit of it, seemed so unbelievably good. And now, in one day, in three hours: gone.

Her mind, as she waited for the bell, was a strained moil of loathsome images that Carol Burcell, the goddam bitch, had planted, and that Ellen couldn't blot out, the images of them together not making love but merely fucking, and the image of him forced to marry her, and, maybe worse, the image of him refusing and then of her goddam vicious brothers beating in his face until the jutting bones were crushed and the delicate concavities lost forever in a pulp of pulverized flesh, or even killing him with one of the goddam pistols out of one of their goddam cars with the goddam dice hanging down from the mirror. And of she, herself: lost and alone and looking forever without ever finding again what she had found and so quickly lost at sixteen.

She shivered when the bell rang, thinking: *"Goddam, I can't tell him. Oh, shit, why did I come back to school?*

She told him, though. With enormous nervousness and a quaking voice she let it out after they met at the bike pile and ridden out to the Trail and down the drive to her front steps, on the bottom of which they sat while she told him.

"I didn't really want to tell you, but—well, I was afraid not to," she said, terrified.

He fell silent for a long, long time, shaking, growing pale, livid, clenching his bony fists until the skin of his knuckles was drawn deathly white, shaking when he finally spoke, almost in a whisper.

"The goddam bitch!"

She waited for him to go on, as he got up, silent again, got up and paced about, kicking at the dried grass, clenching his fists, working his jaw, looking at everything but her, at the sky, the trees, his brown scuffed shoes, the grass, the porch, but not at her, who could now hardly bear to look at him either, except that she was looking at him, was looking irresistibly just as he came to a still slouched but tensed and decisive standing posture that said he was about to say something, he who was now looking straight into her eyes with almost alarming intensity, he who was now talking soft and fast, with tenderness in his voice at the same time as leashed fury.

"Listen, what I feel for you I've never felt for any other person on earth. What I said to you the first night I really meant, only I didn't just think it, like I said, I knew. But I didn't want to say I knew before you knew too. Well, I don't know whether you know yet, because you haven't said, and I don't want you to say now under any circumstances, or ever, unless you really know, and maybe that'll be never. But I want to say to you that I still know, and that's all I want to say right now even though I'm desperately tempted to say a lot more. And maybe you even expect me to say a lot more, to answer a lot of questions you may have, must have. But I'm not going to say any more right now except what I've said. And I'm not even going to see you any more until I get this cleared up. And then I'll tell you anything you want to know. There's not a goddam thing in my life or memory that I wouldn't tell you about. And if I can still see you when I get this straightened out, then I'll see you and tell you anything you want to know. And in any event I'll be feeling exactly the way I know I feel now. I love you more than anything on earth, do you hear me, Ellen?"

He stared with those searing eyes for maybe two or three seconds more, and then abruptly turned about, and took up his bike, and started to pedal off, then braked by putting down his foot when she stood up full of dread and called out: "Henry? What are you gonna do?"

"I don't know," he said. "I'm not going to do anything today."

"But she said—"

"Ellen, I don't give a good goddam what she said!"

Then he was off, down the drive, out of sight, and she flew into the house, upstairs, to her room, and flung herself on the bed, sobbing hysterically.

At midnight she was still awake, her terror of the future unassuaged by her talk on the phone with Claudette, who seemed so blithely sure that everything would work out. Ellen had moped through supper, had barely eaten, had retreated to her room soon after, and now her stomach was not only seething with hot anguish but was growling, and her imaginings were a confusion of grisly and morbid images. Suddenly the big clock downstairs struck *one*. She thought, Oh, God, help me. Then it struck *two*, and she decisively sprang out of bed and drew on her yellow robe as she went down the hallway. She knocked three times fast on Matt's door before going in.

"I've got to talk to you," she said, as he groaned and propped himself on his elbow, and as Mark materialized in the open doorway of the adjoining bedroom.

"What the hell time is it?" Mark said, coming in.

"Crisis time," Matt said, now sitting up and leaning against his headboard as he took Ellen's hand and signaled her to sit down on the side of the bed.

"No jokes," she said. "I'm worried sick." And told them the whole story.

"Whew, what a mess," said Mark.

"Listen, Ellen, why don't we just hang loose and wait and see," said Matt.

"And let him get killed?" Ellen said, aghast.

"It could be worse—he could marry her," said Mark.

"Oh, shit, this is no joking matter," said Ellen.

"Listen, Dumpling, those bastards aren't going to kill Henry," said Matt.

"How can you be so sure? They're practically gangsters!"

"Maybe more than practically," said Mark.

"See? And even if they don't kill him, they could—oh, God, it's awful."

"Dumpling, you really have plumb fallen for that rascal, haven't you?" said Matt.

"I guess so, I don't know, I guess so."

"Well, listen, then," said Mark, "if you'll just promise us you'll go on to sleep—and go on to school tomorrow—and go on and act like nothing has happened—"

"We'll *guarantee* you," said Matt, finishing the sentence, "that this whole thing will be settled, no pain, no strain." He affected the Cajun pronunciation of *garr-ron-tee*.

"That's right," Mark echoed, "we'll see to it."

"Well, what can you do? How can you *garr-ron-tee* that those bastards won't do something?"

"Listen, musclehead, give us at least one or two minutes to

figure it out, for Christ's sake, will you? And, meanwhile, get the hell to bed," said Mark.

"And stop worrying, for God's sake," said Mark.

"Fat chance," said Ellen. "Listen, anyway, I'm sorry I had to wake you up."

"No bother, Dumpling," said Matt.

"Any time," said Mark, yawning. "Twenty-four-hour service."

Ellen turned back at their door. "You really think it'll be all right?"

"Goddamit, didn't we *garr-ron-tee?*" they said, as one.

Tuesday was a fatigued, agonized eternity at school with a few glimpses of a grim-looking Henry who never approached her, and no sign of Carol Burcell, and no one to meet after school, and neither the energy nor concentration to do anything once she had got home, even though for awhile she went up to the skylighted studio that Cliff had made her out of what had originally been built on the roof as an astronomical observatory. She daubed at a painting, but was much too distracted even for that, and so was back downstairs, sulking and hanging around, talking about nothing with Aunt Margaret while her Papa's sister stitched at the embroidery that she had been working on for years but would never explain to anybody.

Ellen haunted the front porch and front windows looking for the return of Matt and Mark to talk to them and find out what they had figured out, but they had neither shown up nor called in as the household sat down for supper: her Papa and Aunt Margaret and the housekeeper, Mrs. Pichon, and two of her half-sisters and one half-brother, all from her Papa's second brood, all of whom had wound up living in California, whence these had come visiting at Christmas and decided to stay on for a couple of weeks.

"Where are the boys?" her Papa asked in mid-meal. When nobody answered, her Papa said: "Well, I guess that's as good an explanation as any." Everybody laughed.

"Basketball maybe?" Cliff asked Ellen.

"Oh, yeah, I think there is a practice game," Ellen said.

Oddly, just then the phone rang in the back hall and Cliff took it and came back to say it was the team manager calling to tell Matt and Mark the practice game was off because the Guard was using the armory for some drill or other.

"I guess they're just messing around," Ellen said, shrugging.

Supper had been done an hour, and four or five of them were slouching around the parlor listening to the radio when the phone next rang. Ellen bolted up to answer, but Cliff was already up and going after it, so she sat back down. He was on the phone for awhile, or at least gone for awhile, and was pulling on the coat of what he called his lawyer-suit as he came back through the parlor door with a furrowed and faintly but not entirely amused expression on his face, a face that gazed at all of them in turn, as though it were about to crack a joke, or something, and then settled on her, Ellen, with its squinty sea captain's eyes regarding her as though she were a culprit. In a slow cool voice, and yet with the expression he might have managed if he were about to make a happy announcement, Cliff said something.

"Well, I've located the lost children at last," he said, sticking his tongue into his jaw as though digging out some lingering morsel of supper.

"Matt and Mark?" Ellen said.

"They're in jail," Cliff said, with some pride in his voice, as though they had just won Rhodes scholarships.

"What on earth for?" Ellen yelled out, bounding toward Cliff as she spoke, as did the others in the room.

"Well," Cliff said thoughtfully, "attempted homicide is one of the charges, according to Matt. But there are a few others, such as assault and battery and reckless driving and malicious destruction of property."

"Great goddamighty!" her Papa suddenly broke out. "Cliff, what the hell is going on? Is this a joke?"

"I'm afraid not, Papa, and I won't actually know what's going on until I get down to the jail and talk with the first three clients I've accepted in two years."

"Three?" Ellen said.

"Why, yes," Cliff said, with that exasperating calm that he always liked to display in emergencies. "Ellen, it seems that your nice young man Henry Rust is one of my clients too."

"Henry?"

"I'll declare, Ellen, for once you must have understood what I said," Cliff said, once again adjusting his coat buttons as though to go.

"Cliff, don't torment me!" Ellen shouted. "What's going on? Why is he in jail?"

"Well, as I understand it, the charges against him are precisely the same as the charges against your dear brothers, with the exception of reckless driving."

"Oh, God, what happened, Cliff?" Ellen said, as though spokesman for all those converged around Cliff.

"I hope to find out soon," Cliff said.

"But, Cliff, isn't homicide *murder?*"

"I'm afraid it can be so construed, depending on the motive and intents and state of mind of the person attempting or committing it."

"Well, did they try to *kill* somebody?" Ellen said.

"Ellen," Cliff said, "I don't actually know, but you tell me something. Can you think of any reason on earth why your brothers and Henry would have gotten tangled up with Jack and Jim Burcell?"

"Oh, God!" Ellen said, gasping and clamping her hand over her mouth.

"Well, Ellen, that along with what Dickey-devil was kind enough to tell me, more or less answers my question."

"Oh, God, help me," Ellen said, almost staggering backward.

"Ellen, while you're calling on Him, you put in a good word for my clients, too, will you?"

Suddenly Ellen bolted out the door into the hallway, saying: "Cliff, I'm going with you!"

"Ellen!" her Papa's voice rang out like a shot, and she bounced back into the room. "Ellen, you're not going any-goddam-where! Now, sit down and listen to the radio! Everybody sit down!" Her Papa was pounding the end of his cudgel-thick stick on the floor. "Everybody sit down and leave this to Cliff! Cliff, get on down there and get those boys out of there if you have to take that goddam jail down brick by brick!"

Cliff was out the door.

"Ellen," her Papa shouted, "I said sit *down*." And then sat down himself beside her on the couch and encircled her trembling shoulder with an arm that crushed her to him like a rag doll while his other enormous freckled brown hand hammered his stick on the carpet in an agitated tattoo.

CLIFTON SHARPE (CLIFF) WORTH:

As soon as he heard footsteps ascending up the creaky stairs within four minutes after he himself had gotten not to work but merely to his office, he knew who it had to be, because, on arriving and parking on the main street down below, he had glimpsed who it had to be sitting with his legs propped up on his desk like two blunt cannon in the window of the *Mirror* office across the street, and knew that he himself of course had been glimpsed by who it had to be, and so was so little surprised when the stocky young man with the hairless globe-like head and the collarless patterned shirt loomed in and barged eagerly through his private doorway, that he neither had to ask nor hear what T.C. Horris wanted but instead silently gestured him into the chair opposite and began talking even as he poured him a cup from the quart thermos of coffee that he had brought in with him under his arm.

He said:

Broadly, it was like escaping from time, like stumbling into some kind of proceeding that might just possibly have occurred accidentally somewhere back before the invention of law. Possibly the very kind of proceeding that might have so impacted on the minds of men as to convince them suddenly and utterly of the absolute necessity either to formulate that mystical fiction we call jurisprudence or else abandon all hope of ever arriving at an understanding or agreement as to who should do the talking, and who should do the listening, and hence all hope of ever resolving any conflict of any nature whatsoever by any means other than incantation or combat.

In short, it seemed, at the outset, like a proceeding without procedure, with those who had called on me as counsel all but physically assaulting the magistrate from one side, while the honorable adversaries of my dear clients assaulted him from the other, not physically but with such a clamor that, had I been he, I would have jailed the lot on the spot with strong recommendations against any subsequent show of mercy or amnesty.

Maybe the closest thing to it I have ever been privileged to witness was the trial and conviction, by forcible exile, of a West African witch doctor who had been accused by his tribe of being a fraud, and who, when I last saw him, was sprinting into the jungle hotly pursued by the jury of tribesmen who, by the very act of the defendant's flight, had become his peers. There were two or three hundred of them in pursuit, flinging spears and knives and axes and stones at the defendant, along with samples of a certain kind of nut that grows to the size of a baseball. Their theory of law was that if he were indeed a witch doctor he would by his powers emerge from the jungle unscathed, and, if not, would be perhaps overwhelmingly tempted not to emerge at all, in which case he might just possibly enjoy life to a ripe old age somewhere else and the tribe, meanwhile, could see to the selection of a dependable witch doctor. Upon close examination, their theory turns out to be exquisitely sound and literally pregnant with the fine juices of both justice and mercy, and possibly even amnesty, which is the most merciful juice of all.

At the moment I got there, to the jail, the receiving room where the deputies had already more or less collapsed in hysteria, it seemed that the magistrate, the honorable one-eyed Charlie d'Iberia, had fallen into the role of witch doctor, with my clients and their adversaries more or less taking the part of the tribesmen, and certainly with none of them showing an inordinate respect for the dignity of a half-blind judge who had just torn himself away from his postprandial cups to answer a call to duty. The whole pack of them, Matt and Mark on one side, and Henry, too, and Jim and Jack Burcell on the other, looked like they had just come in from a street riot that had not quite ended yet. All told, they were as bloody and disheveled looking a bunch as I have seen since a certain untoward event in Singapore. Bruises. Black eyes. Cuts. Splits. Contusions. Lumps. Shredded shirts. You know, the kind of cosmetic effect you can expect when you apply your makeup with tire irons, brass knuckles, pistol barrels, and even plain unvarnished fists and feet. They looked awful, horrible even, though our beloved medical examiner Amos McCall had come in and poured iodine all over them and patched gauze here and there, as well as temporarily binding up Henry's right hand, which, I was a long time learning, he evidently broke in two or three places in exchange for a fascinating new profile that he achieved in the hitherto unblemished nose of everybody's favorite roughneck, Jack Burcell.

I was personally happy to see that Amos was still hanging around when I got there, since my first thought was that his services might be further needed, and this in fact seemed an eventuality that he was prepping for by periodically pouring himself little drinks out of a paperbagged pint into a paper cup that kept dripping down his shirt front. Which Amos kept on doing, and the cup too, even though His Honor, good old Charlie d'Iberia, would look over from time to time, no doubt more out of envy than for the sake of decorum, and caution that there would be no drinking tolerated in this courtroom. To which Amos countered each time by raising the drippy paper cup in a toast and saying: "This is not a courtroom, Your Honor."

Which, after the third or fourth time, prompted His Honor Charlie to personally march all of us out of the receiving office of the jailhouse and across the street and into a courtroom, where he didn't assume the bench but, instead, sat at the counsel's table along with everybody else. Amos McCall came along, too, with his brown bag and cup, and now when His Honor Charlie cautioned him that no drinking would be tolerated, Amos raised up his drippy cup and said, "It's a prescription drug, your honor. I prescribed it myself."

Meanwhile, Sonny Grindell had come in wearing a brand new plaid vest to bolster the case of his clients, the Burcell boys, but was having as little luck in quieting them down as I was with mine, my clients, or at least Matt and Mark, since the Rust boy didn't need quieting down, as he evidently was suffering an anomalous case of good manners. But to shorten it all down, some crude semblance of order finally obtained after I finally managed to catch His Honor Charlie's bloodshot eye and ear and, with as much volume as I could manage, employed a little known defense technique by moving that the court, instantum, find everyone present including counsel guilty of contempt and sentence us all to the county jail until sunrise the following day or until total silence should prevail among us, whichever might come first. At the word "motion," however, Sonny Grindell stopped staring down at his new plaid vest and jumped to his feet to object, and did this in such a magnificent voice that it produced just sufficient silence to permit His Honor Charlie d'Iberia to observe, with admirable clarity, that he wasn't about to entertain any objection simply because he wasn't there to entertain any motion that might be objected to, and in fact was not conducting a session of court nor even sitting as a court but was present only as the magistrate required by State Statute 109.11 to participate at the issuance of any warrants charging a capital felony.

Evidently this was the first moment during which Sonny Grindell quite realized that his clients were in danger of the electric chair, and this brought him once again to his feet, with his coat held apart and his vest well displayed, saying: "Capital? What capital offense?"

"Kidnapping, to name just one," said His Honor Charlie, "and conspiracy to commit murder, to name another. But sit down Mr. Vest—uh, Mr. Grindell—sit down and shut up and let's start at the be-goddam-ginning, and maybe we will be lucky enough to discover several others as we go along, and maybe I will even find out what happened along with all the instruction in law that the complainants and putative defendants have variously been giving me."

And, sure enough, to my astonishment, but not necessarily to my relief, they did—start at the be-goddam-ginning, that is. Up to now, all His Honor Charlie had heard was that long and ever-growing list of charges that the Burcell boys wanted to place against my clients, and those ever-more-imaginative charges that my clients, having had the disadvantage of past association with a lawyer, wanted to prosecute against them. As to what had happened to give rise to all the fury and wounds and recriminations, His Honor Charlie d'Iberia had even less of an idea than I, and I had none at all that was worthy of the name idea, since, on the phone, all Matt had told me that had now been substantially verified was, "Cliff, we're down at the goddam jail with the goddam Burcells, and they're trying to charge us with attempted homicide, et cetera et cetera." But once His Honor Charlie got them started at the be-goddam-ginning, at least some rudimentary outline of the prior and moving events began to emerge.

"Let me hear one side at a time," His Honor Charlie said, and of course, at that, Matt and Mark and Jim and Jack Burcell all began yelling again, but not with their prior force and velocity, and they soon fell silent after His Honor Charlie stopped up his ears with his two index fingers, which, at this dramatic show of respect—the silence—he removed, and then flipped an imaginary coin and pointed toward my clients.

"Let's hear your account of what happened," His Honor Charlie said, and, when Matt and Mark both started talking at once, left it to me to mediate between them and select a spokesman, which I did by applying the seniority rule and designating Matt, who is of course the elder by some very few minutes.

Whereafter we were all ennobled by an account wherein it appeared that Matt and Mark Worth were present at these proceedings first and foremost, and indeed only, as civic-minded defenders of law and order, a role that Matt was enabled the better to intimate by the fact that nobody was under oath, nor was to be put under oath, His Honor Charlie proclaimed, until he had got the stories and until he had decided whether anybody or everybody was entitled to swear out warrants certifying to all the felonies mentioned so far.

Naturally, Matt didn't begin quite at the beginning. He began by describing how he and his brother had merely been cruising about in their decapitated limousine before supper, going no place in particular, just passing the time, when they had driven down the street where their friend Henry Rust happens to live, and had seen parked thereon two suspicious looking characters sitting in a car with overload springs and a pair of oversized dice hanging from the mirror, two characters who on closer inspection chanced to be Jim and Jack Burcell. Well, having decided that for the good of the community and the safety of the neighborhood they should inspect the situation more closely, they had circled a block and come back the other way down said street, and had got back to it just in time to see the Burcell car pull forward toward some approaching citizen who, as it turned out, was their friend Henry Rust. And then, to their astonishment, they saw the Burcell car stop alongside Henry Rust, and saw Jack Burcell get out and, as it appeared to them, force their friend to get in the car, which then drove off.

Well, naturally, as Matt told it, they thought they had eyewit-
nessed a possible kidnapping, a capital felony if there ever was one,
and a crime any citizen is obligated to take note of and act on in some
reasonable way. And so, to investigate further, they had tailed the
Burcell car, keeping it under surveillance as it turned off of Henry's
street and onto the main drag, bearing east, and following it hence
out the highway east of town, their suspicions growing all the while,
to crystallize when they observed the Burcell car turn left onto a dirt
road that everybody who got around at all knew was seldom used
by traffic engaged in normal law-abiding business. All their suspicions were enhanced, of course, by the fact that the Burcells had
Henry Rust sitting between them on the front seat at a time when
the rear seat of the car would have been more comfortable for him
as well as more convenient for the driver and his kindred companion.

Thus my clients decided that the moment had come for them
to do their duty and act on their suspicions in a reasonable way, and
so they gunned their decapitated limousine and drove up alongside
said Burcell vehicle and, with Matt at the wheel and Mark doing the
calling out, had ordered Jack Burcell, operator of the object car, to
stop forthwith. It seems that said Jack Burcell answered this reasonable request not with compliance but with some common abusive
oath, and it was at that moment that my clients invoked the whole
body of the law in the behalf of their mission and decency and
forthwith informed Mr. Burcell that he was under arrest.

They were executing, you see, a citizen's arrest, evidently the
first recorded in the legal history of the county, according to His
Honor Charlie, whose grasp of legal history abides with him even
amidst certain other lapses. Jack and Jim Burcell, however, did not
gracefully surrender at once, and in fact kept driving onward down
the dirt road, all the while addressing my clients in provocative,
abusive, and even threatening language, to their dismay.

At last, when it seemed that Jack Burcell, as well as talking bad,
was leaning forward as though to retrieve from its holster the deadly
weapon everybody knew was usually carried in his car, Matt and
Mark were obliged to make one of those split-second decisions that
are forced on citizen arresters, evidently, as well as conventional
officers of the law. Matt swerved in such a way as to encourage the
Burcell vehicle to come to a halt, and, in fact, it came to a halt with
its front wheels in the shallow ditch that runs alongside that particular road. My clients, of course, immediately leaped out to make the
arrest, but were confronted with totally uncooperative suspects as
well as what they felt they reasonably construed as grave danger.

Just as they leaped from the limousine, in fact, a revolver held in Jack Burcell's hand came sticking out the window of his car, and in fact it was discharged, but fortunately only after Henry Rust, from his place in the front seat, had yanked Jack Burcell from behind, causing the shot to go askew.

"And then," as Matt put it, "the trouble started, Your Honor."

The young, of course, have no sense whatever of beginnings. Even today, Matt likely would resist the notion that the trouble started not then, nor when they saw the Burcell boys, nor when the Burcell boys took Henry Rust into their car, nor even in this epoch, and not even with the birth of the principals in the case, but in some no-time back there when some mysterious nothing on earth was caused for unknown reasons to begin tending toward the occurrence of human life on this peculiar planet.

Of course, the trouble Matt was talking about was that which evolved as the pistol's owner followed the pistol out of the car, and as his brother Jim Burcell, exiting from the other side, leaped over the hood of their car with a tire iron that he planted on Mark's cheekbone. Obviously, the story here must be fragmented, but, as Matt pieced it together, it seems that while Mark was dealing with Jim Burcell, Matt and Henry had their hands full with Jack. That is, while the tire iron befell Mark, Jack whipped his pistol back against Henry's face, after which Matt, with a providentially accurate punt kicked the pistol out of Jack's hand.

Jack's hand had no sooner lost the pistol, which went skeetering down the road, than it dipped into his coat pocket and reappeared dressed with metal knuckles, with which he began chopping into Matt's face, even as Henry, from behind, tried to restrain him with a stranglehold. Which didn't hold, since, as Matt and Mark now admit, and Henry too, the Burcell boys are not putting up a false front when they travel on their reputation for strength and meanness.

For awhile, in fact, Jack, with the help of the knucks, was better than holding his own against Matt and Henry. And, meanwhile, Mark was being spun around like a ballet dancer grasping onto the end of the tire iron that Jim Burcell was of course trying to shake him loose from so as to put it back into productive use. Jim did shake him loose, unfortunately for Mark, and got in two fast clouts on the collarbone and skull. But this, as Matt put it, caused Mark to lose his temper. Yes, to lose his temper so thoroughly that he kicked Jim Burcell where it hurts real bad, which kick, in this instance, caused Jim Burcell to lose all interest in the tire iron, which he dropped, and which Mark deftly retrieved and used to eliminate the possibility of suffering further harm at the hands of this adversary. He knocked him unconscious, in short, and evidently at almost the same time that Matt had leaped down the road and picked up the pistol, which, as chance had it, was at precisely the same moment that Henry connected with a lucky haymaker that demolished Jack Burcell's nose, and presumably his will to resist arrest, as well as Henry's own guitar-picking right hand.

And so it came to pass that, while peace-loving folk everywhere were either contemplating or enjoying or finishing up supper, two deputy sheriffs, both of them quite likely on the private payroll of the Burcell boys, looked up from their domino game in the receiving room of the jail and saw Jim and Jack Burcell marched in at the point of their own gun, it held by the hand of my client Matt Worth, with Mark following close at hand holding a tire iron, and Henry holding the knuckles, all of which items they hoped and intended to introduce as evidence upon the trial of these defendants, whom they announced they had apprehended as citizens acting under State Statute 219.87 as amended in 1891. And against whom, they informed the deputies, they were lodging charges of kidnapping, felonious assault, attempted homicide, disorderly conduct, illegal use of firearms, threatening and abusive language, et cetera et cetera et cetera, and of course, resisting arrest.

I don't have to describe for you the hysterical dilemma of the deputies faced by a demand that they book and incarcerate their moonlight employers, nor the reaction of Matt and Mark when they heard the Burcell boys begin to describe *themselves* as the actual complainants, and when they saw the deputies actually listening, paying attention, with respect, as Jack and Jim began charging *them* with kidnapping, attempted homicide, et cetera et cetera. Which is, of course, where I came in, or where I was brought in by their phone call.

So now, after Matt had done, His Honor Charlie listened to the Burcell side of the story, as told by Jack, according to whose account they had not forced Henry Rust to get in their car, they had only *asked* him to go with them to talk something over, he being an old family friend. Said they were only driving him out to their country house which is in fact just down that country road. Said they had not even got around to talking in the car when, lo and behold, these two maniac kids in the decapitated limousine roared up beside them and told them to get the hell over and turn Henry loose. Said, actually, they would have cheerfully turned Henry loose, if that had been the point, but that the point was, nobody on earth except an officer of the law had any right to drive up alongside them and order them to do a goddam thing. And said naturally they hadn't stopped, and when the Worth kids swerved into them, naturally they had come out fighting. Said, as for the gun, well, he wouldn't have fired it at all if their friend Henry hadn't panicked behind him and, for some reason, shook him up, because he had only intended to use the gun to scare these kids and keep them from trespassing on their rights.

When he had done, His Honor Charlie d'Iberia thought a second or two and then seemed to catch the Burcells off guard. His Honor said, "What'd you want to talk to him about?"

And Jack Burcell said, "Talk to him about? What's that got to do with it?"

And His Honor said, "What'd you want to talk to him about?"

And Jack said, "That's private business, judge."

And His Honor said, "Not any more. What did you want to talk to Henry Rust about?"

Well, the Burcells started to squirm, and Sonny Grindell, with his thumbs in his plaid vest, started to say something, but His Honor Charlie raised a brusque hand to silence him and said, "It's not a trial, Mr. Grindell." And then he turned to Henry, who was sitting there beside me, and said, "Henry, what did they want to talk to you about?"

And Henry said, "Well, all they, or rather Jack, said to me was, 'Carol's talked to us, and you and me's got some talking to do.'"

And His Honor said, "Would that be Carol Burcell?"

And Henry said, "Yes, sir."

And His Honor said, "Did you know what they meant?"

And Henry said, "I didn't know what they had in mind."

And His Honor said, "No, of course not. Did they force you to get in the car?"

And Henry said, "Well, not exactly. Jack just said, 'Get in the goddam car.'"

And His Honor said, "And you got in."

And Henry said, "Yes, sir, I got in."

And His Honor said, "I see." And his bloodshot eye confirmed that he did. And then he turned to the Burcells again and said, "Okay, boys, let's hear about the talking you wanted to do with this young man."

And Jack Burcell said, "Your Honor, we can't talk about that, it was strictly a private matter." They were both squirming good now, with Jim sitting there picking at some shred of his blood-stained shirt, doing that while His Honor Charlie *slowly* got up from his seat at the center of the table, and told everybody to sit still, and went out, and down the hall, and soon came back, and said sit still a little longer, which we all did for about fifteen minutes during which we didn't know what was up.

We didn't have the slightest hint until the deputy ushered her in the door. Actually, I saw her brothers' faces before I saw her, and after seeing them knew that when I turned around I was going to see her, and did. The deputy brought her down the aisle and up to the table facing Charlie d'Iberia, and she stood there trembling, more or less aghast at the sight of her brothers and the others, and soon not looking at anybody at all but keeping her eyes fixed down on the table top while Charlie explained to her, talking very softly, that at the moment he was not holding a trial, but was only trying to find out one thing, and that was what her brothers had wanted to talk to Henry Rust about, and that her brothers wouldn't say, and that it would be unfair to ask Henry Rust to guess, and that she didn't have to say anything at all, but that her name had been brought up in connection with it, and so, if she could and would enlighten him, he would be much obliged and maybe could then proceed to resolve this whole complicated mess if not to everybody's satisfaction at least his own. He let her stand silent and shaking for a long time, and then merely spoke her name very softly—"Carol?"—and then waited again, and pretty soon she spoke up in a barely audible voice.

She said, "Well, I told them I was in trouble, and I guess they wanted to talk to him about that."

And Charlie said, "You mean pregnant."

And she said, "That's what I told them."

And Charlie said, "And you told them it was Henry."

And she said, "Well, they knew we used to go together."

And Charlie said, "Used to."

And she said, "We don't any more."

And Charlie said, "Did you tell Henry?"

And she said, "Henry?"

And Charlie said, "Did you tell him you were in trouble?"

And she said, "No, sir."

And Charlie said, "You didn't tell Henry? You told your brothers?"

And she said, "Yes, sir."

And Charlie said, "If he was the one, why didn't you tell Henry?"

And she said, "I don't know, sir."

Well, by now the Burcell boys were studying their sister as
though she were the defendant and they part of the prosecution team,
silently, of course, because by now everybody had fallen absolutely
quiet, Henry inscrutably quiet, sitting there beside me at the end of
the table, his eyes glancing from her, to his hands, to Charlie d'Iberia,
who suddenly turned our way and spoke.

Charlie said, "Henry, you have anything to say?"

And Henry peered at Charlie for a couple of seconds and then
looked directly toward her who was still standing there facing Charlie, still standing and no doubt still owning the same devastating
shape she's owned for the last couple of years but at the moment
looking strangely crumpled or deflated or something, as you can
imagine. And it was not to His Honor but to her that he spoke,
Henry, quietly and with some immense calm and certainty and ear-
nestness that surely caught me by surprise and obviously everybody
else, too, including her.

He said, "Carol, if you're pregnant I'll marry you."

Well, at that, she looked not merely astonished but shocked, and
the Burcell boys commenced to muttering betwixt themselves as
though they were thinking of inviting *her* to go out for a talk on some
country road, and Matt and Mark at first gaped and then took on that
peculiar look to suggest that they actually knew what was going on,
and Charlie d'Iberia suddenly squinted his thick little eyebrows
together and peered with that bloodshot eye at Henry as either somebody who had just offered him a thousand dollars tax free or maybe
had just confessed to some hitherto unsolved atrocity, staring at him,
in other words, with the profoundest perplexity and incredulousness
until he finally thought of what was on his mind.

And then His Honor Charlie said, "You *mean* that, son?"

And Henry said, "Sure, I mean it."

Well, maybe it was Henry's own cool, calm, perfectly serene
and certain tone of voice that all of a sudden crystallized what His
Honor had probably already begun thinking, as some of the rest of
us certainly had after observing Carol and taking note of her word-
ings. In any event, His Honor now looks not at Carol, whose face
is the picture of arrested consternation and regret, but past her out
among the benches where Amos McCall is still sitting, there with his
prescription drug dripping out of the paper cup that he had stuck
over the one that was previously dripping.

And Charlie says, now very briskly and formally, "Dr. McCall,
how quickly can you do an examination on this young woman?"

And Amos, startled to attention, says, "Examination?"

And all but simultaneously the girl is shouting out, "I'm not going to take a damn examination!"

And all of a sudden her words are hanging there in the room as clear and distinct as a single cloud in a summer sky. And His Honor Charlie just lets them hang there for what seemed a long time to me and must have seemed an eternity to Carol Burcell. Charlie just sat gazing at her now, not like a magistrate at all, but like a loving uncle perhaps, disappointed in a favorite niece, just sat watching her sympathetically and giving her time to discover for herself the meaning of what she had just said, and the implication of it in the light of what Henry had just said. We all sat watching now in utter stillness, until frankly even I felt an impulse to go take her in my arms, and not out of resurgent lechery but out of a feeling kin to that which continued to show on the face of old Charlie d'Iberia. Charlie waited until she had actually begun to sob, had let the tears come running, and still waited, and then just as she began to sob, just as what was inside her demanded to come out more than she could any longer demand that it stay in, until she was sobbing and then sagging into that immemorial slumped posture of regret wherein every human being somehow resembles a question mark, only then did he speak up in the quietest and kindliest possible voice.

Charlie said, "Carol, are you—"

But she didn't let him finish. She said, "I thought I was yesterday, but—No, sir, I'm not." And then she started sobbing and shouting at once. She said, "But I thought I was! I thought I was! I swear I thought I was."

And then all of a sudden her whole upper half fell forward on the table, with her arms in her face, and Charlie pointed a finger at Jack Burcell and said, "Take your sister to a seat and then on home after we finish up, and try to be understanding, you hear me? She's hurtin' enough. In fact, everybody here is hurtin' enough for one day." And while Jack Burcell was coming over and getting her, His Honor Charlie more or less wrapped it up, with a decision that won't but ought to go down in the history not of jurisprudence, which it wasn't, but of humaneness and common sense, which it indubitably was.

He said, "Now, having heard the complaints and preliminary reports in the cases variously of Matt Worth and Mark Worth and Henry Rust and Jim Burcell and Jack Burcell, it is the decision of the magistrate that if *any single one* of the multitudinous charges involved is to be pressed, then all such charges and countercharges will be certified for grand jury action and all defendants incarcerated and held without bail pending possible indictment, and in the event of indictment, pending trial and final disposition. Now is the appropriate time for either any complainant or counsel for same to let it be known whether any single charge is to be pressed."

Well, Sonny Grindell and I both vigorously shook our heads in the negative at once, and then everybody tensed as though to rise, but were signaled to sit fast for one more moment by His Honor, who had only a few more words to say.

Charlie said, "So be it, then, and let all preliminary accusations be expunged from the records, let the matter be forgotten, and let peace and order and goodwill be resumed. And now the court requests that Dr. Amos McCall repair with him to chambers for an examination of the evidence in the case of the prescription drug."

More coffee, son?

1941

End of Summer

3

Henry would be coming in from New Orleans by early evening for sure, but with a little luck just might roll in on the midafternoon bus, and never before had Ellen wished so keenly for just a little bit of extra luck, because never before had she so keenly craved his presence, not that she could remember, and certainly not in this particular way, not simply missing him, not only yearning as usual to see and hear and touch him, and not even merely because it was going to be something special for them to be together on this last, long weekend of summer with everything set for a last, long party before she and her family would head back to McClung sometime next week. Today, this Friday that had dawned fair but now in the early afternoon begun to blow and drizzle, she wished for him as the only person on earth whose presence would surely make things seem familiar and good and steady in a world that had seemed strangely changed since what had happened with Matt and Mark and Mrs. Fielding, what evidently was still happening.

Ellen could find no good words to describe the strange change as she sat with her open loose-leaf notebook before her at the interior end of the long dining-room table. She sat in white shorts straddling the straight-back chair with her bare feet curled around its front legs, and could feel breezy gusts on her back that was left bare by the halter she had made out of two blue bandanas. One gust cutting through the practically doorless downstairs of the house lifted up the uppermost of a stack of paper napkins set at the center of the table, at whose other end a vast window opened onto the high-ceilinged porch and a built-up yard held intact by a four-foot sea wall, and the bay with a few skiffs of fishermen weathering the slanting drizzle, the sloping sandy beach and the bay, and then the Gulf, a vista Ellen had seen and loved a million times but that now, with all else, seemed strangely different, somehow changed as though by a mysterious and incalculable shift in perspective or perhaps a chimerical fading of coloration. It was hard to tell how, impossible.

She gazed through the window, down to her notebook, back to the window, attending her thoughts and mindlessly jiggling the tapered tip of her red penholder between the edges of her front teeth, absently drumming it back and forth in time with the rhythm of the radio music that was filling the house from the big front room across the hall where the others were listening or dancing or talking or something, two or three of the bunch from the new house down the beach, and Percy and Florence, and the new and newly arrived Gebhart girls who had been invited down from McClung for the Labor Day weekend by Matt and Mark. Ellen could hardly think of her brothers now without also thinking of Mrs. Fielding, and they all seemed different, everything seemed different, as though the earth had tilted slightly on its axis. Her brothers seemed so—so—so something that she could hardly imagine them any longer cutting up and having fun with two girls of mere high school age. Just as she was unable to imagine herself talking with Mrs. Fielding easily and comfortably the way they had done from the very outset, almost from the minute they had shown up in July and taken over the rented house next up the beach.

And Ellen had liked her so much and so fast, had liked her easy and open way of talking, had liked that wry self-deprecating laugh she would give out at any compliment, and the gentle and playful way she got along with her children, not only not showing irritation but not seeming to have any, even when they were underfoot or complaining, the boy of four and the girl of two-and-a-half. She had even admired Mrs. Fielding's way of walking with that slow, loose-limbed, long stride, a manner that seemed in perfect harmony with the easy way she talked, gradually divulging a history that had made Ellen admire her even more, because she had survived, with such a good nature, such poignant and tragic events, to which she referred, when she did, with no trace of regret or self-pity, but only with that engaging, gently ironic laugh that she would give out while running her muscular hand through her usually unruly head of cropped and coppery hair.

Corinne Fielding had been born in Boston but brought up in France, where her father, a historian, had taken up residence after his wife and a son had been killed in a car crash in 1923 when Corinne had been seven. At twenty she had married Herbert Fielding, who had met her in Paris and brought her home to the United States and Washington where he was a government careerist now newly assigned to this region as an inspector of defense plant construction or site selection, it wasn't always made clear which. Fielding's assignment, however, had brought them to St. Teresa's, among other places, looking for housing that they had finally obtained, by chance, in the house forty yards up the beach from Sam Worth's big summer place.

And since then, while her husband remained not obscure but extremely diffident and self-contained, a man who was frequently away and uncommonly taciturn even when he was at hand, Corinne Fielding and her children had become familiar figures along the beach. Sometimes, on days when she had help with the children, now and then from a part-time maid and occasionally provided by Ellen, she could be seen strolling slowly along wearing a man's faded chambray shirt that gave her the appearance of having on nothing else underneath.

Ellen had even liked her style of abjuring the conventional beachstuff, of mentioning her age, twenty-five, as though it were merely an interesting fact, and had fully appreciated the admiring ribaldry that her figure and movements had inspired in Matt and Mark from the very beginning. They had maniacally exulted in the shape and flexing of the haunches and behind: *"Two gorgeous melons marvelously come to life, "*one had said. Ellen had hardly been surprised when her two obstreperous brothers had gradually taken to dealing with Mrs. Fielding with open and semicomic flirtations, and would have expected nothing of her but the way she had always countered it, with wry laughter and that look in her gray eyes that said she had a friendly invisible thumb to her nose.

Ellen had simply not even imagined the possibility of what had happened last Tuesday night, of what she at first simply couldn't believe, or could not believe even as she believed it, finally forced to believe what her whole mind resisted with a sharp and mysterious resistance not fully understood, a resistance of unreasoned aversion or avoidance that had finally yielded, not subsiding but surrendering, when it had become clear the following night, Wednesday night, that it was likely happening again.

"Man, you won't believe. . . " they had said the first night in their very first words to Percy, whom she had left sitting on the front steps to come up herself to her bedroom overlooking the porch-roof and the bay. *"Man, what—a—woman!"* the other had said. And she, just then trying to make the right dent in her pillow, had smiled and agreed with Percy's blunt rejoinder: *"Oh, bullshit."*

But something special in their voices had caught her, something excited and urgent, had raised her up to an elbow to listen further, and more attentively, even though she was already feeling guilt that she was heeding at all, already tempted to yell down and tell them to shut up, except that she had deferred the temptation amidst gathering fascination, and so listened on with instinctive incredulousness engendered by their long habit of baiting her and others with patently inflated braggadocio about their adventures and intents, braggadocio that they didn't even expect to be believed. She was held by the something new and different in their voices, not only in their tone but their wish to be believed in this relating of something that even they knew was beyond belief and which had impelled her to sit up and swing about and sit on the edge of her bed close by the big window whose sheer curtains were rising and falling in the dimness before the same breezes that seemed to be bringing their words into her bedroom with uncanny clarity, even when they began speaking in instinctively lowered tones that also caused her to wonder if this were more braggadocio, spilled out for the raw fun of it, or something real and hence requiring their uncharacteristically low voices because, even if it could be told to their closest crony, it could not be flaunted or imprudently divulged.

Percy, that lady just turned two boys into men . . . Man, until tonight we didn't know what it was all about . . . Come on, you expect me to believe . . . Man, I told you you wouldn't believe . . . Percy, to tell the God's truth I can't even believe what . . . Man, we didn't even start it . . . Hell, what we said when we went up there, we were just talking, but, man . . . Listen, we were just sittin' in the yard, chewing the fat, you know, and we had even decided to come back down here, but . . .

The breeze now was bringing her not merely words but images, and Ellen could see them sitting in the backyard close by the children's bedroom so that she could hear in case one of them called out, could see Mrs. Fielding as usual in the chambray shirt over her halter and shorts, sitting and making easy talk, in her way, and running her muscular hands through the unruly hair whose copperiness would be lost in the dimness but that would gleam and fluff about in its way after she had asked them if they were in a hurry, and after she had invited them to come in and have a beer, and after they had followed behind those animate melons and flexing haunches into the kitchen, she pausing at the door of it and then slipping her arms around their waists to usher them in, and then getting out three beers and handing them each one with that here-you-go look in her eyes, those slightly protuberant eyes in the face that was not beautiful but strong and engaging, mobile and set with the strong, faintly romanesque nose and the wide mouth that was forever tilting into that wry self-deprecating laugh or a kindred smile.

Ellen could hear them and see them, too, in the kitchen, just standing around and finishing the beers and then saying, once again, that maybe they had better go, and she saying, oh, don't hurry, and they saying, well, they didn't want to wear out their welcome, and she, giving the first clue to what Ellen also could alarmingly visualize even before they even began relating it, she giving out one of those casual nothing-much laughs and saying:

You must not think much of my welcome. You haven't even started using it.

She would have said that, too, with immense insouciance, probably with nothing at all suggestive in her voice, just tossing it off as she reached for more beers, tossing it off as she did almost everything she said, as in fact she had mentioned that afternoon on the beach that Herb, as she called her husband also with a wry twist in her tone, had gone away for the whole week up to Washington, which had been when Matt and Mark with ribald grins had said, well, they'd be more than happy to come up and help her pass the time, to which she had said it seems to pass all by itself in spite of her best efforts to stop it, after which they had said that, well, then, they would come up and help her stop it, to which she had said, with that invisible thumb on her nose and the lopsided smile on her mouth, oh, well, then, they could come up and chat awhile if they didn't have anything better to do, and if they would stay out of her hair until she had gotten the children down for the night.

Already, even before they had got to where they were going, to where they had to go, and to where she knew they were going,

already she had those sharp and dark and equivocal feelings that were
to gather ever stronger as the voices went on in the late darkness
down below, and as the words breezed up, and the images, old and
new, the old images of Corinne Fielding sunning on the beach and
adjusting herself on her back with those movements of her bottom
that caused her mound to push up in little thrusts that her brothers
and Henry, too, and yes, she, too, had stared at, the old images now
becoming new, as what was almost like a weird and eerie and at once
provocative and disturbing film unrolled before her vision as she sat
on the edge of her bed, naked herself, as always at bedtime, and yet
mindless of it as her mind leaped forth anticipating what it hated to
anticipate and absorbing what it could not help but absorb: Now the
image of them all with the new beers, and her brothers sitting at the
kitchen table, and she in the chambray shirt, now standing and leaning against the sink with her beer in her hand and her legs braced
and her torso loosely outthrust as she said what she would have said
as casually as if she were suggesting it might be nice to have some
lemonade or something, during the dialogue that had so floored them
they had to reconstruct it word-for-word for Percy who was by now
sitting rapt or hypnotized on the front steps below.

She: *Frankly, I wish you could stay all night.*
Mark: *Well, we'll stay a little bit longer.*
She: *Long enough to play?*
Matt: *Play?*
She: *Wouldn't you like to?*
Mark: *You mean?*
She: *I've thought about it ever since we moved here.*
Matt: *You mean here? Now?*
She: *Why not?*
Mark: *Well, for one thing, there're two of us.*
Matt: *And only one of you.*
She: *That's my good luck.*

At that, Ellen had tensed, trembled, and scarcely breathed as
she listened to the voices of those two tall shades of her own blood
whom as a child she had impulsively professed an intent to marry,
each and both of them, and to whom later she had become almost
as a third if late twin, had not quite dared to breathe for awhile as
they went on, without slowing down for Percy's soft expletives of
incredulousness and awe. But then suddenly she was breathing rapidly and struggling against a horrendous upseethe of dark and confused feelings as she heard, no, witnessed the events that she was at
once rejecting and repudiating even as she held her eyes fixed to them
in awe and fascination.

There was Mrs. Fielding with that amused smile and the barely perceptible quirk of the head signaling, and she with her easy stride leading the way, her brothers following at her back, following and no doubt staring and exchanging looks, following her not into a bedroom but into the living room overlooking the beach that she now closes off from view by shutting the blinds, pulling them closed with a brisk snap as at any other bedtime, and then leaving the room to go to the back of the house and look in on the children and pick up the blanket that she carries on her return, unfurling and putting it down as she would unfurl and put down a blanket for a picnic.

You mind? Twin bed's not very big.

There they were, standing, gaping, themselves still incredulous, as she goes from lamp to lamp, snapping them off but lighting the candle before the last, her brothers now watching what causes even them to gasp as they tell about it in the night air below, watching her unbutton her cambray shirt with that same felicitous grace and efficiency that shows in all her movements, staring as she casts it aside, the shirt, and steps out of the shorts, gaping now not only with disbelief but with rapture and with paralysis too, stuck fast in their tracks, so that with her pants still on she comes over to Mark as though he were her four-year-old son and takes the bottom of his polo shirt and begins to shuck it upward—

Hold up your arms.

—with precisely the invitation to cooperation that she would issue to one of her children. And now she had to stretch herself upward like a dancer to get the shirt to clear the peak of Mark's towering upthrust arms, softly laughing as she gently chastises him.

You could help some, you know.

And now there was Mark getting busy at last, reacting to her chastisement by ripping his own shirt upward and over his head, and then discovering that, before he has tossed it behind him, efficient hands are already seeing to the unbuckling of his belt and the unfastening of his jeans at the waist, expert hands that, having given him that encouragement, pass over to Matt and do the same for him who has been trying to do it by himself but fumbling the job. Mrs. Fielding laughs.

I'm good at tying shoes, too.

Ellen by now is actually not believing what she is hearing and seeing as though she were a ghostly witness to it all, as though she were hovering unseen in the lambency of the candlelit room, is not believing but is wordlessly agreeing with the disbelief she still hears in Percy's soft exclamations, and yet watches, stares obsessed and seething as this mother of two with her husband away steps backward a couple of steps from her inseparable brothers and coolly keeps her eyes fixed on theirs, as, with one hand in one movement, she skims her pants down and kicks them backward, then to stand as she might if she had just met them in the drugstore downtown, standing not flaunting or displaying that small portion of her that they had never seen before, but simply possessing it as she possessed her hair or nose or eyes or mouth, possessing all of what Ellen, with some dark inchoate certainty, now knew, while resisting knowing, was about to consume and devour something precious and irretrievable for which she had no words and sought none there on her bed in the dimness with the breeze coming in, sought no words but merely shivered and trembled and shuddered even, growing at once chilled and hot and dark and fiercely luminous somewhere within her own naked body.

Mrs. Fielding was simply walking over, nonchalant, with that which she merely possessed, and was completing the task that only she had had the poise to begin, was drawing down the shorts that they had unaccountably kept on—

You forgot something.

—was doing it for one, and then for the other, and there in the candlelight with her hair glinting like old gold, was still kneeling and calmly looking upward at the two long strong faces that were almost the face of their father, calmly looking up and then down, as Ellen shivered before a violent upseethe within, and then up again into their eyes and speaking in that voice that was as cool and casual as a breeze.

The film had reeled on long after the words had stopped, had reeled across her mind's screen over and over and over, long after the cessation of all the talk below, long after Matt and Mark and Percy had impulsively decided to go skinnydipping, long after they had done it and come back from the beach to the house uttering expletives of wonder and awe and dazzlement and incredulousness, even Matt and Mark, or especially Matt and Mark, in now refreshed and more vigorous voices that all the same seemed so distant to Ellen, so strange, so changed somehow in some way that she could not possibly have discovered or articulated amidst the immense stir and moil and hot rage and confusion of her memories and imaginings, the reeling film of it all that she felt she would have given anything on earth not to have seen, not to be seeing.

When she had lain down, when she had thrown herself back on her bed, she had been able to still it no more than she had been able to still her body, her legs that twitched and kicked as though they wished of their own volition to carry her running out of the room and out of the world, while utterly against her will her body mimicked or emulated the movements of the woman who was gleaming in the candlelight and possessing her brothers over and over, and over and over, and over again. She had clenched her hands underneath her hair to arrest their impulse to run themselves downward across her sweating breasts and pulsing stomach, wrenched with shame at her pounding arousal along with rage and plunging fear, a morbid and unthought intuition that somehow something cherished and inviolable had been betrayed beyond redemption.

For what had seemed forever, she had no clarity at all, only the tumult of feelings, a ferociously seething maelstrom of overpowering sensations beyond sorting, the hammering anger and wrenching aversion along with fascination and melting arousal that filled her with bitter self-disgust even as it permeated her flesh with such a craving that she ached, and gritted her teeth to hold her locked hands against the impulse to placate it. Once she cried out aloud—*no!*— against no single thing but everything, the quaking moil within, and the images that wouldn't cease, and the voices that wouldn't stop, the beloved voices that were at once drowning her and setting her on fire and drowning her again, and violating something precious, betraying something old and cherished and beyond naming.

Several times she had sprung out of bed to stand before the window and let the breezes directly buffet her sweating skin, and even then, already, as she remembered it, the nighttime earth outside had seemed different, changed, alien, and even menacing in the stark emptiness of the precipitate horizon beyond the black sweep of the fertile sea and its hidden freight of myriad life, of prodigal creatures ever-exploding and mutually devouring to explode again. Each time she had flung herself once again onto the damp sheet and crunched pillow, each time desperately wishing that it would stop, or they: that flexing, glinting woman who after awhile had ceased to have any name but had become only an ensnaring presence, an entrapment of flesh that opened and opened again to possess and consume not only her brothers but her memory of them, her knowledge of what they had always been but could be no more, her very mindstuff and lifestuff and hence herself, so that she also was being consumed against her will and consent, consumed and transformed and somehow dispossessed of that cherished thing that was there nameless but indisputable in her memory and knowledge and mindstuff, or had been.

She had thought not in words but in tongueless rage or anguish, *How could she do this to me?*—had thought or felt that long before she had likewise thought or felt, *How could she do this to them?* And, long before she had wordlessly wondered, *How could she do do this to him?* —at last calling to mind, for but a flicker, the husband who was far away in Washington, not nameless but obscure and oblivious, while the mother of his children was on the blanketed floor at home, showing boys who were no longer boys the way to do this, and the way to do that, the way to be there so that she could be there, and the other one there, so she could possess them at once, and both twice, and, at the end, each of them separately in that mutual devouring with each in turn as a witness or spectator—*Did you watch? I sure didn't close my eyes*—as the other discovered in the flickering candlelight the womantaste they had long celebrated, in vain ribaldry, but had never known before now in this place haunted by a husband's innumerable floodings and no telling how many others of strange men and young brothers casually invited to play by that soft-spoken, soft-smiling mouth that was full of its own soft secrets like the silent one below, and that had consumed, like the other, no telling how many before, that secretly hungered to be filled and flooded at once with it, and over and over, and over and over, with him there and him there and then there and then there, and then with his face witnessing while the face just like his went vanishing hungrily at the silent mouth that opened hungering like the soft sly one above, it devouring again insatiably not only him and him but her, her memory and mindstuff and fleshstuff and lifestuff.

Finally the images had gone berserk, the memory spinning, the incessant film racing, accelerating, racing akilter and not only repeating now but inventing until the candlelit recesses of her imagination teemed and thrashed with a welter of faceless nameless golden molten flesh, woman:man, irreducible hungering flesh, demonically hungering and consuming to hunger again, finally inflaming her own drenched flesh until it impossibly ached and burned and hungered, until at last she thought she couldn't bear it, and had uttered some anguished cry and clenched her hands ferociously together before her face and bit her thumbs and cried out or yowled again. And then her unbearable fleshheat had spontaneously resolved itself with shattering flash-flood spasms that had racked and permeated her and that had finally subsided, and then ceased, and left her with emergent relief, of a kind, but also with an inchoate sense of complicity and secret corruption.

She had scarcely slept, if at all, when daybreak showed in her windows. By then the furious storm had waned, but had left some impenetrable inner darkness that she had carried through the day, the darkness and that sense of profound unease and disorientation, as though the world about her, with all its familiar landmarks and faces, had actually changed in some uncertain but irrevocable way, in a mysterious way, a way so sorrowful that her mute rage at all of them had at moments yielded to pity, pity for them all and for her own self, too.

She had got through Wednesday by avoiding everyone, walking miles down the beach ostensibly to collect shells, and had got through supper, where she had closely faced Matt and Mark at last, feeling as though she were in a daze. She had seen them in this new way, as through some weird distorting lens, and had been coiled so tightly inside that she had feared the coming of tears, had feared that and had known that she would be forevermore beyond the reach of the jokes and joshing they had been bubbling over with at the table. She had finally pleaded a stomachache and excused herself and retreated to her room. And there had taken out the loose-leaf notebook that was not a diary or a journal but simply a place to write things down, scraps of talk as well as events, dates and names and ideas, recipes and memoranda and even pen and pencil sketches of places and things. She had decided that by writing she could obtain some clarity. But all she had written down was the date—Wed. Aug. 27, 1941—and a sentence that she had not scripted but printed: "Oh, God, how I wish Henry were here!"

Later, long after supper, through the window that had already told her so much that she wished she didn't know, she heard her brothers on the porch below, casually taking leave.

"Where you boys going?" her Papa had asked.

"Papa, we thought we'd go up and court Mrs. Fielding," they said, not to be believed.

"You keep flirtin' with that lady," said her Papa, not believing, "you'll get your heads shot off and spoil everybody's vacation."

"Papa, she ain't no lady, she's a pure-blooded Yankee."

A long while after they had gone, she had run downstairs, feigned better spirits, and skipped down to the beach, and had stared out across the bay for awhile in a tender night filled up with the lonely clanging of a distant bouy bell. And then had sidled at the water's edge, up the beach, until she was even with the house. And only then, quickly, in turning about to amble back, had stared at the front windows and seen only closed blinds cracked by an illumination so faint she might have imagined it. She had felt sneaky, guilty, and even perverse, thinking, *What in the name of God am I doing?*

She had dreaded going to bed, fearing that what she knew, and what she was now compelled to surmise, might run wild as it had before. As it turned out, it snared her imaginings only for awhile, and then exhaustion had weighted her into a long and dreamless sleep.

Thursday had been better, not good, because she had still felt impossibly walled off, and because she had even felt hateful when she had turned aside her brothers' and Percy's invitation to go out fishing with them, and, yet, it had been better, and certainly it had been astounding, and that two times over.

Astounding onward from the moment when she had done what she would have sworn she would never do again if only because she would have sworn she would never be able to do it again: She had talked with Mrs. Fielding, who had walked up in faded jeans and a chambray shirt this time with the sleeves ripped off at the shoulder, coming up as Ellen sat on the seawall with her legs dangling over, sitting with a sketchbook in her lap, trying to capture, with single swift motions of her pen, the lines of the gulls in flight, filling up a page and then flipping it over to continue. At her approach, Ellen had avoided looking up, had felt a distinct seethe of aversion and hostility that she tried to withhold from her face even as she wondered why, why she didn't go ahead and let go and display what she felt.

"Mind if I butt in?" the woman had said. "I'm lonesome for grownup company." The voice had betrayed nothing, had conveyed only ease and her usual offhand and unpretentious candor about her feelings. And when Ellen had glanced up and noncommittally nodded, as though preoccupied, she saw that the not beautiful but strong, mobile face disclosed nothing either, was entirely inscrutable, or, no, not inscrutable, only interested, believably interested. Mrs. Fielding had hoisted herself up beside her on the sea wall and peered at the page of the sketchbook, saying: "You've got 'em. If I could do it like that I wouldn't have given it up."

"I can't get their motion," Ellen said. "You know, the sweep, the—" She trailed off, almost displeased with herself for having said anything, for having responded at all.

"I suppose your Henry's coming in for the big weekend?"

"Well—I hope," Ellen said, and particularly resented this question, and yet added: "Yeah, he'll be here tomorrow. Tomorrow night."

"Is that lovesickness I hear?"

"You mean me?"

"Well, you've got that thousand-year-old woman sound you get now and then. Don't worry, I like it."

"I don't know," Ellen said, sighing, flapping shut the sketchbook to stare out across the bay with its sprinkling of skiffs and larger commercial boats.

"I've loused up your work," Mrs. Fielding said. "You should've chased me away like a nuisance child."

"Oh, I was just fiddling anyway," Ellen said.

"In that case—"

"Mr. Fielding be back for the weekend?"

"Who knows? He hasn't called. Ellen, Herb's not what you would precisely call an adoring husband," she had said, yielding up one of those laughs of irony or resignation.

"He seems nice," Ellen said in a carefully colorless voice.

"My God, has he actually talked to you? Or are you just making this up?"

"Well, I mean—"

"You don't have to say anything. I'll tell you a secret. He doesn't talk to me either."

"Aunt Margaret says some people just run out of talk at some point."

"Ha! I believe I know what she means. Herb reached that point during our honeymoon on the boat to the States," she had said, and again laughed, as though it were of no importance. In the face of Ellen's silence she had gone on: "I hope Henry does better by you."

Ellen laughed, nervously and briefly, but for the first time since it had happened. She said, "You mean, if we got married."

"Well—everytime I see you two I get the feeling. You think?"

"Hmmmmm."

"I see. Anyway, when I see you two it takes me back an eon of two. Nine years, actually, when I was sixteen and my own first great true love came along. A German, could you believe it? Helmut Koenig. Met him in Switzerland. Skiing. Now, he was a talker, except that he only talked. But I did fall. And while I was still fallen a French boy popped into my life and I almost died when I had to write Helmut. Ellen, you're lucky to be in love with just one man at a time." And there came that laugh again, and suddenly Ellen was wondering what Mrs. Fielding was actually saying, wondering what she was about to say, which in a moment she said, and in an easier and quieter voice than before, a soft almost murmuring voice like some of those that could be heard in French movies. Mrs. Fielding said, "Did you ever wonder how it might be for a woman who fell in love with your brothers?"

"You mean with both of them?"

"Could it be otherwise? Could a girl fall for one without falling for the other?"

"Oh, I don't know, they're different in little ways."

"That the family would notice, but nobody else."

"I always wondered if they might somehow wind up meeting twins somewhere, and—you know."

"And that would be a beautiful dream come true. But I was imagining the plight of just one girl who might happen to fall in love with both of them."

"I guess it would be—what?"

"At least a variation on the classic triangle."

"Not a triangle, that's when a married person gets involved with somebody else."

"*Certainement.* I was just complicating the hypothesis. I was suddenly assuming that the girl who fell happened also to be married." At that, she had jumped down from the wall to the sand, had turned and clapped her muscular hand affectionately on Ellen's knee, had smiled the lopsided smile, saying, "Ellen, I'd give my right arm if it would guarantee that Cecile would grow up to be exactly like you. So long now. Back to the sketchbook."

Ellen had watched her begin to walk away in that long, loose-jointed stride with flexing haunches that now evoked secret images, and had called out: "Mrs. Fielding! I forgot to mention, Claudette'll be coming in tomorrow too, she and Horris!"

The long stride had returned, the mobile face with the slight peak in the nosebone, and the easy smiling face leaned into hers, the wide mouth saying, "Tell her to give me a ring. And, incidentally, now that we know each other, how about calling me Corinne." A dry chuckle, and then: "Miss Worth, don't you know that you're the wise woman and I the child."

Ellen had watched her again swing away across the sand under the cries of sweeping, swooping gulls.

She had drifted off that night—which had been only last night, incredibly, since it seemed so long past, seemed, like everything since it had happened, either long ago or in some eerie way removed altogether from time just as everything seemed removed from any familiar matrix that made sense of it all or of her feelings about it—had drifted off finally wearied not by any wrenching tumult of emotion this time but by a surfeit of thinking and pondering and puzzling about things, things that would hardly stand still to be thought about, so that thinking about it all was like trying to sketch some complex thing that was not only in fast motion but also dissolving, vanishing away to reappear in slightly altered form with variant perspectives.

The face of everything had changed again after what Mrs. Fielding had said on the sea wall, or after what Ellen had surmised or intuited from it, the face and even the tone and juxtaposition of things, the whole spirit of things, with villains seeming victims and vice versa. And then vice versa again, as she had thought on, and then vice versa once more. The older woman who had seemed a consuming, corrupting seducer didn't even seem such an older woman any more but seemed a young woman, and even a girl, imprisoned in some barren if inexplicable circumstance and now, entirely by chance or fate or whatever, smitten by two vital and passionate boys who in fact no longer seemed boys, the twins who at almost eighteen, she suddenly realized, were of an age not only to be sent away to war if need be but of an age two years beyond that at which their Papa had in a single day had the whole weight of a family fall on his shoulders and carried it without pause. And afterward what could she feel for the husband away in Washington? The husband who had seemed to be away much of the time since they had moved in? Suddenly he had loomed, opaque and incomprehensible, as the target of her judgment, an always shiny-shaved, slick-combed government bureaucrat or whatever who sat sullen and inaccessible on the beach when he bothered to come out at all and who had consigned a warm young woman to twin-bed exile and who had dropped some inexplicable screen of silence between himself and his bride before the boat even got them to what was to be their home. "Silence," Horris had once said, "says absolutely and precisely what words of anger and contempt can only approximate."

Still, it was impossible to say, yes, it was all right, yes, she should have done it, caused it to happen, or even let it happen, or, yes, they should have submitted or accepted or whatever they had actually done, whatever they had done with whatever unknown complicity or initiative in gestures and looks and previous overtures. It was impossible to say that, because there were ways and ways to do things, and times to do them, and if her husband was like that she ought to come to terms with it and sever and then the question of obligation and trust wouldn't be hanging there, and—But, no, no, even if she were scot-free and not only severed but never married at all, there was simply no way and no time for falling in love with two boys at once, two men, and taking up with them like that, even if they were exactly alike and even if her love—Except that why not, who was to say, what made that impossible when in lots of places and times it was commonplace for women to have more than one husband and in perhaps even more instances commonplace for men to have more than one wife, as among the Mormons even in this country. And the Lomkubees had really had no marriages at all except for those mutual choosings of men and women for some indefinite season that wasn't expected to last forever, and which she herself had approved, to the astonishment of Mr. Sorrell when he was just getting started on the movie and had talked to her about the aborigines after finding out she had been reading about them all of her life ever since her mother had got her started.

"I'd say you hold a rather advanced attitude," Mr. Sorrel had said.

"*Advanced?* It's only the way the Lomkubees felt centuries ago," she had rejoined.

"Touché," he had said, digging nervously in his ear with the same finger that later had pulled the trigger and guided the pen that wrote the note: *I have felt for you a love that I have never felt for any other person on earth.* And he older than Mrs. Fielding by eight years and she younger by fifteen months than her brothers. Yes, what Mrs. Fielding said could happen, with age not mattering at all, with only something mysterious mattering, something that couldn't quite be seen by anyone except the one it was happening to. Granted the right place and right time, Mr. Sorrel might even have wanted her that completely, only he had never let it show, if it was there, unless it was coming out in those obscure and disturbing/pleasing compliments he had liked to pay her. If he had, if he had felt that way, if the right time and place had come, what would have happened to her attitude then?

Yes, what had happened to her attitude the other night? When they started talking and telling, what had happened to her feeling that it was all right as long as it was mutually loving and the time was right and—and, yet, she had those sharp, dark, even demonic feelings of protest and repudiation. So was her attitude only theoretical, one that sounded all right and seemed all right but that couldn't be lived with or used, one that she could hold for others, other people in other times and other places, but that would always collapse every time it had to be lived with or used, every time it came home?

Anyway, why had she taken it all so personally? Why was she still thinking about it even, this which hadn't actually happened to her, and which wasn't really any of her business? Why had it seemed as though she were a part of it, a victim even? Why had she felt so violated by what they were doing, had done, maybe were doing right now when she was able to think about it and see that it was none of her business? So, for God's sake, why was she even right now letting it go on hanging and running around her mind as though it were something monumental and epic and destructive instead of something as simple and fundamental as thirst and the quenching of it?

Why, even after she'd seen the futility of further thought, had she gone on thinking? Her ponderings had gone everywhere, settling nothing anywhere, villains becoming victims, and vice versa, her intuitions leading her in one direction and her questions diverting her to another as she grappled with notions of duty and trust and fidelity and infidelity.

Suddenly a story that Henry had told her about his early childhood had come to mind: He had been seven, and his daddy had long since taken them from McClung to Louisiana, and he had been lying in bed in the same room with his older sister Polly, she asleep and he awake, and had heard his daddy come in, and had heard some indistinct quarrel going on in his parents' bedroom, and at last had heard his daddy's voice defiantly shouting out those few words that he had not for years comprehended:

"You're right! We fucked! Sure we fucked!" Mr. Rust shouted.

"Ssssshh! The children!" Portia Rust had said.

And Henry had said that for a long time he had thought the old man had referred to some earlier intercourse with Portia, maybe some premarital episode that perhaps had forced them into marrying. What he hadn't even conceived until long, long after was that his daddy had been confirming that he had fucked another woman.

Ellen had been stabbed by the story when Henry had told it. Recalling it last night, she had again felt sharply at the image of a small son overhearing such a thing. Then, with her thoughts on Henry, and urgently wishing to see him, she had thought, *Maybe it's the children and not the grownups at all that the rules are for.*

Today, Friday, in the afternoon, at the head of the long dining table, straddling the chair with her bare feet curled around its front legs, feeling a gusty breeze on skin left bare by her blue bandana halter, hearing radio music from the room across the hall where the others were messing around, gazing absently through the big window beyond the other end of the table at the fine drizzle blowing down and the water growing choppy from a weather change that they said was caused by some distant tropical storm called Beth (which happened to be the name of one of the new Gebhart girls who had come down as weekend dates for Matt and Mark), Ellen suddenly stopped jiggling the tapered tip of the red penholder between the edges of her front teeth and set the pen to the open loose-leaf notebook before her and, on the page under where she had already written only the date—Fri. Aug. 29, 1941—wrote, and then underlined: *"I need him!"*

Then she stuck the tapered end of the penholder in her mouth and bit down on it so that it tilted upward and outward in the way of the cigarette-and-holder the cartoonists liked to draw into the corner of FDR's big grin. She leaned back and looked down the table, off of which gusts were still blowing paper napkins from the stack in the center, and out the window at the beach- and sea-scape that she had seen a million times and that still looked different, changed, even if it no longer looked utterly alien and menacing.

Suddenly two-year-old Cecile Fielding ran into view, trotting unsteadily at an angle across the beach toward the waterline, stumbling there, recovering, stumbling again, and quickly recovering to run on, laughing and looking back and no doubt utterly mindless of her nakedness. In a second, four-year-old Herb Fielding, Jr., in short pants came running after her not in hostile pursuit but obviously with rescue in mind, calling out as he ran, and now overtaking Cecile at the water's edge. He towed her unceremoniously back up the sloping sand, halting when his sister suddenly squatted down not to resist but because something on the sand fascinated her, as it quickly did him also.

The boy hunkered down alongside his little sister and together they studied whatever it was with enormous concentration, heedless of the misty drizzle and heedless, too, of the approach of their mother whom Ellen had not yet called Corinne. She swung into view with her coppery hair dampened and darkened by the rain and the fabric of the sleeveless blue workshirt flattened against the contours that flexed and jerked as she came on in that long-striding, loose-jointed walk, which was bearing her swiftly now but that still seemed effortless and unhurried. Mrs. Fielding bent and, with some word and a smile, snatched up Cecile to her hip in a single motion, and then with a gentle smooth movement of her foot hoisted the boy by the ass into motion toward the house up the beach, and then set out to follow but stopped almost instantly.

Suddenly, as Ellen heard two shrill reports of that crude admiring whistle, and then two more, coming either from the front hall or the front room where the others were, Mrs. Fielding snapped her face about with an enormous laughing grin, searching for and then finding the source of the whistles, and then, after a comic toss of her head, flamboyantly bowed in that direction, straightening and abruptly setting off after the boy, her head suddenly bowed and her eyes thoughtfully studying the sand just in front of her as she strode on at a list to counterbalance Cecile riding there on her bayside hip. Before she passed from view, Mrs. Fielding drew the back of her free hand across her forehead in the immemorial gesture of maternal vexation and resignation, only her mouth fell into that lopsided smile as she did so.

Ellen's pen flew and scratched and captured the gesture in a few strokes, the gesture and then a woman's face that a stranger might have guessed was her own, Ellen's, but that, as she realized only after it was done, was her mother's, a face that even when vexed seemed always on the verge of smiling. The fine rain outside reminded Ellen of the wet streets and sounds of London that time she had gotten that feeling of having almost known or maybe almost remembered that she had been there before, that eerie sense of things that she had known also in other places they had gone—*"Déjà vu, déjà vu, déjà vu. Say it."*—but that she had not experienced in a long time until that night when Henry had started talking seriously of how he felt about children and fathers, the moment when she had decided that it was finally time for her to say what she had, that she now knew: no, not that she decided to say it, had simply known it was the time, had known it because of that feeling, that sense that she not only wanted to say it but actually had to say it, because that's the way it had to be, that's the way it *was,* that's the way it had been in some other place and some other time that she could almost but not quite remember.

And now, once again, she clamped the pen in her teeth like FDR's holder and flipped back the pages of her notebook until she located what she had written down back on Sat. Jan. 18, 1941—a notation that she and Henry had gone to a movie on a double date with Percy and Florence and afterward, when they were alone, had a good, long talk, of which afterward she had recorded:

Me: Can I ask you something?

H: I've told you you can ask me anything any time.

Me: Well, if, just if, she had turned out to be PG, would you really have done what you said?

H: We assume she would have wanted to?

Me: Uh-huh.

H: Then, yeah, I would.

Me: Even feeling the way you do. About me.

(Long pause.)

H: Well, I guess I ought to tell you how I really felt about it. And it didn't really have anything to do with how I feel about you or her. I just felt that if she was, that I ought to see it through no matter what else was involved. (Very serious.) Listen, I think I'd kill myself before I would deliberately leave a child, whether I was married or not, or if I was married, even if the marriage had turned to shit. I think a child could learn to accept my death easier than what he would always feel if I just wasn't there. That's how I felt. How I feel. Does it make you feel bad? The whole thing, I mean.

Me: No, no, I feel the same way you do.

H: You know, Ellen, I got carried away with her, I guess I loved her even, but I really didn't feel this way about her, the way I feel about you.

Me: I know it. I know I feel that way about you.

H: You know it for sure? You needn't say anything until you know.

Me: I know I know it. I know I love you.

H: I love you, Ellen. Goddamighty, how I love you!

Ellen reread, and rethought, and flipped over the pages to glimpse Mon. Jan. 20—*M&M heard that Carol B's gone to Calif. to live with her sister Dixie.* And Fri. Feb. 7—*Happy Birthday, Henry! Seventeen! The doctor took the cast off his hand today!* And Wed. Feb. 12—*Car here at last! Sky blue! Rode around with H til 1:30* A.M.—*freezing with the top down!* Underneath she had sketched the open car, with them in it, soaring through the curve of a fingernail moon.

Ellen looked up from her notebook and back out the window through the blowing drizzle, looked absently and then keenly, then with astonishment and dawning alarm, at first seeing only *something* in the choppy water some yards offshore, the something that might be a creature, and then something that definitely was, only then seeing the clear flash of skin as Cecile struggled to keep her footing only to bob under again, hysteria showing vividly in the face that suddenly tried to look back toward the beach, the beach that was utterly devoid of any other person.

Ellen gaped, paralyzed for an instant, and then bolted to her feet, knocking her chair backward as she lunged toward and through the dining room doorway into the hall where, without pausing, she yelled—"Matt! Mark! Cecile! Out there!"—and then flung open the screen door and, at a flying sprint, leaped from the porch to the yard and then off the sea wall onto the sand where she stumbled and instantly scrambled up again and sprinted on toward the waterline, her first foot striking the water just as her brothers rocketed past her in twelve-foot strides and reached Cecile seemingly in two more leaps.

Matt, by the time Ellen waded up, already held the child upside down like a newborn, while Mark pressed her chest between his hands as though he knew what he was doing. Ellen let an enormous leashed breath explode out as it became plain, quickly enough, that Cecile was all right. The child began squawling and flailing while she was still held suspended upside down. Matt righted her, and Ellen took her and clasped her close, and was amazed that the child became instantly pacific as the three of them waded, breathing hard and now laughing with hysterical relief, toward where Mrs. Fielding was already sprinting up with her coppery hair flying and her face gaping and also somehow receding in alarm, and then flushing, in immense relief, as she saw Ellen, with Cecile in her arms, signaling with a nodding head that the child was okay.

"Oh, my God! Thank you, thank you, thank you, thank you!" Mrs. Fielding said, and embraced Ellen and Cecile simultaneously as she went on saying it.

Ellen relinquished Cecile to her mother, who clasped the child fiercely with one arm while, with the other, she embraced Matt and Mark one after the other, her wide mouth trying to smile but actually struggling against crying out to express what was already bringing tears to her eyes.

"Oh, God! Thank you, thank you, how can I—" Mrs. Fielding was still gasping as she went on. "Oh, God, I had just gone into the back room—trying to get her brother down for a nap—and then I looked around and—Oh, God, Ellen, I can't possibly say—"

"Well, she's okay, so you can stop worrying now," Ellen said.

"Ellen saw her," Matt said. "If she hadn't seen her—"

"Ellen was about here when—" Mark said.

"Anyway—" Mrs. Fielding broke it off, and now merely stood, squeezing Cecile to her, the child now awesomely quiet and observant amidst the furor, the exclamations and chatter now rising from the others from the house who were all gathered around, too.

Ellen suddenly pointed to the two Gebhart girls and motioned them closer, saying, "Liz—Beth—this is our neighbor, Mrs. Fielding —and Cecile—Mrs. Fielding—uh, Corinne—Liz and Beth Gebhart. They're down for the weekend." Ellen, without even intending, watched Corinne Fielding's eyes as she reached to shake hands with the girls she must have guessed or maybe even knew were her brothers' dates. She saw the eyes open and then retreat and recede. Ellen thought, *Yes, she was telling the truth.*

"Listen," Ellen said, "are we just going to spend the afternoon in the rain?"

As Ellen moved as though to go, Corinne Fielding was staring at her with her eyes filming again, and then staring at her brothers with her eyes brimming. And then suddenly the mother moved or almost fell toward Ellen—Cecile still tightly clasped—and embraced her again, pressing her face close, and saying fast but not loud, "Oh, God, Ellen, how I thank you, how I do thank you. How I love you, how I love all of you, so much I can't tell you."

"Listen," Ellen said, extricating herself, "we're having a paper-plate buffet tonight. Why don't you come up, you and the children, and eat supper with us? Okay—Corinne?"

"You don't think you've done enough for us today?"

"Come up about six, okay? Claudette and Horris ought to be here by then."

"If you don't, we'll come over and getcha," Ellen heard Matt say at her side, and suddenly saw Corinne Fielding smile again in her way as though she were almost back to normal, and just then heard her own name being called from the porch steps, where she saw Aunt Margaret standing with cupped hands.

"Ellen, make haste! It's Henry! Long Distance! He's calling from New Orleans! Make haste now!"

"New *Orleans!?*"Ellen blurted to nobody in particular, or to the whole cluster of them standing there in the drizzle. "He's supposed to be on the damn *bus!*" Then she flew away perhaps as fast as she had flown out and down to the water five minutes before.

"You're still in New *Orleans?!*"

"Yeah, but don't worry, I—"

"Don't *worry!?* You've missed the last damn bus, and—"

"Listen, Ellen, I got a motorcycle."

"MOTORCYCLE! And you're gonna ride *it* up here?"

"You don't think I'd roll it up, do you? Listen, the guy's fixing it right now and—

"*Fixing* it?! You mean you've already broken the damn thing? When did you get it?"

"Look, I just got it. It's second-hand. But it's a good bike. This guy says he'll have it ready by six or seven."

"Six or SEVEN? You mean you won't be *starting* til then?"

"Well, I can't very well start until he gets it fixed. But, listen, it won't take me any time. I'll open it up and—"

"Don't you dare open it up! Henry, it'll be dark, and you don't even know how to ride a motorcycle, and—listen, please be *careful!*"

"Ellen, are you mad at me or something? Your voice—"

"Oh, no, no, no, I'm not mad at you. I'm just out of breath. Something just—oh, I'll tell you about it—mainly, I was hoping you'd be coming in on that damn bus in just a little bit."

"Well, this is worth the delay, don't you think?"

"What is?"

"The bike, what else?"

"Listen, it's *you* I miss, not a damn *motorcycle* I've never seen."

"I'll give you a good ride soon as I get there."

"Well, just *get* here, that's all."

"Ellen, you do sound funny. Is everything okay?"

"Henry, I *am* funny. I'm *crazy.* I've gone crazy *missing* you."

"Ellen?"

"Yeah."

"I love you and I'll see you later, bye."

Click.

"How the *hell,*" Ellen said to the empty hall, "could he hang *up* without letting *me* say it, too?"

"Say what?" said her Papa, suddenly barging through the doorway from the dining room.

"Say nothing, say nothing, say nothing," said Ellen, as he came towering over her and imprisoned her shoulders with his arm.

"So that's what you two talk about all the time," he said. "That's fascinating, Dumpling. My favorite subject—*nothing.* And now maybe I'll have two experts right in my own family."

She leaned against the jamb of the open back door, her body slouched but its lines lost with one of the dark blue sweatshirts that fit her brothers but covered her like an outsized shift, tenting her down to midthigh. She looked no longer eagerly but wearily through the screen door that she kept idly pushing open just a bit with her foot, pushing it open and letting it slam, through the screen and up the long, slightly curving lane of crushed shell where he would appear, him and his damn motorcycle, if indeed he ever was going to appear, if he hadn't smashed into a car or a bridge or a tree or one of the damned cows or mules or horses that sometimes just wandered onto the road out of the unfenced pastures along the way.

She leaned, and looked, and crossed her still bare feet, and uncrossed them, and crossed her arms under breasts also lost in the voluminous sweatshirt, and uncrossed them, and bit at a hangnail, and flopped down in a chair at the kitchen table, and got up, and stood again at the door, and sidled over to the sink, and aimlessly turned the spigot on and off, and peered out the big over-the-sink window toward the same crushed shell road that had a wet ghostly gray look. It had stopped raining again.

She heard the sound of the old revival hymns that the others had started singing in the front room after they had clamored in from dancing at Doubloon's, coming in tight and noisy, coming rolling down that same shell lane, the decapitated limousine in front with Matt and Mark and the Gebhart girls all in slickers, and the others behind in her sky blue car, which she probably would have gotten in and gone to find him or look for him if she hadn't let them use it to go to Doubloon's, lending it to them with the thought, at the time, that she and Henry, if they decided to go join them, could go on the damn motorcycle even if it was raining, that it would be wild and good to cling behind him on the damn thing in the rain.

But now, even with her car back, it was too damn late, because she could no longer even assume he was on the road anywhere between New Orleans and here, because if he had ever got started, even if he hadn't gotten started until 10:30, he would be here by now, and, if he had got started, and wasn't here, which he wasn't, then something had to have happened and somebody, the police or bypassers or the ambulance, would have long since taken his body off the road, would have taken him to some damn place she would never find, to an undertaker, or, if he really was still alive, to a hospital. But how could he be alive, since if he had gone to a hospital he would have called, or had somebody call if he was conscious, which if he wasn't, would mean that he was dying if not already dead.

. . . *standing on the promises of God.*

"Come on, that's enough," she heard Florence Ensley say at the end of that one. "We must be keeping the whole house awake." And heard her begging off from playing any more on the piano that she was accompanying with, blushful Florence, who had started playing at Percy's insistence, Percy, whom Ellen had never seen so tight before, explaining to Liz and Beth Gebhart: "Florence is the only Catholic ever to worm her way into the job of accompanyist in the McClung Baptist Church. She's part of Rome's fifth column." And

Florence protesting: "No, they asked me. Don't say that, Percy, I didn't worm in." Everybody had laughed, and her brothers had herded Liz and Beth to stand in a hugging bunch behind the piano, and Ellen, after singing one, had drifted back to the kitchen again, and to the door, and then the window, thinking of how uncharacteristically restrained Matt and Mark had been after Corinne Fielding had come up for supper, how they, who usually practically manhandled their dates, had suddenly begun to seem almost sedate, all but disinterested in these two naïve high school girls newly brought down from Ohio by the father who was a construction engineer or something at the air corps place that was being built up the road from McClung, outside Carterville.

They had been cautious and restrained, too, toward Corinne Fielding, but nobody could say disinterested, after she had almost knocked their eyes out by showing up dressed like that for the first time in those snug white slacks and that brilliant flowered silk blouse with obviously nothing under it except what everybody could practically see made their mouths water at the very first sight of her, she coming in holding the hands of the children but with that mobile face glowing and looking exactly as it had been described by Claudette, who had driven down alone and brought the disappointing news that Horris had climbed on a train to go to Washington for some damn reason that he had explained to her but that didn't make any sense.

Claudette and Corinne, who had got on famously ever since their first meeting in July, had set upon each other like two long-lost foreigners bumping into each other in a strange land, talking in French as they usually did at first and often did all the time, talking tonight as though, without any signal or even knowing why, they had entered some tacitly conspiratorial relationship, sitting there talking after everybody had gone around the table and started eating, as though nobody else on earth could possibly understand what they were saying.

Claudette: You look so good—like a girl in love.

Corinne: Thank you. You may be verging on the truth.

Claudette: Sooooo! Something good has happened?

Corinne: Good and probably disastrous.

Claudette: Such things usually are, is it not so?

Corinne: Too often. And when it is twice as good it can be twice as disastrous.

Claudette: I don't understand. You can tell me?

Corinne: Later. It is not prudent to speak of it here.

Claudette: Ooooh? Then perhaps I do understand.

Corinne: You are clairvoyant?

Claudette: No. Only female.

Corinne: It's enough. Are you free to come talk when we are done? My house?

Claudette: Yes, yes. We can talk. But you do look so—so—delectable.

Corinne: And you. But then you always do.

Claudette: Thank you. If so, it is because I am always in love.

Corinne: You are lucky to have a husband to love.

Claudette: Yes. But one is lucky to have love, husband or not.

Corinne: And disaster or not?

Claudette: Yes. Yes, absolutely. Even food can lead to disaster. An uncle of mine ate himself to death. But we must have food, is it not so? Ellen, you are listening much too carefully, la la!

Ellen: How else am I to learn about life and love?

Claudette: Ha! Experience will soon teach you more than you will care to know.

Ellen: I keep waiting.

Claudette: So? That is life, waiting.

Ellen: And what is love?

Corinne: Love? Love is not being able to wait.

Claudette: And then waiting some more. M. Rust will arrive soon, and then you can instruct us in love.

Monsieur Rust will arrive soon. At the recollection, Ellen thought, *Sure.* By the time the others had spilled out to go dancing at Doubloon's, Monsieur Rust already had not arrived soon, and Ellen had felt only sardonic at the admonition not to worry that she had got from Claudette and Corinne, who had come back to the kitchen to say so long before heading up the beach to the house where they were no doubt having a worldlywise talk about what had happened or was happening to give Corinne that look of a young girl in love. They were probably sitting and talking in the same room where the blinds shut and the lights went off and the candle flared up, probably sitting amidst the lurid ghosts of it all, ghosts that Corinne would evoke never directly and specifically but inevitably with her mood and tone and way. They would go on and on with Corinne talking in her casual offhand style and Claudette, as ever, volatile and animated, sweeping with scarcely a pause from the comic to the tragic, from flip repartee to intricate philosophical abstraction, Claudette who called herself a mystic Catholic who happened to be incompatible with the temporal managers of the Church. Or maybe they would sit at the table in the kitchen where Corinne had first brought it out into the open, brought it out or let it out, leaning back against the sink with those gentle protuberant eyes calmly and warmly regarding them—*I've thought about it ever since we moved here*—whom she had also regarded warmly if discreetly at supper. Simply on observing one of the looks, Ellen had suddenly had that bizarre thought that it not only wouldn't matter but would be sort of weird and droll and fun if this woman-girl could just move in with the family, be part of them, be around as a person never-quite-explained to visiting friends and relatives, and be as an older sister to her, while to the boys she could be exactly what she obviously would love to be. She couldn't quite complete the fancy because it was not yet clear whether they, her brothers, yet had any perception or grasp of the fact that underneath that offhanded ease Corinne Fielding had already grown as serious as she was passionate.

Monsieur Rust will arrive soon. By the time the others had come back from Doubloon's, she thought, *like hell,* because by then she had decided that he wasn't going to arrive at all, because obviously he couldn't any longer, couldn't come charging down that shell lane on a damn raucous motorcycle simply because the damn thing had undoubtedly killed him, and God knows where, maybe even before he had got out of New Orleans, and maybe anywhere along the way on that road that could be treacherous by daylight and at night, in foul weather, an invitation to the undertaker's even in a car. Yet she had kept watch.

At first there had been traffic to watch, cars and lights coming and going on the main road from which the shell lane cut off, and twice she had startled up at the sound of motorcycles that swept by, both coming from the right direction, both going south, both passing without pause right by the lane into the backyard of the house and the shell-covered apron where the cars were parked. Then the traffic had thinned, then it had waned to practically nothing, and now the whole nightscape looked empty and barren and menacing, and sounded eerie with tree frogs and insects trilling the last sad frantic songs of a summer that had been just so damn good, so perfect, so flawless, until the world had started dissolving, the world that now remained so complicated and excruciating, and that now began to seem as though it were absolutely going to collapse and disintegrate under her feet if anything happened to him.

If anything happened that she not only couldn't but wouldn't bear, she would go right out to the bay and start swimming and keep going until she either just sank or the sharks got to her or something, she wouldn't give a damn, if anything happened to him.

They had stopped singing now, had stopped the hymns and gotten quiet, and were no doubt smooching in there, or maybe, since she had heard the screen door up front slam, smooching on the front porch, and so now, on top of all else, she had to cope with the thought that she knew she would have to cope with, the ridiculous thought that they, her brothers, were somehow betraying the illicit love of the woman-girl up the road who of course by betraying her husband had perhaps forfeited her claim to fidelity. But she wasn't going to get into that impossible tangle of thought again. Maybe in fact all *was* fair in love and war, but who the hell knew—not her, who was just now thinking that she could not stand waiting any longer and so just might get in the damn car and go looking even if she didn't have the faintest idea where to look.

Behind her she heard that crepitant step coming from the middle downstairs bedroom adjacent to the back downstairs bedroom where her Papa no doubt was sleeping without a fret, and soon felt the strong, old hand on her shoulder and turned around to see Aunt Margaret, who stood almost exactly her height and who began saying what Ellen knew she was going to say since she had already come out twice to say it before.

"Ellen, standing and staring down that road won't make anything happen or un-happen. Why don't you go lie down, and before you know it, he'll be here."

"If he's going to get here at all."

"Nothing's happened to that boy. Odds are the thing just broke down. You can't trust a machine."

"How could it be that? He just got it fixed before he left."

"You could at least come lie down on the daybed in my room. You can hear from there when he comes up. You keep standing you'll be dead tired when he does get here."

"Well, it's easier to worry standing up. Aunt Margaret, you get your rest."

"How is anybody expected to rest next door to a revival meeting? Ellen, there's something funny about a bunch of heathens singing hymns."

"Heathens?" To her surprise, Ellen laughed.

"What would you call 'em?"

"Well—until I get this mote out of my eye, I'd rather not call 'em anything."

"Whatever they are, I don't want 'em saving my soul after midnight."

"Well, they've stopped now."

"That doesn't bode well either," Aunt Margaret said, going now. "You come on in if you feel like. And if they get noisy you shush 'em. I don't want 'em waking up your Papa this late."

"Aunt Margaret, a hurricane wouldn't wake up Papa."

"I know a hurricane wouldn't."

Now even the others had come back to say goodnight, to console her, to theorize and advise, also to urge her to go on to bed for a dozen different reasons that didn't make any sense, and had themselves clomped up the stairs, still laughing and wisecracking, to beds in various rooms, some of them—Florence and the Gebhart girls—to cots on the screened back sleeping porch upstairs, whence for a few moments had come the northern-accented voices of Liz and Beth exulting with Florence over the time they had had, and over the twins, who had obviously gotten over their disinterest in spite of whatever they might feel for Corinne Fielding up the beach where Claudette evidently was going to sit talking all night as she loved to do sometimes. Ellen glanced at the clock hanging on the kitchen wall and thought, *Good God!*

It was 3:07. And it was just then that she heard, or thought she heard, something in the immense stillness outside, where it was still not raining but nonetheless wet and ominous and barren. Now she did hear something, heard it from the right direction, too, something that could be—but, no, it couldn't be, unless it was one that was indeed about to conk out, because it was only sputtering and not roaring like a motorcycle, and besides, it was going too slow, approaching much too slowly, the source of the sound that had caused her heart to leap but that now, as it rolled into sight, its lights, caused her to sink again.

The lights, diffused by the mist, almost blurred into one in front of whatever it was they were attached to, something sputtering along, imperceptible but probably an old truck that soon would roll past and leave her to concentrate on waiting, and waiting, and waiting for what obviously was never going to come. Yes, she could see now, it was a truck, a farm truck with a big bed enclosed by removable plank siding.

But it didn't go past. It turned in, and at first she thought, *Turning around.* But then it came on and she thought, *Why would a truck—?* But then, quickly, she knew with a sinking feeling that it was probably some farmer who had found him injured and couldn't find a hospital and so—

Ellen was out the back door and out in the yard when it rolled up and jolted to a halt. She couldn't see through the murky windshield, couldn't see anything except that it was a battered truck out of which, now, the driver slowly climbed down: A middle-aged man with a dark face, wearing frayed khakis and a raggedy shirt and a straw hat beaten to pieces by wear, weather, and sweat. He climbed out muttering in Spanish.

"Hello?" Ellen said from not ten feet away, still trying to see when she heard his voice, Henry's.

"Hey, Ellen!"

And then she skipped over to where the driver was standing, waiting, and saw him slipping across the front seat to get out the driver's side, and then leaning back in to drag out his guitar case, only then turning about so that she saw the shock of hair and the full face with the dark brow and the intricate concavities that she loved to trace with her fingers and sketch with her pen.

"Henry, are you all right?" she said.

"Yeah," he said, "just whipped is all." Then he hugged her with his free arm. "Ellen, this is Señor Diaz. *Amigo*, this is my—my señorita, the one I tell you about. Ellen, could we scratch up a little food for Señor Diaz? Maybe something for his family too? He's gone all the hell out of his way to help me. On a night his wife just gave birth. So—"

"Well, let's all go in the kitchen. I know we've got lots, we had a buffet tonight and—oh, where's your bike, and what on earth happened?"

"It's on the truck, and I'll tell you all about it, but first—come on in, Señor Diaz, you're welcome in this house."

"Yes, do come in," Ellen said, already struck by something intense in Henry's voice. Maybe it was fatigue, but—

A few minutes later, when the truck was sputtering away again, and they stood watching in the yard, she was deeply puzzled over what might be going on inside him to make him seem not only intense but grave. Henry had seemed to wish so urgently to give Señor Diaz more than the man wished to accept, had loaded up two paper bags with canned goods from the pantry and the whole remainder of the supper ham, and had carried it himself out to the truck over the man's protestations. Together, they had put down a ramp and rolled the bike, with Henry's gear, off the rear of the truck, and then, when Señor Diaz was back in the driver's seat, Henry had emptied his wallet of everything in it and handed what looked to her like a hundred dollars or more up to the window where the man's eyes gaped as he firmly and sternly protested the size of the payment.

"*Amigo*, only ten of it is for you," Henry said. "The rest is for the baby. And for Señora Diaz. You can't refuse my gift to the baby and the mother. As it is, I can't thank you enough. Señor, I'd be proud to have you as my father. *Gracias, gracias, muchos gracias.* "

The rough browned hand had come down from the window and taken Henry's, and Señor Diaz had expressed his gratitude and friendship with enormous solemnity.

And now Henry had clasped her to his side as they stood watching the truck bounce away up the shell lane.

"Henry, what on earth happened? How did he—"

"Ellen, you should see his family. You should see where they live. How they live. They're migrants, except they've been stationary for awhile. With steady work up the road. And a place to live. Two rooms. Twelve children. And another born tonight. Ellen, I saw a child born tonight."

"*Really?*"

"In a place you and I wouldn't keep a dog in."

"Henry? Are you really all right? You sound so—"

"Listen, I'll tell you all about it, but—Just let me look a minute."

He turned and took her by the upper arms. His eyes were imprisoning her, piercing her, and then they weren't piercing, they were retreating, dissolving, so that she thought he was about to do what she had never seen him do yet, not even over his father—she thought he was about to cry.

Only he wasn't going to cry, his face was working hard to keep it from happening. His hands only got tighter on her arms, and suddenly he said in a strange hoarse voice, "Ellen, goddam, I'm so glad to see you I could die."

He pulled her to him, or she him to her, and he held her closer and harder and more desperately than had ever happened before, and she him, too, until they were pressed into one, and she knew then, yes, more deeply even than she had already known, even though she had clearly known.

He was still holding her, not saying a word, and she him, not saying a word, and she felt almost unbearably glad in a way that washed all memory of the night and all else from her mind, all else until suddenly she noticed that it had started raining again, and then she wondered what was happening to those eyes that were looking somewhere out there behind her out of that face that was pressed so hard and indubitably next to her head.

Whatever had happened had already happened, if it had happened, when at last he looked at her. Rain was streaming down his face and into his dawning grin, as down hers, and into hers, and every stitch they had on was drenched and dripping.

HENRY TALIAFERRO RUST:

He had got up early feeling eager or urgent in spite of the short sleep, and had heard Percy on the lower bunk groan with his hangover when he jumped down from the upper to get dressed, and had gone downstairs where as promised she was waiting to cook the breakfast that they ate together while he told her some of it, some of that which he told more and repeated much while they rolled his conked-out bike up the road to the station and left it, and had walked back holding hands while he talked more still of what was yet on his mind now that they had decided it was too blowy and overcast for swimming but neither too blowy nor too choppy to pull on sweat-shirts and go out in the canvas kayaks her brothers had built and that they now just bobbed along in, resting and drifting as they locked the two frail, narrow vessels together with paddles and hands that couldn't resist touching and as he went over still some more of what she seemed to want to hear more of and what he didn't at the moment seem either able to stop talking about or able to understand fully with that understanding that Horris always said was to look at something not merely with cognition but recognition.

He said:

I just don't know. I don't know whether it was seeing that baby come out or seeing that woman's face or seeing the other kids who were watching it, too, with the oldest one of them delivering it. Or maybe the whole thing, the way the place was, the way they were living, what you could see in their faces as much as you could see in the place, in the ratty beds that they have to sleep in, six or seven of the littlest ones together.

Or maybe it was all of that and something else, too, because it was after that when I realized something had happened to me, that something had happened somewhere inside that wasn't going to let me do what I had thought a minute before I was going to do, and I don't mean right then, I mean with my life.

It first came to me, I mean began to get clear, when we were riding along and he was talking, Juan Diaz, Señor Diaz, so maybe it was what he was saying, maybe it was the stories about that bastard sheriff up in the next county that treats all of them like they were slaves or mules or something, something worse, because he puts them in his goddam jail for nothing and beats the shit out of them when they don't show up for work. Or he'll do it just for nothing, they say, just for some damn mean pleasure he gets out of kicking people around with his goddam fancy cowboy boots.

Maybe it was that, because I sure as hell felt different then. You know what I felt? I wanted to tell him, look, just turn the truck around and let's go up there and kill the son of a bitch. I felt, why doesn't somebody just kill the son of a bitch. Only I just felt it, I didn't say it. Actually, I didn't say anything much, but what the hell could I say?

But this was happening to me then. I guess it had to be a lot of things, the whole thing that got me to feeling so strong, because I think it had started when I saw this baby come out, because when I saw him I suddenly could see him growing up just like the rest of them without a goddam thing to look forward to except scratching in the dirt for some rich son of a bitch and never getting quite enough to eat and never having a decent place to sleep and then getting up one day to have some son of a bitch like this Ellis Kelso kick the shit out of him for nothing with his goddam fifty dollar cowboy boots, size thirteen. Do you know they all know his boot size? Hell, they all seem to know somebody he's kicked, and what the hell can they do about it? When they take a complaint to the prosecutor up there they find out that slick son of a bitch is just like that with the sheriff. And if they take it some place else they find out the whole damn county government's just one big family all in cahoots and paying no attention to anybody except the big growers, the whole damn outfit doing a job on the migrants and the niggers too. Niggers—I don't even like that any more, I don't even like myself when I say it any more.

I don't like it any more after this summer, after playing with some of 'em like Cat Lasalle that I was telling you about, that soprano sax man. I don't want to hear it any more and still I go on saying it out of habit or something, and I guess in a pinch still feeling it. I'm not even positive when I began feeling some new way about this, but I think it was when we went to play that job in Lake Charles, a dance on that pavilion, the boat club thing. I probably told you about it that weekend—Yeah, I remember I did. Cat coming with us to fill in, and when we get there this tub-o-lard club manager says, "We can't have this." And our manager says, "What?" And with Cat standing right there, he says, "The nigger." He says, "It's all right when it's all one or the other." Well, as it turned out, he backed down but then he kept the lights on the bandstand so low the guys could scarcely read, and of course Cat would just sort of disappear at intermissions. And, hell, Ellen, I sat there feeling almost like it was happening to me. I didn't even feel like playing in the damn place, and wished I had just told 'em to shove it, but—You know, what the hell good would it do? Well, of course, we ran into it two or three other times this summer. But up north some of the bands and combos look like checkerboards, and who the hell cares?

Well, you know how things are all around here the same as I do. Hell, a handful of 'em come out trying to vote and all of a sudden we got the Burcell boys and Cecil Drum and all that gang wantin' everybody to put on sheets again and go back to that shit. But actually I'm not just talking about the way things are, I'm talking about what's happening inside me, and last night it all sort of bunched up trying to explode out, and I just don't know for sure when it started or just what started it. Maybe it was even when I was on the road and that thing conked out on me, and I thought about that guy who sold it to me and swore he had it all fixed, I thought, well, there's another one who's just shit on somebody and smiled. Or maybe when I was on the side of the goddam road in the goddam rain and couldn't get a goddam soul to flag down, the few that were coming along, so that it seemed like nobody on earth gave a good goddam if somebody was there waving and yelling that he was in trouble, and how did they know what? And then along came those two farthead deputies, and weren't they a big help, telling me they only wanted to give me a ticket for being on the wrong side of the road. Well, maybe they were joking, I don't know, but I know they sure as hell weren't any help when I asked 'em for a lift. Oh, you know, that was against regulations, and, besides, if I left my bike somebody would steal it sure as hell, one of those thieving "Mexigrants," as they called 'em, would sure come along and steal it.

Oh, yeah, I started to boil then, no doubt about it, and more so after I had rolled that damn thing about five miles or so hardly able to see anything let alone a house with a light on, until I finally saw that one place lit up off in a field. And then when I got there everything in me began to turn inside out in some way, as though I was seeing everything for the first time.

For one thing, this man Diaz, Señor Diaz, was so nice after everything I'd been running into. Sure, he said, he would help me out if he could but I'd have to wait, and then he asked me to come on in, and then for the first time I knew what he wanted me to wait for. And it was something going into that room, all those kids stacked up everywhere and a couple of the other workers and their wives and some of their kids, and this thing about to happen on a bed any minute, and then everybody falling silent when it started to happen. With her, and all the ones she already had, it didn't take long. It was her thirteenth, which is why he was going to give it that name to counteract the bad luck.

But, Ellen, it was something. I tell you, when I saw that child coming out, it was the strangest thing in my life, the strangest feeling, because suddenly I could see me coming out of my mother with her face like that, and I could see you coming out of yours with her face like that even though I never saw your mother with my own eyes. And then suddenly everything seemed just so damned strange or weird or something, so damn sad even with everybody there shouting out of happiness, so damn sad or unfair or something, the way I was seeing it, seeing this baby get born in one place and wind up on one path that's going to carry him to misery, while another, you or me, winds up by pure chance with everything we need, and— But where the hell will a migrant worker's baby Jesus wind up? Where? Doing what?

Oh, hell, I don't know, he may wind up a millionaire, I don't know what I'm saying. All I know is what I was feeling, and I know it was afterward, and Juan Diaz had helped me load that bike on that damn old rattletrap—without even asking me to pay him, you realize that?—it was after that when we were heading down here that it all began to bunch up. It was when he started telling me about that bastard Kelso and the whole rest of his life, of all their lives. It was like the whole summer boiling up in me.

You know, one time down there, down in New Orleans, we were sitting around and talking about the war and all, Germany, you know, and Cat Lasalle said something that just stuck me like a knife, though he wasn't talking directly to me or anybody else for that matter. He said, "Well, you cats got to realize that we could bring Mr. Hitler over here and just likely teach him a few tricks he ain't even thought of."

Well, by God, it's hard to say, but I sort of feel that way now. I sort of began to feel that way last night every time I thought about that goddam sheriff up there. I thought, hell, everybody's all hot to go fight Hitler, but why the hell don't we clean out the bastards here first? And why don't we stop treating everybody like dogs? Why don't we stop making people like Juan Diaz and all of those kids live in a goddam shack where you wouldn't even keep dogs, for Christ's sake.

So finally I wondered if I didn't feel the way Horris did when he was over there after he had left London, when he was over there in Paris all ready to go to Spain and get in the fight against Franco. You know, the way he says he felt when, at just that time, all that pack of state legislators began to stomp on his book and him, too, and all that. So that he said to Claudette that he'd decided to forget about Franco and come fight the bastards at home.

Well, that's how I feel, but there's something else, too. Because as it built up in me I began thinking about this summer, I began thinking about music and everything, playing all those places, and of course I've enjoyed the hell out of it, it's been great. But, Ellen, what the hell has it got to do with anything? That's exactly what I was wondering when we rolled up and I saw you standing there, and I was so goddam glad to see you because I had gotten that feeling that the world was going to come to an end before we got there, you know what I mean?

But I was feeling this other thing, too. I was wondering how in the hell could I plan to spend my life sittin' on some goddam little stage in some damn smoky little joint playing a goddam guitar with all this shit going on? Well, don't tell me the answer, because I'm thinking about that, too. I'm thinking, what the hell can I do? And of course I don't know, I just don't know. Maybe nothing.

Or maybe wind up in the army going off to fight Mr. Hitler. I swear I think that's coming. By God, my daddy might have been drunk at the time but he sure called this thing a long time ago. Still, I don't know that, do I? Who the hell knows what's going to happen.

Ellen, you know something? Ever since that first night, after that New Year's dance, ever since I first touched you that night I've been like a damn little child expecting the world to come to an end any minute. I've been like a little boy who knows he's found the greatest thing he'll ever find on earth, and so now it's time for the world to end and take it away from him.

Goddamighty, Ellen, look where we've drifted to. If we don't get our tails moving we ain't even going to make it back to shore this time—ever. See what I mean?

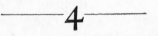

4

She had got up knowing it. The second her eyes had opened to the briefly bright sun she had known it for sure, not merely thinking or feeling or sensing or intuiting it, but knowing it and knowing it so strongly she had written it down.

She had been thinking it ever since he had come Friday night, or actually Saturday morning, had been feeling or sensing it ever since they had been so sealed into oneness and gladness out in the yard that she hadn't even noticed it was raining. When they got up later and ate breakfast together and rolled his bike up to the station, she had still felt that it might be or even probably was.

And then the sense of it or the intuition or whatever it was had gotten even stronger when they had gone out in the kayaks and drifted too far while he talked about what had happened to him and what was happening inside. Maybe it had gotten stronger because now there was such a richness of thinkings along with all else, thinkings that had grown even richer still Saturday night when they had gone dancing with the others at Doubloon's where it had been excruciatingly tender when they had danced slow, and so wild and funky or something when they had let go and danced the fast one that brought them to a sweat, the sweat he could hardly get over with Claudette and Corinne borrowing him along with the others for the now-and-then dances that they said even bachelor wives were entitled to. She had watched him with Corinne with an incipient jealousy that was distinct and yet not even unpleasant, not quite menacing with it becoming ever more obvious that the feeling Matt and Mark had ignited was not waning but growing, showing itself in some not so muted ways through that casualness, that engaging insouciance. Even that, even the incipient pang of possessiveness had heightened her feeling, her intuition that it was, that it was time.

Yet, it had been not when she was close to him dancing or while witnessing his hazardous closeness to Corinne's loose-jointed form, not then that she had thought it most strongly but when she had seen him distantly, when the guy in the combo he had gotten to know in New Orleans asked him to come up and do something with them, and when he had. When she saw him curved over the guitar doing the thing he had begun to wonder whether he should spend his life doing, just then she had a powerful intuition that if it wasn't, then it ought to be.

He had played a light but moody piece, another thing he had written but that was actually mostly improvisation as he rendered it, and that he called "Figgy Blue." It was a phrase, he had announced in that reluctant or diffident way he had of speaking before any crowd, that he had picked up in New Orleans from a red-headed Yankee Irishman named Kennedy.

"He didn't know what Figgy Blue means," he had said, "and I don't know what it means. But maybe you can listen to this song and tell what it means. I'm not a singer, but I'll sing this one myself, since the lyrics are very short."

And he had made the house sit up and then brought it down with the whimsical number full of phrases and turns that seemed to evoke everything in the world that was bittersweet and perplexing, a piece that in fact had no lyrics at all until the very end, when he chopped off a long dirty run with a thick diminished chord and then softly uttered those words: *whang, figgy blue!*

Seeing him on the slightly raised bandstand, seeing him distantly, seeing him at the focus of everybody's keen attention, and seeing him in that state of utter, almost ferocious concentration that foreclosed all else, she had got that feeling that he had somehow gone away from her, that he was not merely across the dusky, smoky room with its musky, smoochy, perfumy reek, but that he was locked away from her at some immense and bridgeless distance. This feeling had been sharpened not only by the song he was playing but by the proximity of Claudette and Corinne with their worldly wise talk that so often verged on what Corinne had previously said and what was on her mind: *Love is not being able to wait.* Suddenly she had hungered to reduce the immense distance between them and to reduce it to zero, and had found herself thinking or feeling or sensing or intuiting it and for the first time forming it into words: *Maybe it is the time.*

Yes, maybe it really was, she had thought, as the night went on, festive and smoky and sweaty and tender and thrumming, with Corinne, after a few beers, borrowing Matt and Mark in turn and dancing with them in a way that even the Gebhart girls noticed, in a way that finally Henry noticed, too, he to whom she hadn't yet had a chance or, in truth, hadn't yet dared to talk to about it. Henry, who at the big, long table was mainly gossiping with her on one side and Florence and Percy on the other, had draped his arm across the back of her chair and let it lightly touch her shoulders, and had suddenly leaned to her ear and said, not gravely or critically but as though mentioning a detail that only he had noticed: "I'll bet you a nickel Mrs. Fielding's got something besides dancing on her mind."

At which she had sighed and looked at him and said, "Could be."

At which he had looked at her and said, "She's a damn good-looking woman, too."

To which she said, "You think so?"

To which he said, "Goddamighty, don't you?"

To which she answered, "I don't think I'll let her *borrow* you any more."

To which he, gazing at Corinne Fielding on the dance floor with Mark, said in words begun in tones of admiring wonder, "Her body—does things—that are almost—as fantastic—" And now he peered at Ellen. "—as the things yours does."

At which her suspense had snapped and she had exploded into a laugh that caused heads to pop around.

She: You realize you were on the verge of getting a glass of beer on your head?

He: A sloshing? For a compliment like that?

She: I mean before that fast save at the end—for which thank you, even if it ain't so.

He: Ain't so! Ellen, when you walk down a sidewalk the air crackles with the sound of male morality disintegrating.

She: Come on.

He: One day when you weren't noticing I saw a sixty-year-old man glance at you and immediately turn and ask his wife for a divorce. Another day I saw an elderly bishop take a quick look and instantly scurry off to confess his thoughts.

She: (Laughing.) Stop it! Enough, enough!

He: You don't even want to hear how seeing you makes me feel?

She: Only that, then. Yes, I'll listen to that.

He: Well, when I see you, I lose my heart, my head—and my nerve.

She: You never lost your nerve in your life.

He: When I see you I know that if the man upstairs had made you any more beautiful he would never have let you come downstairs.

She: (Laughing.) Blasphemy!

He: Well, my natural reverence is just another thing I lose when I see you—along with my sense of direction, my sense of time and my sense of—of—

She: What?

He: Decency.

She: No.

He: Humor.

When they had gotten back to the house she had come so close to knowing it that finally she had had a moment of sharp indecision when they were in the hallway upstairs, whether to pull him on into her room or push him, as at last she gently did, toward the little middle room across the hall that he was sharing with Percy.

But she had opened her eyes today knowing so certainly that she had gone to her notebook and printed the date—Sun. Aug. 31, 1941—under which she had printed: "HR + EW = ∞. The time has come!"

She had known it so indubitably that she had even been impelled to speak her feelings about it to him so that when it happened it wouldn't happen in the wrong way. She had spoken after they had roared into town on his damn motorcycle to get the Sunday paper, after they had gone down to one of the benches under the camphor trees overlooking the wharf, after they had skimmed through the paper and were just sitting there and peeling the oranges they had picked up at the market.

She: Can I talk to you about something special?

He: Listen, musclehead, you don't ever have to ask me whether you can talk to me about something.

She: Well, I've been thinking.

He: That's all right, we all have faults.

She: No joking, now, okay?

He: I wish you would ask me before you talk about something special.

She: Henry!

He: Kiss me, and let's start over.

She: Well, I've been thinking—about the first time we make love.

He: Well, I ought to confess the subject has crossed my mind.

She: Henry! Okay, so I've been thinking of something I would like when it happens, whenever.

He: Okay. Go on.

She: Now, what I hope is—that when it happens, whenever—that at first we can just stand and hold each other—the way we did the other night in the rain. Okay?

He: Okay.

She: For awhile, okay?

He: Okay.

She: And then, when we lie down, I hope we can hold each other and just lie real still for awhile, okay?

He: Okay.

She: And tell each other what we feel.

He: Okay.

She: Do you think I'm silly?

He: Ellen, I think you are something.

She: And then—do you want to hear any more? I mean, is it wrong to think about it? I mean to tell you this way?

He: Oh, hell, no. Tell me. Go on.

She: Well—anyway, there's not much more to tell. But I hope that when we're together, that for just a little while we can still be real still. And look at each other. And say things. How we feel. Will that be okay?

He: Ellen, you may not believe it, but that's exactly the way I'd like it to be.

She: Whenever.

He: Whenever. Now go on.

She: Well, that's all. I think after that it just ought to happen as it happens.

He: Ellen?

She: Uh-huh.

He: You've heard of Tunkintell?

She: *Certainement,* as in I love you more than Tunkintell.

He: You took the words right out of my mouth.

She: And you really feel the same way?

He: Whenever.

She: Tonight? Maybe?

He: Really?

She: If everything's okay?

He: Ellen, would you drive home?

She: I can't drive a damn motorcycle.

He: I couldn't drive a mule the way I'm feeling.

She: You don't feel bad?

He: If I felt any better I'd just fly us home.

She: Me, too.

After all that, after she had known it and even managed to get it out and find out he felt exactly the same way, after the brief sunshine that had gotten clouded over without them even noticing it, after they had roared back to the house with both of them knowing that a golden apple of a day was about to happen, after all that, they had rolled down the crushed shell lane and suddenly noticed people both at the house and up and down the beach looking oddly busy— well, naturally, when they had rolled up to where everybody was they had found out right away that it just wasn't to be, had found out in the flurry of excited yells from Matt and Percy and even the Gebhart girls, who were pitching in and making it sound as though it were going to be a lark, a picnic, a fiesta or something, something they up in Ohio had never experienced before and so didn't know how it was to have the house you were in slammed and hammered as by the kick of an immense and furious horse.

"See?" Henry had said, swinging off the bike and taking her shoulders in his bony calloused hands and looking at her with the face of fate's favorite victim. "Didn't I tell you that as soon as the world found out how I felt it would decide to end?"

So the golden apple had ripened and fallen away in front of her eyes, the day disintegrating into hectic hustling about to the stores reopened for the emergency, dashing around buying candles and batteries and tape for the windows, and canned heat and jugs and buckets for water, and a new gallon thermos for hot coffee, and new line for anchoring the boats after they had been beached and overturned. And scampering about to pick up and stash away the outdoor chairs and everything else that could move. And finally deciding to get plywood for the big front windows on the bay side while letting the smaller ones ride it out, with crisscrossings of wide adhesive tape. And then going to the station to get still another big battery for the radio Matt and Mark decided to take out of the motorboat and bring in the house for when the power failed as it was sure to.

It had passed, helter-skelter, in all that, and then in going up the beach to do it all again for Corinne Fielding who had also never been through one before, and who had already started wondering whether her rented house would stand up, or whether she should evacuate as some of the others would be doing from low-lying coastal areas, but who, it was decided, would come over and sweat it out in the Worth's house with them. Corinne, who after she had gotten home from Doubloon's had received an unsettling call from her husband, a call about something that had come up but that she hadn't yet made clear, unless to Claudette, and that obviously had her thinking somberly about something, something besides a storm that might or might not hit them.

The hectic busyness had got them done by the time the warnings became specific and almost certain, had got them ready with hours and hours to spare before what wasn't expected until hours after supper. Then Henry and all the other boys had gone off to help the crews put in sandbags along the beach to the south where sea walls hadn't yet been built, while all the rest, the females and of course her Papa, slouched around and waited, listening to the radio, with the phone ringing over and over bringing inquiries from Horris in Washington and a report from Cliff saying of course he was battening down everything at home just in case. And there had been a call from Mr. Gebhart, who wondered whether he should drive down and get Liz and Beth and take them home to McClung, to which her Papa had said: "Well, you can if you like, but they're no more likely to get hurt here than anywhere. It doesn't make much sense to run from a hurricane unless you happen to know exactly where it's going and what it's going to hit."

Which had sounded very wise and philosophical and comforting to her at the time, but not now, not at this moment, not with the forecasting all over and the wind in the darkness outside no longer whistling but beginning to shriek, not now that it was about to hit that which it had only been teasing so far, that which it had only been pummeling, spanking, and testily buffeting but not yet hammering and slamming and pounding and battering as it would any minute now, as all of them sat or squatted or leaned variously in the back downstairs bedroom that was her Papa's and the adjoining middle bedroom that was Aunt Margaret's, all of them looking weird and, to her, almost preternaturally beautiful in the light of the candles that had been lit as soon as they had lost the electricity, which down here tended to go out anyway with every heavy dew.

She and Henry, he still gritty from the sandbag work, sat leaning against the side of her Papa's bed on the edge of which Aunt Margaret was perched just above them looking toward but not at her Papa in his wooden rocker that tilted back and forth slowly as though it were a summer day on the porch: he with his long muscular face with its wild brows and browned splotches looking placid or confident or inscrutable, he with his enormous hands stacked on top of his big cudgel-thick stick that he was raising and softly tapping down now every fourth rock, he whose world had already ended so many times and so many times begun anew that he could wait its possible ending again if not with perfect equanimity then without shock and certainly without amazement, and obviously without that feeling that she was having a hard time avoiding, the feeling Henry had expressed and that she at moments also felt, the feeling that it was all happening to her personally and somehow on account of her: all that hell getting ready to gather anew and slam down on them precisely to blow away or wash from the face of the earth the flesh and love and thinkings that were her and Henry and that had just entered into some new prospective realm that day, that morning. She did not believe this with thought words but only knew it as a feeling that her thought words would have repudiated. And yet she wordlessly felt it.

But not him, not her Papa rocking there with even a faint smile on the mouth that didn't grin a great deal but broke your heart when it did, he who at sixteen had run up to the courthouse exactly in time to see the arm of the militia commander snap down and to see not the explosion at the mouth of the cannon aimed toward the doorway but the explosion of his Papa's face and flesh with that of the other Rooters who had decided that, by God, this time they would stand and face down the power that was crushing them all into the dirt from which they were toiling desperately to wring a living. Who had witnessed that while his sister Margaret—she with the long strong wrinkled and now androgynous face peering from its perch on the bed toward things others couldn't see—was in their house or shack out east of town watching their gentle mother die of what nobody understood back then but which probably was cancer or something like it. And without pause had gone on, her Papa, to watch three wives who had come to love him and bear his children be invariably struck down in different ways, as though he were doomed somehow to always be witnessing one world ending and sentenced always to be starting up another, which he had always done with no concern or apprehension that it, too, would end, so that now he seemed almost beyond apprehension, not resigned but simply strong, not cocky, not pretending to know what he didn't and couldn't know and yet knowing without doubt what he did know, that he and they had done what they could do and now it was out of their hands.

"It would take a hell of a wind to take down this house," he had said as they all had gathered back in his room and Aunt Margaret's, the corner of the house most removed from the counterclockwise off-the-bay thrust of the storm. "Cliff designed this thing like a damn ship. I suspect if it blows up a big tide we'd float for a week. Dumpling, if that happens, will you steer?"

Everybody had laughed, and she had too, only she hadn't felt like it sitting there knowing that in fact this world that seemed just so damned unbearably sweet and rich could in fact blow away, as she had seen one blow away when they had been in the Pacific and the hurricane that they called a typhoon had lifted up some smaller houses like they were pods or thistles and smashed others as though they were matchboxes stepped on by a horse. Above and beyond her personal knowledge, the damned radio had taken enthusiastic pains to increase their knowledge about others far worse than the one she had seen and heard and felt down to her quaking bones as her Mama had squeezed her close in their lamplit hotel room.

. . . that swept over Galveston, Texas, in 1900, took a toll of some six thousand lives . . . And in 1928, a hurricane in the Lake Okeechobee area of Florida claimed one thousand eight hundred lives . . . More recently, in 1938, a hurricane that ripped across Long Island, New York, and southern New England left behind six hundred dead . . .

It was not only imaginings but sure knowledge that constrained or modified her laughter at all the brave levity that she understood, sure, without really enjoying at the moment. Long before the wind had even begun to whistle, when this thing with the female name Beth was still merely on the way, it had given them the foretaste of death as hurricanes always managed to do somehow long before they had arrived. Two of the shrimp boats in a covey hastening back to the harbor had collided killing some crewmen. Two men in widely distant towns on the coast had died of heart attacks while toiling in the preparations. No, it was already deadly, and if it weren't going to be worse there wouldn't have been that announcement out of Koppalouka that the radio had brought and was bringing again.

. . . Earlier, in the state capital, officials announced that two tugs sent from St. Teresa's to evacuate all personnel and inmates from the maximum security prison on low-lying Scorpion Island at the southern tip of Los Nubes. Officials tonight said the fifty-one prisoners—all either awaiting execution or considered hard-case lifers—have been landed at the mainland side of the Los Nubes causeway, where they were loaded on trucks for transfer to the county jail near St. Teresa's. Meanwhile, also at the state capital, the highway patrol announced that its personnel would coordinate with the National Guard if it becomes necessary to . . .

Now, as though he had heard or sensed something they hadn't, her Papa said, "Here she comes." And Ellen shuddered, praying, *oh God*, that it wouldn't be the last time she would touch him beside her and see him who had just spoken, him whose seed had found the egg in Emily Boisseau and formed the tiny thing that had multiplied into the billion cells that had become her who had squirmed into the green world while her Mama's face . . .

Whamamamam! Oh, God, yes, there it came. It came hammering and pounding and battering and slamming as though it could not conceivably be merely invisible wind tearing in off the bay at a hundred and ten or twenty but had to be something palpable and implacable and demonic like an immense and incensed horse with back-kicking hooves the exact size of the house. *Whamamamam!* She could feel every *wham* in her bones, and could see what she felt in the other faces, now even in her Papa's, that knowing old face that wasn't beyond flinching, after all, even though it quickly recovered, devoting itself now not to waiting but to sharply heeding.

"Goddamighty, look!" Henry yelled. She, they, everybody, gaped through the crisscrossed back window and saw the world of the back grounds and the road beyond eerily illuminated by sustained and directionless flashes of lightning that starkly disclosed the tall pine trees beyond the road, big trees some of which snapped over like brittle weeds. Even as they gaped at the on-and-off landscape, saw a skiff come from God knows where and go bouncing across the ground like a blown paper cup, rolling and bouncing as though weightless, skeetering across a scape erratically filled not with rain but with enormous wads or masses of water hurled not down but across, wads of it bashing down and exploding on the soil like bombs, saw it and then didn't see it, saw it under weird and garish brownish green light and then saw it all vanish in the inkiest of blacknesses.

The house shuddered. Now the shriek was a hammering howl that didn't even seem abnormal simply because plainly it was going to last forever. The shriek-howl would forever shut out all other possible sounds. It was a shriek-howl of fury, of furious outrage, of the outrage of that palpable kicking thing that the house wouldn't go down, so now in its utterly demonic temper it would have to kick it a million times—*whamamamamam!*—if need be to reduce and obliterate the damned thing, or at least to move it out of the way so that it could plunge on to other demolitions of other houses, other places, where frail, puny, simpering creatures like these huddled cowed and awed and impotent, terrified and cherishing things so trivial and evanescent as to merit not even a breath amidst its enormous demolishing gusts. *Whamamamamam!*

And now again, look: In new flashes outside they could see the lake where the back yard had been, could see it without being able to tell whether it was an inch or a foot, could see only its froth and fury and myriad stir intermittently reliefed by the strange greenish brown light that was winking down out of the hideous gray black mouth or maw that the whole world had become, the ending world.

She knew it was an ending world because even a house built like a damn ship couldn't take much more of what was already making it quiver, what was already quaking the floor and rattling the ceiling, causing it to quiver, too, and so agitating the pullied wires hanging down to the greenglass light shade that her Papa always pulled over to his bureau to shave over a bowl of water, shaving as he always had with a straight razor that he used with fine movements like an artist, that he used almost ritually in a way she probably would never see him do again. She thought, *Oh, please, please help us!*

Her hand was slick and sweaty in Henry's, and she felt she could not possibly clench tight enough the flesh she was already clenching so tightly she could feel the bones of his fingers pressing in on the bones of hers, he clenching, too, his hand and arm and his whole body tensed and drawn close to hers.

Impossibly the slamming and hammering suddenly seemed to get harder, impossibly more furious until not only her hands but her eyes clenched themselves shut, shutting and opening only for a flick to see in the yellow light that everybody else's were squinched shut, too, in this instant, the last instant, she knew, that she would ever see all of these beings who had also sprung up so marvelously from tiny squirmy seeds to what they were and their myriad histories, too, all only to be rent and demolished and obliterated and blown or floated away in a goddam horrendous and insensible wind. *Oh God, oh God, oh God, oh God!*

Suddenly from the front of the house came a smashing, clattering, thumping impact distinguishable even in the rain-thrash and wind-howl. It triggered whoops, squeals and outcries of fresh startlement from the middle bedroom where her brothers were, with the Gebhart girls, and Claudette and Corinne respectively holding Herb Fielding, Jr., and Cecile. At the impact and outcry Ellen, along with the others, glanced back into the middle room. Matt and Mark together had gone out into the hall and were coming back after investigating through the window of the front door, passing the word as they propped themselves in the doorway connecting the rooms.

"Hey, we got a boat on the front steps," Matt said.

"But it doesn't look like the tide's coming up as much as they thought," Mark said.

"Papa, turn the radio back on so we'll know when it's ending," Matt said.

"We'll know," her Papa said but reached and snapped on the radio anyway. It instantly issued forth a resonant male voice that sounded utterly detached and distant and unreal, severed from the knotted and gathered and infinitely vulnerable reality within the room.

. . . *reported diminishing as the storm moved inland leaving behind widespread property damage and at least seventeen dead in the sector of major impact along the Gulf Coast. Winds up to one hundred and twenty knots were clocked at St. Teresa's marine weather station during the first battering of hurricane Beth. Observers at the station estimated that the storm reached its peak at 9:45 with a tide rising to forty-nine inches above normal.*

Throughout the coastal area emergency teams are standing ready to move into rescue and repair operations as soon as the winds permit. And, meanwhile, teams of a different kind were preparing to move out at the first opportunity in a search for four state convicts who escaped custody when a truck bearing them to the county jail near St. Teresa's collided with a utility repair rig early this evening. The convicts were part of a group just evacuated from the maximum security prison on Scorpion Island. They made away during the confusion following the collision on Gulf Bay Highway at the outskirts of St. Teresa's. Authorities have alerted residents of the area to be on the lookout for any suspicious strangers. Though manacled in pairs at the time of their getaway, the convicts are considered highly dangerous.

Now the winds, though still hammering, seemed to have subsided. Maybe they were not going to get the lull and the doublelashing that they would have if the very center of the storm had passed over them. Ellen could feel the slight letup of the fury outside, could see it in the faces of the others, could hear it in Henry's voice as he leaned to her ear.

"It's going to end," he said. "It must not have noticed us."

She turned and studied his face and his faint smile in the weird candlelight. Almost to her surprise, she felt a smile forcing its way to her mouth, though she resisted its spread with pressed lips.

It blew for awhile yet, but then suddenly everybody was getting up, stretching, talking louder, more boldly. A lot of almost hysterical laughter kept bursting into the middle of jokes and comments that weren't all that funny, she realized, even as she found herself compulsively laughing at them, too, laughing and thinking, *Thank you.* And thinking also that now that they weren't going to be wiped off the face of the earth, maybe they would just let go for awhile, and maybe the good feelings would return, and then maybe the day or rather the night might still turn into what she had become convinced it could and should be.

Only she thought and hoped that without foreseeing the inevitable, which came soon: everybody going out to walk and slosh around and inspect what it had left behind, the whole gaggle of them going first around their house from whose front steps the boys dragged down a battered skiff, and then up the beach and around the Fielding house, where Claudette had decided Corinne shouldn't stay tonight on account of the escaped convicts, and then down the beach where the roof of one house had been lifted askew, while all the other

houses in view had substantially weathered the storm. Its most conspicuous memento at a glance was ubiquitous seaweed and little hills
of driftstuff and a number of boats wrenched from moorings or
down-stakings, boats flipped helter-skelter into the raised yards and
onto the sloping ground between the houses and the main road.

She also had not foreseen that after the inspection foray all the
boys would be impelled to abscond to the county courthouse and
offer their services to the rescue and cleanup teams, not that, once
they were gone, they would remain so long, with midnight coming,
and then one, when even Claudette with her predilection for sitting
up through the night had confessed that the strain and excitement
had left her wrung out, with the result that she had instigated the
whole crowd of females to disperse and go where her Papa had long
been, and where Aunt Margaret had been intermittently: to bed.
Corinne and her children had gone to share the room with Claudette
after cots had been unfolded, and Ellen had gone at last to her room.

She had closed the door feeling not chagrin, certainly, nor re-
sentment, but surely disappointment and a kind of snakebit feeling,
the sense that outside events had somehow fallen into unfair dishar-
mony with her own personal destiny. Nevertheless, she felt and said,
thank you, to that whatever-power that she seldom named, and she
was in fact profoundly grateful that the world hadn't ended, that she
would see them all again, those faces, and touch them, that flesh, and
that, and that, of these creatures who, as the world had turned into
a maw and a maelstrom, had seemed so infinitesimal and vulnerable
and impotent as they had huddled in strange union in those rooms
downstairs, all that and so infinitely important. Yes, she would see
them tomorrow, him, and the summer would still end well even if
it ended with debris and litter and gunk strewn everywhere on the
beach. It would end well even if they had to spend the rest of the
time cleaning up and unbattening what they had battened in such
a panic all day long. There was time, and it was still the time,
and . . .

She waked and popped open her eyes not knowing what she
had heard. She popped them open and saw that the first faintest light
of dawn was coming in the only slightly raised windows, the light
and the still restless wash of the bay, and even the early eerie calls
of some gulls. But that had not been what she heard.

Then she heard it again, three swift, very light raps on her door.
She sprang up, taking her blanket with her pulled about her as a cloak
over her nakedness. She pulled the door open a crack and saw the

disheveled hair and querying eyes and tentatively smiling mouth of him who also, coincidentally, was wrapped in a blanket, and who was quickly inside the room with the door softly pressed closed behind him and the hook-lock swung into its eye.

And now without a word they were both in two blankets, a single tent of two blankets held up by two hands clutching the edges together in front of two chests that closed on the hands, until the hands let go, let the blankets slip to the floor and form a crumpled pool about four bare feet. Cool buffeting breezes from the bay through the slightly opened windows played over flesh that was suddenly warm and pulsing, one clasped body of flesh as they stood, and stood, wordless for a long, long while, holding, holding until everything seemed dazed and confused, holding for that long thought out of which arose the strange and marvelous illusion that questing cries of the gulls outside might be emanating from them, from this body with its singular pulse, its singular warmth, its singular severance from and joining with all else on earth, the air, the gulls, the dawn light, and even the forgotten storm.

Wordless still, and needing no words, perhaps even nameless by now and needing no names, with ease already thought and so now mindless and ordained, they were on her bed and again holding, clasping and only that as they had been for the long, long while before the window. They hold and the joined pulse gathers and grows, buffeting warmth and then again an emergent storm. Her eyes open to find his also opening to find hers. Her hand traces the intricate concavities of that face, and his, those tender calloused fingertips discover the lines and contours of hers, and discover the myriad feather curls of strewn hair.

She who had imagined that she would softly speak of her feelings found them as indescribable as the storm, a moil and spill and surge of keen hungering and yearning and thinking, a maelstrom already and still gathering in and about them.

"I feel so good I can't tell you," she whispers.

"I feel so good I can't tell you," he whispers.

Then they were together, and again for a long, long while, faces close but seeing. She felt weightless, and felt that he felt weightless, and suddenly all memory and thinking had fled her mind. They were still, very still, impossibly still, impossible because they were melting, they would melt if they didn't move and rediscover their forms, they would melt and meld with no one or the other but only they indistinguishable. They were weightless and singular, their mind the gull already soaring beyond the reach of wings.

Yet his face was there. She remained impossibly still, and traced it once again, and took it between her hands, claimed it, and brought his mouth to hers, and held his weightless face as though it were a floating luminous ghost in ghostly hands. She was looking and drowning in his eyes.

"I want to tell you but I don't know how," she said.

"I know," he said. "I know. I can't think of anything, only that I love you more than life itself."

"I feel like that. I love you like life itself."

Again she brought his mouth to hers, and then yielded her leashed stillness to tides within and between them, and let happen what happened.

Later, much later, some still new sound brought her eyes open again. She had the feeling that she had not actually slept from the time he had stolen out again, cloaked in his blanket, after they had lain still and quiet for a long while. Afterward, she felt that she had only drifted or floated or wafted.

Now, when she woke up to the sound of voices full of a new kind of intensity and excitement, she was for a moment disoriented. The strange pattern of shadows on the wall perplexed her, puzzled until she glanced back and saw the crisscrossings of tape on the windows through which brilliant sunshine was now bursting.

The voices, not wordy but abrupt and terse and deadly serious, had come to her first from the outside, she felt, from the front porch no doubt. No meaning had reached her at all before they had moved inside, the voices and their owners. Now the talk was a gathering and distinct but indecipherable rumble from the hallway downstairs, an incomprehensible resonant mumbling amidst which she caught a few words, the word *dead* and the exclamation *for God's sake.* These sent her bolting up to tug on a sweatshirt and quickly draw on a pair of white duck jeans.

Downstairs everybody was standing about in the front hall, forming an irregular circle of themselves with Corinne Fielding at the center, Cecile in her arms, her son clasping her leg, Claudette with a hand on her shoulder, Mark and Matt standing by, and the Gebhart girls, and Aunt Margaret and her Papa, so that obviously she and Henry had outslept them all.

As Ellen apprehensively walked up, her Papa was shushing them all and was trying to get some story that was being related not by Corinne, whose face was pale and glazed, but by Claudette, who, it seemed, had just walked with Corinne and the children up to the

Fielding house, only to hurry back, the four of them, to tell what she was telling again now, that they had found Mr. Herbert Fielding in the house dead.

"He was just sitting in the chair," Claudette was saying. "And his chest was all red, and there was no gun or anything that we saw, nothing. Papa Worth, somebody must have killed him, he must have been murdered. It must have been one of those convicts, it must have been somebody."

Now Ellen pressed close to her Papa, gazing at Corinne with a sick and sinking feeling, but trying to listen to what he would say. He didn't say much before he was gone out the door.

He said, "Claudette, you take Mrs. Fielding in there, and the children, and sit them down. Dumpling, you stay with them. Percy, if the phone's come back on, call the police. The boys and I'll go take a look. Matt, Mark. Margaret, you see to everybody."

CLAUDETTE MARIE BEAUVOIR HORRIS:

She had called her husband to tell him what had happened, and to get him to stay in Washington until she got there, since she was going to accompany Corinne and the children on the train that carried the body to his native Baltimore for burial, and, as planned, had rendezvoused with Horris at the superb old hotel that looked out on the park and the White House from the spacious room for which he said the tab would be covered by whom he couldn't say, or wouldn't, just as he wouldn't or couldn't tell her anything substantial about his mysterious trip, or seemingly anything about anything until he had heard everything she could tell him about what had happened and what they knew and what they didn't know.

She said:

It was the absence of any weapon that made us think it was murder, and the first thought that it was otherwise came from the medical examiner who had come out with the police. Of course, we didn't go back until they had come; and *him*, and it wasn't the absence of a gun that struck him but the character of the wound. It evidently told him to his satisfaction that the muzzle of the gun had been pressed directly against the chest when it went off. There were burns that we hadn't noticed, but of course we hadn't studied it as he did, which is an awful understatement.

We had come upon him and almost been flung back by the sight, it was so completely unexpected that anyone would be there, let alone like that. Corinne, after all, had no idea of precisely when he intended to return. All she knew was that some serious trouble had come up. He had told her this when he telephoned late Saturday night, or, rather, very early Sunday morning. We had all just come back from Doubloon's, and when she got into her house the phone was already ringing. He had been trying to reach her but of course hadn't got any answer, and so had this distress on top of the other. Only he didn't really spell the other out. He only said his job was all over and that they would be leaving as soon as he returned. He didn't tell her that even then he was at the airfield up here in Washington waiting for a military flight to Gulfport, and so on Sunday Corinne was completely unaware that he had been closed in over there in Gulfport by the storm.

I don't suppose that fact seems important, but it was just one more that disturbed her very much. Because inevitably she wondered what the outcome would have been if she had been at the house when the army staff car delivered him there early Monday morning. She wonders whether he might have talked to her about it, whether she might have encouraged him, or whether her presence at the very least might have deterred him and—well, you know.

She didn't find the note until after the medical examiner had taken his look at the body and made the comment he did, that if it was murder it was a very unusual murder because of the burns even at the interior of the wound. Until then, of course, we, or she, had no cause to look for anything. And even when she began looking it took some time for her to discover it, although it was right there on the desk in the living room. I didn't notice it myself. And who would have?

He had scratched the note on the back of the notice that they had issued him, one of those dreary government letters with the from—to—subject et cetera at the top and only the single line or sentence of text informing the subject, of course, that his employment with such and such was terminated as of that date. Which was Friday. And which means that he brooded on it up here for almost two days before he called. Or perhaps he was waiting to see about the transportation they offered him before calling. In any event, this letter was simply lying there on the desk face-up and scarcely notice‧able alongside other similar looking stuff. She and I both glanced at it several times before she picked it up at last and turned it over and saw the words penned on the back in that sharply slanting handwriting.

It didn't say much. It said, "Dearest Corinne—It just won't

work any more, and I'm unable to go on trying to make it work. You may not believe it, but I love you all too much to burden you with it any more."

The note, of course, settled the main question, but it wasn't until that evening when they caught the two convicts with the pistol that the puzzle was solved as the police had surmised it. Evidently they had been either on the back porch or perhaps in the kitchen when he had come in. Probably huddled on the porch, if the assumption is correct that when he found the house empty he likely would have looked about, perhaps surmising himself that his family had taken refuge somewhere from the storm. After that, or so it was assumed from the signs of things—the Gladstone bag that was just set by the front door, and the fact his jacket was still on and nothing else disturbed—from all that they assumed that he probably looked around and then took the pistol out of the bureau and put the letter on the desk and—and that was it. And then presumably the convicts heard, and checked, and grabbed up the weapon and fled.

Corinne seemed as dazed as any of us at first, naturally, but at the same time she comprehended as none of us did, and so, finally, she said she wasn't really surprised. Shocked, yes, but not surprised that it had finally come to that. Not surprised that the government had found out, and not surprised that he had found the consequences unbearable. Because his secret had always been unbearable to him, Corinne says. It was something he had never accepted at all, something he had struggled against, struggled to conceal even from himself. And successfully, too, for a time.

So successfully that he utterly fooled her from the time they met until—well, until it was too late, until they were already married. And she hadn't gone into that blindly, either, not impulsively even though it was done quickly. It wasn't out of blind impelling love on her part, and it wasn't that that kept her from knowing about him. It was his effective dissembling or suppressing, whatever. Corinne wasn't actually quote in love unquote when he asked her to marry him. She was fond of him, but— You know, he was with the commerce bureau or department or whatever when he came to Paris that time when they met. Attending some economic seminar or some such at the Sorbonne. Do you recall it? It would have been the first summer you monitored lectures there. I have no recollection of it. Corinne, in any event, was attending parts of it for her father, and so fell into an acquaintanceship, and, well, soon he seemed infatuated, and so—well, to her he seemed a very agreeable man. And perhaps more importantly, he became a way for her to escape what she had begun to feel was the oppressive closeness of her father, of Dr. Bardot, who had, of course, tried to play father and mother to her from childhood. She felt that the only way to get out of her father's shadow was by leaving Paris, and of course his proposal promised this as well as affection. So it wasn't an unfair decision she made, she liked him well enough.

But it wasn't long before she began to suspect, noticing it more in his moods and in his incidental absences than in the constraints that eventually became evident, you know, in the bedroom. So, in any event, as we would say in southern France, she hasn't had an easy row to hoe. Of course, ever since France—poor France—ever since last year she's been worried constantly about her father on top of everything else, with no word whatever so far. She assumes that if alive he's gone underground, and could hardly bear to assume otherwise. Knowing Dr. Bardot's leanings and courage, I suspect it's a safe assumption. Yet, it's only an assumption—like mine about my family. So. So she has had that to bear, and then the move to the strange place, which isn't all that easy, leaving an established pattern in a city like this and plopping down in a place like St. Teresa's. And not only the move but simply dealing with him day by day and month by month—or not dealing but simply witnessing him trying to deal with it himself. For the last while he had become close to incommunicado.

And now, ironically enough, this came along at just a moment when she had begun to feel better than in years. For reasons I haven't yet told you. But that, yes, I can see from your look you've guessed. Well, yes, she fell in love, but even you would never guess with whom, and—Why are you holding up two fingers like so? I see. You've guessed that, too. Well, that's a story apart. But the part that's hers is that she actually was like a girl of sixteen again, only doubly so, in that bizarre situation.

We think of Corinne as someone who is in perpetually good spirits, who has been all along, who is always in repose. But the truth is this is only a tribute to her character—and maybe not to wisdom at all. It's just her way to show us that good happy face and leave us uninformed about the sorrows she carries. But when I got down there at the beginning of what was to be the big holiday weekend —well, she was different. Here was a truly passionate woman truly happy in spite of the dilemma love had trapped her in.

I don't know what you think, but I thought it was lovely. You know, in spite of that easy way, Corinne has never been one for easy dalliances. Her answer to the impossible marriage had never been simply to sleep around. She tells me this, and I believe her, because it's in character, perfectly in character. And—

Well, Monsieur Horris, that's all I know, really. It was a very long train ride. And at the same time, in spite of everything, a very good one. Or do I mean a very rich one, very warm. I felt close to Corinne, which is what I'm saying, very close. We talked and talked and talked, through the night and through all that countryside. Talked until I don't really know how I'm still talking now. I do hope we can keep in touch with her. She's going to spend a few days with his family, and then—well, she didn't know. Of course, I invited her to come stay with us until she gets some direction, but I didn't get the impression she would hazard it. Yet, it would be nice, wouldn't it? I feel close to her, more like a mother than a friend or a sister, which must sound ridiculous, but this is the way I feel.

Horris, I am so glad summer is over. But, God help us, what an ending it was. A hurricane one night and the next morning—oh, God, the horror of it, the pity, the pity of fearing pain more than loving life.

But now you talk to me. I am your wife and I have a right to know what you're doing up here, and you haven't told me anything that I believe. And I want you to tell me, and to hell with security, because in this world there is no such thing.

1941-42
Interim

ELLEN EMILY WORTH'S NOTEBOOK

Fri. Sept. 5, 1941: Home again!
On arrival she had without conscious intent ambled to the weathering mock Lomkubee village where Ben Ezra Sorrel had made his film, and had stayed there only briefly, deeply struck by the fact that already in her life she had seen the strange gray-blue-white faces of two men who had killed themselves.

Sun. Sept. 7, 1941: Horris—"Men own a certain tolerance for pain, and women, too, that can stretch so far and no further, and when its limit is reached, only madness can save them from some unbearable reality whatever it might be. Psychosis is merely one mode of the flight from self or reality of which suicide is the extreme flight and the epitome."

Thurs. Sept. 11, 1941: Drove Henry over to the East McClung to see Jesse Bird about learning those licks.

East McClung was part of the town and yet differentiated both by terminology and the racial cast of most of its inhabitants. They were predominantly Negro, including Jesse Bird, a not-quite-blind guitarist and harmonica player well-known locally not only for his general talent but especially for an uncanny gift, a capacity to evoke colors and events with guitar and harmonica and sometimes with the two flat, black percussion instruments that he clacked between his knee and palm and called "bones." A listener might say, "Jesse, play me a pool game." And he, his eyes grotesquely distorted behind spectacles as thick as the bottoms of Coke bottles, would, with harmonica and bones, evoke the racking of balls, the rising, murmurous tension of the game, and do it so vividly that listeners could almost see the eight ball drop. Jesse Bird played sometimes on the porch of Frizzy's Store, accepting freewill donations in a cigar box beside his chair, and sometimes on Saturdays stationed himself outside the Yellow Dog Pool Room on a side street of downtown McClung.

Mon. Sept. 14, 1941: Papa says two FBI men came by asking questions about Mr. Fielding and Corinne. Supposedly because he was connected with defense work. Also asked a lot about anything she might have said about her father. Strange.

Fri. Sept. 19, 1941: Registration today: European History, Latin III, Chemistry I, Senior Civics, Home Ec., Music. Miss C. says with summer course I could get out early—Jan. '43.

Mon. Sept. 22, 1941: Elected Managing Editor of The Page! Dropped Chemistry.

Fri. Sept. 26, 1941: Henry & I to game. Percy's afterward with M&M & Liz & Beth.

Sat. Sept. 27, 1941: [A line sketch of Henry playing with Jesse Bird on porch of Frizzy's Store, a grinning, jangling street crowd gathered around.]

Tues. Oct. 7, 1941: Warm note from Corinne Fielding to Papa & Family. Answered for him.

Fri. Oct. 10, 1941: Finished Look Homeward, Angel, and agree with Henry: overwhelming!

Sun. Oct. 12, 1941: Last night somebody burned a cross in front of Frizzy's Store! Horris says it's undoubtedly because of Henry playing there with Jesse. Cliff and Horris went and got it and took it to the Mirror office. Henry was right. What a bunch of bastards!

Fri. Oct. 17, 1941: Everybody's talking about Cliff's front page ad in this week's Mirror—"Found: One cross, slightly burned.

Owner may claim during daylight hours only by proving he could not read this ad all by himself."

Sat. Oct. 18, 1941: Somebody threw a Bible through the Mirror window last night! It landed right on Horris's desk. Horris—"No doubt they assumed that, like light itself, it would pass through the pane without resistance." Cliff says they don't know just who but it must be somebody in the crowd the Burcells have been stirring up, and maybe Sonny Grindell and Cecil Drum (ugh!).

Cecil Drum was a town policeman, twenty-five at this time, still notorious or famous, depending on the viewpoint, for having shot down two Negro youths who, while skylarking, had accidentally bumped into and knocked down an aging white woman during a downtown political speaking in the late summer of 1936. The two boys had fled, Drum had given chase, and later claimed he shot them after they tried to overwhelm him. Drum was a tall, hefty young man whose right eye opened much wider than his left. Sometimes contemporaries called him "Dynamite"—much to his chagrin. The nickname had been nailed to him in 1930 because of an episode at the Bulomkubee River, where white boys customarily swam off of one bank while Negro boys swam off of the flat shore opposite. Once in boyish exuberance Cecil Drum had taken the Tarzan pose on the bank, pounded his prematurely burly chest and in clarion braggadocio had shouted: "One hundred and eighty pounds of dynamite!" "Yeah, man," some unknown one of the watching Negroes had yelled back, "—with a two-inch fuse!" On the same day he had shot down the Negro youths, but much earlier, Drum had become the center of a lesser public stir in an encounter with Henry Rust, who was then twelve. Agile Rust, during the political speaking, had scaled the downtown monument to the town's namesake and fitted a condom over the granite sword of Mr. McClung himself. Drum had come running up, ordering him down, and at Henry's descent, had tried to take him in hand. "Boy, I'm gonna take your ass to the mayor," Drum had declared. "You'll shit, too, if you eat regular," young Rust had said, jerking free and fleeing like a streak through the crowd.

Sun. Nov. 2, 1941: Henry & I on the bike all the way to the mountains. Picnic and back. Gorgeous, gorgeous, gorgeous! But sore tail!

Tues. Nov. 18, 1941: Cliff is talking about going back to sea (maybe) since they need masters even if we don't get in the war. Maybe he really wants to get back to England to see if his long-lost Ellen is all right after everything they've been through over there.

Sat. Nov. 29, 1941: Bravo! The committee is going to let Henry get up a band for the New Year's dance!

Sun. Nov. 30, 1941: Sid Fletcher came out of the Texas Cafe, started falling, and fell all the way across the street into Horris's new plate glass window. Horris—"I get the feeling that providence wants me to remain fully exposed to the elements." M&M went to help him board it up.

Mon. Dec. 1, 1941: Corinne F. wrote Claudette from San Francisco. She's going to stay there until it's all over, if ever, and then go back to Paris.

Thurs. Dec. 4, 1941: Henry asked Jesse Bird about playing together some more. Jesse—"Maybe we better wait til spring when it's warmer."

Fri. Dec. 5, 1941: Florence is worried sick about being late or—???

Sat. Dec. 6, 1941: Henry over practicing·six straight hours upstairs while I sketched. With Percy & Florence to Mingo's in Carterville. Weird atmosphere but great shrimpers. Florence okay! Whew! Percy talking about taking flying lessons.

Sun. Dec. 7, 1941: We were playing Ping-Pong with P & F when Mr. Ensley barged in all flushed, saying—"We just got bombed!" Percy was starting to make a joke when he suddenly saw how wrought up his father was. So it's happened! And who ever guessed it would happen this way. Felt so close to Henry. And so afraid, like in the hurricane. Why, why, why, why, why—?

Mon. Dec. 8, 1941: They brought a radio into study hall so we could hear FDR.

Sun. Dec. 14, 1941: H & I to the airport on the bike to watch Percy go up in Mr. S.'s Piper for the first time. Now H wants to try it. If he does, maybe I will. Gorgeous day. Horris and Claudette walked over for supper. Me—"This year I'm not getting the mother-gone pang as much." Horris—"Well, it doesn't mean you miss her less, it means you're growing wiser." (But I don't feel like it.)

Fri. Dec. 19, 1941: Henry hears the committee is wondering whether to cancel the dance because of the war.

Sun. Dec. 21, 1941: Looks like a full house for Christmas. Susan, Tom, William already in with families, and four or five more on the way.

Mon. Dec. 22, 1941: The holidays! Except they don't seem like holidays. They told Henry the dance will be held anyway. Cliff hears the Guard company is shipping out the day after Christmas.

Thurs. Dec. 25, 1941: From Henry—a garnet gold birthstone ring and matching medallion! Gorgeous! Mrs. Rust loves the charcoal of him playing. House is like a mob. Supper in two shifts.
Me—"Do you always remember which are half-sisters and -brothers and which full?" Cliff—"Are you telling me I'm kin to all of these people?"

Fri. Dec. 26, 1941: Papa called me Charlotte today.

Sat. Dec. 27, 1941: H & M&M & I went down early to watch the Guard loading on buses. Nobody would say where.

Mon. Dec. 29, 1941: Family got a late card from Corinne F.—and M&M a separate one! H & I rode the mares down the Trail to Mount Oro this afternoon. Beautiful. M&M saw Carol Burcell downtown. She's quit school and married a sailor!

Thurs. Jan. 1, 1942: Anniversary! Great dance. Here afterwards, and up til dawn like last year. A year—so long but so fast. Strange. I love him more and more. No mention of his Daddy, but I could see him thinking about it.

Fri. Jan. 2, 1942: Matt & Mark are Marines! Snuck up to Riverton yesterday and joined! Quitting school and everything! Papa was so furious Cliff spent the rest of the day quieting him down. M&M went out tonight and came in absolutely looped to the gills! They leave Monday! Damn, damn, damn!

Sat. Jan. 3, 1942: H & I & M&M & L & B & P&F all to the Merry-Go-Round in Taliaferro with everybody drinking too much and M&M trying to talk H & P into signing up right away, God forbid! Wild weird night. Almost went off the road coming back!

Sun. Jan. 4, 1942: Papa says I can skip school tomorrow so H&I can drive M&M up to Riverton to report.

Mon. Jan. 5, 1942: Watching Matt and Mark walk into that building I had the strangest feeling of something awful. I broke down on the way back and Henry had to drive.

Wed. Jan. 7, 1942: Seventeen! Henry gave me another song in manuscript—"Ellen in the Pines." When I read the words I cried.

Without him I'd actually die! Miss M&M so horribly. Why did they have to be in such a damn hurry?????

Mon. Jan. 19, 1942: Had that lost-in-the-empty-house dream again last night.

Wed. Jan. 28, 1942: M&M write—"Why didn't you talk us out of it? Some of these drill sergeants are not exactly polite. Tell Henry and Percy to shoot for the Army Air Corps. We hear those guys have it made in the shade."

Sat. Feb. 7, 1942: Happy Birthday, Henry! Eighteen! When I gave him the drawing of Ellen in the Pines he looked almost like he was going to cry—the way he did that night in St. Teresa's. A million years ago!

This night, which was not warm but not cold either, only mildly chilly, she and he had gone, as they had gone since summer, to a certain one of the lean-to shelters in the reconstructed Lomkubee village, and there had been together in their way, there amidst that mingling of scents, the fertile muskiness of the matted old pine straw underneath and the sharp bittersweet fragrance of the live pines outside, that and the rich aura of their love and mingling, and that other aura, that spectral aura, those presences she always felt there, the presence of the older young man who had felt love for her mutely before he had killed himself, and also the presence, the presences of the people who had once actually lived here on this site, the Lomkubees with their gentle ways, their devotion not to things but to life, to life which they saw as a singular thing inseparable from the earth and the sky as part of which it occurred, the prodigal earth and the immense incomprehensible sky with the stars that their credo admonished all Lomkubees to heed: "Listen with reverence to the silent singing of the stars. They say that we are nothing and everything."

Sat. Feb. 14, 1942: Out to the airport while Henry went up for his first lesson. Mr. S. told him it probably won't make any difference to the Air Corps. H & P are both dead set on getting into it. I'm not so sure I'm going to try flying after all.

Fri. Feb. 27, 1942: Last night they heard that Polly Rust got seriously burned in Natchez. Hotel bed caught on fire. H said she was evidently drinking. They didn't even know she was in Natchez or why. H—"We assume she went there to see the old man's grave or something. Ever since he died she's been in a bad way." So sad.

Tues. Mar. 3, 1942: Florence and Percy have decided to get married sometime after graduation—after he knows where he'll be. She <u>dreads</u> what her mother is going to say. F—"She says it doesn't matter if we are only second cousins, we shouldn't even be going together let alone talking about getting married."

Thurs. Mar. 19, 1942: School let out in the P.M. for the big scrap iron collection. Henry & I rode around in Tom Pickett's wagon with me driving the horse and them loading. Tom's thinking about the merchant marine and wants to talk to Cliff. Henry and Tom in big silly argument over Wolfe and Faulkner.

H—Listen, why don't we agree that Wolfe said everything and Faulkner said it better.

T—Well, the fact is Tolstoi said everything and Dostoevsky said it better.

H—What's that got to do with Faulkner and Wolfe?

T—Henry, the point is that nothing's got anything to do with Faulkner and Wolfe. And likewise they don't have anything to do with each other. Only a nitshit compares one writer with another.

H—You wouldn't be calling me a nitshit?

T—I'm calling us both nitshits. We remind me of those nitshit literary critics who basically hate all books while they're reading them and then palpitate with narcissistic joy when they've discovered some little nitshit category they can put them in or some little nitshit comparison they can make.

H—Agreed. Wolfe's Wolfe and Faulkner's Faulkner.

T—And never the twain shall meet.

H—Now that you bring him up, do you think Huckleberry Finn is greater than Crime and Punishment?

T—Henry, the trouble with you is you're educated far beyond your intelligence. Huck Finn is the greatest novel ever written. Crime and Punishment is the greatest novel ever written. If the subtlety of this judgment baffles you, it's because you don't actually read any of these books. You live them instead of reading them. Henry, what's wrong with you is that you think you are young Sartoris. No, you think you're Raskolnikov.

H—Actually, Joe Christmas. And what about you? Who are you?

T—I am the goddam brothers Karamazov.

H—And what about Ellen?

T—Ellen is Kathy, as in Kaaaaaaaaathyyyy!

Me—No! Absolutely not!

T—Why not? Hell, she awakened love in a churlish bastard incapable of love. She was great!

Me—But she was doomed. They.

T—Jesus Christ! Aren't we all?
Me—No!

Mon. Mar. 30, 1942: Letter from Matt and Mark in San Diego! Not enough leave time to come home. Going to "see some sights." Bet I know the name of the "sights."

Tues. Mar. 31, 1942: Cliff to N.O. to see about bringing his master's license up to date. I didn't really think he was serious. Who the hell is going to be left?

Sat. Apr. 11, 1942: Henry & Percy decided to ask Papa if he would sound out Gene Earley to see if he could finagle and make sure they get an early crack at the Air Corps.
Gene Earley was born Eugene in 1902 in the farmland east of McClung. He was born to dirt-poor parents and had grown up dirt-poor himself until he had gone to work managing one of Sam Worth's sawmills. Young Earley had shown enough capacity and, more important, enough force of person to induce Sam Worth to stake him to successive and invariably successful races for the county board of supervisors, the state senate, and, in 1930, the Congress, wherein he still represented the district that consisted of Bulomkubee County and eleven other counties. The district was called the Famous First and sprawled over the heartland of Nemisisipiana, a region that Horris in 1939 had written, "drains variously into the Bulomkubee River and the capacious pockets of the Hon. Eugene Earley." Earley had emerged as the undisputed proprietor of the Democratic party in his district and increasingly had proved himself to be the master and manipulator of the party's destiny all over the state. He was slight of stature, flamboyant in style, and comparatively unin-hibited in what he did and said. His activity had brought him wealth through an abundance of devious schemes that skirted and occasionally defied the law, and a certain celebrity as a freewheeling personality. His divorce of his first wife and marriage to a brassy showgirl he had met in Reno had nettled Catholic constituents, but at the criticism Earley had said, "Well, they'll get over it. Besides, by the next election, I may be a Catholic myself. I've been drawn to that faith for a long time. Maybe by then I'll even have a Catholic wife, assuming I can find one that'll have me." Throughout his career Earley remained as devoted as a son to Sam Worth, who occasionally took cognizance of Gene Earley's elaborate larcenies without ever condemning them. "Well, hell," Ellen had heard her Papa say, "he's a politician, isn't he? They're the same as us bankers, except that we're licensed to steal. The main thing about Gene is that he's good of heart. He never steals from anybody who needs it more than he does. And above all, he's not a goddam cross-burner. And whatever he's ever done, he's never put on a sheet to do it in."

Wed. Apr. 29, 1942: It's done—Henry and Percy signed up! They'll graduate early and go in May 8! Why the damn hurry? Damn the damn war!

Thurs. May 7, 1942: So he's gone. Last night was gorgeous, but now he's gone. This morning at dawn I was laughing hysterically, but now I'm not laughing. They're rolling across Texas right now. *That night, his last before leaving, she had impulsively led him upstairs to her room, and they had been together not their first time in bed but their first complete night in one, there in the corner room where she had been born and nursed and where sometimes in a sudden updraft of her mind she thought she could almost recall her emergence into the world. They had barely slept, if at all, had dozed perhaps, but had lost themselves not in frenzied passion but encompassing tenderness, warm and insatiable. It was the first time when in that mutual caress she had whispered what she had felt before, had said, "I want you to come in my mouth." Several times they had got to laughing so that she feared Aunt Margaret would come and discover them. "Don't worry, it's me they'll horsewhip," he had said. And of their insatiable hunger for tenderness he said, "Maybe they won't even take me now. Maybe they'll find out I have terminal satyriasis." Laughter had burst out of her that he tried to suppress by burying her head under a pillow. At the first light of dawn they had stealthily left the room and crept downstairs to freeze, in alarm, in the downstairs hallway when they heard footsteps, someone entering the back hall door. It was Cliff, coming from the kitchen, bearing a steaming cup of coffee back to the stairway, thence to his room. He walked toward them, passing by within perhaps two feet but acting as though they did not exist. When Cliff's door had thumped shut upstairs, Henry whispered to her: "Ellen, we've lost more weight than we imagined." She had almost exploded in laughter again but suppressed this which was insuppressible until they had gone through the back doors with the clear red glass windows and across the back porch and out onto the grounds. Then at a certain distance she had let go with laughter that rocketed up through the trees into the brightening sky, laughing uncontrollably. That afternoon, she and Florence had driven them to Taliaferro to get on the train that would trudge them to New Orleans, where they would change to the faster westward train that would bear them deep into Texas.*

Mon. May 25, 1942: Cliff's actually going to do it! He's closing up his law office! Why on earth?
Clifton Sharpe Worth was born in 1883 and grew up to be not a secretive but a profoundly private person whose intents were not always displayed even to those closest to him. He was the third born of Sam Worth's first brood, coming after Charlotte and Seth. By his fourteenth year it was clear that he would have much of his father's long craggy face but a shorter, stock-

*ier physique. At the end of that fourteenth year of life, Cliff had commit-
ted some serious if childish offense that was now forgotten by all except
probably himself but that at the time had chagrined his Papa, who had
disciplined Cliff by ordering: "Don't go off of this property until I specifically
tell you to, goddamit!" And Cliff had stuck unrelentingly to the rambling
place along the river, had stayed there long after Sam Worth had utterly
forgotten the mandate, had not even left to go to school but had made himself
a day-to-day life in the many corners and nooks of the property with its
three-quarters of a mile of riverfront and half-mile width between the Trail
and the Bulomkubee. Eventually his Papa took to asking him now and then
why he never went anywhere. "You ought to know," Cliff would say, and
let it go at that. During his mandated and yet essentially self-imposed confine-
ment, Cliff read his way through the encyclopedia and all other printed matter
that turned up in the house, including all of his older siblings' schoolbooks.
His liberation finally was inadvertent, as it were, coming as it did from a
father who had forgotten the episode that had occurred at the end of Cliff's
fourteenth year. It was at the imminent arrival of Cliff's sixteenth birthday
that his Papa said, "Son, you've been hanging around home too damn much.
I want you to get away from home some and see some of the world." Cliff
had said, "Where do you want me to go?" His Papa, with the habit of mindless
profanity that became the legacy of all the children down to the last, said,
"Anywhere, goddamit, anywhere and everywhere!" With that, Cliff within
a week had departed McClung, wandered first into Mississippi, and soon cut
back across the coastal edge of Nemisisipiana and into Louisiana, and so to
New Orleans. There he had signed aboard a ship as a common seaman.
Twenty-six years later, on Ellen's birthday in January, 1925, he came back
home for the first time, walked in bearing two seabags full of mementoes, a
shipmaster's license and ledgers recording deposits that totaled almost a
quarter of a million dollars in banks scattered all over the world. "How did
you save so much money?" his Papa asked. "By putting it in banks," Cliff
said. At the time he was forty-one and announced that since he had seen all
he cared to see he was retiring. Soon, however, he had enrolled in college and
taken up law, evidently not so much to practice it as to have an office or a
place that needed no explaining, a sanctuary to which he could repair to read
or to talk to the stream of selected friends who could come in without warning,
and who were seldom, or almost never, interrupted by paying clients. In 1928,
Cliff had advised his Papa to sever his own interests from the country's feverish
speculations, and to convert as much as possible into realty and gold and other
tangible assets. His Papa followed his counsel and when the great crash came
in 1929 he and his bank survived not only without a scar but with enhanced
solidity. He asked Cliff, "How did you know?" "By reading the goddam
papers," Cliff said.*

Fri. June 5, 1942: School's out! Signed up for summer school to finish midterm! Papa's going to leave the St. Teresa's house closed unless some of the others want to use it. Tomorrow—Pick up scrapbook for H letters!!!!

Thurs. June 26, 1942: Corinne F. gave birth to twin girls May 27!!! Letter to Claudette! Still in San Francisco! Goddamighty! What now? Must write. But what to say? Wonder if they know? I am so damn confused!!!

Sun. July 19, 1942: Now Horris! Why in hell should he have to go? And why the damn mystery? And how can Claudette run the paper by herself? And—damn, damn, damn the damn war!

All she knew was almost nothing from T. C. Horris, who was going "only up to Washington," he said, and going unexpectedly, and yet obviously going knowing he would be gone for a time or he wouldn't also have said that Claudette was going to take over the paper. All she knew from Claudette was that on the Friday night before this Sunday, the acerbic New Englander who was now an editor in New York City and who had become one of Horris's closest friends when they converged at Oxford as Rhodes scholars in 1934, this sardonic but charming friend had showed up at the Horris home without announcement, had showed up wearing a yellow polo shirt under a seersucker suit that looked as though it had been slept in by entire generations, wearing that and bringing only a small handgrip of fine soft old beatup leather, had showed up and stayed the night and talked privately with Horris several different times, there in the kitchen and again when they had walked away from the house and stood on the bluff overlooking the river. All Claudette knew or professed to know was that when this man named James Guilford had departed Saturday afternoon, still in the yellow polo shirt under the disgraceful seersucker suit, Horris had fallen into a very thoughtful and solitary mood that he had not exited from until midnight when he had asked her to fix him a nightcap and then, after the first sip, had said, "Claudette, it looks like I'm going to be going on a trip."

Sun. Aug. 30, 1942: Strange, I can neither bear the news nor stop reading it. I can neither bear to think of Matt and Mark out there nor stop thinking it. I go around talking and laughing as though I were normal, but inside I don't see how we go on laughing and talking as we do. Florence feels the same way.
Me—"I think I'm actually going crazy."
F—"I think the whole world is already crazy, and us with it." I'm beginning to feel like her sister.

Fri. Sept. 11, 1942: Registration! School Monday! Thank God! The end of the longest and shortest summer in history!

Wed. Oct. 21, 1942: Major T. C. Horris! With the paratroop pin too! He in and out—but where? Horris—"Oh, they'll find some use for a good medieval scholar somewhere over there. It looks as though I'll just be doing some pencil-pushing in Washington. Or maybe London." Me—"They put you through jump school for that?" Horris—"Well, no, that's just so the real soldiers won't look on me with the complete contempt a sedentary coward merits." So good to see him. So sad to see him go. I wasn't created for saying goodbyes.

Mon. Dec. 14, 1942: Papa says yes! Florence and I go out next week to see them get their wings! What a Christmas gift!

Wed. Dec. 30, 1942: GOD DAMN THE WO———

The entry was scored in huge letters, printed with such savagery that the page was torn, with such force that the point of the pen had broken off before she could finish spelling "world." And then she flung the pen across the room and swept her notebook from the desk and raged aloud, screaming denunciations upon all of mankind. She had just come home from the trip she and Florence had made to see Henry and Percy, a good trip with warm reunions, one trip she had loved even when it was over and they rode home wearing the miniature wings. She had been home not long when the telegram came that informed the family that Pvt. Matthew Boisseau Worth had been killed in action, and that Pvt. Mark Boisseau Worth had been severely wounded in the same action, and that each had been awarded the Navy Cross for rare gallantry and courage beyond the call of duty.

MARGARET WORTH:

She had for a week watched her brother's child Ellen profanely shriek at God and the world and man and war, and had watched her lovely eyes grow hollow and dark, and had heard her raging voice grow silent as her eyes began to shriek instead, and now for another week had watched her retreat variously to her room or to the groves outside, hoarding and nursing that which was bearing her into sickness and into dreams the fruit of which could be heard in her gasps at night from outside the room to which now this child Ellen would admit no one, or so declared, none of those who didn't seem to care, who didn't seem to give a good goddam about the goddam war killing every goddam body, a prohibition thus enforced until just now when she had entered softly and encountered not a young woman's eyes but a face transformed into iron and stone and shadows, a face that might well so remain unless she could say what needed saying and what therefore she would try to say somehow even though she had kept it buried within a heart turned part to stone for sixty-eight years.

She said:

Ellen? Ellen? Child, if you don't mind, I'm just going to sit awhile, because I'm tired, too, and a little bit lonely, and to tell the truth I need some help. I mean I need to say something, and I need someone to listen, someone who loves me, and it can't be your Papa because he's carrying all he needs to carry right now, and, besides, even if he wasn't, I couldn't talk to him about it, because he's part of it, in a way, and he might try to shoulder some blame needlessly, as he always does. And I think he's done enough of that for one lifetime, blaming himself for this and that, carrying in his heart, as he does, the feeling that something, some unknown something he might have done but failed to do, might have somehow kept alive the three good women who bore his children, the feeling that if only he had run fast enough when he came into town that day, if only he had run faster and got to the courthouse just a minute quicker, that he might just have gotten our Papa out of that doorway before the cannon went off. And a great many more feelings of that sort, too, in that way he never shows to anybody but that I can see in his eyes, simply because I have been studying his eyes now for one year more than he's been looking out of them, and he's almost eighty-five, will be next summer.

So I don't feel it would be best to talk to him about what's on my mind, but I feel that I can to you, if you'll allow me, because I know you love me and because I know you're very strong, too, stronger in a way than both of us put together, your Papa and me, stronger because at your time of life you love harder, which is, of course, why you grieve harder, which bears on what I need to talk about. I'm not here mainly to talk about your brothers, his sons, my nephews, because it would only break my heart like yours is broken if I dwelt too hard on them. Oh, I cry for them, and right now, even though my old eyes are dry. I cry all the same with only the fleetest thought of Matt being gone from our sight forever unless there really turns out to be something hereafter, which I don't know, although I'm inclined to think exactly like my mama on that, your grandmama, who, like her mama and my grandmama, a Lomkubee woman, I'm proud to say, felt that life, once done, just passes back into life, into the earth and the sky and all that about us which is part and parcel of life simply because without it there wouldn't and couldn't be any life. So I guess that instead of trying to think of him being gone, I think of all that and manage to feel him here amidst it all, a presence with us, a presence still who before he changed had already enriched us maybe even more than we deserve to be enriched. And Mark. I cry at the thought he might be maimed, but at the same time I'm so grateful that his life was spared, and who knows what it will bring to him or to others. I don't.

Child, all I know at my age is that I don't know much of anything. And I surely know I can't tell you how to grieve, but that's not what I'm here for. What I need to talk about is how not to grieve. Because I do know that, Ellen, I sure know how not to grieve, because I did it once and so well I've been the poorer ever since.

Ellen, you know part of this story, the part your Papa talks about sometimes, but I've never told the rest, not even to him, nor to anybody else. And I wouldn't be telling it now, truly, if I didn't need your help to sort it all out and to get my own heart straight at last.

It's about me and that man you've heard your Papa mention, the one that robbed the bank wagon, the one your Papa claims I got the gold from that saved our place from those damn bankers and that gave us a new start. You know how he tells that. Well, I've never called him a lie, but at the same time I've never let on how close to the truth he was coming either, and what I've always said is actually so, that he couldn't know for sure what he claims to know. He couldn't know because it's a fact he was delirious from those snake-bites that he had got that morning. You remember, he woke up with the trots and dashed out of that house and jumped into those bushes, and then before he knew it two or maybe three of those things struck him. He must of landed right on top of 'em.

So he was mighty sick all that day and into the night, and I was tending him, giving him everything I knew to give him and then steaming up that room to sweat the fevers out of him. Well, now, I know he is telling the truth when he says he would have been in on that thing if those snakes hadn't of hit him. Like he says, he had agreed to go in on it with the man who thought it up.

Now this was a man who had always been law-abiding, and he was a neighbor of ours, a young man named Nathaniel Webb, Nate, we called him, and he was a handsome, hard-working fellow who ran the place next to ours, he and his older brother. But then his brother got killed at the courthouse the same time as our Papa, your grand-papa, and in fact Nate's brother was right alongside Papa in the back of our wagon that Sam drove back from the courthouse. That's why Sam had to run in that day, our Papa had taken that wagon in long before daylight.

Well, after the buryings, Nate Webb got the idea for that robbery. Or rather, he got it from one of the drivers of that bank wagon, some fellow who had also lost some kin in that massacre at the courthouse and who was down on the bankers. You need to remember that it was the bankers who got the governor to call out the militia company from up the road and bring 'em down here and set 'em on Papa and those other farmers. You remember this and then you'll understand that when Nate Webb got the idea of robbing that wagon, and when your Papa finally said, yes, he'd go in with him—well, money wasn't even the main thing. Maybe it was part of it, because we were all about to get our places taken away if we didn't get some, but the main thing was to get back at the damn banks. You know today that your Papa doesn't really care about money for itself. All he wants any for is to protect you and me and all of us from the people who prey on those who don't have it.

So that's what they had in mind, and there's no doubt that Sam Worth would have been in on it if events hadn't prevented him. But, now, I didn't know this at the time. I had gotten a notion that something was up, because your Papa was very strung up the night before, and he hardly slept during the night, and then the minute he leaped up with the trots and scooted outside, well, I thought, Sam's afraid of something that I don't know about.

Well, I didn't really know anything about any of it until that night, the night after he got the snakebites. It was while I was seeing to him that I first heard a horse come galloping up the lane toward our place. So I went out into the hall—hall, I call it, but it was just a dogtrot house, you know. But just as I went into the hall, I heard the horse stop and almost at once I heard somebody lunge or fall against the front door. It was a plank door and loose even when it was latched.

Then I unlatched it, and swung it open, and there was Nate Webb standing there, with his hair all wild—he was rusty-haired —and—I say he was standing there, but he was slumping, actually, about to fall already, with his shirt-front all blood-soaked and his face scrunched up in agony. And he was holding this bag in his hand, his right hand, and he tried to raise it, to extend it toward me, you know, and you can imagine the state of mind I was in. No, maybe you can't imagine it yet, maybe you can't imagine it until I tell you what I've never told anybody before, not even my brother, that this man before me was the first and only man I ever loved in my life.

He was the man I was going to marry. He had already asked, and I had already said yes, and we were going to do it and then provide a home for Sam to get in a couple of more years of growin' up, and of course raise up the two littler ones there with us still, that we did raise up until malaria or whatever it was took 'em. So that's who was standing before me, or, not standing, slumping, trying to hand that bag to me and dying as he did it. He reached it out but it dropped to the floor, and then he fell, and in that strange gasp or rasp you hear when a man is dying, he said, "Maggie—Maggie—take it—hide it—keep it—they're sure to be after me—keep it, Maggie—I can't—"

And then he was gone. And I don't know what he was going to say next. And—well, I did partly what he said. I took just a very few pieces out of that bag, and I went back in that room where Sam was lying delirious, and I dropped those pieces in the stew I had put on, a varmint stew, we were down to such at the time. And then I went back and somehow, God only knows how, I managed to get Nate back onto his horse, just draped over it, you know, and I led that horse across the field to their house, and I stuffed that bag in his saddle bag and then let his body—the body of this man I loved—let him fall to the ground. And then I ran like a streak back to our place and got there at almost the minute the posse or whatever was chasing up the lane. I was no sooner inside than I heard them whacking on the door, and so I went, and they wondered if I had seen or heard anybody go by, and I just looked confused, which I was, but which got them suspicious, and then I said, yes, I had heard some horse run by a while back, I thought. Well, when they saw how I was sweating they got more suspicious, and so asked me about it, and so I asked them to come in and took them back into the room where Sam was lying, and of course I had built that fire up something fierce to make him sweat, and that seemed to satisfy 'em. So they left, and of course they right quickly found Nate and the bag and so solved their robbery, except for those missing pieces.

I kept them well hid until later, until just before we either had to put up some money or get off the place. And then I made up a story about going down to below Taliaferro to look up some of our mama's kin, and so got away, but actually drove that wagon all the way down to Law's Crossing and got an old part-Lomkubee trader there to get those pieces exchanged for me. You know, it didn't amount to all that much, but it turned out to be enough, with just a little to spare.

And so—well, child, I had to tell you all of this just to get to what I wanted to talk about. I think it wasn't until I had got everything done that had to be done that night it happened that I started to grieve that man I loved. But once I did, it carried me down hard. And that's what I mean about the way not to grieve. Ellen, I hoarded that grief, and I got filled up with hatred for what had happened, and then I hoarded that on top of the other. I think I had a feeling maybe as strong as yours, because I said to myself what I've heard you say lately. God damn this world, I said, and I meant it, and I meant it in a certain way long after I ceased to feel it in a general way.

What grief, the grief I felt at the loss of that one man I had loved more than anything. Your Papa knew we had a liking, and even teased that we might wind up marrying, but he never knew how I really felt or how Nate felt either. Nate was eight years older than I was, and I was seventeen when it happened, and I don't guess Sam could yet imagine his sister being with a man that much older. So I never talked to your Papa about it. About either the love or the grief. I just hoarded it. I hoarded it and more than that, I nursed and nurtured it.

And in a way that I still don't fully understand, I let it harden and diminish my whole life in a way. Because I told the world—or actually, only myself—I'm not ever going to let anything like that happen again. And I mean never letting myself love a man that way again or encouraging one to love me, because I couldn't bear the thought of knowing and losing it again. So when chances came along, as they did two or three times, something would come up in me that was just like iron, and I would say, no, no, I'm not ever going to go through that again.

So, Ellen, even if I can't tell you how to grieve, I can tell you how not to grieve. I can tell you that grief hoarded and nurtured comes to resemble death itself. And I know you love life too much to ever want to court even a little bit of death. I know this because you're too much like your mother. Now, she was an example to all of us. You know something, even when she knew the end was coming, she owned no self-pity whatever, not a jot. All she felt—and she told me this—all she felt was that she was grateful to have been here no matter that it had to end, grateful to have brought you into the world and your brothers. She reminded me so much of my Mama, who was so brave even when she somehow knew the end was in sight. And, you know, child, you're marvelously like both of 'em.

Listen, Ellen, I'm grateful to you for tolerating me, and for helping me by listening. I feel like I've set down a ton I've been carrying for sixty-eight years. Good lord, sixty-eight years ago. You know, that's when I could love maybe as hard as you, and so maybe could grieve as hard as you then, only I sure did it in the wrong way.

Now, I thank you, again, little Dumpling, for listening, and I'm going to go now, and I'll see you at supper if you feel up to it, and if you don't, well, that's all right, we understand. I'm going to go on now and get back to that embroidery, and you know something? You're always asking me about that, and I'm just going to tell you that, too, if you promise not to tell a soul, because I want to surprise your Papa one of these days. That thing I've been working on so long is a kind of tapestry thing, a representation of his whole life. Did you know I started that thing the day you were born?

Well, Ellen, I'm going now, and if you don't know anything else from what I said, at least you know why I have never let anybody else ever call me Maggie. Not even your Papa.

1944

Late Winter

––––– *5* –––––

"Miss Worth, I'm Jack Jackson," said the unfamiliar voice on the phone outside the dorm manager's office, and instantly she thought, *They've found out for sure.* And the voice went on, "I'm a pilot and a friend of—"

"Oh, I know who you are, Colonel Jackson," Ellen broke in, having already thought, *They know he's alive, they know he's dead.*

"Yeah—well—I guess you would. Anyway, I'm in New Orleans, and I'd like to pay a call on you if I may, if it wouldn't be an inconvenience. Would it be all right if I stopped by this evening?"

"Oh, sure, I'd love to meet you," she said, thinking, *He'd tell me right off if they knew he were alive.*

"Great. I'm looking forward to meeting you. I've heard a lot about you, so—Well, what's your schedule like? What time would suit you?"

"Well, almost any time at all, Colonel Jackson."

"Jack. Okay?"

"Okay."

"I realize it's short notice, but do you think you could spring away from there for dinner?"

"Oh, sure, I'd love to. And, listen, don't worry about the short notice."

"Okay, then, I'll pick you up at—six okay? Six-thirty? You name it."

"Six is fine, and I'll be looking forward to it."

"And the place is Whitcomb House?"

"Uh-huh, it's the first on the left after you've come on the campus."

"Check. Six then. And, listen, maybe it's better if I come right out and ask you—Do you think it'll be upsetting to talk—you know—about Henry and everything? You know."

"No. Don't worry about that," she said, thinking. Don't worry, because nothing you or anybody else can say can send me any deeper into hell than I've already been. From which I have come back only to return so many times that now I can't go back except once for some final time. And now I know you're not going to tell me the one thing that could send me back, because if you were going to tell me they know he's dead you wouldn't even think of taking me to a public place to tell me. And you sure wouldn't tell me in private and then expect me to go anywhere on earth where there were any people to witness me going to hell for the very last time.

"Okay, fine, then, so I'll see you at six," he said, and they closed it out, hung up, and she ducked into the house manager's office and told the chubby manager/house mother Mrs. Whittaker that she would be taking supper out.

She bounded up to her second floor room that had begun to resemble a studio since January when Florence had moved out to go up to Mitchel Field with Percy after their Christmas marriage, Percy who had actually cried last summer when they had left him back as an instructor while Jack Jackson took the whole rest of the group to an unannounced destination that everybody knew was England. Ellen with care removed the miniature wings from her long, roomy navy blue sweater before shucking it off, and then plopped indecisively onto the edge of her bed, suddenly glancing at her watch—4:12 —and realizing she had far too much time to hurry. She glanced over her shoulder toward the bureau where she had laid the miniature wings and where stood the framed, enlarged snapshot he had sent with sardonic apologies, the picture that showed him in the cockpit, not quite smiling and slightly fuzzy, not quite clear enough, not as sharp as the stenciled legend underneath that said—

PILOT—CAPT. HENRY T. RUST
CREW CHIEF—F. C. WILSON
ASST. CR. CHIEF—W. W. ARMOR
ARMORER—SGT. FRIEDRICH
RADIO MECH.—SGT. PULASKI

—nor as sharp as the airy, script-like legend that identified the craft as part of *Jack's Jolly Jackals,* nor as sharp as the neat and precise row of little emblems that announced the pilot had accumulated, by then, kills of nine enemy planes. Though being in no hurry, she went on undressing, kicking off the scuffed and soiled saddle shoes, letting the plaid wool skirt drop to the floor and then kicking it upward into a chair. In a sarong-wrapped orange towel she went out and to the shower, thinking all along.

Yes, he could talk to her about anything, say anything, and she would listen and probably memorize it all. She would listen with keen, warm interest but without astonishment, because nobody could possibly tell her anything that she hadn't thought already, or imagined, or heard, or read in the accounts of others. She had thought and imagined until she had seen and heard and even smelled every way it could possibly have happened, and every way it could possibly have turned out, had seen it a million times in the four months since his mother got the wire he was missing, the missing wire that had come in November and that had sent her yet deeper into that hell that she thought she had already plumbed, deeper into the hell that had now almost been deprived of its capacity to terrify her, because it had become so familiar, she had plunged there so often. Because as Portia Rust had said, a missing message might be infinitely better than a dead message, but it was also worse in a certain way, because it instigated hope without providing any basis for it, and it instigated despair not merely once and devastatingly but over and over again. The knowledge that he had gone down to an utterly unknown end had only assured that she would suffer his death over and over again, just as it assured that over and over she would see him saved and hence resurrected, with the result not of a single transforming anguish but of anguish that had become myriad and almost accustomed, almost a fixture in her state of being and, in a way, an innoculation against any further anguish that might arrive save that which would come only with some final and absolute word that obviously was not at hand.

So, yes, Jack Jackson could talk and speculate to a fare-thee-well. But she had already seen him in that roomy cockpit as the damn machine plummeted into the earth, into the trees, into the unyielding streets of strange cities, had heard the smashing impacts and felt the explosions and concussions, had smelled the flaming fuel and the cherished flesh. And she had also seen him elude that fate in a thousand different ways, had witnessed the canopy flung back and his living flesh flinging clear with the chute snapping and billowing just in time to set him down safely. Sometimes safely, sometimes into the hands of the unconquered Maquisards who Horris and Corinne both wrote her were in fact numerous and diligent in certain areas and who could in fact have recovered and concealed him from discovery by the Germans. But not always safely: sometimes the chute only suspended him as a perfect target for the damned guns of France's conquerors who now annihilated him in midair, or who sometimes took him prisoner on the ground toward a fate conceivably worse, worse for him conceivably, only she did not believe that any fate short of death was worse.

So what could he possibly say to surprise her, what possibility could he raise that her mind had not already raised and actually seen during those descents into hell that she now didn't need to make any more simply because hell fell upon her with the daily sunshine, or the rain, hell was part of her daily bread and her dreams, those dreams sleeping and waking that had at last admitted her to the aching heart of Ben Ezra Sorrel, who had died not simply as an artist unable to bear the murder of the film that was his love child but as a manchild hungering for innocence and love in a world that would not bear or abide either. Horris was certainly right that each being on earth owned some tolerance for pain that would yield and yield and then finally yield no more, that at some unforeseeable point would yield only as a balloon yields to too much air, exploding and hence delivering the being into a realm without pain whether by derangement or the irresistible drive to self-extinction.

What, indeed, could he say that might bring her more anguish than she already had, or give her more hope either, because her hope was as boundless as the despair. Her hope was simply total. She knew he couldn't be dead because she knew quite apart from words that if he was dead on this earth then she would be dead, too, and since she wasn't dead, he had to be alive by one of those miracles that she had also imagined a million times, one of those sequences that had gotten him out of the grasp of that goddam hurtling machine, one of those escapes that were only harder to imagine simply because they were miraculous, had to be, as everything in the nurturing and engendering of life always was miraculous, just as everything in the demeaning and annihilation of life was always mechanical, common-place, banal, unmiraculous, and hence easy to imagine, easy to con-ceive because easy to accomplish with those goddam machines that a moron could understand and use whether an airplane or a gun or a knife or even a stick, or even the hands when they were used against life. Mark in that strange half-absent voice had said he did not even faintly remember what they said he had done, that he had no recall whatever of killing with his bare hands the Jap who had killed Matt after their patrol was surprised. Mark had looked at his hands with disbelief in that one eye that so bitterly sharpened the aura of half-absence that was about him, his gone eye covered by the patch that somehow seemed to sever him both physically and metaphysically from that lost and missed hemisphere of himself.

Mark had come home only for a few days in the late summer, and she had driven him from McClung to here, New Orleans, and seen him off on the train that had borne him back to California, to San Francisco, to Corinne Fielding and the twins who had come in late May of '42 and would soon be two, unbelievably, and she, Ellen, was so damn glad about that, because, who knew, maybe it had been those twins alone that had sustained Mark on the upper side of his ultimate tolerance of pain. She had seen him on the train that would bear him to a destiny neither he nor she could even imagine, and didn't even try to. "Dumpling, let's don't ever fall out of touch," Mark had said, hugging her close by the train step, and she had desperately shivered from that uncanny sense that when he let go of her the always present other would materialize and hug her, too, Matt: *Where?* Mark with his one eye roaming her face had instantly recognized what she was feeling, and had spoken of it without men-tioning it, had spoken in that somehow depleted, energyless voice, saying, "I know, I know. I feel it every minute."

So what could call-me-Jack Jackson of *Jack's Jolly Jackals* possibly tell her that would astonish or dismay, even if he were reduced to celebrating the goddam death machine that he flew, they flew, the goddam machine that they abstracted as the P-47 and vaingloriously christened the Thunderbolt and in fact more often called the Jug as though it were either a jail or a vessel from which some bizarre intoxicant were dispensed, or imbibed, when they got in, when they left that old farmhouse or manor house in England and went out and climbed in and headed east to look for bridges or buildings or trains or bodies to obliterate or to fend for the bombers while they did the obliterating. She would listen to all of that, too, without letting on that she had read and heard so much she practically knew the feel of the cockpit and could feel the thunder of what the aviation writers coyly liked to call those two thousand horses that could send the goddam death machine with its freight of guns and even a big bomb into screaming dives or send it flashing and skeetering across the treetops of France and Germany at the cost of weight that gave it, as one could even hear in the servicemen's centers where she had for awhile sketched free portraits, the gliding capacity of a brick once power was lost.

She could and would listen to whatever he might have to say, even if it all had to be repetition. There was no need to let on even that Horris had already dug out and written her everything that the group records had on it, the last sighting of him over France, the trouble he had reported, the last talk amongst them on the radio right up to when he peeled away, saying simply *"I've got to get the hell out,"* cut away and down only to have vanished into or through some lower cloud cover by the time the other plane had gone down to check. Which still, Horris had said, might have left him altitude enough to get the hell out. Horris: who had still never plausibly defined what he was doing, not even to Claudette as far as she could let on, except that he was in England doing something, but whose letters suggested if nothing else that he had sources of information that with luck might hear whether a downed pilot had wound up in the hands of the underground or otherwise.

The miracle was possible, yes, and likely call-me-Jack wished only to remind her of that, was only carrying out his duty to someone who had been not only his charge and colleague but his friend. She would listen as she listened to all of those who, in the end, never actually seemed to own as much hope as she, the owner of hope that had to be total because if it turned out to be groundless she would not merely fall but would die even if she went on living, would die at least in that certain way that Aunt Margaret had died when she had opened the plank door in 1874 and seen her one love with his chest turned to blood and his hand reaching and his voice sinking into its last gasp before it ceased to remain silent forever.

His name was John G. (Jack) Jackson, and he was a full colonel at twenty-six years of age, and he had shot down nineteen enemy planes personally, and the group he commanded was likely in any given week to be either tops or runner-up in the total number of kills, and it was invariably the best in the kill/loss ratio, but he wasn't telling her all of this which she already knew but that she imagined he might enjoy mentioning under other circumstances. He was telling her how unexpected it had been to get ordered back stateside to do three weeks of song-and-dance and God-bless-America, as he called it, on a circuit of defense plants around the country.

"I pretended to object," he said, "but that was only to insure that they wouldn't cancel me out. No, actually I have mixed feelings about it. It's good to get a breather, but—But, anyway, it's worth it just to get to see New Orleans and meet you. I got them to work New Orleans into the itinerary just in hopes I'd get the chance."

They were sipping their first drinks. Rather, she was sipping hers. He was already tilting his empty glass, rattling the ice as he absently fingered the encyclopedic menu of the famous old restaurant whose rooms were filled with uniforms and a surf of chatter-and-babble that was probably louder and brasher than that which would have been heard in the place before the war. He held up his glass, saying, "I wouldn't mind another. You?"

"No, thanks, this'll hold me for now," she said.

He had a narrow, angular face and dark hair that had been recently cut and was already thinning and brown eyes that would glance restlessly about then focus for a moment on her, or on the table, or absently on the menu lying across his bread plate. She thought that in the flesh as in the snapshot of all of them that Henry had sent he did somehow resemble the whole bunch of them, in the way that they oddly resembled each other, not because of the uniforms or their studied negligence in wearing them but because of something else which certainly wasn't their varied faces or their individual physiques, but perhaps the way face and form were juxtaposed, the way something had conditioned them to stand with a certain tilt of the shoulders and with their heads carried at a certain subtle tilt on their necks. Whatever it was, it was his, too. She wondered whether his way of talking might be characteristic of all or most of them, the tendency to sardonic understatement of certain things, the leaning toward self-deprecation that was never quite reached.

"Cheers," he said when his second drink had come. "Sure you wouldn't like another?"

"Well—maybe in a bit. But you go ahead. Don't mind me. I've been told that one's too much for me sometimes." She heard herself laugh softly and half-apologetically in a way that reminded her of Corinne Fielding's way when she had first known her on the beach at St. Teresa's that summer.

"Now, who would have told you a thing like that?" he said.

"Well—my father, for one. And Henry, for another." She laughed again, offhanded but disproportionately, she felt.

"You mean they don't want you to drink?"

"Oh, no, they don't care. They only mean that sometimes one makes me slightly hysterical."

"Come to think of it, Henry mentioned it. Said he feels like a great comedian when you've had a couple. That's it—he said it raises your mirth quotient out of sight."

"I hope he didn't tell you about my cry quotient, too."

"Oh? No, but meet a kindred spirit."

"You? I can't imagine it."

"Well, I save it for the dark of night. I discourage publicity on it. I couldn't afford to go down in the books as Jack the crybaby, could I?"

"Oh, come on now."

He was draining his second drink when some of it spilled around the left corner of his mouth and onto the rows of ribbons above the pocket of his forest-green jacket. "Damn!" he said, daubing with his napkin. "I tell you, Ellen Rust, I need a nurse, not a waiter."

He gave no sign of realizing he had called her Ellen Rust, a slip that caused her to shiver. As he daubed at the spillage, she took up her menu. She said, "So what do you feel like? The trout amandine's always good."

"Well, the scotch was good, too, until—You think I can manage to keep a trout on my plate?" He took up his menu and went on: "Everything on the bill looks good to me. In fact, this whole town looks good so far. I think I'm finally really glad I'm here. You know, Henry was always talking about New Orleans. That is, he was always talking about you or New Orleans or music."

Was, she thought. He had said *was,* and was staring down at the menu now realizing he had said *was,* and now was glancing at her and peering down again knowing that she had noticed he had said *was,* maybe knowing that she now knew that no matter what else he said, *was* was what he really believed.

Now he looked up from the menu with a sudden smile that was like an unexpected lightning bolt. He said, "I should add that he turns in a very good report on you. And that, unlike most of us flyboys, he obviously tells the truth."

"Thank you," she said, thinking, now he has resurrected him with *turns* and *tells* and the *was* is to be forgotten as though it hadn't been uttered, so that later it won't seem implausible when he says that, no, you never can tell, and, yes, miracles can and do happen, and, besides, it wouldn't even have taken a miracle but only a little bit of luck for him to have chuted down and eluded capture. Now, as he began saying something more, she decided that, no, maybe she was wrong, maybe he wasn't going to be glib and glossy and pro forma at all.

"I think I've gotten off to a bad start," he said. "I'm sorry. I think I came here to do something I don't really know how to do. Or don't really know quite what. Listen—" Now he extracted an envelope from his inside pocket and handed it to her. "Here's a copy of two things I thought you might like to have. They were both in the works before—uh—before that last mission."

She unfolded and read, first, a mimeographed copy of an order awarding Rust, Henry T., a second DFC, and, second, an order promoting Rust, Henry T., to the temporary rank of major. She slowly refolded the two sheets and returned them to the envelope which she set down in her lap as she looked up and spoke in a voice that had no certainty as to what it should say.

"Thank you," she said. "Thank you very much."

"Ellen, I'm not even sure I should have done this, given you those." Now he looked up at the waiter who had come up. "I think I'll follow the lady's leadership and have the trout." He gave the order and also held up his glass to the waiter. "And how about hitting me with another scotch and soda. Ellen, you game yet?"

"Well—why not?" she said. "But mine's bourbon, remember."

So he ordered the drinks and returned to what he had been saying. "All I'm sure of is that I wanted to do something, wanted to look you up, wanted to say something to you. And now I guess I'm finding out I'm not a chaplain after all. Just a dumb cowboy."

"Oh, stop it," she said, suddenly feeling a welling of warm sympathy for him, even liking. She also became aware that from the moment of his call she had regarded him not only as an unmet friend but also as the enemy, as an agent of and inextricable from that whole large dark pervasive thing that was the war and that annihilated so much that she loved and that threatened to annihilate more, and perhaps had, and that hence was her nemesis and personal enemy quite apart from all the imperatives of survival and national duty that might be recited in vindication of it. But now at his floundering she saw at least the possibility that, even though he was inevitably an agent and arm of that dark thing, he might be its victim as well, its hostage. And, with this, she lowered the baffles and guards she had erected within and saw him as flesh, and in his restive eyes saw a certain bewilderment and loneliness as clearly as she could see the discomfort or embarrassment he felt at his failure to have done well what he had come to do. Now their drinks materialized, and he began talking as he took his up and after a silent salute took his first gulp.

"Okay," he said. "Why don't I stop trying to do perfectly what I can't even do well and just do it. Look, I don't know whether he's dead or alive. I know he could be alive, and I know he could be dead. In the last year or so I seem to have lost the ability to feel either optimistic or pessimistic. God knows, I hope he lucked out, and not only for him and you but for me. Because I feel that way, I loved him. There, goddam, I did it again, killed him again. Ellen, I loved him if he's dead and love him if he's alive. You wouldn't believe how I love all those crazy bastards in that group of mine. The ones who go and the ones who might go tomorrow, who might have gone since I left. But, you know, when they go I can't afford to despair or hope, because when I despair I get paralyzed, and when I hope—well, that's when I find myself crying in the middle of the night. Jesus Christ! Just like I'm doing. Excuse me."

He was gone, at a very fast walk, dodging among the tables as his hand grabbed at his hip pocket for a handkerchief. The trout had come when he returned, and she had sampled it, and was chewing when she got up at his approach and gave him a hug and then let him seat her again, and felt his hands grasp the top of her shoulders with a grateful squeeze. She drained her drink and watched him sit down looking composed but still taking a couple of deep breaths to make sure, a faint smile of lingering embarrassment on his mouth.

"I took the liberty of ordering two glasses of wine," she said. "You mind?"

"Perfect," he said. "For a start. I feel like I could use a couple of bottles tonight."

"Why not," Ellen said and herself signaled their waiter. *"Garçon, nous avons décidé avoir une bouteille de Mouton Cadet, le meilleur, s'il vous plaît."*

"Well, you do that beautifully," he said. "Where'd you learn it?"

"My mama. She was born here, and French was her first language. Her maiden name was Boisseau."

"I hear that *was* again."

"She died when I was ten."

"Mine, too. Only I was twelve. Mine—uh—killed herself."

"Oooooh."

"Sleeping pills. Or something of the sort. I'm not even sure, but she drank a lot, too. She was always very lonely. Typical Army wife in some ways."

"Your father's a professional?"

"All his life. He was out in the Pacific, but he's in Washington now. I sort of suspect him of rigging this charade they brought me back for."

"Good for him. You have any brothers? Sisters?"

"One brother."

"Older?"

"Two years younger."

"He a pilot, too?"

"No, he went the Marine route. He's *was,* too. He got it on Guadalcanal."

"Ooooh. One of mine, too, one of my brothers, and the other one was wounded there."

"On Guadal?"

"Yeah. Isn't this strange?"

"They were in the same outfit?"

"Yeah, they were twins, so they kept them together."

"God, Ellen, you're getting more than your share of this goddam mess."

"You, too. I guess we all have. But, listen—"

"Ah, the bottle, mine redeemer."

"—listen, why don't we consider everything said, and just enjoy now, okay?"

"Done," he said, looking at her now in a way he had not yet looked, with his eyes not so lost and restless but still and tender, and with an incipient smile creeping into the lines of the narrow angular face that somehow resembled all of them and even Henry. He said, "I'll say this, it's very easy to enjoy sitting opposite you."

"Ditto," she said, and smiled a tilted smile as Corinne Fielding might have done.

"You know something, Ellen Worth, I have the feeling that you're so much stronger than I am that it's pitiful."

"Fat chance. Is the wine okay?"

"Perfect. And here's to you—perfect."

"To you, too," she said, again with the tilted smile with which Corinne Fielding had always seemed to meet new situations and possibilities.

"Another?" he said, already pouring it.

"Why not?" she said.

Now they were sitting side by side in wooden captain's chairs with their feet propped on the raised hearth of the see-through fireplace that divided the rooms of the famous old cafe/saloon that bore the name of the famous old pirate, and he was saying—saying in a voice whose slurs and thicknesses by now seemed utterly natural—

"—so I can either weep for 'em or live for 'em. And so which should I do? Weep? I don't believe it, because I don't believe that's what the whole goddam thing is all about. I don't believe that it's to sacrifice some of us so that the rest can weep and moan. I believe we're doing what we're doing, no matter how horrible, so that those of us who live can go on *living*, by God, and feel joy and tenderness—"

—And she could not have agreed more, could not have felt more profoundly and warmly in full and absolute agreement with what he was saying, and what he was about to say, too, what she knew he was either about to say or eventually would say, simply because he was already saying it with his eyes and with the free hand that reached over and placed itself on top of hers from time to time, the hand that had tentatively reached for hers and got it when they had finally left the famous old restaurant and started walking aimlessly through the narrow streets of the Quarter until he had suggested another drink and steered her into the place where two blondes at twin pianos were singing bawdy and insinuating songs that had added not to the warmth she already felt but to the sense of volition-less abandonment that had begun to overtake her even before they had left the supper table.

They had sat at dinner for hours, gone through the bottle of wine and then a brandy that she could remember at least sipping, as she laughed and confessed it was going down on top of more than she ever had taken to drink at one time in her life, a confession she had made not on the basis of estimating the volume of her intake but on the fact she had just noticed that she had glimpsed a double image of him and that her talking had grown thick whereas his talk by then had begun to seem like the only way he ever had talked or could talk. Somewhere along the way of their rambling talk, somewhere that she couldn't have put her finger on, and didn't even care to, the deepening sympathy she had felt for him had turned into distinct warmth, a gathering impulse to comfort and console this new friend who seemed less and less a lethal warrior and more and more a lost and lonely boy who had been deprived of roots all of his life and betrayed by his mother in the flush of boyhood, and who, like them all, had been merely caught up in the great kill-machine that mankind had long ago invented as the nemesis of simple love and tenderness and caring among people.

"Who's to say who's had enough?" he had said. "You know,

Ellen, there's something more than mere poetry in that eat-drink-and-be-merry stuff."

She had recalled the time she had resented Matt and Mark singing that song at the New Year's dance before the war, and thought now that, yes, sure as hell they were right, that it was good that they had eaten and drunk and been merry as much as they could, because, as the not earnest but convincing voice across the table was saying, you only go around once on this green earth and you sure as hell never know when you're going to leave it.

"I agree," she had said, and had leaned across the table to peer at him more closely, because he was blurring, as she went on. She said, "Jack, did you know that during the Dark Ages when the plague swept Europe, the revels of life went on amidst mountains of corpses?"

"More power to 'em," he had said, and she could not have agreed more, could not have been more absolutely in agreement with his agreement to what she had forgotten to tell him had been said not by her but by Horris.

"Horris said that," she had said. "Horris remembers everything."

"That's too bad," he had said. "The trick is to forget everything."

"I agree," she had said, suddenly remembering what she had forgotten for an hour or so now, and what, now as she remembered it, suddenly fled her mind again.

"I could use some air," he had said.

"It's indispensable," she had said, and he had laughed, and she, too. They had got up and woven their way amidst the tables, and she had gone to the ladies' room and grinned pleasantly at herself in the mirror, and felt foolish for doing it, and laughed out loud, and adjusted the miniature wings she had pinned to the simple navy blue frock whose front her brothers would have said looked like a shirt full of goodies, which maybe it did, even if she thought so herself, now aware, as she squinted to examine and give a finger-combing to that mass of feathery curls, that whatever she had been feeling about comforting and caring for, suddenly she felt like receiving some, too. And why not?

So outside when he had reached for her hand she had yielded it with a squeeze of his and looked at him with the smile that told him, yes, it was good to be with him, too, and got the flicker of the smile in return, that look of his eyes briefly receding and growing darkly earnest as he stopped walking, paused, turned, and—

"Ellen, meeting you is the best thing that's happened to me in a long, long time."

—and, with that, leaned over and against no resistance kissed her very lightly on the lips.

They had ambled on, aimless, she not thinking but simply knowing that, yes, the sympathy had turned to warmth and the wish to be tender had multiplied into a wish also to receive tenderness of the kind she had not received since whenever the hell it was that she and Florence went off to the wings ceremony just before she got back and everything went to hell, but be damned if she was going to think about that right now, not tonight, not with him who got enough of that day by day and month by month at the base in old England out of which this country was launching its half and more of the hell of war.

"The later it gets the better New Orleans smells," she had said, with pointless laughs ringing out. "Early in the morning it smells like wet hemp."

"Ellen, you're a born poet," he said in that half-dragging, half-lurching voice that now sounded not only natural but very comfortable, too, very reassuring, very easy, very promising.

"No, no, no, no, no, I'm an artist," she said. "Would-be, would-be, would-be. I'd love to sketch you."

"You think I'm scratchable?"

"Did you say scratchable?"

"I said sketchable. I know I'm scratchable."

"Oh, sketchable. Sketchable. Sketchable. Jack, I'd say you're the most sketchable colonel I've met all day."

"Well, that says a lot. You gonna sketch me?"

"You are definitely sketchable."

"You think I'm scratchable, too?"

She had wagged a finger at him, and squinted, and said, "I'm not going to say. I think you're just begging for another compliment."

Then he had suggested the drink, and they had gone into the place with the two blondes at the twin pianos, and they had listened and laughed and had the drink that he called very weak, and then she had suggested the famous old cafe/saloon named for the famous old pirate with the built-up hearth and the see-through fireplace dividing the two rooms where, on this breezy and chilly eve-of-spring night, they had even had a fire that had now fizzled away.

They were in the captain's chairs with their feet propped up, with her hair no doubt askew but who cared, and with his jacket unbuttoned and his tie at half-mast, with the two of them in their own island of talk even though the place was three-quarters full of men in both uniforms and civvies and women youngish and oldish growing mostly murmurous and affectionate as the clock on the wall crept toward midnight, as she could see when she squinted, and he was talking about living, which was absolutely right, and about joy, which was absolutely right, and about tenderness, which was absolutely right.

And now he was saying what she had all but known he was going to say and to which, even before he said it, she knew that she wanted to answer in kind, because the warmth and pulse and hunger within had become general and powerful now, both that hunger to give and to be given to also, so that she felt one of those sudden little fleshquakes when he said it, that which she knew he was going to say, lowering the voice that suddenly stopped lurching and grew distinct and keen even though it was only a low whisper.

"Ellen, I'd love more than anything on earth to be tender to you. To have you—be tender to me."

She glanced for only a tick at the eyes that confirmed what he had said, eyes that were studying her, and then she looked back into the raised fireplace at the small fire that wasn't there any more, and felt his hand reach over once again and stack itself on top of hers where it suddenly was not merely resting on the chairarm but gripping it. She was almost surprised that she had not said, yes, at once, that she had not at once confirmed the powerful impulse inside, that she had not instantly admitted, yes, that's what I would like, that's what I need.

She was murkily surprised that instead her mouth was involuntarily smiling, as though to announce her pleasure at what he proposed, this even as something in the dizzy veiled deeps of her mind began to grapple with that part which was smiling, something that all the drinks and the hours of conscious, defiant, yea-saying, life-celebrating good spirits had dispersed or coated over but that now began indefinitely stirring and emerging. It was only emerging, this older feeling, and had not yet overturned her wish and intent to say, yes, and had not even yet brought it into counterbalance or equilibrium so that her mind confronted a dilemma. It did not yet face a dilemma, as she sat gazing with her signal smile into the fireplace, but only sensed the emergent dilemma that had not yet fashioned itself into words but had only entered like a returning shade or ghost into the pleasurable and gauzy haze of the intoxication and warmth, the warm and now perhaps even hot yearning to give tenderness and to be given it, the yearning which had somehow summoned up and summed up all of her experience of fleshhunger and passion unmodified by thinkings, summoning it up and awakening it within her alongside that telescoped vision of time wherein it seemed that life existed only today and that tomorrow all bypassed feasts and passions would occur only as mocking fantasies.

She glanced at him again, and again with the involuntary smile that might even have said already that which her tongue still wasn't saying, and again looked away, while he waited for some spoken word that the pressure of his hand on hers was bringing closer, because she realized now that she even yearned for this gentle pressure, this visible and slight mingling of caring flesh. In the instant of the step she was about to take, the word she was about to utter, the affirmation she was about to make, but to which she had not yet given word, she grew so warm and pulsing within that she felt almost on the verge of spontaneously coming, and yet increasingly sensed the intrusion or resurgence of that shade or ghost amidst the keen and dizzy tumult within, that ghost out of some deepest part of her, that part of her that had been vehemently and joyously defied and banished during this evening of awakening pleasure and gathering abandonment.

It had not even fully emerged, not fully defined and identified itself, not fully been remembered but only intimated, its presence, when, still smiling, she closed her eyes and removed her hand from under his and put it on top as perhaps another way of saying what she still couldn't say, and wouldn't say now until, in the private darkness behind her eyes, she had located whatever it was that was intruding, that emergent cloud or ghost within. The dulled edges of her thinking couldn't quite locate it, and so now she sighed and made some resigned surrendering plea to that unseen and unidentified power of life that she addressed in many moments of jeopardy or stress, that she addressed without ever thinking of the appeal as prayer. She thought simply, *Help me.* And then she heard him saying something else in that low resonant whisper.

"Ellen, if—if things were different—I would ask you to marry me. That's how I feel. I mean, if everything was settled, and—the God's truth is no other girl has ever made me feel the way I feel right now. I wish with all my heart that nothing else was hanging over us right now. But I hope to God we don't sacrifice this moment and lose it forever."

Now she pressed his hand, but without looking up or over, because she couldn't bear to look, and she agreed absolutely about the moment and other things, or felt agreement even if she didn't think it, and yet she didn't speak, nor stir as to go, which would have said it without speaking. And she had begun to wonder if she would or could speak with whatever it was holding her back, checkreining her words while the other highly distinct and almost palpable thing burned within and kept her mouth in a half-smile not only of warm spirits but of anticipation. Once again she sighed, and gazing into the small dead ash where she could almost see the enactment of the fleshhunger within, she thought that now, yes, she would go ahead and say it, go ahead and speak. And she was just about to when suddenly she almost leaped from her chair at the sound of her name and at the instantly recognized voice that practically shouted it out from above and behind her.

"Ellen! Goddam! What a relief to see you! I've been over there looking for you all over the goddam moors! Stumbling around through the night yelling, Ellllll-len! Ellllll-len!"

Her head snapped about and then up, and then up again, as at the Eiffel Tower or a tall pine. It was who it had to be, Tom Pickett at six-seven, his face now weathered, looming theatrically in grubby khakis and a tieless dark shirt under a jacket that might have cost one hundred dollars or ten, and, as always, preempting and commanding all other presences in the room partly by his towering presence and otherwise by animated gesture and the voice that rang out heedless of who might hear whatever he might elect to say. In a whirl she was up and hugging him and remembering that if he were in New Orleans then Cliff likely was, too, because Tom was sailing as a seaman on Cliff's ship. After her impact against him she found herself lifted an additional foot and an inch or so into the air so that he could look squarely into her face. Then she got set down and turned about to see that Jack was also on his feet, his lean angular face a construct of frustration and exasperation comingled with astonishment and consternation. She briskly introduced Tom Pickett to her good friend and Henry's, to Colonel Jack Jackson, who was Henry's group commander and who had been kind enough to take her out to dinner and let her talk his ear off all evening. And then she turned back to Tom.

"Cliff? Is he here?"

"Oh, hell, yes," Tom said. "We just tied up this evening. I just left him at the hotel."

She turned to Jack and said, "Cliff's my brother, I think I mentioned him." And then back to Tom: "What hotel?"

"Is there more than one?" Tom said. "Listen, he would've called you tonight, except that it was too late, so he wanted to wait. Or maybe he tried after I left. He's got something for you."

"Listen," Ellen said, "why don't we walk over there? What's he got, Tom? I want to see him." And again turned to Jack and said, "Cliff's a master."

"I gathered," Jack said, not abject but descending from a moment of high expectancy. He was still regarding the presence of Tom Pickett with disbelief.

"Walk over, hell, I just walked over here. Why don't I give him a ring?" Tom said.

"Well—Listen, what's he got for me?"

"Hell, I don't know. He doesn't even know. It's something we got from Horris."

"You saw *Horris!?*"

"Hell, yeah, we had a great time with him. We got into London this trip, and—"

"Well, what is it you got from Horris?"

"I just told you I don't know."

"You mean you saw it but you don't even know what it was?"

"Look, I know he gave Cliff an envelope, but I don't have the faintest idea what's in it. I gather it's the most important message since the one to Garcia. He said he couldn't send it in the mail, and couldn't wire it, and couldn't put it in military channels. Hell, Cliff and I decided you're part of some goddam spy ring. Colonel, is that so? Is that why you two are hanging around this tawdry tourist trap murmuring in low voices?"

"Absolutely," Jack said, "until I was so rudely interrupted I was just telling Ellen the only secret I have that's worth telling—at a bargain rate, too."

Ellen glimpsed the wry grin on Jack's face, and quickly turned to Tom again and said, "Listen, Tom, let's go over, so—"

"Look, sit down and relax, and I'll go give the old bastard a ring. He'll still be up. Hell, Ellen, he never sleeps, anyway. I've never been on a watch when he wasn't up and prowling around. I asked him to come over here and have a drink, but he said he doesn't like to be seen where genteel people might accidentally stop in, and besides, he said he doesn't like to fraternize with a hired hand, particularly one who feigns intelligence. But, of course, what he really meant was that he wanted to get up to his room so he could prowl around and pretend he's listening to the engines and probably make a few entries now and then in the Gideon Bible. Here, lemme go call. Colonel, you may resume the exchange of that sensitive information while I'm gone." Tom clapped a condescending hand on the shoulder of Jack's unbuttoned jacket, and Jack looked upward at the face that was regarding him with a miscreant's speculative look.

"Son, tell me," Jack said, "how's the weather up there?"

"Tom, don't you dare!" Ellen snapped just as Tom was about to speak. After which Tom merely smiled and turned and receded to the back of the famous old saloon, toward a public phone hidden in a corridor close by the restrooms.

"What was it he wasn't supposed to dare?" Jack asked.

"Well—I'm not sure his standard rejoinder to that question you asked would breed good will."

"How does he answer it, then?"

Ellen lowered her voice, which was growing giddy, and said, "What he usually says is, 'Crawl up my ass and check for yourself.' "

Jack exploded into inordinate laughter, which released, it was quickly evident, the coiled frustration that had begun to accumulate from the moment of the interruption that had, for better or worse, resolved Ellen's own dawning dilemma.

The two of them sat back down in the captain's chairs, and she was grinning into the fireplace and wondering, when for the second time in fifteen minutes, and while Tom Pickett was still back at the phone, and just after Jack Jackson had said, not with fervor but matter-of-factly and believably—"I meant what I said awhile ago" —when for the second time in fifteen minutes she heard the abrupt sound of a dear and familiar voice and so snapped her head about once again and then leaped up with her arms spread out.

"By God! Is that our Dumpling hanging out in a notorious dive at this ungodly hour of the night?"

It was Cliff, and she was up and in his arms, and then was introducing him to Henry's commander, as Jack stood trying now not to be abject, the colonel who had been kind enough to take her to dinner and let her bend his ear all evening. Then she explained that Tom Pickett at that very moment was trying to get him, Cliff, on the phone.

"You know," Cliff said, "that's characteristic of Tom. All his instincts are sound but his disorientation is absolutely beyond repair. He's always looking for something that doesn't exist or else looking for it where it isn't. Since I'm here, why do you suppose he would be trying to reach me there? No, in fact, Tom asked me to come over here with him and I turned him down so emphatically that I got to feeling guilty and thought I'd come buy him a consolation drink.

Colonel, can I buy you one? Ellen? Ellen, am I correct in assuming that you have already had an apéritif?"

"Apéritif!" she said, laughter exploding. "God, Cliff, I've drunk more tonight than I ever did in my life."

"I never would have guessed it," Cliff said, gravely, "although when I first saw you I thought you might have been a member of my crew, very few of whom show any weakness for moderation."

"Oh, stop it. Now tell me what Horris sent me."

"What? What? What's this about Horris?" Cliff said.

"Tom said—"

"Tom said what? You know, Ellen, along with the rest of his immense collection of flaws and disabilities, that boy has no goddam discretion whatever. Do you mean that he mentioned to you, in this public place, that Lt. Col. T. C. Horris had dispatched in my care some illicit and probably dangerous letter to you?"

"Are you going to tell everybody about it?" Ellen said. "Come on, and let me have it."

"Dumpling, doesn't Tom realize that we could probably all be put in jail for committing a deed like this. I wouldn't be a damn bit surprised if the colonel placed us all under military arrest this moment."

"If I had my jacket properly buttoned I might well do that," Jack said. "As it is, you're safe."

"Well, thank heaven for your disloyalty. Now, here comes Tom, and, see, it only took him five minutes or so to discover that I wasn't where he thought I was. Ellen, would you agree with me that Tom Pickett is the best argument available for the abolition of book-learning?"

"Cliff! I'm dying of curiosity!"

"Colonel, my little sister no sooner got away from home than she utterly forgot her goddam manners her Papa toiled so hard to drill into her curly little head. Ellen, for goodness sake, I offered to buy the colonel a drink. And I'll even buy you one, even though I suspect that'll be taking coals to Newcastle. But at least let's sit down and feign civility for a moment or two. Besides, I'm sure you wouldn't care to read your illicit mail in the presence of others."

"Well, you're wrong—and you're torturing me on purpose."

"Nevertheless—here, Tom, walk over to the bar, carefully now, and get us four tall, iced crème de menthes. I don't know if that's what these people are having, but it's what I'm buying. So, walk carefully, Tom, and try not to bump into anyone or say anything uncivil along the way. And if you need help, just send for me."

"Cliff, you're awful to him," Ellen said. "Jack, don't you think he's awful?"

Jack, with a barely repressed smile, held his quiet, but Cliff, dragging a chair between their two and taking his seat, said, "No, Colonel Jackson would intuitively understand my felicitous treatment of Tom Pickett. It improves the fiber of his soul. Ellen, a frail sense of self is not among Tom's innumerable defects. He's a gifted young man, but he still mistakes his gifts for self-created virtues."

Only after Tom had brought the frappés and sat down to Jack Jackson's left, and only after they had sipped did Cliff slowly reach to his inside jacket pocket and take out a plain manila envelope that bore no writing and hand it to Ellen.

"I would surmise," he quietly said, "that the mystery is not to protect whatever information this may contain, if any, but only the source of it, if any."

Ellen unstuck the envelope closure with an index finger and took out a single folded sheet that also bore neither salutation nor addressee nor date nor signature. She read it, and then looked up at Cliff, with eyes already filling, and then at Jack, at Tom, with eyes now filled, filled as her ears were filled with roaring, looked at them and at first tried to say, without being able to say, what she finally said in a voice that was half croak and half whisper.

"He's alive."

"He's alive," is what she croaked or whispered, and then, more clearly, "He's alive! Oh, God, he's alive!" And then stared at it again, and then handed it to Cliff and said, "Cliff, isn't that what it says? Isn't that what it says?" Then, barely able to see him, them, she listened as he read it aloud, softly, but in that calm, methodical, lawyer/seacaptain voice.

"One unconfirmed unconfirmable but plausible transmission from a certain part of the old world suggests that an unexpected uninvited drop-in guest with the designation HTR-0147 is safe and recovering. Take heart but pray on."

When he had read it, Cliff said, "Why, yes, Dumpling, I believe that's what it says without saying it absolutely."

Now she looked at all of them, or tried to, looked at them through those strange watery lenses that caused them all to blur and lose shape, and began to tremble as though a volcano were going to erupt inside her, and then began laughing, first in hysterical spurts that ricocheted off the ceiling beams like missiles or palpable objects, and then uncontrollably, causing all heads in the place to pop around and converge on whatever madness was occurring or about to occur.

And then she gasped, and interrupted the simultaneous laughing and sobbing, and during the interruption managed to say or shout, because she had no choice but to shout, because the volcano made her shout, which she did in a way that didn't seem to annoy the others in the room so much as to enliven their faces with some strange pleasure at the ecstatic joy that they witnessed without comprehending.

"He's alive!" she shouted. "Oh, thank God, he's aliiiiive!"

COLONEL JOHN G. (JACK) JACKSON:

He had been climbing toward this heaven he didn't believe in, had gotten shot down, had crashed, had suffered, had raged, had died, had found himself resurrected, had found himself flying again as he saw her face, those eyes, heard her voice, that ineffable joy and exultancy. He had soared with her, had been redeemed by it, cleansed of sin, saved from betrayal, and finally had said goodnight and left her in ecstatic hysteria with them to whom she belonged. Still flying, he had walked back to the hotel, whistling patriotic tunes that ordinarily made him want to retch, and had swung himself across the lobby as though entering some blue yonder of which he was the lord and proprietor, and had slipped a ten to the bell captain, whispering, and had gone to his room, leaving the door ajar, and had stripped to his shorts and, after dropping five twenties on the bed, had sat down at the desk facing out the window. He had been there when someone came in to whom, without turning about, he had said, just make yourself comfortable while I scratch this note, and pour yourself a drink, and heard her say that for that kind of change she would be an overnight guest, and still without turning about had said that, yes, that was what he had in mind since he had just fallen in love and wanted to pretend it was his honeymoon night, and heard her say in the voice that he already liked, that that was the sweetest thing she had ever heard and that she would make sure it was the best honeymoon he had ever had, to which he said he loved her voice, but just let him finish this note that he was writing, and was still writing when the voice said that she saw he was a bird colonel, to which, looking out the window, he said, yes, he was one of the great heroes of all time except that he had just found out that he was really a fifteen-year-old boy incapable of standing up against a fifteen-year-old girl, and now if she would just give him a minute he would finish this little note and then they would commence the honeymoon, because he already loved her from her voice alone and knew that if he turned around and looked he would be reduced to rubble in ten minutes if he was lucky and five if he wasn't, which was why he wanted a whole night's honeymoon, since he had just discovered for the very first time in a life during which he had not loved anything but flying that falling in love was an aphrodisiac against which there were no defenses and for which there was no antidote as far as he could imagine, and now, and now he had only a line or so to go, and if she would just enjoy her drink and just avoid letting her hands get too far down on his shoulders, because he was madly in love with her just from that one touch, and now he was done, and so he was going to get up and turn around. Which he had done and found that she was absolutely gorgeous, and so with tenderness that obviously amazed her he took her to him and kissed her face and touched her lightly with his hands and closed his eyes and kissed her mouth and after awhile gently took her to the bed and told her that they would leave the bathroom light on with the door ajar because in the darkness he often cried the way heroes are supposed to but with that little light he would lie with her without crying all night and if she didn't mind would call her by the name of the girl to whom he had just written and sealed the note that he was going to mail in the morning.

He had written:

Dear Ellen:

Meeting you is the greatest thing that has ever happened to me. Witnessing you at the moment you found out that my friend and your love is alive is the most splendid thing that ever happened to me.

I thank you for a time that I'll never forget. I called you in the clumsy hope of cheering you, but it was you who lifted me out of a pit darker than you might have guessed. I thank you, and I suppose it is obvious that the effect was overwhelming to me.

My move at the end was of course unforgiveable, all things considered. Yet, I can't bring myself to say I'm sorry. It was simply inevitable. It was only what is bound to happen when a movable object is beset by an irresistible force. You are something.

My song-and-dance tour lasts another week, and then I'll be going back. I'll take a great deal of joy back with me as the result of the good news. I do think that your friend's advice to "pray on" is pretty good—because unfortunately, this thing isn't over yet. I'll tell you what—I'll be doing something I haven't done in awhile, I'll be praying with you.

Good luck, and if I can ever be of service, I'll always remain,
Your devoted friend,
Jack

1946
Winter–Spring

——6——

The earth was green again. The air was good. The sun was warm, and the rain was sweet, and on clear nights she listened with reverence to the silent singing of the stars.

Even time was different. Time had been different since the moment two years before when she had learned he was alive. After that, the past had at last begun to recede, and the future lost its ineluctable ache. She had been delivered from that stifling and baffling texture of time wherein the past was not quite past, the future not quite future, and now not quite now.

Then the present had returned.

The invasion begins. They sweep across France. The telegram arrives, incongruously flip, and fills her with heady joy: "Back from vacation. All's well. Writing instantly with boundless love. Henry."

The first letter comes: He is to remain there on duty but without flying. Amazingly the letter bears no mention of his epic adventure.

She writes, asking, and soon receives an elliptical account: He had jumped at low altitude, landing in some woods close by a village outside Châteauroux sixty-five miles south and west of Paris. He had broken one leg and the other ankle. Someone with the Maquisards had sighted, saved, and concealed him at great risk until the Americans came along.

She works better through the rest of '44, and better yet through '45. Her work becomes a nutrient instead of an anesthetic, her art teacher says she is beginning to find her way.

She cares for his regular letters like treasures. She flattens them, fixing them chronologically in the special leather-bound scrapbook, attaching the envelopes to pages facing the letters.

She drives home more often, visits Claudette at the *Mirror*. Along the leafy streets of McClung she glimpses familiar faces and forms in a world no longer alien but infinitely mysterious still.

She glimpses Claude Atwell the dentist who habitually whistles but only with an insuck, Shorty Haines the mailman who collects everybody's foreign stamps, Annie Buckleman who in her husband's absence once got drunk and painted their bedroom, linens and all, George Appleman the electrician whose father had been tried and acquitted for his mother's death by shotgun, Doug Lenoir who would leave a customer waiting in his shoe store while he strolled down the street for a drink, Sidney Carter Fletcher who had once been a minister and who had fallen across the street into the *Mirror*'s plate glass window, Connie Singleton whose no-longer skinny daughter Dora had married an Army captain, Nub Cachet who spent most nights in his woodwork shop, Frances Whitcomb the seamstress who at three had seen her drunk father tumble backwards down the stairs to his death, Bill Turnbull the hardware man who had committed his father to the asylum and banned his younger brother from their house, Jack Burcell who was still running Jack and Jim's although Jim had also been killed in the Pacific.

She hears that Maynard McComb the lawyer who used to be seen sometimes sitting under his banyan tree during thunderstorms had died of cancer, and that John Edgar Heever who had grown chubby eating Post Toasties so he could get Junior G-Man stuff with the boxtops had had to be committed to the state asylum after the FBI turned down his application, and that Dixie Burcell who had gone to Hollywood with one of Mr. Sorrel's technicians had married the wealthy owner of a Bolivian tin mine.

She thinks of Mr. Sorrel and of the film he had made and begins to comprehend the effect of its theme on her, she who in her own life had wished and still wished to emulate the scene in which he had filmed two young Lomkubees tenderly standing still, and then lying still, before yielding to their passion.

She visits the Temulca Preserve of the Lomkubees and acquaints the aging matriarch Bema with her projected paintings depicting the customs and rituals of the aborigines. She and Bema become warm friends.

A letter comes that discloses by its return address that he is a lieutenant colonel. Among other things, it says:

"Rank in the air forces is said to have evolved out of the Mexican revolutionary army's discovery that a colonel is less likely to desert than a private—the principle that gave the Mexicans such an abundance of the former along with a chronic shortage of the latter.

"As you know, my days now go to the chore of selecting, notching, branding, and marking the officers and men for going home. My superiors have provided me with a motive to keep going by informing me that when all the others have shipped out, my time will have come. Actually, I might have sprung out a little earlier, but I wanted to help out Jack Jackson in this last little way, because he has always been superb to me. I know you'll understand this.

"In any event, very soon they'll all be cleared out and it will be my turn to be notched, branded, stenciled, etc., and certified as a fortunate cull to be sent back to the civilian market. Meanwhile, my boss has been generous enough to approve a brief furlough during which I'll shortly bum a hop across the channel and make one last visit to that not entirely quaint little village near Châteauroux and pay my thanks to someone whose nerve and courage undoubtedly saved my life. I have nothing grand in mind but only feel a need to offer my full gratitude to this benefactor (known in the underground, preposterously enough, as Mickey Mouse) for letting me stick around to come soon back to you with of course all of my love."

It is late 1945 when that letter arrives, and it fills her with happiness. She thinks of their reunion and her hunger to be in his presence.

Later a letter comes that says:

"Of all the goddam things, Jack Jackson got killed in a goddam car crash in London—while celebrating his engagement to an English girl. To have lived through all that he did and then get it like that is more than I can bear to think about. I'm awfully glad you got a chance to meet that man. He was more than a good friend and comrade, he came close to being like a father to me, though I didn't realize this until now when I feel so close to tears."

She thinks of the night they were first together when his father had just died. She thinks of Jack Jackson who had professed such instantaneous love for her and toward whom she had known such impelling warmth. She thinks of Mr. Sorrel who had professed that extraordinarily disturbing hidden love in the note to her. She thinks of Matt. She thinks of Mr. Fielding, loveless. She thinks of all of those who have gone. She thinks, *Where?*

She thinks of Mark and Corinne, now married—how strange —and now writing that they and the children—the twins Anne and Marie, and Cecile and Bert—will be going to Paris to live before long.

She thinks, works, dreams, enjoys the world and finds its mysteries impenetrable and marvelous.

He lands in the States in January, and an immense good tide begins to rise within her.

She hears nothing more until he calls and says he is in New Orleans. He is heading out. She waits outside Whitcomb Hall. She sees the brand new motorcycle he hasn't mentioned. He is not in uniform but in common pants with a yellow sweater over his shirt and a twill jacket over that. As he pulls up he is grinning almost as maniacally as Matt and Mark used to.

They are one. They clasp silently for a moment. He owns her. He tilts back her head: "Goddam, I still think I love you."

She is wordless, brimming, exploding, and to the mysterious something, she thinks, *Thank you, thank you, thank you.* She reclasps him and tries to squeeze him to death.

They walk the campus, sit on the benches. They go to supper. They stroll the Quarter. Together they know the smell of wet hemp at dawn. It is cold but warm.

He takes a room in a boarding house close by. Warm days come. She is on the back of the goddam bike. They roar toward St. Teresa's and a cottage owned by the dealer who sold him the motorcycle.

He cuts off and stops to inquire at the migrant quarters where Señor Diaz used to live. They learn that the Diaz family stays on the road all the time now, hauled hither and thither in trucks by a man who contracts field labor all over—Florida, California, Texas, New York.

The borrowed cottage on the northern outskirts of St. Teresa's lies on a spit of bayfront land. They watch evening fall over the water. They stand embracing, they lie embracing, they let happen what happens. At night the stars sing, and by day the gulls cry and play over the fertile sea and its hidden freight of myriad life, of prodigal creatures ever-exploding and mutually devouring to explode again. They walk the sand with luxurious indolence. They dance at Doubloon's. They get their fortunes told by Annamelio, a glistening, golden, laughing woman from the strewn islands called Los Nubes. They lie down in the afternoon and can still hear the clamor of the gulls. He whispers, "I want you in my mouth."

They talk about the marvel of the world, the strangeness, the impenetrable sadnesses, the unutterable joys. He recites "The Song of Wandering Aengus" to her against the background of his guitar. They talk about her work, about what he may do.

He says, "I don't know. I may be too rusty to get back into music. I may be able to make a better living flying. I ought to check out the airlines soon. Actually, I ought to go on and get some college. Why don't I matriculate with you next fall? You mind being seen with an underclassman? Hell, it'll be a shame to waste the GI Bill money. You could go on and get a master's. Or a doctorate. Think of that. Dr. Ellen Worth. Hell, I wouldn't have to work at all. Aaaaaah, shit, Ellen, I don't know yet. I don't even want to think about it for awhile. You know something? All I really want to do is be with you. And live. Just be with you. Why don't we dedicate the summer to that? Hold my hand. You know something? When you're not holding my hand I get the feeling some malevolent wind may blow me right off the face of the earth. Ellen, I could eat you up."

Their old married cronies Percy and Florence Ensley join them the second day at the borrowed cottage. Henry says, "It's a good thing you've come. A little incest will add moral tone to the place." They laugh wildly. They watch evening fall over the bay and the Gulf beyond.

He sits in with some members of the old band in New Orleans. He says, "I'm just not cutting it. I've got a lot of work to do if I'm going to get it back."

Spring burgeons into a feast, gaudy, redolent. Life is a dance, a song, a saunter, tender, without fury. She loves, works, thinks.

The term ends. They set off toward McClung as a convoy of two, she in her much-traveled convertible, he on the goddam bike. They stop off at Temulca Preserve. She introduces him to the matriarch Bema. "Ellen is ours," Bema says. "Ellen is mine," Henry says. They all laugh up into the leaves of some camphor trees by the river where they are standing.

They get a sandwich lunch in Tamerdes, seat of the county in which Temulca Preserve lies, the county of Sheriff Ellis Kelso of whom Señor Diaz told Henry long ago. Henry says, "Maybe I ought to come down here and run against the son of a bitch." She says, "Don't say that too loud or we'll wind up in his damn jail."

They go on to McClung. Cliff will be at home, retired from sea for the second time, and also retired, he says, from the toil of practicing law without a clientele. Almost everyone is back home except a few, and except those who are gone forever. Tom Pickett is still going to sea.

They come to McClung. At her house he goes in to say hello to everybody. On the front porch he says, "I'll see you later, okay?" She says, "Okay. You mind just sitting on the porch tonight?" He says, "Ellen, it's okay with me if we just sit on the porch forever." He roars out the drive to go to his house where his sister Polly is drinking so much that Portia Rust is concerned.

"Dumpling, it's good to have you back," her Papa says. "Let's sit down out here and visit a little. You and Henry decided anything I ought to know?"

She laughs. She says, "No, I don't guess so. I mean, except that we're gonna be together and have a good time this summer. Papa, does that sound okay? I mean, if we just laze around and enjoy for awhile? You know, without even trying to decide anything? Does that make sense?"

SAMUEL WORTH:

He listened as they sat side by side in rockers on the front east-looking porch of the big house that he had now inhabited for fifty-five or maybe sixty years, he didn't remember offhand, and at her question he thought awhile as he rocked and rapped his favorite thick stick on the floor at every second rock, and then began to speak, glancing over from time to time to see not only this his last child but the mother she marvelously resembled and the fleeting span of years that she represented, twenty-one of them now, fewer than a fourth of the now almost eighty-eight he had lived, not quite a third of the sixty-seven he had already lived when he begat her.

He said:

Dumpling, it makes as much sense as anything I might say or suggest. The only thing that life's taught me is that if I do decide something, then something else is going to undecide it for me. And, on the other hand, if I don't decide something, something else is going to decide it for me.

It looks to me like a goddam question of six and half-a-dozen. So, yes, I think you make sense, but of course I always think you make sense, as much as anybody I've ever heard on the face of this earth. Which may be saying a lot but on the other hand may not be saying much of anything, if you understand what I mean. And I, of course, include myself in any judgment you might infer.

Dumpling, the best thing you and I can know is that we don't know what the hell is going to happen. Granted that, and I hold it to be irrefutable even though it took me half-a-century or so to learn it myself—granted that, the only thing that does make much sense is to go on and enjoy and let yourself love and be loved and let the goddam future take care of itself.

You know something, Dumpling, in my early years I damn near drove myself mad trying to make sure about the future, and every time I thought I had that son of a bitch in hand something snatched it right out, and there I was again not knowing a damn thing about what was going to happen.

Why, I thought the future was settled for good when I first brought our family to this very house. Let's see, in 1877 I had married Susanne Sharpe, and then in 1879 Charlotte came along, and then in 1880 Seth was born, and then in 1883 Cliff—Clifton, and you know, from the moment I laid eyes on that child I knew he was going to be absolutely unpredictable; he looked up at me and rolled those damned eyes as much as to say, look, here, Papa, I'm yours but I'm one mule you're not going to put a halter on whenever you feel like it. Yes, sir, I should have known then the future was beyond settling.

And then, let's see, in '84 Susan came along, and then Thomas Worth, and then William, and then in '87, the year Ruth was born, well, Susanne died, and that was the same year Thomas Horris walked up to the house and became like one of our own. And then in '88 Elisabeth Freeman suffered that fortuitous lapse of judgment and consented to marry me, so in '89 Sam Jr. was born and of course died within the month, and, you know something, I had always felt that if I named a child for me it would hex him, and I don't know why the hell I did unless it was that I just let Elisabeth talk me into it. Well, anyway, that was about the time we moved here, that was in 1890, and then a year later Elisabeth was born, and then Luke in '92, and Aaron in '93, and then Anne and Edward, the other twins, in '95. And then Robert and Freeman and Victoria, each one year after the other.

And then, sure enough, I thought the future was settled. But, sure enough, along comes 1922 and Elisabeth dies, and I thought, well, I'll just pass on out now in a state of widowerhood, but, of course, I was wrong about that, too. Thomas Horris inveigled your precious mama up to these parts and I—to my astonishment, I must say, since I was then well past the flower of my youth—I flat fell in love with her, and to my even greater astonishment she consented to marry me. And even appeared to like me a little, or at least tolerated me—no, she loved me, Emily was a very loving woman—but, anyway, there I was with a brand new future. And then along come Matt and Mark in 1923, and then, the same day that rapscallion Cliff shows up, on January 7, 1925, along comes Ellen Emily. So how can I possibly regret that the future I thought was settled got unsettled.

Well, ever since then life hasn't been a damned bit more predictable than it was before. Maybe even less. Dumpling, I could sit here and grieve over what life has taken away from me, or I can sit here and rejoice at what it's given me. Well, there are times when I do one and then the other. Fortunately, I'm doing the latter right now, and as a direct consequence I feel very good.

It's good to have you back here. For whatever your while is going to be. For however long I can keep you. Maybe I'll just chain you to the porch post and—Well, no, I've learned that lesson, too. I know better than to try that. The last time I ordered Cliff not to go off the place he hung around for damn near a year after I'd forgotten all about it. Then when I told him he ought to get out and see something of the world, the damn child left and didn't come back for twenty-odd years. Let's see—twenty-six, I think. You know, Charlotte, I still wonder where that scoundrel got all that money he saved up while he was at sea. You suppose old Cliff was a pirate or something? I wouldn't put it past him.

Charlotte. I just called you Charlotte, didn't I, Dumpling. You know why that is? You probably think it's just age and lapse of memory, but that's not the whole story. You know, Charlotte was something very special to me, she was my first born. And you're something very special to me. And sometimes I just get these special things switched around. Dumpling, you're my last born but you're first in my love. You're my child Ellen, my only child Ellen.

BOOK II

1946
End of Summer

That hot Saturday morning when he neither called nor came by Ellen was sharply aware of it and even peeved, not directly because of this trivial absence but because of her impatience to tell him what she had decided to tell him, what she had waked up knowing it was finally time to tell him. When she had heard nothing from him by the end of the usual afternoon rain, she grew intolerably impatient but not yet alarmed. She grew alarmed or certainly anxious and mystified only when she finally phoned his house to be told by his mother not simply that he was not there but that late in the night Henry had evidently gone out of town. Quickly Ellen asked the inevitable questions which Henry's mother answered in a friendly but resigned tone. No, she did not know where or why or for how long. Henry had not said.

Ellen stayed in her house the rest of the day, struggling against anxiety and rising anger. Every minute she expected a phone call that would end her suspense. She called the only two persons to whom Henry might conceivably have confided some private plan, but each

171

said he had heard nothing. Ellen actually could not imagine Henry having confided to anyone if not to her. She was not only mystified but incredulous. She scarcely slept that night.

On the second day a moil of fretful feelings seethed within, and she yielded to a flight of lunatic skepticism. She imagined that Henry was actually at home confined by some grisly situation his mother was concealing for some incomprehensible reason. At midmorning Ellen stopped unannounced at the Rust house and found Portia Rust in the middle of dressing to go to church. Henry's mother seemed vague as usual but persuasive as she repeated that Henry had merely stuck his head in her bedroom door and casually informed her that he had to go away for awhile.

"I'm not even sure what time it was," Mrs. Rust said. When she got up the next morning, that was when she noticed that Henry had taken his old blue canvas overseas bag. "I didn't realize until then he meant he was going out of town," she said, adding, "I swear, Ellen, if he was going to tell anybody he would have told you. Frankly, I'm surprised he didn't. But you know how men are sometimes. Anyway, maybe he's only planning to be gone a little bit."

A succession of torments heaved over Ellen like the breakers of a steadily rising surf, and she felt herself floundering. She found herself utterly unable to dream up an acceptable hypothesis that explained Henry's abrupt departure. Nor did she immediately hear any plausible theories. Flights of unreasoning disbelief in his absence recurred, a desperate sort of skepticism. But this ended on the third day when Percy Ensley said he at last felt obliged to reveal what Rust had asked him to hold in confidence: that Henry had come by his house quite late Friday night and borrowed five hundred dollars.

"All he told me was that there was something urgent he had to do," Percy said. "I asked him if you two weren't about to run away and get married. To tell the truth, when he denied it, I didn't actually believe him, although I couldn't figure why he would lie to me. Of course I knew I had been wrong when you called me last Saturday and I realized he was gone somewhere by himself."

So despair began encroaching. It had gathered over her like a mountain by the moment she woke up the fourth morning. Now she felt not only alone but buried, weighted down, and yet also burning brightly in a deep secret fathomless way.

By sheer concentration Ellen tried to tunnel out of the gloom. She read an entire book on Indian lore during the morning, and then almost ferociously she thrust her attention to the composition of metaphysical poetry. After a nibbled lunch she shut herself up in her rooftop workroom and began fashioning Henry Rust's head in clay. As the afternoon downpour began crashing onto the skylight she flew apart.

Ellen hurled the almost finished head against the wall. It flattened and stuck, impaled on a wall hook, the face's blank eyes staring crookedly somewhere across the room. Ellen dropped her face into her arms and sobbed as the rain crackled onto the glass panes above her. Amidst that tintinnabulous sound she thought she heard the phone ringing unanswered. She rushed out and down the stairs to find out that she had been mistaken.

That night she walked half a mile up the river and visited Horris and Claudette. Horris speculated that Rust might have been impelled to go off and settle some private thing that had befallen him during the war.

"You mean a woman," Ellen said.

"No, but if I did mean a woman, I wouldn't mean a woman in the way you mean a woman." Horris absently tugged at the rim of his collarless shirt.

Ellen hurled herself through the fifth day. She rode a horse for two hours. She played four sets of tennis with Florence Ensley. With Cliff she undertook three almost wordless rounds of croquet. She visited Aunt Margaret in the old woman's room with its perpetual aroma of jasmine. She watched as Aunt Margaret whipped stitches in and out of an encircled segment of a large piece of very fine and exquisitely light silk, a piece so light that it would collapse into a small wad that the old woman would drop into a brocade bag between times of working on it.

"Can't I tell Papa what it is? It'll make me feel better," Ellen said.

"You can tell him it's nothing," Aunt Margaret said. "Now, do you feel better?"

In the evening Ellen sat stoically alone through a movie about pilots. The show featured Thunderbolts, the kind Henry had flown and been shot down in over Europe. Home again, she took a hot and cold shower and shampooed her hair. She studied it in the mirror and decided to crop it, and so got Aunt Margaret to help with that. While the outermost of her prolific dark curls spiraled and spilled to a newspaper on the floor Ellen harangued once again for a better answer about the embroidery but got none.

Later she got dressed again and had a glass of milk in the kitchen and took a second up to her room. She stripped off the short-sleeved jersey and soiled white duck pants she had been wearing daily since Saturday. Stitchless, she propped herself up in bed with a writing tablet on raised knees. For a long while she concentrated intently, setting out to record or evoke all she had felt and thought and been aware of the night before Henry departed.

It had been a very good night. They had eaten a fish supper on Percy's boat. Later, with her in front steering, they had roared home on Henry's bike, cooling off. Then they had walked down to the big spring and made love on the pine-quilted ground just above it. Afterward they had strolled slowly back to the house. On the porch he had kissed her goodnight and spoken of his feeling for her, had spoken so poignantly that she had been tempted to tell him right then what only the next morning she had finally decided it was time to tell. He had walked with crunching steps down the pea-gravel drive and started up his bike and eased it down toward the road, gunning it there as he always did in an invisible second goodbye. He had left her feeling warm and good, free of all uncertainty.

Ellen's effort at recall resulted in a long soliloquy, tender and sensual. Upon ending it, she flipped back to the first page and inscribed a title: *Complicity in the Pines.* That done, she issued an inchoate howl and hurled the tablet across the room. It splatted against the wall and fluttered to the floor as Ellen exploded into sobbing and shrieking.

She leaped from the bed and stomped the floor and pounded the wall. Erupting anguish so blinded her she did not notice that her bedroom door was soon jerked open by Mrs. Pichon, nor that Aunt Margaret and Cliff Worth almost instantly joined Mrs. Pichon in the doorway. When Ellen finally realized they were standing there in a bewildered vigil over her tantrum, she lunged toward them with flailing arms.

"Get out!" she shouted. "Get out of my goddam room so I can have some goddam peace and quiet!"

Like amazed ghosts they faded back into the hallway. Ellen whipped the door shut with a shattering impact that dislodged the framed manuscript of Henry's first song. It landed face down. She leaped and came down with a stomp on the fallen memento.

Blood squirted from her left heel where a metal protrusion of the frame cut it. She squeezed her eyes shut and shouted: "Shit! Shit! Shit!" Then she dove crosswise onto her bed. She lay there, belly down, heaving with gasps that quaked her buttocks and set her dangling feet to twitching like branches in a storm.

Blood pulsed out of the cut, crossed her heel, curved into the recession of her high arch. It bent to the outside of her big toe whence it dripped to the orange and brown rug beside her bed.

Soon and softly Aunt Margaret reopened her door and came in. She daubed at the bloody foot with a wadded handkerchief. She went away and returned with a damp washcloth and bottle of iodine. With a thumb and forefinger she held open the wound and poured the medication copiously into it. Ellen's foot jerked. Her gasps subsided.

"You want to talk? Or can you sleep now?" Aunt Margaret said.

"Maybe," Ellen said.

"Maybe which?"

"Maybe I can sleep."

A disturbing dream visited her. Somehow she had remembered that Henry would be at the very bottom of the big spring, and so she had raced wind-fast to it, and from a great distance had plunged in, and only then had seen that he was not in the water but on the bank, that he was standing on the bank with the bridegroom Indians, standing there and, like them, holding a burning taper in his hand. And then the taper went out, burned away, and so signaled her to go to him, so she tried to, but strangely couldn't, something wouldn't let her swim. The water, the icy water, had turned not to ice but to something hot and thick, viscous, and she could not swim in it, it was pulling her down, she struggled futilely, sinking, and he could not hear or see her, she sinking with her choking stomach about to explode.

Outside, out the tall windows the gentle gray light was diluting the darkness. The earth seemed perfectly still. Her heart pounded from the terror of the dream that she did not at once remember clearly. She peered through her tall windows at the silent earth and soaring trees as at something just discovered. And now suddenly she knew.

Now suddenly she knew that Henry was gone, had gone, was gone. Now suddenly she became conscious of a conviction that he would not soon be back. It was a conclusion to which there had been no conscious prelude, no flickering ratiocination. She became aware not of the conviction arriving but only of the fact that it was there, insistent, implacable.

But still his absence made no sense. Even with this deep unmistakable knowledge of it, the reality remained somehow beyond belief. Things had been so good, things between them. From the time he had come back from the war they had been as indivisible as before he had gone away. They had relished an almost flawless summer. As summer had begun to draw to an end they had begun talking to settle on a day when, together, they would go back to New Orleans. He had seemed indecisive, yes, but certainly definite about going: Already he had written New Orleans in the hope of taking the same room he had rented earlier in the year.

So she did not feel that she suddenly comprehended his departure. Now she merely grasped the fact of it. She thought, *It is this way, and I don't know why.* At this, her memory began to disgorge seemingly every detail of her years and minutes with Henry. Episodes returned with almost palpable reality until the sheer weight of memory grew heavy. Closing her own eyes, she clearly saw his, eyes of a pale almost translucent blue. As they filled her mind she suddenly recalled that she had never seen him cry.

And so recalled that she had in a sense cried for him at moments when he couldn't, or wouldn't, as on the night they had first been together, when his father had just died. *Actually, I guess I don't give a good goddam,* he had said, and she had found herself silently crying, and had known keenly that there was some special warmth between them. Matt and Mark had roared up the long drive in their roofless old limousine, both boisterously drunk, piling out of the car and dragging their dates into the house to cook up a supper. Then, when they had spotted her and Henry sitting to one side in the dark, they issued a barrage of affectionate joshing and with their girls serenaded them loudly to the tune of the childhood birthday song:

Happy one nine four one . . .

Henry at first hadn't wanted to join the others in the kitchen. But finally he had and stayed long after dawn. Just before he walked away he had caught her face between his hands and examined it as he might have some curious novelty. And had said, *Goddam. I think I love you.* And she had nodded, yes, yes, yes, and said nothing.

Once more Ellen peered out of the tall windows at the gathering light and the tranquil earth. She felt, except for one elusive and restless spot within her, profoundly leaden. She stayed in bed into the afternoon and remained silent even when Mrs. Pichon called up two or three times to say that she was wanted on the phone.

After the rain ended she toilsomely got to her feet. She surveyed the disorder left by her tantrum. She retrieved the writing tablet from the floor and, with a toe, gingerly nudged the fallen manuscript away from the blood splotches near it. She tucked the tablet into the drawer of her night table and noticed one phrase—*impaled on henry's tender wit*—as she pressed the drawer shut. Before dressing, she sat momentarily on the edge of her bed, elbows on knees, chin on joined fists. Finally she was up again. She pulled on a fresh paisley shirt. After a moment of hesitation, she morosely climbed into the soiled white ducks. She studied a small calendar on her bureau for a long moment before she figured out what day it was. It was Thursday.

Downstairs in the big kitchen alone she heated, poured, and gagged on the dregs of coffee that, as always, had been made corrosively strong to start with. She went prowling about the vast cavernous house looking for her Papa.

She found him by a bay window at the front of the house. He was sitting in a creaky old leather chair, his right hand atop his cudgel-thick stick that he idly tapped on the floor as he placidly surveyed the freshly washed afternoon.

Ellen sat herself on the window seat facing him, legs adangle. He smiled with pleasure as he examined her. He shifted his stick to his left hand and with his enormous sun-browned right enfolded both of her small lean muscular hands.

"Dumpling, you look scrumptious even in britches," he said.

"You like my hair?" she said.

"Love it. Reminds me of your mother's."

"You noticed I cut it?"

"Absolutely. Margaret warned me. Now, tell me, what was all that hell-raising upstairs last night?"

"Didn't Aunt Margaret tell you?"

"You tell me."

"Well—I just went to pieces. I was upset about Henry."

"And what's the matter with Henry?"

"You know—he's gone away somewhere."

"And what's so wrong about that? He's a grown man."

"But I've got the feeling he's not coming back."

"Dumpling, he'll come back, don't you worry. He may have some wild hair right now, but that boy's not a big enough fool to forsake you."

"But, Papa, something tells me he has, and I'm *sick* about it."

At her insistence, the old face flared. Thick eyebrows shot upward. His hand tightened its hold on hers.

"Goddamit, Dumpling, I don't want you to worry. I say, don't worry yourself about him! Screw him!"

"But, Papa, I *can't* unless he comes back!"

A raucous whoop whipped out of her father's throat. Ellen felt a grin fleetly crack her face for the first time in days. She saw the concentric creases of her Papa's long weathered visage fly apart like the lines of some marvelously expanding target. His whoop grew into a torrent of laughter. Quickly it turned into a paroxysm of coughing. His face grew purple. Even beneath its deep freckled brown his hand turned green-white around the thick stick it clenched. As the cough wracked him he wildly hammered the stick on the floor, implanting dents over a big area of the heart-of-pine planking.

After his spasm subsided, Ellen walked her father back to his bedroom. She fed him two soupspoons of cherry-red syrup and insisted that he stretch out on the bed to which he was always reluctant to yield in the daytime. Lying down, he visibly relaxed and then clutched her hand to his vast chest. He looked fondly at her face and directly into her eyes.

"Thank you, Charlotte," he said. "I do love you dearly."

Outside his door, Ellen felt like a solitary seed within a strange steadily contracting shell. Some untouchable weight all about was trying to choke and crush her. It resembled what she had felt when her mother was suddenly gone, dead, and she wanted to be dead, too, and so plunged into the big spring intending never to come up. Each time her father's mind lost its hold on her she felt somehow annihilated. It was not as though he were confused but that she was. Now a wrenching yearning for Henry freshly awakened, swarming up out of the restless hot place within her. She hungered sharply to clasp and absorb him and be absorbed. Ellen trembled, as though of a quick chill, and abruptly fled the house.

Out back the reverberant crack of a rifle shot punctured the hot afternoon murmur. It was followed shortly by another. She imagined one of the tiny slugs plummeting out of the sky and piercing her skull to scatter all of her thoughts and memories: *where?*

She sat sprawled at the top of the high back stoop. For a moment she listened to the shots. Then she leaped down the broad steps three at a time and slowly walked toward the sound of the firing.

She passed a helter-skelter woodpile, a chicken yard, a garden, prowling cats, an arbor of muscadine vines, a wire pen within which an old setter lay dozing and two young beagles stood attentive to the sound of the rifle shots. She passed a barn, stables, immense oaks and gums festooned with pendant graygreen moss. From two hung swings of thick old rope that looked wet and viridescent.

A dragonfly lit on her nose or hovered close, flitting away a few inches as she protruded her lower lip to direct a stream of suddenly blown air against it.

She vaulted a low tilting fence enclosing a pasture in which two horses and three tan and white cows browsed. Ellen shrilly whistled, and the horses started toward her. Then they stopped and looked puzzled, as she raised a negating hand. She bent and climbed between loose strands of barbed wire at the pasture's other side and entered onto a worn path that passed amidst brush and mixed hardwoods and cedars and pines.

The path ascended gradually and crookedly to the edge of the bluff overlooking the river.

She could see him first at a distance through the trees: Cliff. He was sitting on a stump, throwing bottles into the air over the river and snatching up the .22 from his lap and firing as he sighted by feel.

Cliff acknowledged Ellen's arrival with a nod and a glance, but he did not interrupt the motions of his next shot. From the pile of bottles on the ground he took up a small capped medicine bottle and flung it in a high parabola out over the river. In a single smooth flashing movement he plucked the automatic rifle out of his lap and aimed and fired; the bottle disintegrated in midair.

"Perfect," Ellen said.

Cliff feinted as though intending to toss the rifle. Then he tossed it and at once threw another bottle up and out. Ellen snapped the rifle up and fired holding it free, and then watched the bottle splash onto the surface of the muddy water below. She lowered the aim, fired again, the bottle vanished. She tossed the rifle back. Cliff caught it, propped the weapon against the stump whose rotten center contained a residue of rain. Cliff stood up and propped one foot close by the rifle and then hitched up the waist of his khakis.

"Ellen," he began. His voice was gentle, yet commanding. He paused, ruminant, before he went on.

"Ellen, there was only one woman I ever truly loved. And I went away from her without a single word of notice or warning. Or explanation. But I didn't do it with any intent to violate either my love for her or hers for me. I wasn't repudiating her or forsaking her and certainly wasn't wishing to be rid of her. And maybe I was just a damn fool. No, probably I was, surely I was. But whether or no, I was answering to something in me that I really had no choice but to answer to. And in truth I intended to go back. But—one thing and another. Well, it's neither here nor there now, I guess, but I wanted to mention this just on the chance it might make a difference in the way you feel. It's not always easy to guess what's going on in a man's mind."

Suddenly Cliff snatched up the rifle and lobbed it to Ellen again. Another bottle sailed out, and she fired, and it vanished, and she tossed the gun back.

"Thanks," she said. "You may be right."

Ellen turned to go, but spun half about to listen as his voice came again.

"And, of course, actually there've been two I've truly loved, and if I were a bit younger I suspect I might try to talk you into marrying me."

Ellen's head snapped back with an abrupt laugh that speared the sky. She said, "But I'm your sister."

"Well, hell, if I was younger I'm not sure I'd give a damn about a little technicality like that."

Another terse laugh shot out of Ellen and into the treetops.

She left neither by nor in the direction of the previous path but through the thinned but still dense riverside woods, thinking, *I've never heard him say so much about it before.* Such was his mode, not of secrecy but privacy, that she had never heard Cliff more than vaguely allude to the woman who had played such a strange distant role in her own naming. Nor, though his special affection for her had always been clear, had Ellen ever heard him make such a bald affirmation of his fondness.

It had caused her a sharp but not unpleasant twitch of embarrassment, but this had passed now as her thoughts yielded up a recollection of the strong fleshhunger she had once felt for her brothers, a thing she had known even before she knew its name. Once she had announced her intent to marry both Matt and Mark, and they in almost a single voice had rebuked her, saying, she recalled, substantially what she had just said to Cliff: *But you're our sister*, they had said. And she had yelled back, *I don't care. What difference does that make?* Matt: *Where?* Matt and Mark: *Happy one nine four one.* Mark and Corinne in Paris.

At the edge of the woods was the continuation of the low fence of barbed wire. She climbed over it and passed onto the neck of open pasture. She crossed it at a run, slowing at its other side. There she entered the grove of tall old pines. The trees soared up out of ground that gradually sloped down toward the big spring.

The hot bittersweet air, the resinous scent evoked Henry. Everything about the grove did. The ululating hum of the trees. The spongy tread of the ground with its carpet of ancient layers of needles. Ellen seethed with fresh anguish and a clear burning fleshhunger. She was the seed choked to bursting within the shrinking shell. She thought, *Here. Craving his flesh where it was mine. Gone. But it is not the absence of flesh that is unbearable. It is the loss of something weightless, something inextricable like breath or blood or thinkings.*

Ellen lay down with knees raised and hands laced under her head. She stared up at the flittering jays. In broken planes shatterings of the sun glanced through the myriad humming limbs. *in the pines i seem what he says of me . . .*

Words she had set down last night in the tablet uttered themselves in her ears:

my thoughts resemble him i am his words his mouth evokes me dispels me conjures me consumes me ellen blindly i-less in the pines impaled on henry's tender wit

ellen/henry henry/ellen miming oneness beneath the moon in complicity with all creation: discovering as it was a million years ago lust transformed to startling love that drives us on feverish odysseys among the soaring trees jabbering in search of a way to utter it

She sprang up. With long slow stretching strides she descended toward the spring. She snatched at the needles of low-hanging branches as she went.

The surface looked silver-black and motionless even though the crystalline water moved incessantly. It arose in a constant icy flow from a reachless depth underground. An abundant overflow slid smoothly over a spillway that was mostly concealed by overhanging brush at the containment's distant narrow end. There the water emptied into a gully, a deep cut that meandered to the river.

Ellen was unbuttoning her paisley shirt as she approached the bank. Then suddenly for the first time her waking mind disgorged the dream that had come to her that morning at dawn. She felt a tremor. She was standing where Henry and the Lomkubees had stood with their tapers.

The dream had fashioned itself partly out of the spring's actual history, and out of a scene that Mr. Sorrel had filmed. The spring had been a sacred place to the Lomkubees. They had used it in part of their ritual not of marriage but of choosing.

On a night of the full moon a chosen maiden was obliged to remain at the icy spring's center while her chosen man waited on the bank holding a taper of bark that was set afire at a certain signal. When it burned out the chosen woman was permitted to come to her bridegroom to be taken at once to a warm lair in the nearby trees. There the feast of joining would begin. The chosen woman who came out of the water before the taper had burned out faced a gentle rebuke. The successful one was deemed to be an elect handmaiden to the spirit bridegroom Tomachen.

Tomachen was believed to be the source of the spring. So the legend went, Tomachen ages ago had refused to choose any save a woman perfectly virginal in both fact and mind. For many epochs he had wandered all the earth amidst all tribes in search of such a woman. At last despairing of success, he had retired to the earth's depths. There, out of inconsolable eyes, he wept icy tears at his destiny. The Lomkubees pitied Tomachen's fate but laughed at his original naiveté. The tribe put no value whatever on virginity but, to the contrary, held it to be wrong for a human being to starve any of the body's hungers.

On the wide short jetty at the widest side of the spring, Ellen shook the shirt off behind her. It dropped in a limp multicolored crumple on the cedar planks. She kicked off her open leather sandals and felt the wood's warmth pour into her feet. She peeled off the white duck pants, reversing one of the trouser legs. At the jetty's edge she paused. A hovering dragonfly inspected her forehead. She leaned, braced her hands on her knees and drew in a series of deep breaths before one final profound insuck. At that instant Ellan saw a flicker of khaki through the distant trees toward the river: Cliff in his solicitude becoming watchful. She thought, *He really tries to be my mother.* Her lean sun-browned body tautly lanced the still surface with a trivial splash lost beneath the racket of the jays.

Icy cold encased her, a violent enwrapment. The cold seethed deeper as she descended. She breasted down slowly and at a low angle at first. Soon she flipped over and looked upward. She saw the sky as through a marvelous lens, and at some impossible distance the top fringe of the surrounding trees.

Her dream returned again, but now it aroused not terror, not anguish, but detached amusement. She heard her own voice as though from a long way off: *He didn't leave with any intent to violate either his love for me or mine for him.*

She stroked downward, now sharply. A huge familiar catfish slithered across her path. She passed within a foot of the cat's face. She spit a tiny spurt of bubbles toward him. Small trout, bream, cutting schools of minnows shadowed her arrival.

The cold seeped deeper. Her reserve of inner warmth retreated. It shrank at last to a point at which it became nothing. The last warmth within went out like a snuffed spark. The cold permeated. For a flash it became a reaming core of heat. The heat fled too. She felt neither cold nor warm.

Now she felt free of gravity as though she were soaring, not diving. She was without the moil of thought, fancy, anguish, and craving that had been storming about her mind at the surface. It had at some point seeped out of her. Her conscious sphere seemed vast and still, very still. Now it ceased to perceive itself in its habitual way.

To itself it seemed a luminous awareness not that she held but that held her: no, it. Now darkness broached upon it, a strange speckled and resonant kind of darkness. It was time to rise. Its body kicked and very slowly began to ascend.

With a ravening gasp Ellen broke and surged into the air. She heard the bird cries and sucked her lungs full of air and pine-reek. She hoisted herself onto the jetty and rolled her body onto the warm planks, feeling the heat flow as though it were liquid into her face and breasts and stomach and thighs and toes. Soon she scampered up to her feet to bounce and shake off water. She whirled and tossed her head wildly. Then suddenly—as a voice rang out toward her from the other side of the spring—she erupted in a sharp startled laugh.

"You scare the hell out of me staying down there that long," Cliff said.

Ellen glanced over her shoulder and shouted back: "You might have the decency to turn your back."

"Goddamighty, child, don't you know I'm sixty-three years old?"

"So what? Papa was sixty-seven when he begat me."

"Well, you better take the precaution of wearing something next time you try to drown yourself. I was on the verge of coming in after you. You were down there seven or eight minutes, for God sakes."

"Six," Ellen said.

In a few seconds she glanced back again. He was indolently retreating toward the river, the rifle held across his neck, arms dangling over butt and barrel.

She clambered into her shirt and pants, took her sandals in hand, and trotted back through the pines and across broad rolling untrimmed grounds toward the house. It commanded a small rise and looked out on all sides at decorous trees. It was situated almost at the center of a half-mile wide sprawl of property that embraced three-quarters of a mile of river front.

Running, Ellen could see her room, the room in which she had first breathed life, the room in which she and Henry had spent not their first full night together but their first full night in a real bed, the night before he was to leave and enter the Army Air Corps. *Maybe now I won't have to go at all. Maybe you've given me terminal satyriasis.* Dawn, and they had sneaked laboriously downstairs, heading out. Henry saw Cliff coming into the hall from the kitchen and said, *Oh shit!* Cliff, carrying a steaming cup of coffee, walked by them in the back hallway as though they were invisible. Henry had whispered, *Ellen, we've both lost more weight than we think.* At a distance at last from the house her lunatic laughter seemed as though it were spiraling up to the vanishing stars.

Now running, Ellen suddenly grinned.

At the drive she stopped and sighted down the perfectly aligned row of tall oleander trees that bordered it. The drive ran a quarter-mile east to the Bulomkubee Trail, the arterial macadam highway that ran approximately parallel to the river from which it took its name. At this end the drive led into a wide shedlike carriage house with space enough for four cars, though it contained none except the old decapitated limousine that had been owned by the twins. Ellen stared. There were lawn mowers; garden tools; a thicket of tilted bicycles, some of them partly dismantled; fishing gear; paint cans; an upended wheelbarrow.

Her father's old heavy car and her own were parked on the gravel apron outside the garage.

At the back steps Ellen paused, turned about, and looked toward the river. Far away over the vast swamp and lowland that lay to the west of the Bulomkubee she saw circling black specks, buzzards. Cliff wasn't shooting anymore. Her mind cast up a saying from the credo of the Lomkubees, and her lips moved to its words though she uttered them only silently:

Step with reverence on the earth, breathe with reverence of the air, look down with reverence from the burning sun, and listen with reverence to the silent singing of the stars. They say that we are nothing and everything.

She entered the back hallway through double doors inset with red windows, panes of a transparent but deep red that her mother had found and loved when they had visited Italy on the round the world trip they had completed not long before Emily Worth died. Light passing through them gloomed the hallway where she picked up the phone. Ellen asked the operator for number 321. A rumbling voice answered with astonishing quickness, even before the ring was complete:

"McClung *Mirror.* Horris speaking."

"Can I stop by and talk for a minute?" she said.

"Uncanny, you are uncanny," he said. "I was just reaching for the phone to call you. There's something I want to tell you about."

"I'll be there in a few minutes."

"You sound good. Feeling better?"

"I think so."

Ellen slid herself onto the edge of his desk. She sat alternately leaning back on her arms or folding a knee up under her chin.

Horris habitually sat on a raised swivel chair with his thick trunk tilted back and his short legs propped up onto the desk like two short cannon aimed through the plate glass window that looked northward out onto the town's main street. The thoroughfare dropped like the stem of a T out of the Bulomkubee Trail; beyond McClung it became the highway that led to Mississippi.

With one hand Horris was holding the phone receiver to his ear, with the other he clasped a long flat ruler-like piece of printer's lead with which he alternately scratched his ankles, and his neck at the rim of his collarless striped shirt that was one of an enormous store of such shirts that his long deceased father had once accepted in payment for six sets of encyclopedias. His hairless, globe-like head glistened with sweat.

As Ellen slid onto his desk Horris gave her an affectionate whack on the thigh with the printer's lead. Now he extricated himself from the phone conversation.

"By God, Dumpling, you *look* great, too," he said. "You out of the pit at last?"

Ellen shrugged. An oddly ambiguous smile overtook her mouth. "Maybe," she said. "Right now I'm crazy to hear—whatever."

"Well, it's just a trifle, but—"

"But what?"

"But it makes what I was saying the other day more interesting. Of course it doesn't prove anything."

"Well, what is it?"

"It's just a thing I heard about from Shorty Haines."

"The mailman."

"Right."

"Portia got a letter."

"No. *Henry* got a letter. Last Friday. The morning of the day he left."

"Well, I haven't forgotten the day yet."

"And this letter stuck in Shorty's mind. This morning he knocked on the door over there and asked Portia about getting that stamp off Henry's letter, and that was the first Shorty had heard of Henry being out of town. And he happened to mention it to me when we were gossiping across the street in the cafe awhile ago."

"You're torturing me on purpose."

"No, no, I'm not, Ellen. I just wanted to give you the whole insubstantial context of things."

"So what was the letter?"

"Well, that we don't know. What we know is where it was from. And as Shorty remembers the markings, it was from France— Châteauroux."

Now Ellen realized that her mind had striven with theories all that it could. The fact Horris had just related was up there. But her thoughts made nothing of it.

"What could it mean?" she said.

"Well, as I said, it may add a *little* something to what I was speculating the other day—that it was something in or around the war that pulled him back over there. Plausibility isn't the right word. But this adds just a little weight to that idea."

"But what? I still don't see."

"We don't know."

"What do we know that we didn't before?"

"Not much really, but if we wanted to begin some inquiries we at least have something to start on now. Some place to start. Would you want me to see what I can check out?"

Ellen silently shook her head. "It won't help," she said.

Horris sighed. He chopped at his creased black shoe with the printer's lead. "Well, anyway, you seem to have your problem in hand," he said,.

"That's not quite where I've got it," she said. Her mouth tilted again into the equivocal smile.

Puzzled wrinkles ran all the way up toward the polar region of Horris's head.

"You're enigmatic," he said.

"No. I'm pregnant."

Horris swung his legs off the desk. He popped to his feet. He tossed the printer's lead onto the desktop with a dull *thwap*. He looked about, he tugged with the fingers of both hands at the sweat-moist neck of his collarless shirt. He began to grow suffused as he expressed amazement, or began to—not at what Ellen had just disclosed but at what he took to be the fact that Henry Rust had fled in the face of the situation.

"It's not a damn bit like Henry to have—"

Horris ceased, fell silent, in the face of Ellen's raised hand and vigorously shaking head.

"He doesn't know," she said.

"He doesn't know," Horris said.

"I hadn't told him," she said.

"You hadn't told him," Horris said.

"I hadn't decided it was time to tell him until I woke up last Friday."

"You mean you weren't sure until then?"

"No, I was sure, but I didn't think the right time had come."

Horris shepherded her away from his habitual work desk at the front window. They went into his private cloister in a front corner of the *Mirror* quarters. It was a room walled with shelves of strewn books. Other books lay scattered about on tables, on the surfaces of chairs, on the floor, on his desk, many of them opened face down.

Now Horris sat behind the desk with his legs sprawled underneath. Ellen took a chair just opposite him and propped her sandaled feet up so that they framed her view of him.

"Why don't we take the radical step of pausing for a minute or two of thought?" he said.

"As soon as you stop to think about it, you'll see there's not much use in thinking about it."

"Ellen—you just summed up the colossal failure of five thousand years of intellectual toil. Nevertheless—"

Horris closed his eyes and leaned his glistening globular head back as though to take in the stirred wind from the ceiling fan that creaked and clattered overhead. Ellen felt confident that he would shortly see the situation as simply as she. She felt even certitude that he would advise no step that she would find unacceptable. He would of course avoid any mention of abortion. The notion would arise in his mind to be quickly disposed of. He would cast it aside not because he would grasp her unspoken attitude and not even out of moral principle but because of his own experience and Claudette's: Early in their marriage she had three times got pregnant and each time miscarried, the last time with complications that put child-bearing out of the question for good. So he would discard the notion of abortion not as morally repugnant but as incomprehensible or unthinkable. Nor would he likely suggest adoption as a bearable alternative, though this possibility likely would pass through his thoughts. So he would set aside the common paths and solutions and finally would be driven first to optimism about Henry's return and second to approval of whatever course she might follow.

"You know," he said at last, "you may be right. There's not really much to think about. Except that I don't think we should conclude that Henry's gone for good."

"I would only assume he'll be gone too long."

"And you don't think this is a good reason for checking out what we can?"

"It won't help, Horris. He won't be back in time."

"Ellen, what makes you so sure?"

Now her eyes closed briefly and reopened in a quiet and serious gaze. She said, "Everything, I guess. The way it's happened. The silence mostly. Before and now."

"Well, if you're right, I guess the only real problem you face is to reconcile yourself to certain realities. A baby out of wedlock carries certain problems."

"For me or her?"

"Her?"

"The baby."

"You know that, too?"

"I have a feeling."

Horris shook his head in wonderment. He said, "I guess I meant both. But to tell the truth I don't seem to worry too much about you in this instance. What your child might face would be real, however. It's probably less today than long ago, but there's still a stigma."

"That's unjust."

"Yes. But real."

They fell silent for a moment. The ceiling fan above them clattered ferociously in their silence.

"Of course," Horris said, "you might go away somewhere and—"

"No," Ellen said, "no."

"I don't suppose you've spoken to—"

"Nobody. You're the only one who knows. Except me. And—" Ellen's mouth tilted satirically.

"And what? Who?"

"And her."

They talked for awhile longer. Horris asked about school, and she said, yes, she would be going back in a few days.

"I want to get back early and finish up all the Indian paintings before the workshop exhibit. So tomorrow and the rest of the week I'm going to have to finish my sketching here at the mounds, and maybe take another look at the stuff in the library, and—Oh, I thought I'd buy myself a new car. And on the way down stop for a day at Temulca and sketch some of them from life. If they'll let me. I think they will."

"You won't have any trouble. You've been there before."

"Yes, but never *staring* at them with a stupid pad in my hand and—Horris, wouldn't it be great if we were all Lomkubees?"

The letter had passed from her thoughts by the time she got home. Aunt Margaret and Mrs. Pichon were putting supper on the table when she walked in. Her aunt spoke to her and Mrs. Pichon merely laughed softly. Mrs. Pichon was capable of going for weeks without uttering a sound except for soft-spoken salutations and inexplicable soft laughter at things said to her. She had first been hired as a nurse at the time of Emily Worth's illness. Afterward she had stayed on as a nanny of sorts and then as a housekeeper, more or less, but in truth not because her services were needed but because Sam Worth found her unobtrusive personality pleasant to have about. As Ellen entered her Papa was already seated and asking for coffee to start with, and Mrs. Pichon laughed and got it. Cliff was already sitting down, too.

Ellen yielded to a suddenly enormous appetite. And she began to feel even good as the family, as happened from time to time, lapsed into a disjointed dialogue at the last part of the meal. Cliff, for no good reason, got it started, deciding to take note of the fact that she had gorged herself on the fried fish.

"Son of a bitch," he said, as she was picking her fourth portion from its bones, "no wonder she doesn't drown."

"Were you talking to me?" Aunt Margaret said.

"I was talking to myself."

"Then maybe the term of address was appropriate after all."

Ellen burst into a laugh that expelled cornbread in a fusillade of crumbs across the table.

"Ellen, don't you like the cornbread?" her Papa said.

"Sam, why do your children wind up so foul-mouthed?" Aunt Margaret said.

"Son of a bitch if I know," Sam Worth said.

"Papa," Ellen said, "I've decided to get myself a new car."

"Well, Dumpling, is that any reason to blow cornbread all over the table?"

"What kind do you think I should get?"

"If I were you I'd get a good one," Cliff said.

"Ellen, that's very sound advice," Aunt Margaret said, "so you pay no attention to everybody telling you to go out and find a bad one. Sam, Cliff's got a head on his shoulders, all right."

"So that's where it is, huh?"

"Papa, what do you think?" Ellen said.

"I think it's going to get a little cooler tonight. What do you think?"

"I think I'm too full for any dessert."

"We don't have any dessert tonight," Aunt Margaret said.

"Then let me have Ellen's portion," Cliff said.

"Margaret," her Papa said, "don't you give Ellen's dessert to Cliff. I want it."

"Sam, I said we've got nothing for dessert."

"Then go ahead and give Ellen's to Cliff."

"No," Aunt Margaret said, "Cliff's getting too heavy as it is."

"No wonder," her Papa said, "hogging all the dessert."

Aunt Margaret pushed back her chair and from her brocade bag in the vicinity of her feet took up the mass of large light wadded silk and began embroidering.

"What are you making now, Margaret?" Sam Worth said.

"She's making our dessert," Cliff said.

"Ellen can have my portion," her Papa said.

"Aunt Margaret, why don't you admit it's not *nothing*," Ellen said.

"Ellen, you've made me see the light," Aunt Margaret said. "All this time I thought it was nothing, but now I see it's not nothing. Cliff, do you want me to embroider you a not nothing?"

"No, thank you. I've got a sea bag full of them. Bought a gross in Hong Kong in 1911."

"Is that how you saved all that money?" her Papa asked.

"Papa, I told you I saved that money by putting it in banks."

"Mrs. Pichon, would you like me to embroider you another helping of dessert?" Aunt Margaret said.

Mrs. Pichon covered her mouth and laughed and began to clear the table.

"Mrs. Pichon, what kind of car do you think I should get?"

Mrs. Pichon laughed again and went about her business.

"Maybe Aunt Margaret is embroidering you a car," Cliff said.

"Where are you going to get the money?" her Papa said.

"Well, I'm twenty-one, so I thought I would start spending some of Cliff's money now."

"Your money," Cliff said.

"What does that amount to now?" her Papa said.

"More than I could ever spend."

"Don't put that to the test," Aunt Margaret said.

The distraught coil within her had left. It was followed by a feeling of deep weariness.

Ellen took a long hot and cold shower and at last tossed the soiled white ducks in the dirty clothes hamper. She went to bed early.

Stitchless, she took the side of the bed close to the windows. A breeze not chilly but cooler blew in with some prescience of summer's end. It passed over her skin like a light veil or a cool tender breath.

Her mind grew very still. She lay on her back with her head of mussed cropped curls rolled slightly to the right. Her legs were slightly spread and her arms lay alongside her body with the hands facing almost palms up.

It was the Lomkubee attitude of listening rest.

Her consciousness became a luminous sphere. From behind her eyes it seeped down gradually like a drifting vapor. It spread and expanded until it infused her whole body, inhabited it.

It filled her from skin to bone, permeating tissues, viscera, heart, lungs, channels, connections, and joints, some sentient awareness discovering and releasing taut muscles and ligatures.

At last her conscious mind was not distinct from but coincident with the flesh it inhabited.

Ellen sighed.

A deep long insuck of the cooling night air filled her chest. The permeating consciousness reduced itself. It became a lens upon her womb, a presence there, a small vivid locale of awareness about the womb, discovering within it the amorphous and elusive but unmistakable hot squirm. Her eyeless vision fixed upon it, and she thought, *Now the being of this body and this mind animated by this life has only the purpose of serving that, and that, animated by that which is also this.*

Ellen's eyes opened. She stretched her body. She raised her knees, straightened them, stretched again. She ran her hands with firm pressure across her thighs and stomach and breasts, across her neck and face, through her hair. She stretched her arms above her and then clasped her hands behind her head. Through the tall windows she stared at the diminishing contrast of the silhouettes in the deepening night outside.

She thought, *It's important to remember constantly that he didn't know. That if he had known nothing would have impelled him more.*

Ellen recalled the ferocity of Henry's feeling about paternal obligation, what he saw as an obligation to be present even when it might be impossible to be good. Once he had expressed it with savage vehemence: *I think I'd kill myself before I would deliberately leave a child . . . even if the marriage had turned to shit. I think a child could learn to accept my death easier than what he would always feel if I just wasn't there.*

Suddenly Ellen bolted up. The letter rushed back to her thoughts. Two letters: the one he had recently received from Châteauroux and one he had written and had sent her from England.

She sprang out of bed, flipped on a light. She whipped open the bottom drawer of her bureau and dug out the scrapbook in which she had chronologically preserved all of Henry's wartime letters and wires. Quickly she located the one she sought.

It was the letter he had written late the previous year, in 1945, had sent not too long before he was to come home. On the album page opposite was fixed the envelope in which it had come, the first that had brought the news of his promotion to lieutenant colonel, to which event he had opened the letter with that sardonic style of deprecation he had always larded on each new decoration they pinned on him.

Rank in the Army Air Corps, he had written, *is said to have evolved out of the Mexican revolutionary army's discovery that a colonel is less likely to desert than a private—the principle that gave the Mexicans such an abundance of the former along with a chronic shortage of the latter.*

Ellen tore her eyes away from what immediately followed. She was searching for some particular words that she only murkily remembered. Now her racing finger found them, yes, there:

Meanwhile, my boss has been generous enough to approve a brief furlough during which I'll shortly bum a hop across the channel and make one last visit to that not entirely quaint little village near Châteauroux and pay my thanks to someone whose nerve and courage undoubtedly saved my life. I have nothing grand in mind but only feel a need to offer my full gratitude to this benefactor (known in the underground, preposterously enough, as Mickey Mouse) for letting me stick around to come soon back to you with of course all of my love.

With a big yellow towel wrapped about her like a sarong Ellen stood at the phone in the back hallway downstairs and heard Horris rumble not his name but a resigned hello.

"I just called to ask you something," she said brightly.

"Oh, I'm glad it's you. Somehow I expected a creditor."

"Well, I have a question."

"Anything."

"Horris, do you remember, when Henry got shot down, do you remember anybody of the ones who helped him out who was known as Mickey Mouse?"

"Why, uh, yes, yes, as a matter of fact I do. It comes right to mind. There was a party with that code name. Have you found out something?"

"You say *party,* a *party* by that name."

"Yes, there was, I—"

"Why do you say *party?*"

"Oh. I see. Well, Dumpling, I say party to avoid saying anything else."

"It was a woman."

"I guess I didn't want to give you fuel for imagination."

"Well, you haven't. It was in a letter he wrote."

"A letter! When?"

"Last year. While he was in England. Just before he took that last trip over there."

"He mentioned the girl?"

"No. He only said it was to say thanks to somebody. Was she a girl or a woman?"

"Both, really. Michelle. She was about your age. Some of the things she did you'd have thought she was girl, woman, and man, too. Ellen?"

"I'm here."

"I hope you aren't leaping to too many conclusions."

"Don't worry about that. The conclusion just leaped at me. I know what was in that letter he got."

"What do you mean?"

"She was telling him his child had just been born."

"Good God, Dumpling, what makes you think *that?*"

"The timing, among other things."

"But that's quite a leap you're taking. What else?"

"Well, actually, it's about the only thing—it *is* the only thing that would have made him feel obliged to go away. If it had been anything else he would have told me. If it had just been the woman, the girl, a greater love, he would have told me. A child is the only thing he would have felt forced to go for and would have been unable to tell me about."

"All this just came to you?"

"I guess."

"Am I permitted to say that we still don't *know* all of this?"

"Oh, sure, but don't you see, it's the only thing that makes any sense."

"How does the idea leave you feeling, Ellen?"

"Relieved, I think, in a strange way."

"Dumpling, to feel so sure, you sound very forgiving."

"No, it's not that. There's nothing to forgive, actually. He just did what he had to do."

"If it's true."

"Yes, if."

"Well, it's futile, I know, but I sure wish he had known about you. He'd never have—you know."

"Maybe it's better that he didn't."

"I don't understand."

"Maybe it would only have torn him in half."

"Ellen?"

"Still here."

"I'm glad you're my friend."

"I'm glad you're mine. Listen, I've just decided to go on down to Temulca in the morning, so I won't be seeing you til whenever."

"What's your hurry?"

"Well, none, really. But I'll get some sketching done and I thought I'd go on and go through the *bakana oro.*"

"And discover your destiny?"

"Oh, no, just so I'll know what it's like when I paint. But maybe the other too."

"Okay, Dumpling, but you keep in touch."

HORRIS:

He hung up and told Claudette what Ellen had figured out, or thought she had figured out, and related her plans to go at once to Temulca Preserve and to undergo the *bakana oro,* and then he took from a shelf a copy of *Journey to Amaomanta,* the book that the young Spanish explorer Bartolome Jose Caldas had written as a confession four centuries ago after he had had a long adventure among the Lomkubees, and that Horris had discovered and translated and edited now almost ten years ago, and had published and from which Ben Ezra Sorrel had extrapolated the material that he had fashioned into a filmplay that had been duly produced and duly killed or banned, and with the copy of the book opened and the pages riffling, talked on while his wife sprawled in a big chair close by listening and manicuring her fingernails.

He said:

It's interesting the direction she's turning for sustenance now, interesting that now that she has seen civilization at its lovable best, she is hungering more than ever for the old innocence of the Lomkubees. And I suspect not only because she has that splash of their blood in her. I suspect that it's at least partly in the way Ben Sorrel did, or the way he seemed to have done as he was coming to the end of that filming. You know, when the drama or fable or whatever it might be called, when the thing he had put on film began to seem more real to him than the actual world about him. Of course, I don't think Ellen's letting that happen, because she grasps the whole situation too concretely. I'm not suggesting that.

But her reach for what the Lomkubees have to offer is just as clear as Ben Sorrel's was, and I would suppose a great deal more accessible to her, to the extent that it's accessible to anybody in this day and age. This afternoon when she came down, she said, among other things, that if only we were all Lomkubees there'd be no problem. And of course she's right, because there was no such thing as illegitimacy among them, nor, as you know, even such a thing as marriage in the way we know it, only decisions or choices by a couple of lovers to live together for some certain or rather uncertain season, or until the passion had calmed down. And, of course, every adult Lomkubee functioned effectively as a parent to every Lomkubee child, so—well, hell, her wish may have been wistful but it was very sound at the same time.

And I think it reveals the direction she's leaning in, or rather searching in, of trying to find some ancient way to accommodate her particular realities to a world that behaves rather stupidly about such things. And now with her thinking about undergoing this *bakana oro,* I think it becomes very clear what's working within her. I just wanted to refresh my thoughts on that thing. You remember, don't you, that it was the filming of that scene, of the *bakana oro,* that set off the first batch of rumors that the wild man Ben Sorrel was down here putting a sort of pastoral orgy on film. You remember that? Ah, the gossipers had a time with that—the outrage of showing anything as disgusting as some portion of the human anatomy on a movie screen, and not only that but proposing to show it to all of those people none of whom would ever before have seen anything as lurid and suggestive as the human anatomy. I suspect it was as early as that that the money boys made up their minds to do what they finally did only a year or so later. But anyway, somewhere in this damned testament, Caldas describes that thing, or at least quotes the old matriarch, or does both, and let's see. Yes—here it is:

"The Lomkubees claim that the *bakana oro* is not sorcery although it strongly resembles such. The words of this curious ritual actually mean 'the birth of light' or 'the birth of illumination.' The matriarch Lunama says that the purpose of the *bakana oro* is not to tell the future but to discover the harmonies which a person has with life. The person, man or woman, undergoing this strange ceremony lies nude along one of the diameters of a circle painted in green on an area of smooth glazed earth. One diameter is painted in red and a diameter at right angles to it is painted in blue. In the four distinct phases of the ceremony the person faces his head in turn in the different four directions.

"A thin disc covered over with a light layer of reddish dust is placed on the stomach of the subject undergoing the *bakana oro*. While some elder of the tribe instructs the subject on what thoughts to have, another elder observes the lines that form in the dust of the disc, evidently as a consequence of the changing pulse or slight movements of the subject. From these lines, which to a stranger seem as nothing, it is believed that the harmonies of a person's heart *(kubee)*, thoughts *(oabao)*, spirit *(kumanta)*, and body *(tumba)* can be determined. The reading of the heart is undertaken just after the sun has set, the reading of the thoughts just at dawn, the reading of the spirit at high noon, and the reading of the body in the darkest part of night, although small fires are kept burning when the ceremony is acted out. During the reading of the body it is customary for the subject to be touched and rubbed by a young man and young woman, the purpose, so the matriarch Lunama says, being to awaken the body completely from its hidden slumbers."

Ah, yes, and then our old friend Jose Caldas goes on, of course, to mourn the sinfulness of it all and recounts that he then made still one further effort to persuade the Lomkubees to give up their pagan ways.

It'll be fascinating to know, if she elects to tell us, what harmonies Ellen shows up with. And fascinating to see where it all leads her. Actually, considering all she's facing, I think she's doing goddam well, don't you?

But that Henry. Well, I think she's right about that, too. Events just happened to touch a mania of his, and he had no more choice about going than a rabbit can choose to sit still when a gun goes off. But you know something? No matter what she says, and she's probably right about that, too—about it being too late—I think I'm going to get moving and try to track that rascal down. It may not be too late to turn this thing around. I think there's a couple of people in that Paris embassy might be able to—Claudette, what time would it be over there right now?

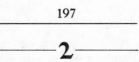

2

To her skin the ground at first seemed very smooth, almost like marble, and slightly cool. And then it felt warm, still with the feeling of glazed smoothness where it touched her shoulders, her buttocks, and her heels.

Now the sun was well down and the twilight deep and made deeper by the trees about them.

At last she lost the sensation of the ground. It was as though her flesh had become part of it. There was no feeling of numbness about her skin, but it brought her no clear perception of where the earth ended and her body began. She tried to think as Bema had told her. She thought, *earth, earth* . . .

She ceased to have any distinct sensation of the large circular disc that rested upon her. Its surface of taut thin hide extended from the base of her breasts down to the upper surface of her thighs. At first she could feel its bottom surface, too, could detect a faint friction when her deep even breathing expanded her chest and stomach. But at last it seemed as though the disc with its upturned rim were not there, and as though she were not physically distinct from the earth.

When breath entered into her it was as though the earth were breathing. Now as she heard the slow even beat of her heart even this did not sound as though it was going on inside of her: it seemed like a very resonant but gentle *ka-boom, ka-boom, ka-boom,* that was arising somewhere in the earth just beneath her, or perhaps throughout the space of ground on which she lay. She felt more than heard it. It might have been the concussion of some delicate measured pounding upon the earth close by. Then it became not like a pounding upon the earth but a pulse arising from the ground of which she seemed such an inseparable part. This drew her thoughts into the earth. Suddenly it seemed that it was the earth itself that was thinking.

Ellen lay within the center of a perfect circle drawn on perfectly cleared ground, its surface scraped and packed and baked and glazed so that it shone almost like polished stone in the firelights. She lay so that her navel was just at the center of the circle, which was divided by two lines drawn across two diameters. There was a diameter of red along the east-west direction and a line of pale blue at right angles to it. Around the circle, at the main points of the compass, burned four tiny steady fires arising from burning woodchips.

She lay centered along the red line with her feet toward the west where the last glimmer of the sun had just vanished and left the thick grove where they were in darkness, a darkness made strangely fluid by the wavering lights cast up by the tiny fires. The disc that rested upon her, the upper perimeter of its upcurled edge tucked against the very seams of her breasts, was covered over with a thin and smoothed coating of a very fine powder not of red but of some elusive shade of ochre or salmon or orange. Once the disc was upon her Ellen could not see its top surface, but when she opened her eyes she could see the elder peering at it with eyes that gleamed in the firelight.

The elder Raos, who looked so much like young Kimo, sat or squatted with his legs folded under him, his knees close by her hips, his arms drawn behind him, and his neck and head craned over the disc in such a way that he could scrutinize from directly above the tiny lines that would appear in the powder, lines caused by impulses emanating from her. Once it had begun Ellen had opened her eyes only once and had instantly felt Bema's hand pass like a whisper across her vision as a reminder to keep them closed.

"Think earth," Bema had softly reminded.

This would be the reading of the heart. It was the first of four readings of the exploration that the Lomkubees called the *bakana oro:* the birth of light or of illumination.

Afterward, Ellen and Bema alone remained in the woods. They talked long into the night, sitting and lying close by the small steady fires that they fed with the casual tossing of woodchips onto the coals.

Bema listened as Ellen spoke of her thought that perhaps her impulses were revealed in the faint and subtle lines that emerged in the powder on the disc in some way similar to the recording of bodily impulses by modern electrical devices.

"Perhaps it is true," Bema said. But she also laughed and shook her head. "Bema does not know. It is enough to know that it tells us important things. Perhaps there is no way of knowing exactly how this happens. Not even the elder could tell you."

"He resembles Kimo," Ellen said. She had gotten to know Kimo among the Lomkubees who had come up in 1940 to play in Mr. Sorrel's film.

"Raos. Yes," Bema said. "He is the son of the sister of the grandmother of Kimo. He is Kimo's uncle, in your word. He does not appear to be as old as he is."

They slept at last wrapped in blankets upon a thin canvas pallet.

Just at dawn there was the reading of the thoughts. Ellen lay then on the blue diameter with her head to the south. She thought of the wind until the wind seemed her thoughts. This time she remembered not to open her eyes at all until Raos raised the disc from her body.

When it was done she ate of a great bowl of steaming broth, and then was left alone to remain so until the elder returned alone for the reading of the spirit, *kumanta*.

At noon Saturday, Raos returned to the place in the grove away from the stir of the village and the weekend sightseers. Ellen was scarcely aware of the elder's motions as the disc was raised from her. At that moment her consciousness had fallen in a state of vast stillness. Then, just as the disc was raised, her profound quietude was interrupted by a sharp, shouting female voice, a sound not too far away, the voice rising and flinging out along with the sound of some running through the trees.

She opened her eyes and rolled her head to the side and, through the trees, saw first a child, a boy, and then a flash of bright fabric. The stir, the sounds, came from a small boy being overtaken, by his mother perhaps, by the woman who had a black object in one hand, a camera. The woman in the bright print dress snatched up the boy and glared toward Ellen and the elder. Raos was still kneeling by her and was with careful delicacy setting the disc upon the glazed smooth earth where he would give it final scrutiny.

The woman, yes, the mother was dragging the boy by the arm, retreating now through the trees back toward the shelters. Once she glanced back with a look that was both amazed and fearful, maybe outraged. And then she ran on, her flowered print dress soon vanishing from view.

Stillness returned. The elder, Kimo's uncle, went about his business as though he had been unaware of the interruption. But he spoke of it when he had finished his scrutiny of the disc. Ellen was on her feet, dressing, when Raos glanced up at her, his mouth uncharacteristically tight in a downturned sort of smile.

"Visitors," he said. "They did not belong here. The boy wandered, and his mother came to find him. It was nothing, but it is good we had finished, because the disturbance is not good." Getting to his feet, he went on, "Now I must go on the river to see after some lines. But I will be back tonight for the last reading. And Ellen is no doubt growing curious to find out, true?"

"Yes."

They ate sitting cross-legged on blankets spread about a low round table on the ground alongside the village's center shelter where Bema was quartered. Visitors, sightseers in pairs and small groups, walked about the village staring, sometimes snapping pictures.

Bema spoke of the tourists in a dry complaint. "It is not good," she said, "but they bring in a little money. We always seem to need that even though once we did not know what it was. Ha!"

Ellen became sharply aware that she herself looked on the tourists as intruders, aliens. But the talk at the meal was good humored. Ellen asked Bema what the readings so far had told. Bema said nothing could be disclosed until the *bakana oro* was completed.

"Tonight," she said, "we will wake up Ellen's body if it is not too deeply asleep." Bema laughed at her own mock tone of foreboding.

Kimo and his companion Puana grinned through Bema's drolleries. Ellen sat opposite the matriarch with Kimo at her left and Puana at her right. Bema ate slowly, deliberately, dropping chunks of bread into the bowl of fish gumbo and then fishing it out with her fingers and sucking them into her mouth with high gusto. Bema would cradle the bowl of gumbo in both hands to drink down the soup. At certain moments Ellen would be surprised to discover again the innumerable creases and crevices in Bema's face. Her age seemed at odds with her aura of vitality, her youthful spirit.

It was first Bema's face, a sudden gape of surprise and outrage and even ferocity, that told Ellen something unexpected was at hand. Even before Bema had uttered a sound Ellen glanced back over her own shoulder and saw them. They were rapidly striding toward the center shelter, led by a tall, burly man whom she had never before seen in person but who was unmistakably the one she had first heard about from Henry the night long ago when Señor Diaz had driven him to St. Teresa's, the one of whom she had heard so much more since and all of it so bad as to seem incredible. She had even heard more of him on her arrival at Temulca the day before, when she had told Bema of being paced by two deputies who had teased her in the Tamerdes cafe where she had stopped for a late breakfast, and whose car, when she left, followed hers almost all the way to the Temulca Preserve.

"Kelso!" Bema had said, turning her head to the side and vehemently spitting into the air, and then had reiterated a sardonic parody of the name that had sprung into use among the Lomkubees as well as the Negroes of the county: "Kill-so, Kill-so!"

"The others have been bad," Bema had said yesterday, "but he's the worst of all. He *will* not leave us in peace. He and his hirelings lie in wait all the time on that road, and when one of our men is driving home they will stop him for nothing, for nothing, and if he has the smell of drink, they put him in jail and usually beat him. But it is not even necessary to have the smell of drink, because the truth is nothing to them. Nothing. They will tell anything that suits them.

"People think it is worse for the black people. But it is worse for us all. The truth is nothing to them. The law is nothing to them. Kelso thinks that he is the law. He is not authorized to enter the Preserve except by request, but when he is after one of us he comes in and is deaf to all protest. Sometimes he does not even bother to lie to invent crimes. He has beat men for refusing to work in the groves or the fields.

"Ellen, he is so evil, so evil, and he goes about hiding behind such a false picture of himself. You have heard of him, true? Yes, you told me. Oh, he *struts* about in that costume of the cowboy, with the big hat that hides his lies and the big boots that have weapons for heels. And, oh, he *plays* with such cunning at seeming so friendly and so fair. But he is so evil, Ellen, and the ones who believe he is not are fatally fooled.

"Ha! Even his own story is a lie. He makes of his father a hero, a poor man who toiled long and hard to provide bread for his children. Ha! His father was a maker of whisky, and he let his children run wild. You could not have heard of this, because the papers cannot print this much of the truth. This Kelso tells the papers that his father was killed in an accident while hunting, but those who watch things closely tell a different story. They say it was Kelso himself who killed his own father and created a false picture to make it appear otherwise.

"He will lie about everything. We know that he lies about his father's ear. Kelso likes to tell that a black man cut off his father's ear in an unfair fight. But those who know will tell you that the truth is far different. Ha! It is a good story even if it is sad. As it is told, the father of this sheriff who exalts the white man above all others is said to have come upon his woman joined with a black man. And then is when the fight came about. But the truth is it was not between the whisky maker and the black man. It was between the sheriff's father and his woman. It was the mother of the sheriff who cut off his father's ear with a heavy knife used in the slaughter of hogs. Ha!"

There he was now, Sheriff Ellis Kelso, with the two deputies who walked behind her at the cafe and tugged on the shirt hanging outside her white duck jeans, who had laughed and said, "Little boy, yore shirttail's hanging out," and who had later tailed after her for no good reason. There came Kelso and the two deputies and the woman in the bright print dress, she whom Ellen had glimpsed through the trees, the mother grabbing up her wandering son and then glaring at her and Raos with the face that she could now see clearly and that wore a mask of determined bitterness.

The sheriff was walking in the lead, his rancher's hat adding to the impression of enormous height, as did the elevation of the ornate cowboy boots that his feet were flinging toward them in fast implacable strides. The narrow trivial string tie at his neck emphasized his great bulk. An enormous silver buckle glinted at his waist; it seemed a signal of something unyielding in the man who wore it.

With one deputy at his flank and another following with the woman in the print dress, Kelso came on with his head oddly tilted to one side as though it were tipped over by the weight of the long dark cigar that stuck out from the right side of his mouth, the dark cigar on which he was said to suck constantly without ever lighting it. His mouth, though distorted by the cigar, formed itself into an almost prissy little half-smile as he walked up.

The face of the woman in the flowered dress seemed smitten by a very foul taste or smell. Now Ellen heard Bema's voice, not loud but crisp and emphatic.

"Mister Kelso, you are not supposed to be here without our request."

They were still yards away and came on as if they had heard nothing. Now Kelso was before them, his enormous hand sweeping out of his hip pocket and swinging in a point toward Ellen. Without quite turning his face away, he spoke over his shoulder to the flowered dress.

"Is that her?"

"I think so," the woman said. "Yes, that's her."

"Ernie," Kelso said to the deputy at his side, "put her under arrest."

The deputy called Ernie moved toward Ellen. Now Bema was coming around to that side of the table. The old woman stepped between the deputy and Ellen.

The sheriff pointed at Kimo.

"Mister Kelso," Bema said, trembling, "we demand to know what you are doing here."

Kelso went on as though he had heard nothing. His hand was almost touching Kimo's face.

"Is this the boy?" he said to the woman in the print dress.

"It looks like him," she said.

"Mister Kelso! I demand that you stop this." Now Bema sounded fierce.

Kelso turned slowly toward the matriarch. He said, "Old woman, if it weren't for your age I'd teach you a lesson in manners. Now, don't you interfere, and get out of deputy Pack's way there. Ernie, I said put that girl under arrest."

Then Kelso turned to the woman in the flowered dress.

"I asked you, is this the boy?"

The accusing woman took a deep breath. Her head shook uncertainly, but then she said, "Yes."

The sheriff spoke to the other deputy. "Charlie Joe, you take the boy."

Now deputy Ernie Pack had grasped Bema's arm to get around her to Ellen. But Ellen suddenly leaped to face the deputy with a shrieked protest.

"Don't you touch her!" Ellen commanded.

Kelso suddenly whipped around to look at her.

"Girl, you're under arrest, so you watch your manners, too. You're the cause of this whole thing, so I'm not about to put up with any interference from you."

"The cause of *what?*" said Kimo, his face storming. Kelso's head snapped back to him.

"Boy, you just keep your mouth shut good, you hear? You ought to know what. This lady—" Kelso jerked his head toward the woman in the flowered dress. "This lady right here swears she saw you with this girl out there in the woods. So you're in trouble, too, boy. Okay, Charlie Joe, take him to the car."

Ellen saw Kimo wince under pressure of the arm the deputy suddenly pressed behind his back. Simultaneously Puana leaped toward the deputy, who fended her off with his elbow and sent her sprawling almost to the ground.

Ellen snapped free of the tentative clasp of deputy Pack's hand on her arm. She strode to within defiant inches of Kelso and felt Bema quickly press to her side.

"He wasn't in the woods with me!" Ellen shouted.

Kelso stared at her. His odd smile was back. It grew a little more emphatic around the unlit cigar on which he was still sucking.

"I hear you telling me you *were* in the woods," Kelso said, triumphantly. "So tell me this, too. Did you have your clothes all off like this lady says?"

"It didn't have anything to do with what you're thinking," Ellen said. "And he wasn't there at all."

"Somebody else can decide that," Kelso said. "Did you have your clothes off?"

Bema was close to Kelso's face now. "Mister Kelso, you don't have any right—"

He cut her off. "Old woman, now I don't need any crap out of you. Don't you talk to me about rights. These two don't have a right to do what they was doing. Not where a little boy can see 'em. Let's take 'em to the car, boys."

All the way to the parking lot Bema stuck with them, Puana at her side. Her long old fingers clasped at the sill of the window of the sheriff's car until, suddenly gunning, he backed with a roar and spinning tires that whipped a huge cloud of dust and gravel across the lot. As they pulled off Bema was calling out.

"I'll get some help," she yelled.

Ellen and Kimo sat in the back seat of Kelso's car. The deputy named Ernie Pack was driving with Ellis Kelso beside him, Kelso smiling and waving at pedestrians along the streets of Tamerdes. The woman in the flowered dress had gone ahead in the other car driven by the deputy Charlie Joe.

A Saturday crowd was about the town as they wended to the sheriff's office in the jail behind the cream-colored Bienville County courthouse set amidst decorous oaks, maples, palms, and camphor trees.

In the receiving office where another deputy was booking three Negroes, where a fourth Negro, a young woman, was sobbing hysterically, and where, unaccountably, a small black-haired, brown-eyed boy who looked Mexican sat on his heels against a wall looking lost and sorrowful and yet full of wonder, the sheriff had turned her into the hands of a matron who, gripping her arm, had steered her not toward the door to the cells toward which Kelso had pushed Kimo but up a flight of steps to a hall and into a second floor door stenciled Detention Room. The matron with hair the shade of iron rust had said, "I'll be back in a minute and search you, so don't get to playing with yourself yet," and then had let slam the door with the four-by-four-inch window that looked opaque from the inside but through which, as they had come up to it, she had glimpsed the long bench that was the only piece of furniture in the room.

As the door had slammed shut, Ellen in her solitude had known with savage clarity for perhaps the first time in her life that, yes, by God, she, too, could kill, and in fact yearned to kill, and in fact, granted the means, would love to kill that goddam evil and queerly unctuous and sanctimonious sounding sheriff who went around pushing and shoving and stepping on any-goddam-body he felt like. Would herself and only wished she and Henry together long ago had come up and killed the son of a bitch and would get him now to come kill him or get Matt and Mark to rip him apart, except that she was having crazy thoughts in this fury because Henry was gone, gone, goddamit, and Matt was dead and Mark was in Paris, but she would get Cliff to come and shoot the son of a bitch in both of his eyes or her Papa with his stick to beat him to a goddam pulp as he would, and the goddam snickering deputies, too, as soon as he found out, as soon as she could get to a goddam phone that the arbitrary son of a bitch sucking on his little cigar wouldn't even let her use, and the goddam deputies and even the goddam matron giggling when he said, "Oh, you know your rights, too, huh? Well, girl, you tell us all about your rights after you tell us about this Indian-screwin'. Edna, take her on up to the detention room and search her real good."

Horrendous rage and murderous violence had hammered within her, pounding at first, and then coiling and uncoiling, and then rolling or pulsing in waves like a surf whose periodicity she could hear in the roar in her ears and even see in her vision wherever she looked in the room with its floor of concrete and the walls filthy from scrawlings and the touch of innumerable hands and bodies. Two small windows not quite opaque looked out of its rear wall, windows also filthy and not barred but covered on the inside by a frame of steel mesh screen bolted to the wall. The vista of the court-house square and of a street running between it and the jail could be seen only obscurely with all shapes and figures distorted by the pebbling of the glass. The room contained only the bench opposite the door with its peep-through glass, the bench with the dirty smooth shine of age and use about it, a wooden bench bolted to the floor against the wall.

She hardly knew whether ten minutes or forty had passed when she heard two resonant measured bongs of a public clock, probably at the courthouse, sounds that suddenly retrieved a memory of London long ago, of her with her mama and that feeling of déjà vu, and then the matron came in with the iron rust hair and the badge on her blouse held up almost horizontal by her breast, came in with a grudging suffering look on her face as though the duty of the search was an imposition not on the prisoner but on herself. That face full of oddly curly lines and shapes, the face of a cherub sculpted by a demon. That face under that hair the shade of iron rust, hair set in precise waves and contours as though by some metal stamping process. That face, that hair, and that drawling tone as of an irascible mother full of weary exasperation in dealing with a slow miscreant child. She had told Ellen to stand at the bench and take her clothes off.

"You think I've got a gun?" Ellen said.

"Honey, whatever you've got I don't want to catch it. Just be a good girl and take 'em off."

"I don't have anything hidden."

"I believe you. Now just strip and get it over with."

"I don't see any reason for it."

"Listen, honey, if I have to call for help you're not going to like it."

Ellen felt an almost nauseous clutching at her stomach at the threat of physical humiliation the matron had thus evoked. She stepped toward the front wall to avoid the vantage of the peephole.

"By the bench," the matron said.

"Why should I stand where they can see me?"

"It's not so they can see you, it's so they can see I don't get hurt. But go ahead and stand where you like. From what I hear, though, you're not so timid out in the bushes. Likely nobody's watching now anyhow."

Ellen moved swiftly to get it done with. She shucked off her work shirt and white ducks in a furious flurry of fingers at buttons and hooked tugging thumbs.

"Once you get to it you peel 'em off like it's your business, honey," the matron said. She took a step over and picked up the garments from close by Ellen's feet. She ran her hands into one pocket after the other and then stood holding the clothes in a wad in front of her stomach, staring at Ellen, who felt blood pounding up into her neck and face. At the matron's order, Ellen turned around. She struggled to suppress all the words that vehemently wanted out. The matron's voice drawled on, intermittent.

"I recognize your type. Drifter, right? Snatch and grab it. All I can't tell for sure is whether you sell it or give it away. You don't look like you'd let yourself get hard up enough to take on one of those Indians, though."

Ellen glared as the matron stood gazing never up to her eyes but all over her body. After awhile she tossed Ellen's clothes back.

"You can put 'em back on now, honey. I guess it's safe for the sheriff to come talk to you. You wouldn't likely beat him up very bad anyway, would you?"

Ellen swiftly and silently dressed while the matron watched. As she was leaving, Ellen said, "When can I make a phone call?"

"The sheriff'll tell you all about that. I guess it'll depend on how nice you are." The matron unlocked the door and glanced at her once again. "He'll be in in a little." Then the door had thudded shut behind her.

After awhile it opened again to admit not the sheriff but the deputy called Ernie Pack, a man in his midtwenties, much shorter than the sheriff, and stockier, with blondish hair that was now freshly dampened and combed, and with a ruddy, tightly structured face that seemed constantly ready to issue a grin for no reason at all, and with blue eyes that had at once something predatory and furtive about them.

She was leaning with arms folded against the wall by the door, and he leaned against the wall at the end of the bench, almost opposite her.

"You could sit down while I ask you a few questions," he said. His voice was solicitous, not loud, almost offhand.

"I want to make a phone call," Ellen said.

"Well, you'll get to make one. Who you want to call?" he said.

"I need to call my family," she said.

"And where's your family?" he said.

"I told them that. In McClung."

"But you got a Louisiana tag on that car of yours."

"I told him I go to school in Louisiana."

"You go to school dressed up like this?" His voice was not harsh but one of friendly joshing. When she didn't answer, he went on, "It's too bad you don't have any identification we could check your story by."

"Listen, I told him—or her—or, I don't know—my driver's license is out at Temulca in my bag. Why the hell didn't he give me time to get it?"

"Now, wait a minute, miss, don't start fussing at me. Actually, I'm only here to help you out. If you cooperate with me, it's gonna be a whole lot easier for you when the sheriff comes in. So why don't you just tell me what happened out there, and—"

"Listen, I've already said—I told him it was nothing but what they call the *bakana oro*, but he—"

"Yeah, I've heard tell of that. That's the thing with the witch doctor and all that, right?"

"Listen, it's not a witch doctor, it's just an elder of the tribe, and it's their way of trying to find out about—"

"Elder? That boy that was with you don't look any older than you."

"Oh, God, he wasn't with me, I've told you—"

"Well, that lady that made the complaint, she says he was the one. Now you want us to think a nice lady like that would just come in here and lie for nothing?"

"Oh, what's the use?" Ellen said. She folded her arms tighter, propped her left foot onto the wall she was leaning against, closed her eyes. And while she stood thus, Ernie Pack began talking in a still new tone of voice, a voice that was not only soft and solicitous but insinuating:

"I get the feeling you and I understand each other underneath it all. Fact, I could go for somebody like you. You a right good-looking thing if you'd get out of that sharecropper's shirt. Get yourself a little fixed up you'd knock somebody's eyeballs right out. You know? There's no need for a girl like you knockin' around in that old car pickin' up any-old-body. I speck if you'd use your head you could make a pretty good life for yourself. And have your fun, too. You know what I mean? As far as the Indian goes I don't feel quite like the sheriff does about that. I mean, I don't blame you for doing what you feel like doing in that way. Myself, I don't have much use for 'em, any more'n for niggers, but that just goes for socializing. I don't think that goes for private business."

Some quirk in his voice might have been a muffled chortle. Ellen fleetly glanced up and back to her hands. His eyes were upon his own hands. They were interlaced and flexing upon themselves.

"You can talk if you want to," he said.

Ellen nodded but said nothing. He went on.

"To tell the truth, I'd have to deny it if you spilled it, but I'm colorblind when it comes to that, anyhow. I guess maybe you and me feel just alike about that. I been in the hay with light ones and some so black you couldn't see 'em in the dark. And I got no regrets even if I couldn't admit it in public. Heck, my brother taught me the facts of life when I was just a tad. And he was a real heller hisself. My old man give him hell once for playing around with a nigger girl. And my brother, he said, 'Daddy, you don't know what fuckin' is 'til you've fucked a nigger.' And Daddy, he comes back with, 'Boy, you wrong. You don't know what fuckin' is 'til you've watched a *nigger* fuck a nigger.' " Pack hoarsely guffawed. He said, "You ever hear a thing like that?"

Ellen reluctantly opened her eyes and felt a sharp feeling of alarm upon confronting his smiling mouth. She felt a powerful impulse to break in and destroy the flow of his talk. At the same time she felt a distinct fear of engaging him, of directly acknowledging what he was saying. Quickly she shut her eyes again. She heard his feet subtly shifting and knew his weight was rocking from foot to foot.

"Well," he went on, "he was right. I came to find that out. I've watched 'em, and they got some things to teach us, sure 'nough. I mean they go at it like it's supposed to be. And, myself, I feel that way about it, too. Something just tells me you do, too. I tell you, you just got that one hundred percent *woman* look about you. You know? I mean even in pants and that shirt. I was just kiddin' when I called you 'little boy' in that cafe. Truth is, even right now you just look like all woman, and no doubts about it. I mean I'd love to be just as sweet to you as I could be. That's how I feel about a real woman. I don't go for a whole lot of hurry and haste. I just like to lay there and be sweet to 'em for a *long* time. You know? I love it every whichaway."

Ellen said nothing. She heard his feet shift, maybe he had sat down on the bench. His voice drawled on.

"Now, Kelso, he's not like that. He's a bim-bam man. I'm telling stories out of school, but you watch him at the end of the day and he'll go back into the back storeroom with that Edna Boyles, she's the one searched you, and he'll be out in a minute or two, and nobody on earth would guess he's just had a blow job. To him it's just sort of like taking an aspirin, and of course it's just like drinking a coke to her, though I'll say she can be right nice in a pinch. Sometimes Ellis takes us up to weekend shindigs at this cabin he's got up along the big bluffs, and when he brings Edna along damned if she won't put every one of us to sleep when she gets a little high. Goodnight kiss, she calls it. She'll put one to sleep and then wake him up later and put him to sleep again. But of course she's not the kind of woman I'm talking about, not the kind I like to get close to and stay a long time. But, I'm telling you, you are that kind of woman for sure. And if we can get along, well, I think I just might be able to help you out of this jam. So what do you think?"

Against her wish and will, Ellen glanced up at Ernie Pack. He was still standing. She saw first the conspicuous sign of his arousal, then the tentative grin on a face that was at once hungry and pleading and menacing with its veil of gathering sweat. Quickly she looked back down at her hands. She thought, *He's going to rape me.*

Just then the door rattled, and Ellis Kelso came in and glanced quickly at her and then strode over to the deputy.

"She cooperative, Ernie?" he asked.

"I got a hunch she wants to cooperate," Pack said.

"Well," said Kelso, taking a seat on the bench, since you two ain't using it, I don't guess you mind if I sit down here and take the load off my feet." His hat was off and his forehead bore a fresh crease where the band had rested.

"Sheriff, I want to call my family," Ellen said, still standing with arms folded and foot propped, leaning against the wall by the door.

"You actually got a family?" Kelso said. That odd listing smile was on his mouth again, more as he removed the unlit cigar from its corner. The end of the cigar was sodden. "I wouldn't a-thought a girl with a family would be carrying on with some Indian out in the bushes."

"Can I use the telephone?" Ellen said.

"Well, you might as well hold off until we know what the bail is gonna be," the sheriff said.

"I'd like to call now," Ellen said.

"You're a stubborn little thing, now, ain't you."

"Don't I have a right to make a call?" Ellen said.

"Well, now, you're smart, too, ain't you. I'll tell you, an accused person, sure, has a right to make a call. But if you want to get technical, you're not properly accused yet. You see, we still haven't decided just what charges we going to put against you."

"Why don't you know that?"

"You know something? I'm the one that's in here to ask some questions, but it looks like you're just set on stealing the show. Something funny about you, too. You just don't talk like you look."

"I have a right to know what I'm charged with." Ellen shifted her right foot against the wall behind her.

"Watch your foot there, honey, or you'll get the wall all dirty," Kelso said. Deputy Pack emitted some sound between a grunt and a chuckle. Kelso went on: "We'll know what we're going to charge you with, I guess, after this little talk and maybe after we consult with the state attorney. So you just tell me something now: Just what went on out there between you and that boy upstairs?"

Ellen stood silent. Her gaze swept past the deputy. He ostentatiously tugged his pants leg in the vicinity of his groin. She fixed her stare at the far corner of the room to the left of both of them.

"It'll be better for you, now, if you'll just come right out with it," Kelso said.

"He's right," Ernie Pack echoed. "It's hard for us to decide what to do until we know just what went on."

"That's the ticket," Kelso said. Now he had propped his hands on opposite ends of the bench and was leaning his weight back against the wall. He crossed his long legs and set one of his embossed cowboy boots to swinging. He said, "It's one thing if you two were just out there, you know, playing around, and another if—well, the real question is, what was going on when that kid saw you, and his mother."

A long ticking silence followed, a drawn stillness during which Ellen could hear both a pounding in her ears and the coming and going in the offices of the jail. She heard the muffled grind of a truck on the road behind the building. Her mouth felt sandy dry, her stomach was like a cauldron of capped lava, churning, boiling.

"Ellen? That her name, Ernie?"

"Uh-huh. Ellen. Ellen Worth, I believe it was."

At this exchange Ellen felt that she was plummeting into some nauseous darkness. She clenched her teeth. Kelso went on.

"Ellen, when the kid come up on you, did he have it in? The Indian? Did he have his thing in you then, Ellen?"

Kelso's voice had taken on a soft and oily tone.

Ellen stood silent, her arms across her chest, each of her hands desperately clasping onto the opposite bicep.

"Of course, Ellen," Kelso said, "it's only officially that I need to know. I ought to admit that as a human being I'd just rather not know. In fact, I can hardly stand the thought of a white girl taking on a damn Indian. Honey, I think if you told me you sucked him it would make me downright sick."

Silence again. Ellen stared with demonic concentration at the corner until something forced her eyes to shut.

"How does that notion strike you, Ellen? Is that the way it was?" Kelso had lowered his voice almost to a hoarse whisper. "Or was he sucking at you? The lady seemed to think that might have been the way it was. Not that she said exactly that. But she did see that Indian boy kneeling over you. Was that it, honey? Was that redskin sucking on your little thing?"

In the silence Ellen felt she were hearing the explosion of innumerable suns. Now Kelso's voice laid aside its unction. Now he sounded righteous.

"Girl, we can't make you tell us what went on, of course, but I can sure tell you it's going to be easier on you if you stop being so stubborn. And I can tell you something else you ought to learn before it's too late."

With her eyes squinched shut, Ellen heard Kelso stand up. His voice approached her.

"I don't know what that family of yours has taught you, but

I know somebody ought to teach you that screwin' around with an Indian ain't a damn bit better than screwin' around with a nigger."

Suddenly the pounding within her exploded, and now she was almost shrieking at him.

"Who taught you all of this, Mister Kelso? Your mother? Did she teach you all this while she was cutting off your father's ear, Mister Kelso? Why don't you tell—"

His hand, the enormous back of it, smashed against her head like a swung bat. Then the palm slapped her on its forward swing, and then the back of it again. The blow impacted at the base of her chin and neck. It sent her not tumbling but sliding along the wall toward the corner. She saw a flash, a vast luminous sea of red, and felt her right shoulder jar into the corner. She came to rest there, astonished to be still on her feet. She was aware that she had heard, even as she had plunged into her outburst, a shocked electric hush in the room. Ellis Kelso's face had grown livid, pale, livid. But she had not seen his motion. She only felt the impact, the flash, and saw the red, and felt the wall come to her, the corner. Then she heard the door slam with a horrendous crash.

Now Ellen realized she was trembling inside and out. She was unraveling. Tears were running down her face but her throat was emitting no sound. Her eyes were shut tight. Rage that seemed as palpable as hot lead spread through every particle of her consciousness. Murderous images flashed upon her mind, left, and flashed again. She with her grandmama's blood was a Lomkubee and Kelso all the whites who had murdered the tribe in 1813.

Her Papa would kill Kelso. No, she would tell Cliff, and he would kill him at once. Ellen could see two bullets piercing each of Kelso's eyeballs. She herself would kill him. Once out she would get a rifle and stalk him. No, she and Cliff would implant his head on a stake at the entrance of Temulca. The head on a stake in the way of that tribe in Borneo. And—*oooh shitshitshit*, she thought.

Her left hand reached up now to the edge of her jaw and her neck. Where Kelso's hand had landed the flesh felt not pained but oddly numb except for the skin of the neck, which felt scalding hot. Her eyes were still shut. She began to collect her breathing. Again she was alone in the filthy room, she thought.

So she gasped and almost screamed when she opened her eyes and saw the deputy Ernie Pack still standing by the bench. He was regarding her steadily. His expression was utterly ambiguous. He did not speak at once. Ellen instantly closed her eyes again. Slowly she yielded to a wavering feeling in her legs. She lowered herself to the floor. She leaned her back against the wall and tilted her head into the corner. She sat for what seemed a long while before she spoke.

"I need to call my family," she said, begging. The deputy's voice came back sounding weirdly, eerily friendly, even though his first words were a remonstrance.

"That wasn't a very nice thing you said to the sheriff," he said.

Ellen now glared at him with a feeling of fierce detestation, but he went on in that almost grotesquely good-humored voice.

"Looky, I can't be all that bad for you to look at me like that. It wasn't me that hit you, remember. And you stop to think about what you said to the sheriff, that about his mother, and you ought to see how come he lost his temper. I tell you, you're lucky he didn't kill you, and you better remember you not out of here yet. People just don't say things like that to Ellis Kelso. What I mean is, I don't think you helped yourself any by saying that. I know if you'd been a man you'd be dead yet."

"If I tell my brother he's gonna be dead for hitting me," Ellen blurted, seething.

"Well, now, let's cool off a little. Your brother wouldn't be the first to think about doing it. But doing it is something else. Right now, if you want my advice, you better think about yourself. There's no telling what he'll try to put on you now. But I still think I can make it lighter on you if we can just get along."

Ellen suddenly squinched her eyes shut again, and wished she could vanish into the corner she was tucked into, half-squatting and half-sprawled, the fury boiling within, fury utterly frustrated and feeling as though it would explode her very skull. She retreated microscopically, jamming her arm and back harder against the wall, as deputy Ernie Pack's voice went on, now returning to the language and images of passion and fleshhunger that she had always held in tenderness and that he was overlaying with a vileness that she despised as it entered her ears and thoughts, vileness in spite of or maybe somehow because of the matter-of-fact and mock-friendly way he was talking, imagining no doubt that he was courting her and arousing her by describing his ways and what he liked, and describing again the ways of the female deputy and matron Edna Boyles with the son of a bitch Ellis Kelso alone or with all of his cronies at his hideaway lodge on the river, and now, oh, God, even describing with that casual chuckle the time Edna had got carried away and started playing with one of Kelso's dogs while all of them hollered and cheered her on and after that made it a regular part of their outings and getting some of their other lady friends to try it, too, when they took them up including that girl that was cashiering at the cafe where she had been sitting when they kidded her about her shirttail but were only trying to get her attention, he was confessing again.

"Cause to tell the truth, I liked you a whole lot right from the start," Pack was saying, and now, even with the thunderous surf in her ears she could hear his feet beginning to move toward her. "I thought to myself, now there is a girl I'd just like to keep to myself and lie around and please all day long, just lie there with my mouth in the right place as nice as a little dog and just lick and lick and lick until kingdom come, and then do it some more. And then I thought, no, maybe if she really does like it as much as she looks like, well, I might be willing after awhile to take her out to the lodge and let her have a bunch of us all at once and maybe even one of those sweet little shepherds with the juicy red goodies that Edna's got to liking so much, and them others, too."

Now he was standing above her at the corner where she huddled. Now she suddenly realized anew that they were beyond the view of the peephole in the door. Ellen could hear the cloth of his pants rustle. His voice was low but urgent.

"Come on, Ellen, open your eyes up. I'm just a plain old human being like you. Come on, open up your eyes, and just put your hand on this sweet thing and I just bet it makes you feel better."

From the movement of the air itself Ellen could measure his strained closeness. She felt a shriek arising, a gathering impulse to leap to her feet, claws ripping. But she was paralyzed by some equivalent horror of even looking, of looking and confirming what was happening, not because it could be doubted but because intuitively, in a way that she did not grasp until later, she profoundly wished to prevent the actual image of him from entering her mind.

Ellen cringed.

Then in a swift sequence she heard the metallic rattle of a key being inserted into the outside lock of the door. She heard Ernie Pack's furious rustle of trousers, the sudden zip of the closure, and felt, more than heard, his sudden leap back to the room's center. As the door opened she heard a man's excited voice, a voice she didn't recognize, evidently the voice of one of the other deputies.

"Ernie, we can't locate the sheriff anywhere right now and the governor's office is on the line and they want to talk to whoever's in charge—and right now! That's you, so you come take it, and whoever it is is shore in a bust-ass hurry, so—"

Ellen heard Pack hastily stride from the room, and overheard the man who had summoned him now say in a low voice as Pack passed out of the door: "I think it's about *her.*"

Then the door was pressed shut. In the room's new emptiness she could hear a roaring, a pounding from within her as of some diabolical surf. Now her burning eyes opened. Before she felt them, she saw them—tears splattering on her shirt, suddenly released and pouring down to make large dark splotches on the faded chambray.

From the street outside came a piercing cadenza of youthful laughter. She peered intently through the filthy window and could see murkily the distorted gymnastic forms of skylarking youngsters.

Now the sound of the clock began again. It was 4:00 P.M. At close to the same time a week ago she had called Portia Rust and found out Henry had gone somewhere. The time since seemed like a million years.

Ellen heard a key being fitted once again into the door behind her. She thought, *Yes, Bema must have called Papa. Papa must have called Gene Earley.* The Hon. Eugene Earley in 1944 had settled a dispute between would-be contenders by deciding that he himself would enjoy a term as governor and so had turned his congressional seat over to his younger brother Dilworth Earley as caretaker while he ran the state house for four years beginning in 1945.

Later, Ellen was taken down, Cliff was in the receiving office, and Horris, and the lawyer Aaron Hatch, and Bema. The old matriarch was standing and waiting as she had been ever since she had gotten there. She had come right after she had gone to the village commissary to phone Ellen's home. Bema had gotten not Sam Worth but Cliff.

Kelso was nowhere about when Ellen came out. Nor had Pack yet ordered Kimo brought down from his cell. Aaron Hatch was a wiry compact man with a thatch of gray hair carefully brushed back from a sharp face that brought to mind a ferret or perhaps the blade of an ax. He seemed brisk even when he stood, brisk and commanding, yet amiable in a sardonic way. Horris looked stern, knowing, patient, an abbreviated juggernaut.

Cliff's face looked harder than Ellen had ever seen it. It was an icy mask constantly threatening to fragment with an eruption of leashed fury. His eyes gleamed with the lethal ferocity of the eyes of a hemmed cougar she had once seen by torchlight on a night hunt. Cliff gave her a quick crushing hug and then drew his face back from hers to whisper a series of questions that she was suddenly afraid to answer candidly.

"Any of them hurt you?" he said. "Any of them bother you?

Insult you? Demean you? Any of them mistreat you any way?"

"It's all right," Ellen said. "I'm all right. It's so good to see you."

Then Cliff's eyes swept about the room, reaching out like stabbing icepicks toward deputy Pack and five others of the sheriff's official family. Cliff began to speak, raising his voice not to loudness but to its restrained norm that by its intensity suddenly dominated the murmur within the room.

"Every decent man knows," he said, his eyes flashing from face to retreating face, "that this sheriff's office is in the hands of a goddam sadistic savage." Cliff turned back to Ellen as she reached out and clasped his hand. "Where's your friend?" he said.

"They haven't brought him down yet," Ellen said.

Cliff called over to Hatch, who was by the main desk talking softly with Pack.

"Aaron," Cliff said, "tell 'em to bring Ellen's friend down."

"Cliff," Hatch said gently, "that's what we're trying to work out now."

"Aaron—" Now Cliff's voice grew softer but even more implacable. "Aaron, don't try to work anything out with 'em, *tell* 'em to let him go. Or can't these sons of bitches understand the English language. Aaron, maybe you'd better just bark at 'em."

At this, Pack bristled and looked with dodging eyes toward Cliff. "Mister," he said, "that kind of talk is just slowing things down, so—"

Ellen felt Cliff's hand release hers, and she grabbed it back as he was about to take a step toward Pack. Now Horris drifted up to Cliff to put a hand on his shoulder. Horris said, "It'll only be a minute."

First they heard the steps on the stairway. Then they saw a turnkey appear at the barred door opening into the jail wing of the building. Then they saw Kimo, and saw Bema rush toward him. Ellen followed close behind her.

Kimo's right eye was swollen shut, the corner of his mouth split and puffed. There was a raw abrasion at the corner of his forehead.

Hatch glared at deputy Pack and bitterly said, "I suppose he tripped and fell."

"I don't know anything about it," Pack said. "I haven't been in that part of the building even."

Kimo's one open eye was roving over the room. It looked exactly like Cliff's eyes had. As he came out of the door Bema grasped his big shoulders as though they were a small child's. Kimo seemed scarcely to see her. His eye kept looking about. His shirtfront was crusted with blood.

Ellen felt Cliff press past her and himself enfold Bema's shoulders with an arm as he asked Kimo: "Who did that to you?"

Kimo said nothing. The good side of his mouth quivered and jerked as though it were trying to smile.

Ellen brushed past Cliff and Bema and embraced Kimo. For a moment they were all just standing, and Bema was embracing Kimo again. Suddenly Ellen noticed that the small black-haired, brown-eyed boy she had glimpsed earlier was still squatting against the wall in an out of the way corner of the room, looking about with uncomprehending wonder, looking lost and sorrowful.

As Horris began organizing their departure, she went over to the child and spoke to him. He simply stared at her until she spoke again in Spanish. She got little out of him, except that he was lost from his parents, and had been told to wait.

"What is your name?" she said.

"It is Diaz," the boy said. And Ellen wondered if he could conceivably be of the family of the Señor Diaz who had helped out Henry so long ago, whose wife Henry had witnessed in the delivery of a child.

"What is your given name?" she asked.

The child remained silent.

"Well, I'm sure they'll take care of you. They'll probably find them," she said. And now Cliff was touching her shoulder, and she walked back to where Horris seemed now in charge.

"Aaron," he said, "you stay here and get this record cleared up, get it eradicated, and we'll take Kimo by the hospital clinic, and then we'll come pick you up and go out to Temulca and get Ellen's car and let Cliff drive it back to McClung."

At this moment Bema studied Horris as though she had just seen him. She pointed a finger at him and said, "We met long ago."

Horris nodded. He said, "In 1935. You were the guest of honor at the Lecture Club at Oxford. Afterward you were generous enough to tell me that I didn't know everything there was to know. Since then I've rediscovered that every few weeks."

Ellen felt astonished. She said, "You never told me that."

"Sorry I left something out, Dumpling," Horris said. "Let's go."

While they waited at the clinic Ellen raised a question about the arrangements Horris had proposed. She said she intended to drive on to New Orleans. But he had turned her stubborn insistence aside.

"Listen," Horris said, "Papa Worth knows you've been in jail. So does Aunt Margaret. And they're not going to stop worrying until

they see that you're all right. So you're going home, let them look
at you, and tomorrow I'll run up to Riverton and put you on the
plane. You're gonna get a new car, anyway."

As Horris drove them all to Temulca, Bema sat on the back seat
between Ellen and Kimo. The old matriarch held a hand of each. It
was a short trip, silent save for an exchange or two between Horris
and Hatch.

At Temulca village they tarried beyond sundown. Horris and
Bema fell into a long reminiscent conversation. Cliff's face began to
let go of some of its hardness.

Kimo sat with them at first. He vanished to seek out Puana but
returned as they were beginning to talk of departure. Except for a
word or two, Kimo had kept silent until now. Now he expressed
gratitude to Horris, Cliff, and Hatch. Then, as a grotesque half-smile
formed on his battered mouth he asked permission to steal Ellen for
a short walk.

They walked in silence away from the shelters, to the river.
There under the pair of camphor trees he spoke at last.

"I'm glad this happened," he said. "Does that sound strange to
you?"

Ellen nodded. "I don't really understand."

"It cleared my vision," he said. A glitter almost as of a tiny
bursting rocket flashed in his single open eye. Ellen felt a chill pass
through her. Kimo went on: "I see things now I had blinded myself
to—about them." He jerked his head in the general direction of
Tamerdes. "I think it has made me see what I need to do."

"I think I see what you mean," Ellen said. "Do you know what
yet?"

"No, it's not all clear. I hope I can talk to you about it again.
Will you be back to see us?"

"Oh, yes. I've still got to have the last reading. But I'd be back
anyway."

"There's another reason it's good this happened," Kimo said.
Now he was propped against a low limb of the camphor tree, his eye
staring up into the leaves. But suddenly it fell upon her. "It binds
us in a certain way," he said.

"Yes."

"I know you are chosen," he went on. Ellen waited. He said,
"I'm glad you are. I wish he were with you. I am unhappy at your
unhappiness. This is how I feel. Bema says you are one of us. I think
she's right. She is always right. We are all one, Ellen. Those of us
who see it."

In the silence, swelling up in the twilight, arose the twitter and drone of summer night sounds. Ellen said nothing. As Kimo took a step as though to return to the shelters, she reached out and took not his hand but his little finger, hooking her own in it as they walked.

"Was it Kelso?" she said at last.

"Yes," he said. "He came in like a madman, and started—for nothing. I hadn't done a thing."

"Something I said enraged him," Ellen said. "He beat you because of something I said."

"He doesn't need a reason to beat one of us. Or a black man."

"I suppose I gave him a reason to hit me."

Kimo stopped, whirled. "Kelso hit *you?*"

Ellen had taken his hand then and pressed it between both of hers. "It wasn't bad. But I want you to promise me, swear to me you won't say anything about it."

"I'll do anything you ask, but why? Why wouldn't you want it known?"

"It's Cliff, the way he is right now. I think he'd kill him if he knew."

"That's how I feel, too. Do you know that? This is one new thing I feel."

"Kimo. I felt that way, too, I did, while I was in that room. But this is the really terrible thing about men like that. They make us hate them so much we become just like them. We do if we aren't careful."

"Let's put it behind us for now," Kimo said. His mouth grotesquely worked at smiling again. Suddenly he laughed at his futile effort. He said, "You must imagine that I am smiling."

Ellen's throat issued a sharp terse laugh—two—that shot up like darts toward the awakening stars.

Soon they departed and, just below the city of Taliaferro, stopped at the oyster house for supper and then drove on steadily but without haste up the Bulomkubee Trail. She and Cliff rode mostly in silence, but it was a silence without distance.

He drove with eyes that kept intent watch on the road and the rear-view, an alertness that impelled her to imagine him in his years in command over ships. Again and again the lethal hardness of his face in the sheriff's office returned to her. Now as never before she could envision this half-brother whom she knew as easy-going and soft-spoken—she could see him as a different entity around those boisterous, brawling ports of call that she had glimpsed as a tourist child but never experienced concretely. Once, she knew, Cliff had shot and killed a sailor who was one of several who rebelled at entering a certain river in Africa. Now his face was a private house of vaguely smiling seams and crinkles that came not from his advancing years entirely but from old habits of watchfulness. From time to time, he would, with a glance and a few words, admit her into his privacy.

"Came close to letting myself go back there," he said once.

They were in her rattling blue convertible with Horris and the lawyer Aaron Hatch following behind in the big car that had brought them all down after Bema had called.

The big car belonged to Hatch, an expensive machine that he seldom used around McClung. After everything had been done, after they had left Temulca and stopped at the roadside oyster house, while they were still eating, Hatch had wryly apologized for having decided to use his big car.

"Practicing law is very simple," he had said. "If the enemy is an Ellis Kelso you arrive in a Rolls. If your adversary is a Vanderbilt, you come up in a Chevvy and make sure it rattles a lot. Retrospectively, I suspect it wouldn't have mattered if we had hitchhiked to Tamerdes so long as we had Gene Earley on our side. I knew the governor would put the fear of God in Kelso, but I was surprised that he went into hiding. Too bad, too. I wanted to test his dedication to law by telling him I had parked my Rolls in that no parking zone."

Ellen had found out they were on the way down as soon as she had found out there would be no charges against her. Deputy Ernie Pack had come back from his talk with Governor Earley's office to release her instantly, carefully deferential, regarding her with a mixture of awe and fear.

Now suddenly she felt Cliff's powerful fingers mussing the top of her hair.

"Wake up, Dumpling, we're almost home," he said. Two of his fingers tapped the headband that Bema had given her and that she had put on and utterly forgotten. "Ellen, you don't make a bad Indian child at all," Cliff said.

The Trail itself only skirted through the westernmost fringe and purlieus of McClung. Now they had passed these and turned off into the drive to the house. The lights of the big car swung in behind them. It was past midnight.

There was the house with evidently every light in it burning, even in its unused rooms. And there at the edge of the front steps stood the tall figure of her Papa. He suddenly thrust his heavy stick up and into the air as though it were a triumphant rapier. Sitting on the top step close by him was Aunt Margaret, peering up from her embroidery.

Ellen felt very glad that she had yielded her wish to go on to New Orleans at once. Tomorrow, flying down from Riverton, would be soon enough.

In a shadow Mrs. Pichon was leaning against a post at the top of the steps. She was leaning where Ellen had leaned eight nights before as she watched Henry walk with crunching steps down the drive to his leaning bike to roar away. *Where?*

Ellen felt very strange, but good, very warm. The bright burning inside did not seem menaced now.

ELLEN'S NOTEBOOK:

On the flight out of Riverton to New Orleans she opened the notebook that was labeled simply *Notes on the Lomkubees* and read some of the words of Bema that she had written down during their long talk Friday after she had sketched and before they had started the *bakana oro.*

She read:

"*Omanta.* Family. It really means all of us together in oneness. Yes, the aim of every ritual was to deepen the unity of the family. But this word does not say what *omanta* meant to us. Their books have spread much that is false about our language, or false because it was not understood. Our language does not possess a word that means what they mean by family. We did not conceive of a woman and a man and the children out of their seed as a group outside of the *omanta* or even distinct from it, from us.

"We have a word that speaks of a woman and a man who have chosen each other to bear and ripen children. But this word arouses the thought of them as an inseparable part of the whole of us. Bema has never gone over this word with Ellen, but it is simple. It is *omantakubee.* Like that it is said: *o-mahn-ta-ku-bee. Omanta,* Ellen knows. *Kubee* means life and it also means heart or the beat of the heart, from which the word was taken in the beginning, according to the story. *Ku-bee, ku-bee, ku-bee.* It is more the feel than the sound of the beating heart. So *omantakubee* arouses the thought of the woman and man who have joined, and they are the life of the *omanta,* the life of all of us, our heartbeat, our flesh blood.

"So it is not at all the same as the white man's family. This word speaks of a little group apart, distinct from and even hostile to the whole. But, of course, among the whites there *is* no whole. Ellen knows this. Anyone with eyes knows this. There are only symbols representing a whole that does not exist. There is the pretty flag that is said to be the symbol of a single nation. But what is the truth? The white man pays homage to the flag with his words and his salute and then turns upon his brother and beats him or kills him or treats him like a slave.

"We did not worship symbols of our unity or even take them seriously except as things for teaching the very young and reminding us all. The reality of oneness was everything. This we did not worship except by living it. Our language shows this. All the rituals that Ellen is painting show this. She must keep in mind that the rituals were not worship. They were a part of life itself, preparation and practice for the acts of living.

"It is hard to bear the sight of the walls. In the good days the lean-tos all would be open-sided except when protection was needed against the weather. But now they demand that we put up those screens or foolish walls so that we cannot be seen without clothes. And here is one of the ways that they are killing the oneness that even the Great Murder could not kill. Some of our own children have begun to feel shame at uncovering their bodies in front of others of us. It is so foolish, so sad. Why should we hide from each other when we are all one? What thought does it put in the heads of the children when they see the screens and walls that the politicians have forced us to put up? Without realizing it they begin to think that we are *not* one.

"So this is the way it will end. It has come down to what is here before our eyes. Our home from the dawn of time was the whole region of the ridges and forests on this side of the river. Bulomkubee. Its name means of us. You know this. Where you live, the region around McClung, was the heart of our home. But it extended to the Akana, the mountains. Each year we marched to the mountains and in this way opened what you call the Bulomkubee Trail, its upper reach. Its lower reach, down to here, we blazed, those of us who were left, after the Great Murder.

"No, Bema was born here. But that long sad march down the river to Temulca lives in my thoughts as though these feet had walked it. This was also part of our domain, but we had never come here to live, because it was not so hospitable and fruitful as the other. Now these few fields are all that remain for us, and these few shelters, and perhaps not quite fifteen hundred of us.

"And now they are killing the oneness. You see our men. The

young ones wear shirts of the *omanta* and pants from the store. Some think it is a slight thing, but it means divided thoughts. Divided thoughts. Even the language we are forced to speak gives us thoughts that are not at one. Even Bema. Our tongue has no word that is quite the same as *I*. But in English—see? It is this way: In English, I lapse and am almost forced to lapse into the constant use of *I*. So even Bema's thoughts come to see her as something apart and distinct from the *omanta*. Ha! It is an impossible trap. Ellen sees.

"You are very wise. You sound *bumanta*. You sound like you *are* of us. The best life is built by doing with grace what your being leaves you no real choice but to do. The difficult thing is to see the lack of choice. The tragic man is only one who never discovers what he must do, so his life becomes a futile struggle that is like a death in life. His is the same fate as the man who decides that he does not need to eat. You yearn for your chosen, true?

"A woman of the *omanta* is not allowed to suffer in such a way in the absence of her chosen. She is not forced to walk and sleep alone and endure the hunger of the flesh. The white man's way seems so strange and cruel to us. It is as though the woman is to be punished for some absence she did not cause. Still, we can see it, of course. The white man is not at one with any of his brothers. And this is why he sees it as a betrayal for his woman to fulfill herself with any man but him. This we did not suffer. The woman, like the man, is of us, and to fulfill her in his absence is no more than to feed her in his absence. It is the same, and it is not a betrayal but an act of life, an obligation of life. In the *omanta* the most mournful tragedy was for one of us to withdraw unto himself. I do not mean into solitude but to withdraw in spirit as a part of us. And, oh. What must happen to the woman who must suffer hunger when her chosen is away. She is soon in a crisis of spirit. In the *omanta* she is expected soon to say to one of the men, *meshamantakubee*.

"There is no good way to put it into English. Let's give ourselves in life, this is what it means. She is expected to say this to a man, or he to her, if the chosen is absent. And so they fulfill themselves, and it is not an offense against the chosen. In the old days a Lomkubee man could not have *comprehended* us if we had asked him whether he were offended that his chosen woman had joined with another of the *omanta*.

"For we were all one, each nourishing all. Even this is changing. We are too close to the others on the outside who do not understand. Yes, this is still our way, but now we must go, *sshhhh*, and teach our children to keep it secret on the outside. You see? So once again they begin to wonder if it is wrong. And their thoughts about man and woman grow confused, as do other things, by the language. They hear the word *fuck* as the white man says it, and this arouses contradictory thoughts about our ways. Our language does not contain a word like fuck.

"*Meshamantakubee.* It is not a thing that one of us could even think with himself alone in mind. And of course we do not have the *I* to think that way with. So it is really not possible to think of using *meshamantakubee* as the white man uses the word fuck, as an oath. It would be like saying, shit on life. Ha!"

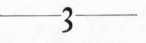

It was Friday—thirteen days later.

Ellen negotiated the busy noontime traffic with the quick ease of a child at play. The new car was sky blue, lowslung. Its top was down.

She made her way toward the big hotel where he always stayed, invariably and with the invariable explanation that he didn't know why he stayed there because the place was too much for him but he never could think of any other place to go.

Once again he had so explained when he had called from McClung the night before and asked her to come have lunch with them.

She saw him standing out front, alone, wearing that vaguely fussy look that he took on whenever he added a white collar and necktie to one of his striped shirts as his concession to what he called the cult of gentility.

She waved and caught his eye and jounced the car to a stop at the curb, and was out and on the sidewalk, her shift of soft cream-colored linen yielding loosely before the breezes of the balmy day.

Horris for a moment raptly gazed at the car, nodding with approval. Then at her.

They stood almost face to face, and he hugged and bussed her before stepping back for the ritual inspection. He tapped the headband across her forehead in a way that evoked Cliff, rapping it lightly at the front where its lines of blue and red and green were painted.

"Still playing Indian, I see," Horris said. "I like the dress.

Where'd you get it? I'll get one for Claudette." Across its chest were repeated the markings of the headband.

"Made it just for you and Claudette," Ellen said. "Where is she?"

"She made off to a shop. There's a clerk there who speaks her native tongue the way she likes it. She takes my French only as comic relief. Why don't we go inside and I'll try one of their famous exotic alcoholic beverages."

In the cool cavernous musky semigloom of the lounge they took two big wine-colored brass-bound leather chairs that flanked a tiny table.

"You know you love this place," Ellen said.

"I know. I just hate to admit it. It reeks of vice and malignant politics." Horris sipped from a tall drink with an ornate name. "A desecration of good liquor," he said, "but good. How's the sherry? Well. Sherry's sherry. Ellen, I grow depraved whenever I get to New Orleans or Paris or London or Rio or Key West or Los Nubes."

"Tell me the news you heard," Ellen said.

"Tell me about yourself first. You all set for tomorrow?"

"I think. Yes, I think so. I feel so. I did the last bit yesterday. Or what I hope is the last bit. And it's been great. I don't think I ever worked better. Actually, it hasn't even seemed like work. You know? I got down that Sunday and got my room and everything, and then I just parked myself in the workshop and the whole thing just carried me away. Except for a couple of errands, it was that morning-to-night thing. I'd hate to see the light go. And I'd hardly be able to realize that I'd been there since morning. So I finished up seven panels. Which is what I wanted."

"And you're pleased with them?"

"I think so. You never know how you'll feel after a little bit, but right now—Oh, the faces is what makes them, I think. I had all the scenes down to start. What I've been doing is really putting in the real faces that I saw at Temulca. And I think it—Oh, I'm just full of it. I won't know until somebody else looks at them."

"And you put them out tomorrow?"

"All day tomorrow and all day Sunday—weather permitting. There are supposed to be twenty-three of us exhibiting, and we'll be all around the whole square. You won't be leaving too early to stop by, will you?"

"We wouldn't miss it. How're you feeling about other things?"

"You mean—"

"Yeah."

"Oh, pretty good, I guess. I haven't let myself fall to brooding. I think about it, but—what can I do? I guess the only thing I can do actually is with what's here for me to do something about."

"You seen a doctor yet?"

"Uh-huh. Last week, I—Horris, I didn't expect to feel so *odd* when the nurse asked me if I were married. And I felt the strongest temptation to say yes. You know? And then I thought of what you said to me. I was just feeling the *aura* of disapproval. And I thought, well, *damn*—so I said, 'Not just yet.' And she gave me this weird look. And then the doctor asked me the same thing, you know, when he told me the result, and so I gave him the same answer. And he was so completely different. He just laughed and said, 'Well, missy, it might not be inappropriate if you started thinking about setting the date.'"

Their laughter bounded up amidst the cherubs and gargoyles peering down from the high vaulted ceiling.

Horris passed his two hands over his face and back across the hairless reaches of his globe-like head. He sighed, and after that, said, "So you were right."

"Looks as if," Ellen said. "She's squirming away somewhere in there."

"Well—I'm here to confess that I did something you didn't want me to do. And it looks like you were right about something else, too."

"Henry," Ellen said, whispering.

Horris sipped his drink. He set it down with fastidious care on its scalloped blotter-like coaster. He shifted his chair a few inches closer to Ellen's. He reached and took her left hand between his two.

"First, you've got to forgive me for butting in," he said.

"Oh, don't say that. Whatever you do is okay with me. So, come on, just tell me. Anyway, if it's what I think, it's only what I already know. Almost."

"Well, you certainly knew closer than I thought you knew. Listen, I had a friend of mine from the old days discreetly check around through the embassy in Paris and a couple of other places. And it seems that Henry flew in there out of New York a couple of days after he left here. Or McClung. And it seems he did show up in Châteauroux. And it seems that he did leave there on a bus with the, uh, with Michelle."

"No baby?"

"Well, you were right there, too. My friend turned up the fact that she gave birth in late July."

"Are they married?"

"No sign of it. In fact, that's about all we know."

"Where are they now?"

Horris shook his head. "That we don't know. We know they got tickets on the local bus to a junction. But where they went from there, if anywhere, we don't know."

Horris was squeezing her hand now between both of his. She wondered why what he had told her had not seemed more of a surprise. She had over and again thought, yes, that is the way it had to have been. And over and over she had concluded that nothing else made sense. Yet, she also had remembered Horris's admonition: *We don't really know.* But maybe she really had known.

They sat in silence for a moment. The lounge's subdued murmur had swelled and become intermittently raucous with the laughter and chatter of a group of college students who had come in, some of them wearing the emblems of the school whose football team would play in the city tomorrow. Ellen took a tiny sip of the sherry in its fragile crystal glass.

"Ellen, I feel that there's a certain kind of relief in sure knowledge," Horris said. "Even when knowing might at first cause some pain."

"Horris, it's so funny. I felt the pain at first—not just now but when this possibility first came to me—but it isn't quite that now. I mean, I think at first I really felt a bitter jealousy. But, I don't know, I don't feel that now. I just miss Henry horribly—when I let myself —but I don't feel that hateful *anguish* that I did at first."

"I marvel that you don't get some of that hopeless what-might-have-been feeling. You know—that hating yourself for not having told him what probably would have kept him from going away."

"Not much, not now. I'm not even sure how I feel about that. One time I'll think that if I had told him it would have torn him in two, and another time I think, well, maybe—" Her sentence trailed off. She shrugged and saluted Horris with the sherry glass.

"Who knows?" Horris said, returning the salute. "To fate, providence, fortune, destiny, whatyouwill."

"Who knows?" Ellen said. "Maybe if I had told him he could have just taken me with him."

"It would have been complicated."

"Oh, at this point I'm not so sure *I* would mind being part of his menage."

Ellen giggled. Horris began laughing, too. Then he pointed and said, "Here comes Claudette."

She came up dumping parcels on the tiny table and drowning them in cascading chatter as she drew Ellen to her feet and gave her a hug. Claudette had arrived speaking French still, and now they all fell into the language, drawing glances from the patrons at nearby tables.

"*Ils sont surpris d'entendre une Indienne parler français,*" Horris said. ["They're surprised to hear an Indian speak French."]

Claudette stood perhaps three inches taller than Ellen and the same height above her husband. A shapely, even voluptuous woman of thirty-three, she moved with easy ungirdled grace. She was wearing a smart sans-serif street frock that Ellen was praising.

"*Ta robe est plus jolie,*" Claudette said to Ellen. ["Your dress is more beautiful."]

"*Merci, attends une seconde,*" Ellen said. She sprang up and ran from the hotel to her car, returning a moment later with a brown paper bag she had taken from the back seat. "*J'ai passé beaucoup de temps à envelopper ton cadeau,*" Ellen said. ["I spent a lot of time wrapping your gift."]

She handed the grocery bag to Claudette, who kissed the homely package with mock ecstasy before peeping in. It contained a dress identical to the one Ellen was wearing, and a headband that she had also made identical to the one Bema had given her.

"*Oh, qu'elle est belle. Une minute,*" Claudette said. Then she sprang up and at a fast walk vanished to the ladies' room. With astonishing swiftness she returned wearing Ellen's gift and the headband, her frock in the brown bag. A flurry of compliments and thank-yous as she sat down. Claudette pointed to the markings on the headband and breast of the dress; saying: "Now, tell me, is it a symbol, or—" [*"Explique moi, c'est un symbole, ou—"*]

Ellen: "It means you are ready to be chosen." [*"Cela veut dire que tu es prête à être choisie."*]

Horris: "What!" [*"Quoi!"*]

Claudette: "To be chosen by whom?" [*"A être choisie par qui?"*]

Ellen: "It means you are looking for a man."

Claudette: "*Merveilleux, merveilleux. Et c'est vrai—je cherche toujours.*"

Horris: "Ellen, this won't do."

Ellen: "*Trop tard.*" ["Too late."]

Claudette: "*Il est toujours trop tard, mais il n'est jamais trop tard.*" ["It's always too late, and never too late."]

Claudette winked extravagantly at a college boy at the next

table. He blushed violently, and the three of them burst into uncontrollable laughter, laughing until their eyes watered over.

Later they lunched expensively and long at a celebrated restaurant in the French Quarter. Then Ellen took them on a long ride around the city in her new sky blue car.

He looked inexplicably familiar when she first saw him but she did not at first remember why.

It was early afternoon, and he paused at the exhibit to her left. When she glanced over and saw him he was not looking at the paintings but staring at her sideways. When her eyes caught his he quickly looked back at the exhibit before him and pointed at one picture. He made some remark to the sharply tailored older woman at his side.

He was tall but not strikingly so and had even features that should have added up to a handsome face but somehow didn't. In some way that she could not at once figure out there was some want of symmetry that lent his face a certain suggestion of—what? Shyness? Furtiveness?

Some sign of irritation also flickered across his face as though he did not really care to be doing what he was doing. Then he and the older woman detached themselves from the exhibit to her left and moved toward hers. They both paused before it. But the woman glanced only for an instant, glanced not at the pictures but at Ellen, and then at once moved on to the exhibit on her right. He stood for a few seconds with his hands stuck behind him in his hip pockets, his wrists raising up the edges of the red and blue coat sweater that he wore though the afternoon was very mild. He examined her work with a seemingly casual look and took a hesitant step or two toward her.

Ellen sat on an upturned apple crate, leaning back against the wrought iron uprights of the fence that partly enclosed the park within the square. He nodded without smiling, nodded in response to her acknowledging nod. His voice sounded tentative, diffident.

"I think I've seen you on the campus," he said.

"I'm Ellen Worth," she said, leaning forward to extend a hand but without getting up.

"John Eubanks," he said.

Then Ellen remembered the many times she had heard and read about him and seen his picture in the papers. During the war years he had been a star, maybe *the* star player on the football team of a college in Mississippi. And in 1943—or was it 1944?—he had made a stir in the papers by quitting the game to go to work part time in a defense plant. Now he was a senior law student at the university in conjunction with which her own woman's college operated. She had heard him mentioned in gossip as a loner, a grind, even something of a recluse.

After a second of hesitation he shook her hand by the fingers and turned back to her exhibit. He said, "Are these—" but dropped whatever he had thought of saying when the older woman crisply called out his name from the next exhibit.

"John! If we are going to see them all *and* get to the game on time—"

"Okay, mother," he said, and quickly left to join her, glancing once again at Ellen, who smiled and shrugged. She was amused at the quickness of his response, but not only amused: she felt something like sympathy and decided that his mother was the cause of the irritation she saw in his face.

Probably he had no interest at all in the pictures but had been dragooned by a mother who—from the cut of her clothes—probably had no more than a fashionable interest in seeing the exhibit: That is, she would have less interest in seeing it than in saying later that she and her son had seen it. Ellen wondered about the shell of shyness about him. Most football players she knew were boisterous clods incapable of even imagining that their companionship was not the first yearning of every girl.

Pedestrians passed into and out of Ellen's field of vision, going by as in a drowsy unorganized film. During the time of the game the sidewalk crowds grew much thinner. But already the exhibit seemed a success. It had not drawn (did not usually draw) a crush of spectators. Viewers came in trickles, many of them indistinguishable from the common pedestrians and tourists.

The morning had been the best. Horris and Claudette had come by at midmorning and taken her away to the cafe across the street for a coffee. Then they had set out on their drive back to McClung.

At first Ellen had felt a strange tension as her seven panels fell under the gaze of strangers. Within her she felt some amalgam of fear and desire: she both wanted the work to be seen and was apprehensive about the exposure. She felt pleased that her work captured the attention of the passersby at least as much as any other. And was distinctly pleased when the director of the senior workshop stopped by to whisper that her things were provoking more comment than all of the rest.

Several times photographers stopped to shoot her and her work. Three of them seemed professionals. One had identified himself as a hand of the *Times-Picayune.* Ellen had felt tempted to ask the others about a rumor that had early started going among the exhibitors, that a national magazine also had a photographer on hand to do a story on the event. One photographer had shot what seemed a hundred exposures of Ellen. He had talked in the accents of an outsider.

"Baby, I'm afraid you're the only real work of art on the square," he had said. "I like your work, but that smock is what I'd like to buy for my collection. I can't offer more than a grand, though."

Ellen had felt herself blush as she laughed. She had for luck decided to wear, over her denim shirt and light gray flannel skirt, the smock she had used in studio every one of her college years. It was by now an explosion of variegated splotches.

"Not for sale," she had said to the cameraman. He was a man of perhaps thirty-five, with a swarthy leathery face, a soiled shirt and gleaming but disheveled hair.

"Well," he said, "why don't you just run away with me, and then I won't have to buy it."

Ellen's laugh had startled a flock of pigeons feeding at the curb. Suddenly she had thought that what she felt on displaying the pictures for the first time was similar to the feeling she got on encountering undisguised lust: she felt somehow stripped and on exhibit herself before an audience of exceedingly uncertain affection. She was, of course, aware of the frequence of incidental lust she seemed to precipitate, but did not tend to take it as complimentary. Sometimes, when it was gross and pathetic, it bit at her sharply. There was such a moment as the afternoon waned.

A man with a red face and graying hair and a spittle-filled grin paused unsteadily on the sidewalk by her and propositioned her directly.

"Just a friendly little party up in my room," he said.

Ellen clenched her teeth as she looked at him, not with disapproval but pity. His face began to dissolve under her gaze. Finally she said, "You look so unhappy."

He seemed startled. He broke his gaze away from hers. He looked up into the trees of the square.

"Yeah," he said at last. Then he walked away, shaking his head as though trying to clear an ear of water.

Ellen watched him recede. He crossed the narrow street without noticing a cab that screeched to a stop within inches of him. Then, for some reason, she thought of Henry's father, of the years of his wandering that Henry could only piece together from the few letters his father had written. He would write only when he could enclose some money. She remembered a note scratched on some cafe menu, a note in which Henry's father had apologized for sending so little. *I've been doing handsprings for hamburgers,* he had said.

As twilight fell over the old quarter Ellen and the others carried their work to a nearby commercial gallery to be stored overnight, convenient to setting up again on Sunday—weather permitting.

Sunday, as it turned out, was beautiful.

To Ellen's surprise, John Eubanks came by again. In midafternoon he first walked past her exhibit and turned to nod and then suddenly stopped and approached her as though the idea had just popped into his head that instant.

"Maybe I can finish my question, anyway," he said. His mouth began but did not quite complete a smile. "I wondered about the Indians. Are they real, or—"

"They're the Lomkubees," Ellen said. "They're real. I didn't see the actual rituals, but I reconstructed them from, you know, studying about it. I also happened to see some of them acted out for a film. I sketched some and—sort of worked it out. Are you interested in Indians, too?"

He had nothing ready to say. He peered intently at the paintings for a moment before he went on. "Oh, I don't know too much about them."

"You probably know more about the Cherokees and Choctaws."

"I don't know, except that I've heard of them."

"They were over in your state. Or partly. The center of the Lomkubees region was close to where I live."

"Where *are* you from?" With this question he seemed comfortable for the first time.

"McClung. Do you know it?"

"I've heard of it. Isn't it close to Riverton? We used to play the college over there."

"We're fifty or sixty miles south of there."

"I've seen you around the campus. Are you in the university or the other?"

"The other," Ellen said. Suddenly she noticed that the man with the red face and the graying hair was standing hesitantly on the sidewalk looking toward her. He seemed very shaky. This time his hair was slicked down, and here and there about the shiny suffusion of his face were pale splotches. His expression was grim but somehow expectant or perhaps abject. Ellen's gaze flicked back to John Eubanks, then to the man when he spoke in an uncertain voice.

"Miss, I just felt I wanted to thank you."

"Oh?" Ellen feigned an expression of greater bewilderment than she felt.

John Eubanks whirled and stared as the man went on.

"For last night," he said. "I wanted to apologize and thank you. Just for what you said. Strange thing. It helped me. Thank you."

Ellen grinned. Abruptly the man turned and walked down the sidewalk whence he had come.

John Eubanks looked puzzled, undecided whether to ask a question that might enlighten him. Ellen broke the strained silence with a comment that seemed to astonish him.

"I guess in law school you don't have a lot of time for outside things," she said.

"How did you know I was in law school?"

Ellen laughed. She propped a foot on her apple box and an elbow on her knee.

"Oh, don't be so modest," she said. "You're famous."

Eubanks's mouth broke into a profoundly ambiguous smile that conveyed partly satisfaction and yet some curious bitterness.

"Well, in a way," he said, "probably the wrong way."

Ellen found, as she had from moment to moment, some distinct feeling of sympathy arising within her. She immediately turned the conversation back to the exhibit, wondering what else in it had caught his eye. After a few faltering words, he checked himself and confessed ignorance and indifference to it all.

"Now, *that's* the right way to deal with a subject you don't like," she said, laughing.

"I guess I just wanted to meet you," he said.

"Thank you. I'm glad you did," Ellen said.

"I guess you can tell it isn't easy for me."

"That's not necessarily a mark against you."

"There was something—" He trailed off, looked away.

Ellen waited.

"Well, I just wanted to meet you," he started again. His mouth tried to smile but curled down somberly. Then briefly it smiled. "I wonder if you'd give me a date sometime."

"Tell you what," Ellen said. "Help me load up my stuff here when we close and I'll take you to supper."

He seemed astounded. He said, "Tonight?"

"Sure."

"Well, I—"

"If you're busy, don't worry."

"No, I—"

"All you owe me is an answer." Ellen sat down on her apple box and leaned back.

"Well, I'll be here. What time should I—"

"We close down at sundown."

"Where do—What should I wear?"

"What you've got on," Ellen said, laughing. "You like gumbo? I'll take you to a seafood place over by the lake."

"I don't have a car."

"I do. So—done?"

He talked some that night, which ended early. He talked a bit more the next and increasingly opened up as the week went by. Eubanks asked to see Ellen every night of the week. He asked for Saturday and Sunday, too, and seemed greatly disappointed when she said, no, she was going away.

Ellen didn't say where. He looked as though he very much wanted to ask, but he didn't.

"When do you get back?" he said.

"Sunday night, maybe, maybe Monday. I don't know for sure," she said.

The indefinite answer troubled him, Ellen sensed. But he said nothing about it. He had not yet held her hand. At moments he had taken her arm to guide her in his markedly diffident way, but even in this his touch had seemed only formal. Nor on taking her back to her house after each date had he even attempted the expected ritual goodnight kiss. Ellen felt great sympathy for his shyness.

After her Saturday classes, and after lunch, Ellen, wearing her headband and the shift that she had designed after the style of the *omanta* shirt, wove through the pregame traffic and out of New Orleans. She followed the road that skirted the lake and skimmed out of Louisiana into her home state.

She relished the first open road test of the new car. She raced easterly and then northerly, picking up the road that took her soaring over the Bulomkubee and thence back onto the riverside highway, the Trail, and up to Temulca.

Tonight she would submit to the final reading of the *bakana oro*. The meantime she would spend with Bema whom she had written of her hope to do this now and who had written back: "Come. Be with us. Kimo is well now. Puana is here. They will help us."

After the evening meal, Bema and Ellen walked to the river.

They sat under the camphor trees while they waited for the later hour, the deep darkness required for the reading of the body. Ellen was talking as the time approached, talking as she had been for a long time, now, telling Bema of new things in her life.

"So," Ellen said, "I get the strangest feeling that this person is going to ask me to marry him, and now I have begun to feel that if he does I will say yes. And yet I don't know. Would it be right? There's no real love between us—well, yes, some warmth, some friendship, but no deep warmth, no pulse of heat.

"I don't think my reason would be evil, but I don't think it would be enough. It wouldn't even be in my mind unless I—Bema, there's something I haven't told you. It's—I'm pregnant, I'm going to have a baby. Henry didn't know when he went away. So that would be my only reason for even thinking what I'm thinking. And I don't know, of course, I don't know any of this. It's just the way things have happened that give me this feeling. This is what I wanted to talk to you about.

"Maybe you'll think it's all foolish. Maybe it is. I felt one way at first and another way later. I had only heard about the feelings about illegitimate children. I had never had that feeling hit me until the nurse of a doctor I went to asked me whether I was married. Suddenly it became very real to me, and that—well, I don't know. I think I've said more than I need to say."

In the hush that followed the cessation of her voice she heard shrill crickety sounds and the absurd chirruping of tree frogs, a night chorus soaring up in immense concentric swells, filling the mild breezy air about them.

Bema was sitting with her body forward in a meditative curve over crossed legs completely tented by her shift. After a long silence she began to talk.

"I had wondered whether you were carrying a child. You have had that look about you at certain moments, but I was not sure. You have said very much, and I—Bema, Bema, Bema—how I detest the *I*—but it is too late—I am not sure I need to say as much. In truth I can say little more than what you already know. And you already know that no child is illegitimate. No child is that. The idea of a child coming into the world without legitimacy is one of the most evil ideas perpetuated by any of our cultures. The born child holds a legitimacy that the inventions of man cannot touch except in violence. I know you feel the same.

"And in further truth, Ellen, any step that you might take to protect your child from violence or violent attitudes needs no motive beyond that. We, the *omanta*, could not in the old days have conceived of the idea of a child being illegitimate. There was no such notion in our language. We also could not or would not conceive of a child growing up without a man of his own. Even the word that we translate to mean father did not quite mean what it does in English. It meant seed-man. Seed-man, the one from whom the child's seed came to the mother. Our word for mother meant more accurately nest-woman or womb-woman.

"In usual times a child's man would be his seed-man, and he would be regarded more as the possession of the child than the other way, though even this did not entail the idea of possession as of property. More closely the seed-man was the right of the child, the child had a right to his continued presence. But what if the seed-man were gone? What if he were killed? Lost? What if he lost his senses and went away alone? The child still had to have his man. Just as we could not bear the idea of the woman suffering constant hunger of the flesh simply because her chosen might be away, we could not bear the idea of the child going without his man. So the mother, with the help of the child if it had years enough, would select a man.

"And it was that man's obligation to be the child's man. It was not a choice but a duty, but it is also closer to the truth to say that the man thought it a great honor. This was not the same as the woman, whether a mother or still childless, choosing a man of the *omanta* to join with her. I told you of that before. One says to the other, and it can come from either one, *meshamantakubee*. But it is not the same when the mother picks a man for the child. With that man she might or might not join for any reason, including the reason of age if an old man was so chosen. But that was a different question.

"Now. Ha! Just as our language cannot be carried exactly into English, it is no doubt difficult to translate our practices directly into the terms of the white man's customs, his ethic, as he likes to call it. But let us ask—who on this earth could guess what would ultimately be just and right for the person you describe. What is clear to me is that if you decide whatever you decide entirely on the basis of what is good for the child, then you have done right by the highest wisdom Bema knows of. But this is not simple: it also means that if in so deciding you damage yourself so that your value to the child is lessened, then you may have considered the well-being of the child but you did not consider it fully or wisely.

"So I am not solving your dilemma for you. I am not quite that arrogant. I can only tell you that your thinking, so far as I know it, seems clear by my standards, clear and honest. I do not need to say that if the person should ask what he may or may not ask, it is not Ellen who is putting words in his mouth. Ellen's obligations may be complex, as they must be if she is to look out for an unborn child. But her obligations do not include looking out for the rights of a grown man. Nor is it for Ellen to know whether what she is prepared to offer this person, whether this is more or less than he is made to expect. There is so much we do not know, and that includes all of the future. All that we can prepare for and know is the frame of mind with which we meet the future.

"Ha! Perhaps we will know just a bit about Ellen after the readings are done and the elder decides what they say speaking singly and together. After you have left the circle tonight, Raos will go over it with Bema, and tomorrow Bema will tell Ellen. Now. It is time for us to go. If my bones and gristle will lift me one more time."

Bema arose slowly. She stretched her arms high and emitted an enormous sigh and yawn. She scratched her belly vigorously. Then she put out her arm in an embrace of Ellen's shoulders.

Together they walked across the field toward the woods.

She had come full cycle. Now her head lay to the west, her feet to the east. Tiny fires glowed and flickered just beyond the end of each diameter of the great circle of glazed and polished earth.

Puana kneeled on her heels behind the fire at Ellen's right. Kimo kneeled at the left. At her feet the elder Raos kneeled, too, as he smoothed the orange or ochre powder in its thin layer over the thin stretched hide that, upturned around the circular rim, formed the disc.

Bema was just behind her. As she centered herself on the painted diameter of the circle Ellen saw the heavy shadows in the trees above yield liquidly before the faint gold flickerings of the little fires. The smoothness beneath her quickly grew warm. She lay with her face upright. Her arms lay alongside her torso, slightly removed, her palms up. Her legs were slightly separated and her feet tilted relaxed at an angle.

At the sound of Bema's voice Ellen's recent thoughts of other places began to dispel themselves. Bema spoke softly, almost whispering. The flow of phrases from her took on a singsong cadence, became almost a chant.

"We have heard the heart and the thoughts and the spirit, and now we will hear the body. We are one, we are *omanta*. Ellen closes her eyes and is with us. We are one together. This body is of us. This body is ours. This body is us. This body is of us, by us, for us. We will awaken this body unto us, and it will speak of us and to us as it speaks of itself. This body is ours, and we touch it with reverence. This body is us and wakes to nourish us."

Ellen heard only the voice now, no movement, but felt a brush of close warm wind at her forehead. Wind. No, it was a very light breath. Warm breath. At each side. It was single, but it was two. Her forehead felt the lightest of touching flesh. Two mouths. A warm wind coursed down from her skull to her feet and out.

"This body is of us and we take ourselves to it and nourish it. This body is our vision and we take our sight from it."

At once the faint warm breath passed across her eyes, to her eyes. Fleetingly a warm mouth encompassed each closed eye. The voice was filling her, and an awakening tremulous warmth that was not quite heat, a permeating electric filling.

"This body breathes of us and into us. This body is of us. We be one breathing one air on one earth under one sky."

The touching mouths passed across her nose and now the words befell her as a soft incessant irresistible breeze. She felt the warmth at each corner of her mouth and then it was as though the two mouths had beome one and enveloped her whole mouth. Then they/it passed on.

"Our nest is in its limbs, our milk in its breast, our strength in its arms."

Suddenly her hands were clasped warmly, strongly, her arms simultaneously raised. A hand slowly ran up and down the length of each arm, and then each was returned to its place beside her and released with such gentleness she scarcely knew the touching hands were gone. She did not see so much as feel an immense light that was not without but within her. It began as a globe of exploding yellow gold in her head. As she listened it filled her.

". . . is filled with the sun, is warmed and filled and awakened by the sun and to the sun. This body awakens to the light and speaks to and of us. It feeds to us the life we feed to it. We are one, *omanta, omanta, omanta.*"

The warmth was upon each breast and at once seemed a part of each breast, closing upon them, briefly closing upon the nipples, breathing heat upon them and passing on. Inside she became a seethe of hot golden light that now seemed both within and without her. Now it seemed an emanation both from and to her, from her even into the earth which felt a part of her. On top a phantom veil came down, the faint delicate coolness of the sky. Now the warm mouths seemed part of her flesh. They did not descend to but emerged from her stomach, each in turn, indistinguishable, covering her navel to breath into and out of it. She knew some strange and literal transmission of lifebreath through her skin, into her flesh, and from it, from it into the breathing mouths that were strangely also a part of her. Two seeming one moved across the contour and seams of her pelvic mound.

"We are one, out of one nest we come, out of this our body."

The singular touch of the lips, those lips, her lips, our lips. The touch awakened the sky that lay upon her like a veil and the warm earth beneath her. She saw in the dazzling gold light within/without that she was this: blood red between and at one with the blue and green of creation. Now the light within her took on a sound as of a mighty surf or an enormous wind strangely without force. Her body emanated to the sky and to the earth and was joined with them. She was everything, she was nothing, she was nothing and everything. Ellen was scarcely aware when the mouths caressed her feet. There was only the brush of the faint warmth on the top of them and then on the tender skin of the arch. Bema's words came to her as though from an enormous distance.

"On its feet we stand and by its feet we fall. We revere these feet. We wait to hear this body speak of us and to us and for us. It is ours. It is us. *Omanta. Omanta. Omanta.*"

She was soaring, expanding, phantasmal, flaming, melting. She was a spill of sun and heat upon the earth. She was a bubbling of sunlight up out of the earth. At her side wings lay unused. She was the blown wind, the warm flooding prolific river. She thought not with words but with knowing until in the instant that she felt the disc gently set in place with its rim at the seam of her breasts. Some words broke through the burning pulsing warmth, and in this instant she thought, *oh god it is alive everywhere.* In this instant her mind seemed to struggle trying to think something which it could not. Only later did she realize what: it could not think *I.*

Suddenly she realized it was very still. She could hear the faint popping of the little fires. The disc was gone. It was over. She had fallen asleep. They had left. No, she could hear them breathing. There was Bema's voice, murmuring, murmuring indistinctly.

Bema had moved. Or had she herself moved? Was it over? Ellen wondered whether to open her eyes. Yes, Bema must be talking to her.

"Yes, it is all done, our child."

Ellen looked about her. She wondered if it had been wrong to fall asleep. Kimo and Puana had moved too. They were sitting together, tossing chips into one of the fires. As she saw them, they grinned.

"You can dress," Bema said. "We will have nothing to tell you until tomorrow." Bema and the elder Raos were mumbling to each other as he scrutinized the disc. "Kimo and Puana will go with you. Bema stays here and pretends to talk wisely. Ha! Ellen will find a pallet in Bema's shelter. It is late. Goodnight. You will not see me until morning."

From the slight rise at the edge of the woods they could see with some perspective the concentric circles of the village streets. The shelters at this distance seemed merely darker squares upon the darkness.

Kimo and Puana walked on either side of her as they crossed the field. They walked in silence, strangely communicant in the silence. At the outer ring of shelters Puana embraced Ellen and then Kimo. Then she ducked through the canvas drop that covered the front of a plank hovel that crudely evoked the lean-to design of the traditional Lomkubee shelter.

Kimo and Ellen walked on toward the village center. They walked slowly. Only the ancient night sounds broke the stillness, the ceaseless insect twitter, the mindless rustle of restless bodies within some shelters. From one came the rasping cough of an old man, then a rattling sigh. From a distance beyond the shelters, from the village produce farm, came the uncertain crow of a rooster. A dog barked.

The stars were brittle and bright and full of motion. Ellen wondered if from them emanated the plangent thrum she heard within herself.

At the center shelter they stopped. Both looked upward again. Ellen discovered that the ground felt oddly gentle beneath her bare feet, almost yielding. A sudden breeze cast the hem of her shift against the sensitive flesh behind her knees. Within her the extravagant vibrancy she had felt in the woods had moderated. It was a persisting pulse of nourishing warmth.

Seen in the faint light a contour of Kimo's cheekbone suddenly evoked a certain concavity of Henry's face. In the wind she could taste him, could taste him in the ineluctable waft of pinereek.

They had stood for how long she did not know. She did not know when they had stopped looking at the sky and begun gazing silently at each other.

They stood a few feet apart, but Ellen felt no distance between them. Suddenly she moved her lips to say something, but no sound came out. She heard the dog bark again, its sound not distinct but seeming only a part of the inextricable oneness of the moment.

She moved her lips again without making a sound. Kimo closed his eyes as though trying hard to hear.

Ellen trembled.

Again her lips moved, and a sound emerged, hardly more than a breath.

"*Meshamantakubee.*"

She wondered if she had only imagined that Kimo had slightly nodded. His face was very still, free of common language. She could not make out the slight bruise that lingered yet around his eye. His mouth was not upturned, and yet it told her he was smiling.

She wondered if she had really made a sound. Then his head moved again, moved in a barely perceptible nod. She didn't know what to do. Kimo comprehended her uncertainty. He nodded toward the shelter.

Ellen shivered and went in.

Her eyes would close and it would be Henry turning to Kimo. They would open and it would be Kimo turning to Henry. There were no words, and it was without haste.

He delicately brushed her face with his mouth. Fingers scarcely touching threaded up from her neck through her hair, yielding to tangles. He took her nether lip whole into his mouth. It was without haste, and the yellow-gold warmth filled her again.

It was Henry, without weight, tremulous, tender.

His breath and wetness filled her breasts. She flowed out to him. It was as though there were no roof, and the sky was a veil upon the earth, chimerical, and they were without substance between, blood-red and shot with sunheat. He breathed across her stomach, and her warmth arose about him and bound them into oneness. His lips pressed weightless upon her nest and wafted down and took her, and the brittle stars rained down, singing.

She opened her eyes as his face drifted to hers, and her fingers took his hair. It was Kimo becoming Henry. He came into her without haste, and held her with his flesh close but his weight strangely nothing. They lay still for a very long time, mergent and emergent, his mouth hers, hers his, tongues annealed, inextricable, and deep within her, deep within the seethe of molten sun, a gathering, a coiling, a writhing of tenderness that would, yes, that did: galaxies exploded and her face their faces vanished from the earth and they were a hot turbulence of born life, a soaring plummeting joy unutterable and then her throat constricted in its futile toil to utter and only gasped and then gasped again and then released a coiled laugh brief and primordial to erupt and shoot through the roofless roof and out among the startled dazzling brittle stars singing in the sky.

She did not know how much time had passed when she realized that silent unsorrowful tears were pouring from her eyes. Kimo was taking them with his lips and touching her cheeks and hair with the tips of his fingers.

He was on his side, still close. When she opened her eyes she felt his fingertips pass over her brows and move on to trace with a delicate touch the terrain of her face. She was breathing profoundly but not sobbing. Now the tears stopped spilling out.

She could see the lines of the planks in the shelter ceiling. She heard a distant train whistle and now the lines looked like innumerable railroad tracks. They recalled Henry climbing aboard the train in Carterville the day he left to report. His words had been sardonic but his embrace had crushed the breath out of her. Suddenly she saw him boarding a bus with Michelle. Then they came close. Michelle looked like her. She was not looking at Henry but at the baby in her arms. Ellen audibly sighed. The end of it almost triggered another laugh, but she shivered instead.

Kimo's hand passed across her face, a fleeting shadow. She turned her head and their eyes joined. The uncurbed smile was on his face. Until now he had not uttered a word, and now he spoke for the first time.

"He is of us, too," he said.

Ellen's lips curled in between her teeth, and fleetingly she gnawed them. Her eyes let go of Kimo, and she nodded.

Kimo reached behind him and pulled a blanket over them. For a long while they lay in silence, only the faint nightstir falling upon them, and the sounds of pulse and breathing. Then he began to talk of other things.

He spoke of his plans, his new purpose. His plans were still vague, unformed, but his purpose was clear. He said that he had decided he wanted to make of himself in some way an enemy of Ellis Kelso and others like him. How, he did not know yet.

"It is not in the way of the Lomkubees to be aggressive," he said. "I respect this, but I no longer agree. Perhaps if we had been different, we would not have been murdered. I don't know what I will do. But I don't intend to let myself be beaten again without a fight."

Ellen rolled her face to his again and saw that his eyes were glittering as Cliff's had that day. She touched her hand to his forehead. He drew it down to his mouth and kissed her palm.

"He is one of us," she said. "He is."

"It is so," Kimo said.

She woke up late Sunday afternoon. She could not remember Kimo taking leave. She felt very good and very hungry. The shift she remembered dropping to the floor was hanging on a nail, her headband with it.

She found Bema outside.

"Ha! You have decided to come to life, lazy child. You are beautiful. You will have to eat without me. I will cook."

"No, no, I will," Ellen said. On a pump-up camper stove she cooked four eggs, singing as they sizzled. She wolfed them along with chunks of bread torn from the French loaf she had brought from New Orleans. She washed the food down with grapefruit juice drunk out of a clear mason jar. As she ate she could feel Bema's gaze upon her. Irresistibly she kept breaking into a grin. Once she looked up at the old matriarch's creased and lined face and it looked young and eternal to her.

"Oh, God, I feel good," Ellen said, and shivered. Then she grinned again.

"So when you are done I will tell you what the *bakana oro* seemed to say."

"I'm very curious. And after that I guess I'll have to go."

"Don't make us think of that," Bema said. "Ha! We may not allow it!"

They sat by the river again amidst the sparse grass and worn earth under the twin camphor trees. Bema talked at length about the readings of the heart, of the thoughts, of the spirit, of the body. And then she told how the elder read them together, how he brought them into a complex synthesis. And finally she summed up.

"It tells, Ellen, that in all of your aspects you have very unusual harmony with life. It does not mean that you will be spared sorrow and grief. It means that if you remember these things you need not fear sorrow and grief, because if you can only go as you are life will prevail for you. It means both that life is in harmony with you and you are in harmony with life. It is not infallible. I must tell you that. Our eyes are fallible, and sometimes do not read the markings right. Raos was amazed at the tracings you gave off in each reading and even wondered if he were not losing his perception. But he was very careful. So. Ha! We have predicted nothing, we cannot. But it seems this way: that what you truly desire, life will give you in some way, somehow, but not necessarily without pain. All that you need is to be patient and not expect to know what you cannot know, and be yourself, and grow."

It was time to go. As they crossed the field to the shelters Puana ran out to them and embraced Ellen in the way that Bema always did.

"You will be back?" Puana said.

Ellen nodded, yes.

From Bema's shelter she walked alone to the parking area, her small brown leather bag slung over her shoulder. Kimo was sitting near her car, sitting astride one of the low posts through which a single cable was strung as a border to the parking lot.

He stood as she saw him, and she paused, and their eyes held fast for a moment. She extended her hand. He took it in a firm grasp.

"You will be back?" he said. It hardly sounded like a question.

Ellen's eyes left him and swept the sky, the long shadows spilling across the field from the trees. She nodded, yes, and he released her hand. She got into her car and drove off, waving, departing as she had come, not by the public road that led to Tamerdes but by a trail through the Preserve.

It exited at Temulca's southern limit directly onto the end of the Bulomkubee Trail. Soon she swung onto the long high bridge that vaulted the river. Bearing south, she came to the Y-fork of which the left arm spun off sharply to the southeast thence to pass by the fringes of Los Nubes and lead to the seaside town of St. Teresa's. Ellen took the fork to the right.

It curved to a southwesterly bearing and then beelined toward Louisiana. A throbbing streaked red-gold color poured up into the western sky. She pressed the accelerator down. Wind whipped against her face and tore some of her dark hair out of its binder. Ellen drank in the sky color and thought, *Gorgeous.* Then she went faster still and shouted aloud into the fiercely buffeting wind: "Gorgeous!"

She laughed aloud at herself. And then spoke aloud: "By God, for her I'll do it that way!"

Soon she began passing signs giving the mileage to New Orleans.

1946

Early Fall

----4----

Now the signs were giving the mileage to St. Teresa's. It was four days later, early Thursday afternoon.

The lowslung sky blue roadster was skimming along a low-lying road bordered by marshes, bayous, salty sandy flats and reedy growth. Bait shops flew by, tackle shops and, as St. Teresa's grew closer, the tacky windows of souvenir stores. Gulls hung on the wind above them. Now and then an inscrutable pelican squatted flatfooted on some piling by the way.

John Eubanks was in the passenger seat, his white shirt and necktie fluttering and flapping incongruously in the sporty wind.

They approached the place where a fork to the left led onto the causeway system that connected the mainland with the sprawl of innumerable islands know as Los Nubes. Ellen banked around the right fork, keeping toward St. Teresa's, but pointed toward the causeway and shouted across to John Eubanks.

"Did you ever happen to get down there?"

"To Los Nubes?"

"Yes."

"No, no. I've heard about it. I've heard it's dangerous. Did you?"

"A friend and I went there once. Just to see one of the mescalino festivals."

"The what?"

"They have these celebrations all the time and they all take mescalino and everybody goes sort of looney. It's a fantastic party."

"What's mescalino?" Eubanks yelled. His feet kept grabbing at the floorboard as he tried to break down Ellen's abandoned speed.

"It's derived from mescal, only it's more so. I don't know what else they put in it. You know mescal? The Mexicans use it a lot."

Eubanks shook his head, yes. "I think I've heard of it."

Only the wind's roar was heard for awhile. Then Ellen shouted again. Her hair was blowing wildly. She had put away the headband and now wore a smart creamy linen frock. A tiny nosegay of small flower blossoms was in danger of being blown off her left breast.

"That J.P.'s place isn't far," she yelled. "How are you feeling?"

Eubanks's mouth tried valiantly but futilely to smile.

"Okay," he said. "Good. I hope the Doubloon's got my wire."

"Don't worry. They won't be crowded. If we run into trouble I know a place we can go."

"Yeah, but I asked for the, uh—I asked for the bridal suite."

"You *did?*" Ellen laughed hysterically. "Don't you know that puts us center stage?"

"Do you suppose they would tell everybody—the other guests?"

"Oh, they're probably all waiting right now to ambush us. They don't have anything to do but try to guess who's really married and who's faking it?"

The roar of the wind again. Eubanks looked very tense.

Ellen had told only one person. That morning the first thing she had gone to the "mother" of her residence house, Mrs. Whittaker, a chubby bouncy gossipy widow whom she had always liked. Ellen had felt no real need to tell anyone and wondered whether she was confiding in Mrs. Whittaker only to indulge her pleasure in knowing secret things.

"I just wanted to tell you," Ellen said, "that I'm going away for a few days."

"Home?"

"No. A trip. And when I get back Monday I'm going to be moving out."

"Oh?" Mrs. Whittaker sounded astounded. "Ellen, you're not leaving school?"

"No. I'm getting married."

"Ooooooooh!"

"We're eloping."

"Oh, how romantic. You're not even telling your family?"

"Nobody on earth will know but you—until we get back."

"Well, Ellen. So who's the lucky man? I've noticed you with—"

"John Eubanks?"

"Yes. Yes. Oh, Ellen. Well. I do wish you every happiness. He's a lucky, lucky man. He strikes me as a nice boy. Very quiet. I hear he works hard in law school. Well, Ellen, if you—"

"You'll keep it between us for the moment, won't you?"

"Oh, certainly, Ellen, I won't breathe it. John Eubanks. I'll declare. He was quite a famous athlete, wasn't he. He seems a nice boy."

As Mrs. Whittaker reiterated the phrase Ellen had realized that she herself had come to think of him in much that way. A nice boy, with something about him that called up a strain of sympathy in her. Perhaps it was the inner struggle that he had increasingly revealed as the days had gone by. Perhaps it was just his painful shyness. Or perhaps the two things were so related that they were inextricable, one thing.

Eubanks had had one public life and an inner life of an utterly different order. In the 1941 season, as a sophomore, he had emerged as the ranking star of his football team in Mississippi. The next year he had even been mentioned on some of the All-America teams. He had played both end and in the backfield, and sports writers celebrated both his versatility and his ferocity. He had been known as well for his fanatic year-round training. He abstained not only from tobacco and alcohol but from female companionship.

Then during the 1942 season he had made news of a different sort. He had been turned down first by the Marines and then by the other services to which he offered himself before his draft was due. Finally, even the draft rated him unfit for military duty for reasons that had never been spelled out in the papers. His difficulty was recurringly described as a minor but uncorrectible imperfection in his hearing. Finally, in the middle of the 1943 season, Eubanks had created a considerable stir by announcing his retirement from football. He quit the game to go to work in a defense plant near his college. The papers had duly printed a statement by his mother applauding his decision in patriotic language.

With Ellen, he had gone over it all. His disability had left him embittered at himself, feeling ashamed to be playing a game while his contemporaries were fighting battles.

"They liked to talk about my fanatic training," he said, "and I guess it was partly true. But—but I ought to tell you I didn't abstain from all the girls out of a fear of breaking training. They crowded around all right, or tried to, but I just couldn't let myself go around them. I think this was partly the other thing, that shame. Somehow it made me feel I had no right to. But I couldn't even really talk to them. You know, some of the sports writers used to say my mother helped me ward them off. Well, she has her way, but I didn't need any help. It was just me, something inside me. I would be there in the middle of a bunch of coeds and feel like the loneliest person in the world. It was torment."

His story had come out gradually. He often mentioned his mother, who had never missed one of his games, but spoke only hazily and fleetingly of his father.

"He's away a lot," he said. Finally Ellen even had to ask what work his father did. "He's a businessman," John Eubanks said. He had had a brother who had been killed accidentally as a child. Ellen had found his manners so guarded as to seem almost stuffily formal at first. As days had gone by he had begun to loosen up. Several times he had told her, "You're the first girl I've ever felt at ease with."

On Monday, the day after she got back from Temulca, he acted as though she had been away a year. Ellen sensed in him some desperate yearning that never quite articulated itself. It was to this, whatever it was, that some strong sympathy in her seemed to answer. That Monday night it took him awhile to get up the nerve even to ask where she had been.

"Oh, I just went to see some friends," she had said. He was clearly curious, even jealous, but didn't pursue the matter. Later that night he had for the first time reached to take her hand. He held it briefly just before saying goodnight.

Tuesday he had asked her to have lunch with him in a campus sandwich shop and that evening took her to supper, talking about himself with an openness he had not before achieved. Wednesday, taking an oblique tack, he had brought up the subject of marriage.

"The reason I've been telling you all this is, uh, I just think you have a right to know if, uh, when—when I ask you if you would marry me."

She had fallen silent, waiting, and soon he went on.

"Do you think—knowing it all, do you think, uh, that you might?"

"Well, I'd never answer a question like that unless it were actually asked," Ellen had said.

He thought about that and said, "I see what you mean. Well, let me ask you and get it over with. Would you marry me?"

"There are things you don't know about me," Ellen said.

"I think I know enough," he said.

"I have a certain feeling about getting married," Ellen said. He waited for her to go on, fretting with the crease of his pants as he did. "I don't think I should try to answer you until you know about it."

"Well," he said. "Can't you tell me?"

"I have the feeling that when two people get married they shouldn't wait. They should decide and go ahead and do it without waiting."

"Well, I don't see anything wrong with that. It could be worked out. We both graduate next June, and—"

"If I were going to get married I wouldn't wait that long. It wouldn't make any sense to me."

"Well, tell me what would make sense."

"The only thing that would make sense to me would be to do it right away."

"Well, we could work it out if—I mean as soon as arrangements could be—or whatever you do."

"Well," Ellen said, "I don't think you feel the way I do, so I don't think I'd better answer."

"I'm sure I feel the way you do," he said. "I just don't know how to put it. Whatever you want I would want."

"If I said yes, then I would want us to get married tomorrow."

"*Tomorrow?*"

"I wouldn't want to wait at all."

"But tomorrow?"

"It's very simple. It can be done fast in our state. There's a justice of the peace over at St. Teresa's who marries people all the time on five minutes notice."

"Tomorrow," he said. "I'm not even sure mother could get there by tomorrow. In fact, I haven't even told her about—I haven't even told her I was thinking about this."

"Well, that's another thing," Ellen said. "I wouldn't want any-body at my wedding except me and the person I marry. I don't like weddings as social events. So maybe you just don't feel enough like I do."

He had stood up and passed a shaking hand over a perplexed face that again and again manifested some want of symmetry she couldn't quite define. He took a pace away from the stone bench on which they had been sitting. Suddenly he shook his head as though clearing it.

"Well, why not," he said. "Why not. Tomorrow's fine with me. So what's your answer?"

"My answer's yes," Ellen said.

Eubanks had awkwardly touched her mouth with his for the first time. His face was perspiring heavily. His skin felt chill.

Ellen felt the small burning inside her. She very clearly focused a thought into words: *I am prepared to give whatever he asks in exchange.*

Something in his face retreated, and she realized she did not know what it might be.

The J.P. had not needed any notice at all. He stamped the license, pocketed the change at a signal from her. He slipped off his khaki windbreaker and slipped into a shiny black suit jacket. He called forth his skinny wife and a jovial fat brownskinned woman from the back of his house to act as witnesses.

Now as Ellen Worth Eubanks pulled away with her wedded husband John beside her, those three stood in the J.P.'s sand and gravel yard and waved them onward.

"Don't overdo," the brownskinned woman yelled out.

"Go ahead and overdo," the J.P. yelled.

The air was full of gulls, the beaches were growing wider. Cottages by the road or beach popped up more frequently. The wind was salty. Fat clouds sped overhead. A high wind current would likely push them northwesterly. By midafternoon these or some like them would probably dump rain around McClung.

Ellen thought of the rain that had spankled down on the skylight panes the moment she hurled the clay head of Henry against the wall where it was still impaled on the wall hook staring blankly across the room.

She glanced at and examined the face of her—of John Eubanks: the word husband did not want to form itself in her thoughts. He was sitting leaning against his door, studying her.

"Now that we're married, uh, could I ask you to slow down some?" He smiled a downturned smile. He looked relieved but still somewhat apprehensive. Ellen laughed and responded. She let the car coast down to an easy breezy speed.

"It's a gorgeous day," she said, glancing over. Eubanks peered up at the sky as though expecting rain. Ellen said, "They'll blow over in a bit."

"Have you been over here much?" he asked.

"Now and then," Ellen said. "My family has a place here."

Soon they passed a hook of sandy land on which stood a single small cottage almost at its point. The cottage overlooked water at its front and sides, its barren almost nondescript back to the road. It was more or less an oversized shack of plank, and was owned—or had been—by the New Orleans dealer from whom Henry had bought his motorcycle when he first came there at the start of this year. The dealer Emile had liked Henry and so lent him the cottage. They had roared over this same road with her clutched behind him.

Inside the shack was a single good room with walls of burnt pine. The time was beautiful, too chilly to swim but clear, a time of shimmering colors ever-changing in the water. She had fallen for a moment into a blue mood. It had seemed so lovely she had grown sad that it would end. Insane. Henry had come up behind her and rubbed her neck. *Let's go back to bed*, he had said. *We just got up*, she had said. *Yes, but the only absolutely sure way I can make you laugh is to make you come*, he had said. An irrepressible burst of ribald laughter had erupted out of her. Five or six times before summer they had come back at some ridiculously cheap rate. Percy Ensley and Florence had come down to meet them there. Henry had said, *A little incest would improve the moral tone of the place.* That night when her throat had constricted and forced out that inevitable gasping laugh, Percy had said, *What's so goddam funny over there?* And Henry had said, *Only my lovemaking. But it's improving. Usually she hisses.* They had all gotten up and sat up all night and watched the first light fall over the sea.

John Eubanks pointed at the cottage as it receded.

"Who would ruin a piece of real estate like that by building such a dump?"

They passed a shack on the landside of the road. A weather-beaten sign in the yard advertised the fortune teller named Annamelio.

"Don't you think we had better get our fortunes told?" Ellen said.

"Do you believe in that stuff?"

"It depends on the fortune teller. Annamelio's very good. She's from Los Nubes."

"Well, maybe."

"One day while we're here?"

"I'll go with you, anyway."

Ellen grinned impishly. "You're not afraid to know your future?"

"The future's what you make it."

"Annamelio wouldn't agree."

"I take it you've been to her."

"Yes."

"Did she tell you about our getting married?"

"In a way."

"How?"

"She said I would be going on an unexpected journey."

At a glance she saw John Eubanks shaking his head, soberly scoffing. She smiled to herself. She thought, *Mr. Eubanks.*

Doubloon's Inn was named for a long dead man who had in turn been named for the coin. It was known as the biggest and best of St. Teresa's seasonal hotels and lodgings. It was a drafty old place within, and all of its exterior rooms opened onto the galleries that encircled the main structure at each level. It faced the water from broad but mostly barren grounds, and it commanded the widest beach of the shore.

Their registration passed smoothly enough. The desk clerk displayed no more than a friendly smirk when John Eubanks asked for the suite that he had wired about. He briskly walked out with the porter to get the bags. When they came back Ellen was standing at the base of the stairway. The porter was grappling with Mr. Eubanks's two large suitcases while clutching her small leather grip under an arm.

"Was, uh, was this all we had?" her—the word came hard—husband asked.

"Believe so," Ellen said. She felt faintly absurd at the contrast in their luggage. She thought, *He's worried that the porter will think something.*

She thought the room looked beautiful. It was full of light. It commanded a corner of the third floor. The management had put bright bouquets on three of the tables. On one of them stood a large silver bucket with a huge bottle of champagne packed into the ice.

The room was large though not literally a suite. It had a distinct dining nook and, just outside the bath, a semi-enclosed dressing area.

John Eubanks tipped the porter extravagantly. As the door clicked shut Eubanks peered about the room with close scrutiny. He looked at everything except the big high tester bed.

"It's lovely," Ellen said.

"Not bad," he said. Then he added, "Well, Mrs. Eubanks, here we are."

"Yep," she said. She rubbed the tips of her fingers across the icy moisture of the champagne bucket. "It was nice of them," she said.

"You know," he said, "I can't imagine I'll ever have a better time to celebrate. Do you think I should give in and at least drink a toast to the bride?"

"And the bridegroom?"

"What do you think?"

"It's up to you."

"Well." His voice sounded brighter than his wrinkled brow looked. "Maybe later. First, I think we ought to get in a good swim while the sun's good. Damn, it's been a long time since I had a good swim. The beach looks great, don't you think?"

He was standing at the window, one of the floor-to-ceiling windows at the front of the room. Ellen was still musing at the silver bucket. She walked over to his side. His hands were stuck in his hip pockets. She put her right arm across his shoulder, grasping his right arm.

"It really is lovely," she said.

"But maybe you're not in a mood for a swim," he said. He turned in a way that dislodged her hand.

"No, no, I'd love it," Ellen said. "Let's do." In two steps she was out of her white cross-strap sandals. By the time she reached a chair by the vanity her dress was over her head and off. In a singular motion she peeled her underpants down and off her feet. Thus she stood stitchless when John Eubanks turned about from the window.

He looked startled, flustered, and all but averted his gaze. Quickly he strode around the bed and busied himself with the unsnapping of his bags.

"I'll unpack while you go on and change," he said.

Ellen by then stood beside him fishing her pale yellow swimsuit out of her grip. Eubanks buried his head in one of his open bags as though diligently searching for something. Ellen walked to the center of the room and stepped into briefs cut trimly on the European model. She fitted the bra over her arms and was behind Eubanks again. When she spoke she felt him jump.

"Mr. Eubanks, how about snapping this for me?" she said.

"Oh," he said. "Yes. Let me see." He fumbled for a long while but got the bra snapped at last. Then he turned back to his suitcase. Ellen felt almost ready to laugh aloud at his consternation. Then that feeling of sympathy welled up. She approached the bed and leaped onto it, landing backwards. She began raising and lowering her out-stretched legs.

"Ah, here it is," he said. Now he was standing. He held his trunks up for display, proof. He watched her leg movements for a second. "That's great for the diaphragm," he said. Then he strode toward the bathroom. He said, "I'll only be a sec."

Ellen heard the bathroom door close. She squinched her eyes shut and stretched her arms out far and sighed a deep groaning sigh. Then she popped her eyes wide open and stared at the tester over the bridal bed. Within its crocheted pattern she saw a depiction of ribald cherubs, barely discernible, but suggestively at play in a field. Ellen whooped a laugh up into the canopy. She raised her legs toward the cherubs, extending them almost to the canopy as she rolled up onto her shoulders. Then she let herself collapse. She thought, *I just don't believe it.* And laughed again.

"What was so funny?" Her—her Mr. Eubanks was out now in navy blue trunks. His body was broad but not beefy. He had a well conditioned look. He seemed relieved. "What was so funny?" he said again.

"Everything, everything," Ellen said. "I just felt good. Ready?"

"Towels, we'll need towels," he said.

He was a good swimmer. Powerful but not playful. He swam as though the water were a foe. Ellen led him out a great distance at first, but when she tried to tease him into play, skeeting water in his face, he seemed leashed. When she fled him he gave chase, but when she stopped and turned, so did he, skeeting water at her but never engaging.

She floated on her back and enjoyed listening to herself breathe. The clouds had blown away, and the sun was good. The water was cool but felt delicious to her. He was floating, too, with some look of consternation now and again coming upon his face: two not quite vertical lines between his eyes. She thought that his face, with its wet sheen over the emergent shadow of his shaved but heavy beard, was taking on a beautiful look. But it vanished, retreating somehow, when she called over to him.

"Do you like swimming in ice cold water?" she said.

"It's not my favorite," he said.

"Too bad. At home we'll swim in the big spring most of the time. It's like ice."

"You mean your father's house?"

"It's mine, too. I told you I'd die there. Now so will you, I guess."

"You mean I've got no choice?"

"Sure you have," she said, skeeting water toward him. "I'm the one who doesn't have any."

Ellen gasped down a great breath and dove deep under the water. Slowly she breasted toward the shore. She swam until her lungs began to pound. She thought, *four minutes.* She surfaced and looked about. Her—her Mr. Eubanks's head was darting about in all directions. Now she was perhaps sixty yards from him. She yelled shrilly.

"Come on in, the water's fine!"

His face jerked toward her, incredulous. Now on the surface she raced to the beach. She was sitting, catching her breath, when he came dripping out of the water.

"You really scared the hell out of me," he said.

Ellen kept her face expressionless. "You mean you missed me?"

"Well, I thought you had drowned."

"But I told you I was a good swimmer."

"Good swimmer, hell, you're a fish."

"My mother is a fish."

"What?" He was sitting down at a short distance, his breath heaving.

"Faulkner."

John Eubanks shook his head in bewilderment. He said, "I think I've had enough."

Ellen hopped up, stropping her shoulders with a towel and taking a second towel to her—her Mr. Eubanks. She placed it about his neck with a squeeze of his upper muscles. He grabbed its ends and began running it back and forth where her hands had been.

"Well, this was great," he said. "I also think that celebration is at last in order for me. Don't you? Twenty-four years on the wagon isn't a bad record, is it?"

"Not bad at all," Ellen said. "Around McClung some kids start drinking around fourteen or fifteen. My brothers loved beer when they were thirteen."

John Eubanks's face clouded over. He said, "Now every time I think of your brothers I get that feeling again. Why couldn't it have been me instead of them? Or instead of anybody? Or at least why couldn't I have been there to take a chance, too?"

As he spoke, without turning about, Ellen studied the back of his head. She ran her fingers through his sodden hair. She said, "Hey! It's a *happy* day. Let's go toast it."

Three gulls swooped past them as they crossed the highway. The birds suddenly banked down and then darted out across the vivid blue sky over the water, screaming out into the salty air. Up the broad sidewalk they saw the approach of what seemed like hundreds of girls, all wearing identical sweat suits, shepherded by nuns, a chattery mob.

"They're from St. Teresa's School," Ellen said. "The sisters march them down for a swim every good day. We'll have to remember to get to the beach before them—or after. Once they're here, all is lost—for us heathens."

John Eubanks looked thoughtful. He said, "Did you ever hear of the two guys at the bar, and one of them asks the bartender, 'How tall is a penguin?' And the bartender shows him, 'About this tall.' And the other guy says, 'I told you that was a nun we ran over.' "

Ellen laughed riotously not because she was that taken with the story but because it was the first joke he had ever tried to tell her.

"Oh, yes," he went on, "the two guys were drunk. My father told me that a long time ago. Before he started going away so much. I didn't really get it until a long time later. But when he told it to me I laughed until I cried almost."

In their room, he went immediately to the bath to take off his trunks, and to shower. He showered so long she had almost dozed off. He emerged scrubbed and combed and even wearing his tie.

"Well, I'll wait for you before we pop the cork," he said. In less than a minute she rinsed and dried and slipped on flannel slacks and a paisley shirt whose tails she tied at her waist.

So he popped and poured. Almost at the first sip he seemed unaccountably different. He did not in fact sip but drank down the first glass like water.

"Hey! This is great!" he said. "Why did mother keep telling me it was all awful?"

Ellen laughed sympathetically. Later she felt he had said more or less the same identical words perhaps a hundred times or so. She drank two glasses of the champagne with him but left untouched the third that he poured. He drank the second two as fast as the first. On his fourth he began laughing without cause. She laughed in response. Then he seemed to laugh at her laughter. Then he abruptly ceased, and creases appeared across his forehead.

"What was that you said about a fish?" he said.

"It was you that said I was a fish," Ellen said, smiling.

"And then you said something."

"What did I say?"

"I've got it on the tip of my tongue, but—"

Ellen laughed at this, but then his face took on an odd cloud.

"What are you laughing at?" he said.

"Everything," she said.

He guffawed. "That's right, everything, everything."

He put off the idea of eating until he had finished the big bottle. It was then eight. He seemed steady on his feet as they went downstairs, but his voice grew louder. It reverberated through the sparsely populated dining room when he promptly ordered another bottle of champagne.

They sat at a table for two. It was decorated with a candle in a squat old liqueur bottle with a chocolate-colored label. An odd sweet smile or half-smile fixed itself on his mouth to remain regardless of what she or he was saying. He said less and less.

During his long silences, Ellen chattered on, good-naturedly (but with a clearing sense of futility) about the locale, the day, the region, the state, St. Teresa's School, her new car, the apartment her hall mother had told her about, the part of her house that they could turn into a more or less private apartment, the fortune teller Annamelio, T.C. Horris and the McClung *Mirror*, the governor of the state Eugene Earley who had been a congressman before deciding to take over the governorship and who would be a congressman again afterward from the district that he more or less owned, the Famous First, which included McClung.

"Politics," he said. "Maybe that's what I like."

"You think you'll go into politics?"

"What was that you said about fish?"

Not long before ten the waiter came over to remind them the kitchen would shortly be closed.

"Then we'd better order," Ellen said.

"Would you like a cocktail?" the waiter said.

"I don't think so," Ellen said. "We'll just order. Why don't you just bring us both trout amandine."

"Wait a minute," John Eubanks said. He still wore the odd little smile. "This is a special thing, so why don't we have the cocktail. I'll have one, waiter."

"What would you like?"

"A cocktail, a cocktail. Isn't that what you said?"

"There are many, many kinds of cocktails."

"Well, bring me whatever you think I would like."

Shortly a whisky sour in a tall narrow glass appeared before John Eubanks. He took an exploratory sip.

"Hey! This is even better," he said. His eyes had lost focus, he seemed to be looking around either side of her. "Why did my mother keep telling me all this stuff was awful? Hey! You're Mrs. Eubanks now. Ellen Mrs. Eubanks." He drained the whisky sour in a series of gulps. "What was that you said about a fish? That's what I need to know."

"I said my mother is a fish."

"Your mother is a fish?"

"It's just a line, Mr. Eubanks." Ellen laughed, half-despairing.

"Hey! That's the first time you said that."

"It's never too late," Ellen said.

Their waiter slid the plates of trout before them. In a moment her Mr. Eubanks suddenly discovered his as though it had been delivered by miracle. Then his eyes struggled to fix upon her. They were expanding and contracting in the candlelight. He grinned wetly down at the plate and said, "My mother?" Inordinate laughter came out of him, volcanic. His voice was collapsing. "No, you are the fish, you are my fish. That's what I said. You said my fish is my mother."

An expression of immense and impenetrable perplexity suddenly contracted his face. Then, almost as though it had been severed from the rest of him, his face, his head, fell forward directly into the beautiful untouched golden trout. Ellen called for the check and a porter.

At 10:30 with the help of the aged night porter she walked him up the stairs from the dining room. In the climb he tried to help, with the movements of a faltering automaton. But as she opened their door, his exertions ended. He pitched forward. Only the grasp of the old porter prevented a bad fall.

Together she and the porter worked him onto the bed. Ellen gave the porter a five dollar bill.

"Thank you, mam," he said. He paused and added: "This ain't the first time a man's had a little too much on his marrying night." Ellen smiled, and he went on: "Fact, I passed out cold as dead just after we traipsed out the church." He started to go then, but turned back again. "What I been wishing ever since is that I had passed out dead before I went into that church." He chuckled. He said, "Miss, you can't win 'em all." Then he vanished, closing the door inaudibly behind him.

So she undressed her Mr. Eubanks, whose eyes seemed tightly sealed. She neatly hung up his clothes, piece by piece: his jacket, his shirt, his tie. She was emptying the pockets of his trousers to put these too on a hanger when suddenly she hardly knew whether to laugh or weep.

Along with a mass of change, one pocket contained a fresh packet of condoms tightly wrapped in unbroken cellophane. The notion of a rubber contraceptive had always brought Ellen mingled feelings of distaste and amusement. Like her, Henry had disdained them on mystical grounds. Now she was suddenly imagining John Eubanks scurrying around on Wednesday night—or maybe even Thursday morning—searching for a drugstore with an acceptably understanding face that he would order from. But what did she know? Maybe he bought them all the time. Now she did laugh, calling to mind Henry's tales of drunk officers who would fill rubbers with water and leave them on the bunks of others to be—with luck —exploded by a sudden grasp to remove it. Well. Who knew? Maybe he was a secret swordsman. Dragooned into marriage. *I need some condoms, please, I'm going on my honeymoon. Oh, I guess three will do it.*

Ellen returned the condoms, change, keys, wallet, handkerchief, and short comb to his pants pockets and hung the trousers by the beltline on the top corner of the closet door. She left untouched on the bureau the new pair of maroon pajamas that he had left out as he unpacked.

It had happened to him so fast, so smoothly, with so little fuss that it seemed now that it couldn't really have happened at all.

She never went to sleep—or even felt like sleeping.

At dawn Friday Ellen thought, *Wouldn't it be funny if the thing I didn't know was that I wouldn't be asked to give anything. Ever.*

Their room faced east-southeast, so the tall spacious windows caught the very first light. With her head turned on her pillow Ellen saw it come.

She lay at a wide sprawl over the right half of the bed. Her Mr. Eubanks lay clutching a thin blanket about him. He was doubled up in a stuporous sleep at the far left.

At seeing the first trace of a new day come without the transition of some moment of sleep, Ellen felt a peculiar weary elation. She had passed the night vividly awake. Now as she saw the window grow gray she felt a sharp hunger for coffee. She did not know what time it was. She guessed 5:30 or so. Nothing would be open downstairs.

The sound of his breathing was regular but still slightly labored. It was punctuated by occasional snorts and grunts. His right forearm was pressed to the side of his face and its hand clasped the back of his skull.

Now she got out of bed and walked to the window just before the sun burst over the rim of the earth. It came exploding an infinitude of deep oranges and blood reds and silver/black speckles across the waters. She slipped out onto the gallery in front. With her elbows propped on the bannister she watched until the sun had risen to its full diameter. The startling beauty of the vista seemed to sweep her back a million years. She thought, *This earth, this garden. How can we have this and give so much of our lives to pain?*

On the road below she heard a crunch, a screech: a milk delivery truck had run up over the curbing, its driver disconcerted by the sight of her. Suddenly she realized she was naked. He was still staring. She waved and fled into the room. Maybe now they would have coffee made downstairs.

The lobby was very still, the coffee shop unlit. The clerk behind the desk, a young man, said nothing would be ready until seven. It was 6:10.

"You a guest here?" he asked.

"Room 301," Ellen said.

"Oh, the newlyweds!"

"I guess the word travels," she said.

"Well, as a wedding present I could let you have a cup out of my thermos. Could you use that? No bad germs. You mind going in stealing a cup off of one of those tables?"

Carefully Ellen climbed the stairs with the brimming cup. She waited until she was back on the gallery before sipping it. The coffee was strong, rich with chicory, delicious. After it she undressed again and flopped back on the bed and went to sleep, sprawled on top of the cover.

She woke up not so much to a sound that he made as a certain jerky movement. It was hours later, the room was dancing with bright midmorning light. Still wrapped in covers he had raised his head and glanced back and forth from her to the bureau, from there to the entrance of the dressing room, the bath. His expression looked urgent, almost desperate. He was swallowing repeatedly, or trying to.

Suddenly Ellen divined his dilemma. She sprang across the room and snatched his robe off a hook on the bathroom door. As she brought it to him, he did not meet her eyes. Nor did he move while she stood before him. She flung herself back to her side of the bed. Then Eubanks, with panicky swiftness, emerged from under his cover into the covering of the robe. With urgent strides he went to the bathroom.

Ellen could hear him being sick. He remained there for a long time. Finally the shower began running. When he emerged Ellen was already dressed. She had on white ducks and the paisley shirt she had worn the night before, again knotted at her midriff. Then she went into the bath and spent perhaps half a minute. When she came out he was already dressed. He was standing at one of the front windows overlooking the beach.

"Good morning," she said brightly. Eubanks glanced over his shoulder at her. He responded in the same words but with a heavy puzzled voice. Abruptly he sat himself down in a rattan chair, sprawling back. Ellen said, "You feel better?"

"I think so," he said. "Wonder what got me sick?"

"Maybe it was something you ate," she said. Her voice was satirical but not sarcastic.

John Eubanks stared at the ceiling. "I have the feeling that things didn't go right last night."

"They went fine," Ellen said. She sprawled into a nearby chair that also flanked one of the small tables still bearing a gift bouquet from the management.

"They *did*?" he said.

"Sure," Ellen said.

"Everything?"

"Everything was fine. Is something the matter?"

"I don't know, I, uh, have the funny feeling I didn't, uh, that— What could I have eaten that, uh—you know." Creases of bewilderment filled his face.

Ellen sensed his odd blankness of memory but decided not to mention it. She would wait. "Shall we get some breakfast?" she said.

"Well, yes," he said, "but do you mind waiting a minute? Maybe we could walk and get a little air first. Isn't it sort of warm in here?"

The beachside walk was breezy, the air full of bright gull cries, the sun benign, the sky sparsely dappled. His color grew even. He drank gluttonously from a public fountain. Several times he seemed on the verge of saying something that he suppressed. Then finally he asked, blurting.

"What did we have for dinner?"

"Oh, you're teasing me," Ellen said.

Eubanks stopped. He took a seat on one of the green slat benches that were spaced along the beachfront walk. Ellen stood close by and propped a foot on the bench.

"No, I'm not," he said. "I can't remember eating dinner."

Light traffic wheezed by. Ellen thought for a moment.

"Trout amandine," she said.

"Oh?" His facial color was wavering again. "Did, uh, did we

—Where did we eat? I wonder why the hell I don't remember."

"Oh, it's probably just all the excitement," Ellen said. "We ate in the hotel. We'll find another place tonight, okay?"

"Excitement?'"

"I only mean getting married and everything. There's been an awful lot in a short time."

"I guess so. And you're sure everything went okay last night?"

"Sure it did. It was fine. For me. Were you unhappy about anything?" His hand was in his pants pocket. Ellen thought of the contents.

"No," he said. "Nothing specific. It's just that I have the feeling that—To tell the truth, I don't remember *anything*. Are you sure it was all right?"

"I don't have any complaint," she said. "I'm not sure I know what you're driving at."

"Well, I'm not really driving at anything. I'm just trying to remember. I, uh, I'm just glad everything was okay. I have the feeling I was a—"

"Oh, forget it. I imagine the nausea has just upset you."

"Well, did I—was I—What I mean is, did I take precautions?" Ellen's laughter rang up amidst the gull cries.

"Mr. Eubanks," she said, "last night you didn't seem to have a worry in the world. So why worry today." His face was a perplexed mix of alarm and relief.

"Now I've started thinking about calling mother," he said. "She's going to be hurt if I put off telling her too long. When are you going to call your family?"

"I thought when we get back Monday."

"Monday," he said. Ellen thought he might secretly be counting off the coming days as a sequence of torments. But perhaps—

Breakfast seemed to restore him. Before the swim they took a long walk to the southern edge of St. Teresa's, to the harbor where most of the shrimp fleet was out. Ellen bought an orange from a vendor. She peeled it with her fingers and offered her Mr. Eubanks half the sections. He ate them singly. She devoured her half in two enormous juicy chewings, remembering when she and Henry had sat there eating an orange and she had told him how she hoped it would be.

As before, he swam out with her, but he returned almost at once to the beach. There he lay stomach down in the vivid sun while Ellen played on. She plunged and surfaced like a manatee, and floated. Slowly she drifted on her back to a distance quite far out.

She was lying facing the open water when she saw, for one quick rippling, the fin of a shark. It seemed headed not toward her but athwart her line of vision. Then she saw a second, a flash, and mercurial ripples. They seemed to be bearing toward some point far to her left.

But her heart pounded. She began swimming on her back at a furious stroke and a fast kick, heading for the beach. She kept her eyes on the suspicious water but saw nothing more until she had reached a point where she thought she could touch bottom.

Then she saw another flash of fin but was confused about the direction it indicated. She began kicking and stroking with new fury, trying to thrash the water violently as she fled. She was still stroking when her hand suddenly dragged into the sand.

Ellen scrambled to her feet and sprinted with high splashing steps across the broad space of very shallow water to the beach. She threw herself onto her stomach into the hot sand gasping for breath, eyes closed. She began to laugh hysterically but quickly ceased. She opened her eyes and peered over at John Eubanks. His face looked very peaceful. He was sound asleep.

Beyond him, perhaps ten yards away, a darkly tanned couple with thick black hair were dozing on a blanket, face to face in a loose embrace. They looked perhaps thirty-five. The sight of them called up some recollection of the beach or rocks she had seen on Capri as a child. For the first time she had seen or for the first time noticed old people displaying gestures of affection like those of the young. Her mother had said, *Oh, yes, Ellen, us old folks love each other, too. If we didn't you wouldn't be here.* And she had said, *Why not?* And her mother had said, *Why not? Because your Papa's seed wouldn't have fertilized the little egg that you once were. That's why not.* And she had burst into wild giggles at the thought of herself as an egg. She had finally said, *Humpty Dumpty is an egg.* And her mother had said, *Yes, and a walnut, too.* Ellen had caught on and giggled insanely again. On Capri her Papa had used the word shark, and she had not known what it meant. He had said, *It's a mean fish that will eat you up. It's kind of like a banker.* Now Ellen thought of the racing fins and shivered and loved the gritty-wet feel of the sand against her thighs and belly and face. Her big toes moved back and forth digging two short arcs in the beach, as long ago she had seen Corinne Fielding do. She—they—would have to go see Mark and Corinne in Paris.

At dawn Saturday she thought, *Maybe what I also didn't know was that the sympathy I felt was not sympathy but pity.*

She had slept a few hours, waking up after a plunging dream.

She had evidently dived from the swaying, impossibly tiny, upper-most branches of a tall tree, had dived toward what must have been the big spring but which turned into the vast open mouth of a fish, perhaps a catfish.

She woke up in darkness, her heart violently thumping. As it subsided, she heard the snorts and grunts of her Mr. Eubanks, again deep in a stuporous sleep. It had grown cooler during the night, and she was under a sheet. When the first light came she slipped her oversized navy blue sweater over her head and issued up a message of gratitude that she had thought to buy a thermos and have it filled with coffee for the room.

From the gallery she saw up the beach indistinctly the slender forms of two lovers joined standing in an interminable kiss. She could taste Henry. They were only a darker gray in the dawn's first gray. Small wisps of steam curled up from the coffee in the bright red cup whose aluminum sent heat directly into her thumb and fingers. She set the cup on the gallery bannister. She thought, *Or did I feel contempt? Do I? Yes, some. But pity, too. Pity.*

Low fog was thickening over the channel. From far away came the hoarse measured hoot of the warning horn, and the erratic and oddly merry clang of buoy bells. Even after the sun was up the dawn stayed the shade of first gray. A light drizzle began to fall on the street below, a misting rain that blew onto the gallery and in a million tiny glistening droplets across the front of her big sweater and over her face and hair.

The milk truck approached and passed, and the driver who had seen her naked the morning before looked up with a face that she thought must be Cajun. She waved with a grin, and he laughed and waved back. He honked his high-pitched horn—*toot tutu toot toot*—and rolled on. Ellen felt she had made a friend.

She drained the now tepid remains of her coffee and went back to their small dining area to pour another from the thermos. John Eubanks's hands were clasping the pillow over his head.

Their second night had started out with a certain resemblance to the first. Ellen again had been puzzled by the almost instant transformation that had come over Eubanks after he had taken only a small amount to drink. He had begun in late afternoon when they had dressed and decided to get some refreshments at the small tables of the open air cafe on one side of the ground floor gallery.

Before they sat down he had spoken of having iced tea but had changed his mind when the waiter—hearing him complain of feeling hot from his sunburn—suggested, "How 'bout a cold beer to cool off?" So she had had one with him, and had even ordered a second, knowing she wouldn't finish it. He had finished it, however.

"It's sort of bitter," he said, "but it—I remember my father said cold beer is the best thing after you've been drinking the night before." Then he had looked thoughtful and said, "You know, when I call mother it'll be just as well if we don't mention that—well, that I've broken the vow. She always said she'd rather see me dead than have me pick up a drink." After he had downed the last of her second beer he had begun studying the drink list. He said, "Whisky sour— that sounds kind of good. Are they actually sour?"

Later he had turned aside her suggestion that they try another restaurant. They went again to the dining room in the inn. It was much busier with the Friday night contingent of a usually larger weekend crowd arriving.

By ten, Eubanks's mouth had taken on that same fixed irrelevant smile. Ellen had the feeling she was living through a film of the previous night, except that this time she got their orders in early so that they would have more time to eat.

Eubanks had wolfed down a steak and afterward complained of being full. A waiter, overhearing this, said, "A crème de menthe frappé'll fix you up." Cliff buying frappés for Jack Jackson, Tom Pickett, and her at the Lafite in New Orleans back then—ages.

After he had taken his first sip of the icy green liqueur, Eubanks could be heard throughout the room. "Hey! Mrs. Eubanks! It's like magic. It's like starting over again!"

Then he had had three, and his eyes lost all focus. Ellen said, "Why don't we go up to the room, I'm kind of tired." And her Mr. Eubanks had seemed to be mulling this when suddenly a loud unfamiliar voice exploded toward them from the dining room doorway into the lobby.

"Eubanks!" it said. "Johnny Eubanks!"

The loud drunken voice had belonged to an old teammate named Billy Brism, a boyish looking man with wavy blond hair, a florid face, and the beginning of a premature belly. He had obstreperously barged amidst the tables of the dining room towing with him, almost dragging, a petite woman with purplish hair and precise lipstick and with anger lines that flickered up between her eyes even when she smiled. She, whom Brism called Mimi, seemed in her mid-twenties and was packed into a snug satin dress of some color like burgundy, an iridescent frock.

Eubanks had lurched to his feet at their approach. Ellen thought it the first dramatic show of emotion she had ever seen him display.

The two men had boisterously exchanged greetings while Billy Brism's companion stood for a moment ignored, her face guarded by a sardonic smirk. Watching the two, Ellen thought, *Good ol' boys.*

Yet, in a way, she almost welcomed the signs of vitality that the moment seemed to awaken in Eubanks. This feeling passed quickly. Billy Brism had hardly sat down before she began to dread the sight of him. He was full of braggadocio: Yes, he was making it, getting well, cleaning up. He had latched onto an automobile dealership, and was all but rolling in money, yes, and he told of it in a voice that the entire dining room could share. In fact, he had just gone over from Jackson to New Orleans for a dealers convention and there had picked up Mimi.

"Man, we got to having such a time we just decided to up and come over here and have a convention all our own," Brism said, grabbing Mimi behind the neck as he might have a dog. He went on, "Now tell me where you got that pretty little thing."

Brism was leering at her, his mouth curled into a grin that he no doubt took to be charming. Ellen began studying the candle on the table. Her Mr. Eubanks, with that look of dazed or glazed concentration, and wearing that waxy smile, was listening but not answering. And while Billy Brism went on, Ellen tried to engage Mimi, who sat with her head tilted in some exasperation toward her escort.

"Have you been here before?" Ellen said.

"Uh-uh. I just work New Orleans," Mimi said. She pronounced it New Or-leens. Mimi examined Ellen's ringless left hand. She said, "You work this joint?"

Ellen had laughed. She said, "No, we're just staying here. John and I just got married."

Mimi looked at her hand again. She said, "Uh-huh. This John?"

Eubanks had incoherently tried to explain to his old teammate that he had met Ellen in New Orleans. But now Brism wasn't listening at all to what in any event was never made clear. Right after they had come over, he had introduced Eubanks to a drink called a stingeree. And Ellen had watched as the glazed face grew almost paralyzed.

John Eubanks's grin had widened and remained fixed, still. His eyes had begun to roll. Once again he began saying, "I don't know why my mother told me all this was awful."

After awhile Brism had drawn Mimi's chair close to his. He began fumbling with her breasts. She would laugh, her mouth sharply in conflict with the flickering anger lines.

"Billy, honey, not right here in front of God and everybody," Mimi said again and again.

Ellen wondered if she had said it a million times. John Eubanks seemed to be witnessing what was going on but showed no sign of comprehending. Mostly he just stared, grinning emptily at Brism.

Brism finally had begun suggesting a get-together in his room. "Johnny, let's all go up to my room and have a little party."

"Good idea," Eubanks said. "Good idea." But he made no move to rise.

"I'm too tired," Ellen said. Brism looked at her in annoyance. Then his mouth turned up again in his curly smile.

"Aw, come on," he said. "Mimi'll teach you tricks you've never even heard of over here in the sticks."

Suddenly Ellen had thought of Ernie Pack the deputy and of the joke his father had told him.

Brism turned from Ellen to Mimi and pointed at his companion's mouth. "After all," he said, grinning, "she's French." He chortled, and a fleck of spittle flew from his tongue toward the candle.

"*Merde*," Ellen said.

John Eubanks now was staring at Mimi; his eyes seemed to peer around either side of her.

"Good idea," he said.

"Great!" Brism shouted.

Brism got to his feet. Her Mr. Eubanks had started to rise.

"What does this John like?" Mimi asked her.

"Football," Ellen said drily.

Mimi burst into a scream of laughter just as John Eubanks's face fell precipitately downward onto the table.

The impact overturned several glasses and knocked the candle out of the squat liqueur bottle with the chocolate label.

When John Eubanks woke up Ellen was in the bathroom throwing up. As she emerged he half-raised from the bed and spoke in a hoarse whisper.

"You, too," he said. Then, as before, he sneaked into his robe and rushed for the bath himself.

Rain fell throughout the morning. They went down to breakfast late and came back to the room. Ellen quickly saw from his puzzled questions that he remembered seemingly nothing of the evening. Again his probing was hesitant, fumbling, embarrassed. He seemed remorseful, oddly, about things of which he was unaware. At last—with excruciating circumlocutions—he wondered whether he had let her down in any way.

"No," Ellen said. "Everything was fine. Your friend was very funny. All told, it was a very sexy evening."

"Did, uh, do you, uh, did you you catch his name?"

"Your friend?"

"It seems to have slipped away from me."

"Billy Brism."

"Brism," he said. "Yeah, old Brism. He's a good ole boy."

"How'd you like Mimi?"

Eubanks ran a hand across his forehead as though attacking some web of bewilderment. Then he grew pale.

"You seem to recover so fast," he said. "You were sick too but you don't—"

"Maybe mine was just morning sickness," Ellen said. "Maybe I'm pregnant."

Eubanks fell silent.

When the rain stopped, it was he, to Ellen's surprise, who suggested they go to the fortune teller's. She was cheered even at the possibility of some diversion from his gloom. For the first time since their arrival she cranked up the sky blue roadster.

Eubanks did insist that she go first.

Without hesitation Ellen ducked behind the curtain that Annamelio held back.

Annamelio showed signs of recognizing her from the past but made no comment about it. Ellen and Henry and Percy and Florence Ensley had come to her. Annamelio worked only by looking and listening to a client. She had no use for the reading of cards or leaves or palms. She professed to being clairvoyant without claiming infallibility.

The fortune teller's calm narrow face was of a caramel hue, and enormous but thin gold rings dangled from her ears. Her hair was piled high on her head. Previously, when Ellen had directly asked, she had said that her gift came from an understanding of many bloods.

"In Annamelio," she had said, ticking them off on long slender fingers, "there is French and Spanish and English and Dutch and Indian and—who knows?—a little bit of everything. So I listen and things speak to me. Here it is unusual. In Los Nubes it is not."

"What did she tell you?" Eubanks instantly asked when Ellen pushed aside the curtain into the tiny vestibule where he had waited in a cane chair.

"After you hear yours I'll tell you," Ellen said.

He came out tense and excited, impressed even though he was somewhat incredulous.

"I couldn't believe it," he said. "She put her finger right on it.

She said that I was upset because I had just gone through a strange darkness. You see? You see? My memory. So I asked if I would go through it again, and she said, only when I wasn't looking for it. What do you suppose that means?"

"Maybe only that it'll happen when you don't expect it," Ellen said.

"Yeah, that could be it."

They walked back across Annamelio's small yard as he talked. Ellen slid into the driver's seat.

"So what did she tell you?" her husband said.

"She said that I was either very fertile or already pregnant."

"Are you serious?"

"That's what she said."

"Weren't you kidding back at the hotel?"

"Not really. I have a feeling I'm pregnant."

"*Already?*"

"That's a funny question," Ellen said. She broke into a sly grin. "After all, it only takes a minute."

Her Mr. Eubanks fumbled in his pants pocket. Ellen thought she heard the faint crack of splitting cellophane. She started the engine and gunned the car onto the highway. With the weekend here, the traffic was growing thicker.

Eubanks pleaded a need to sleep when it came time to swim. Ellen went alone. Again she swam far out. She was floating on her back when a skiff driven by an outboard came not toward her but just across her seaward vision.

Two men and a women were in it. They were dressed for swimming. One of the men suddenly squinted into the sun and pointed at her.

"Hey! Isn't that a girl?" he said loudly.

The man at the back of the boat cut the motor and stood up.

The sun behind her was falling upon them, a brilliant spotlight. She saw that the man who had stood was the deputy Ernie Pack. And just as she recognized him she heard him say, "I can't tell, but if it is, this is right where I want to fish." Then he was yelling toward her.

"Hey! Good-looking, are you a girl?"

Ellen began imperceptibly stroking backwards. She saw that the women in the boat was the jail matron who had searched her.

"Hell, I'm going to go see," Pack shouted.

He sounded intoxicated. He dived off the boat. Ellen appealed to the unnamed power: *Don't let that son of a bitch get me.*

Ellen spun about and at a sprint-crawl began driving hard toward the distant shore. She thought she heard a scream and heard some muffled shouting. Minutes later she glanced back. It looked as though they were helping Pack back onto the boat, but she couldn't see it clearly.

In their room John Eubanks was still deeply asleep.

Ellen fished a notebook from her bag and took it to the spindly desk that stood between two windows: *Notes on the Lomkubees*.

She wrote for a short while. Then she pushed the notebook to one side and took up a color postcard depicting Doubloon's Inn. She addressed it to her hall manager, Mrs. Whittaker.

At around seven she tried to rouse Eubanks to suggest supper. He only murmured and then fell again into deep sleep, breathing profoundly. She decided to go get a bite alone.

Ellen walked to a nearby hamburger shack. At the door she saw the purplish hair of Mimi. The petite woman was sitting at a stool before the not quite full counter. Ellen paused, thought of turning back. She decided to take the stool next to Mimi.

"Where's your boyfriend?" Ellen said.

Mimi snapped around with surprised and at first hostile eyes. Then the hostility passed away, and she displayed only vivid irritation.

"The son of a bitch ditched me," she said.

The counter man set a plate with two chili-drenched frankfurters in front of Mimi. Ellen ordered a hamburger. Mimi took a huge bite of one of the franks and with a paper napkin wiped away drippings of chili from her chin.

"Son of a bitch owed me another hundred, too," Mimi said. "What about you?"

"Well, I haven't been ditched yet," Ellen said.

"You hustle this joint all the time?" Mimi's eyes darted fleetly behind her and all about the room as she talked.

"It seems more like a vacation to me," Ellen said. Suddenly she realized she was enjoying herself.

"I know what you mean," Mimi said. "Around this hole the ones with the green got their wives with 'em and the ones that need us are sons of bitches. Broke."

"Was Billy broke?"

"Broke? Him? Are you kidding? That son of a bitch was loaded. But he ran up some extras last night and skipped. I wonder you didn't hear him. Crazy bastard went knocking on doors last night until he found some other john to come in and do a trick with us. Oh, that son of a bitch just had to play three-way horsey, don't you know. Well, I said, 'Look, Jack, this is another fifty,' and he said, 'Sure, sure anything.' But by then I'm too drunk already to sock it away, right? Now, honey, don't you know what a fool I was. So the way it goes, I'm still *talking* about the fifty when this big tool comes between us, and how the hell can I talk then, you know, me with a mouthful and him slobbering all over it, too, and then of course pretty quick it's too late to talk anyhow. So big shot Billy's passing out, and he's saying, 'Later, later,' and so later comes, and I'm going to the bathroom this morning and come out to find out he's long gone. I'll tell you this, honey, I'll never trust one of these football jocks again. Don't you know all that son of a bitch could talk about was sucking. You know, I got a suspicion all these football boys are cocksuckers at heart. Haven't you noticed that?"

"Well," Ellen said, "I always kind of wonder about the ones that ask for the three-way horsey. But I'm not so sure about those that want the double-ended snapjack. Unless, of course, they want seven or eight people in on it."

"Jesus Christ! I never heard of that. What the the hell kind of a routine is that?"

"You must not really be French," Ellen said.

"Are you kidding? That was just some of big shot Billy's shit."

"Mimi sounds French."

"Now you got to be kidding. Next thing you'll tell me you go by your real name. Now, tell me, is your name Ellen?"

"Sure it is."

Mimi's laugh hit the ceiling like a flung bucket of tacks.

"Damn," she said. "You know, I kind of take to you. Everybody in our business takes it so seriously. We could use more like you. You give me your number, I'll pass some tricks along your way."

"I appreciate that," Ellen said, finishing up her hamburger. "But I guess I'm strictly a loner."

"I might have guessed that," Mimi said. Ellen climbed off the stool. Mimi said, "You got some class about you, honey."

"Thank you," Ellen said. "You do, too."

At dawn Sunday she thought, *Yes. What I didn't know is that it was pity all along.*

Ellen remembered it was Sunday when the milk truck didn't pass by in the early light. She had slept well and felt rested. As she watched the day arrive, she also felt an extraordinarily powerful urge to return at once to New Orleans. It was almost as though some invisible wire were pulling her there. Once she even walked up to the bed thinking that she would violently awaken John Eubanks so that they could start right away.

As she observed his deep slumber, however, she decided to wait him out a few hours. It was hard for her to understand how he could sleep so long. Doubtless he would welcome the suggestion that they end the honeymoon early. Ellen studied his sleeping face, the limp curve of his hands, the position of his legs. They seemed bent as in some mode of running. Suddenly she thought, *Now I am his mother, and he is his father.*

"I wrote it—but forget to mail it," Ellen said. She handed the postcard to Mrs. Whittaker. The chubby cheerful housemother held it high to inspect the picture.

"St. Teresa's!" she said. "So that's where you went. And no wonder you came back early, with all those *sharks,* for goodness sake."

"What about sharks?" Ellen said, puzzled. She hadn't mentioned the sharks even to John Eubanks.

"Oh, it was in this morning's paper. I would have thought you would have heard."

Mrs. Whittaker picked up the *Times-Picayune* news section from the Sunday paper strewn on her sofa. She leafed through until she found an item which she now scanned again.

"Here—" she said. "It was some deputy sheriff, it says—horrible—almost eaten alive—and, yes, it was right off St. Teresa's—swimming off of a fishing boat—still alive when two companions brought him ashore—let's see—Ernest L. Pack, 26, critical condition—terrible—he's from Tamerdes—his wife and six-year-old son Ellis Pack brought to hospital by Sheriff Ellis Kelso—yes—terrible, Ellen—leg amputated—" She tossed the paper aside. "You get the impression the thing just ripped him all away *down there.* Horrible. And, oh, what a horrible thought to welcome you back on. Now, let's see, Ellen—will you be staying here tonight?"

"We decided to batch it tonight and try to line up that apartment tomorrow. That's one reason we cut it a little short."

"I see. Well, you've got some messages somewhere—and, oh! —oh, Ellen!—I do *wish* I'd known you would be back here today. There was an overseas phone call for you—just a few hours ago."

"A foreign call?"

"Oh yes, it had *everybody* excited. Paris calling Miss Ellen Worth."

"Well, who was it?"

"Lord, Ellen, I just don't know. I talked to the operator, and she said she had a party on the line calling Miss Ellen Worth, and I said you weren't here. And she asked when you were expected. I said not for a few days, or something like that. And then—oh, I don't know whether I should have, but I just couldn't resist—then I said when she gets back she will no longer be Miss Ellen Worth, she'll be Mrs. John Eubanks, because she is honeymooning right now—Ellen, did you mind?—I know I broke the secret, but, after all, I knew you only meant not to the girls around here—"

"What did she say then?" Ellen felt the earth opening beneath her.

"Well—she spoke to her party, I could hear that. She said, I believe, '*Monsieur*, could you hear what the answering party just said?' And then she began talking to me again—I hadn't heard a thing—but she said, 'That will be all, thank you, the calling party has signed off.' And then before I could *ask* her who it was, well. Now let's see."

Mrs. Whittaker had turned her back and was rummaging on her desk. Ellen abruptly sat down on her couch. Now the housemother was speaking again.

"Now there are some other messages that some of the duty girls took. Oh, here they are. Let's see. There's one from Mr. Harris—by golly, they're all *five* from Mr. Harris. Friday and Saturday and today. Different times. Urgent. Or is it *Horris?* Yes, Horris. Urgent. Call back. Et cetera. Et cetera. So. Would you like to use my phone, Ellen?"

Ellen was not looking now but knew that Mrs. Whittaker had turned and was looking at her.

"Ellen?" she said. "Ellen? Are you all right?"

Now she was sitting down beside her. Ellen felt her arm come around her shoulders, but she was still plummeting through the open earth.

"Ellen? Ellen, did I do something wrong? Did I say the wrong thing?"

Ellen tried to speak. She tried to say, no. But nothing came out. Nothing.

1946-55
Interim

May 1, 1947

    *CABLE—TO MR MRS MARK WORTH 71 RUE TUILE PARIS
—EMILY WORTH EUBANKS BORN TODAY SEVEN POUNDS
EXACT—BEAUTIFUL—ALL WELL—ELLEN & CO.*

June 30, 1947

    *Horris to Claudette: "Looked across the street and saw a fellow scratch-
ing old Cliff's gold letters off the windows today. Ellen's getting it all
fixed up for Mr. Eubanks to move in."*

August 10, 1947

    Dearest Corinne:

    Thanks for the lovely letter.

    *Yes, we're all settled in now, even if settled may not be the exact word.
I'm not sure you ever experienced exactly what I am experiencing, but
I think you've experienced enough to make me wish I had a chance to*

*talk to you. Which I will one of these years when Emily is a bit older.
Or when you two come over here—with the menagerie that is welcome,
as you know.*

Emily seems to be thriving, which is what matters most.

*Tell Mark hello—and not to be so damned impatient about learning
a little technique before he uncorks his masterpiece.*

*Love,
Ellen*

November 20, 1947

Dear Percy:

*Here at last is at least part of the $500, along with my assertion that
it is not to dodge a bill collector for the rest that I'm not giving you
a return address.*

*The fact is that I'm leaving Châteauroux in a couple of days and going
to Paris where there is at least a possibility that I can latch onto some
more or less permanent work.*

*I've been here with Michelle's family for the last two months. They've
been great to me, and to Henri, and might even be happy to have us
stay on indefinitely. I'm sure they'd love for the boy to stay for good.
But I have the feeling that it's time for us to go. For one thing, I've
gotten a little self-confidence back, and there is this prospect or possibility
of something dangling before me in Paris, although as I understand it,
I might be traveling a good deal if it materializes.*

*During the last two months here, I've managed to pull myself together
for the first time since Michelle got killed. Or, more exactly, from that
day when I got out of the hospital and made that call to New Orleans.
Until then, I guess I was hanging together by a thread, but when I heard
about Ellen it snapped, and so began what has got to be the worst year
I can have this lifetime. A year of darkness is all I can call it. I should
have learned from my old man that booze won't do the trick. The trouble
is that even after I realized it wouldn't, I had a hell of a time cutting
it out.*

*I remember dimly writing you about all of this some time ago, but I
haven't the faintest idea what I actually said. No matter. Anyway, I've
decided that I'm one of those all-or-nothing types and that, with me,
it's got to be nothing, because I can't take it the other way. I can see
myself sitting lost in the fog at the Texas Cafe with Sid Carter.*

*As you damn well realize, the money this brings isn't even the important
part of the freight. It brings my boundless affection to you and Florence
(and any progeny I might not have heard about) and a pledge to send*

*you a return address as soon as I have one, because I would dearly love
to hear from you about yourself and Florence and all of your neighbors,
too.*

*It's strange how I've managed to screw up so many people so fast in
such a short time. I'm in a mood to do better now, however, and intend
to—if possible. This brings the best from babbling Henri as well as from,*

Your devoted friend,
Henry

April 9, 1948

Dearest Claudette:

*Mark and I have been at a loss as to whether to write Ellen about this,
or, indeed, whether to write anybody. We decided to write you and
Horris and leave it to your discretion as to whether it would be wise
to mention it to her—or to anybody, for that matter, because it involves
some sensitive matters.*

*In a nutshell: we bumped into a certain long-lost party here in Paris
a couple of weeks ago, and had three good visits with him, and he retains
now the feelings he had when circumstances, as he felt them, obliged him
to go away. When we first encountered him, quite by chance, he was
already making final preparations for a trip and job that he says will
take him (and his son) by a circuitous route to the ancient East where
he will be operating a machine in a certain civil controversy.*

*As I said, we're in doubt as to whether to mention it at all, and as you
can see, I'm afraid to spell it out even here, knowing how certain things
are being watched these days.*

*Anyway, when we see you, here or there, I'll tell you more if you wish
to know. Meanwhile, do as you think.*

Love,
Corinne

June 15, 1948

Dearest Kimo:

*I'll be driving down to Temulca this weekend, Saturday the 19th, to
talk to Bema about some things, and I'd love to see you. Best to Puana.*

Love,
Ellen

ELLEN'S NOTEBOOK

June 21, 1948:

Who can calculate
The arcane equities of love?

Who can tell you:
Stay,
Your fire disrupts
Some wan gentility?
Do you heed,
Quell the spark
And tend the pallid ash?
Who bears the pall
If forbearance stifles all?

ELLEN'S NOTEBOOK

July 2, 1949: Emily <u>swam</u> in the big spring today!

April 1, 1950: Richard (Dickey-devil) Devers to Horris: "Horstantnomarjatalldonchunoat? [Horris, it ain't no marriage at all, don't you know that?] Datfelmitswellbeinvsblmanaswathes. [That fellow might as well be an invisible man as what he is.] You see him come up across the street there getting to that office right at the crack of nine all spick and span. Sho, and you see him right here through this window pop back out at twelve sharp for a bite of dinner down there at the drug store. And then pop back in, still spick and span, and then pop back out at five sharp. And you know he don't go home. You know he goes right out to that country club and shoots that golf. And then comes in from shooting that golf and sits down and starts to drink. And don't stop drinking until he feels like conking off to sleep. And goes home then and conks off to sleep. You know that well as I know that. And then gets up and gets all spick and span and comes back down here and pops up in that office at nine sharp. Elnworth mights well have an invisible man as to have that kind of man. I don't know how she stands it. You know all that you don't have to pretend to old Dickey-devil. You know old Dickey-devil knows all sees all. Horris if you don't know all that you might as well be an invisible man. Now you tell me something I don't know. Tellmeowcomshedonkickimoutadehouse. Senimawnysway. Come on you know what I mean."

July 3, 1950: Horris to Cliff: "After that speech at the Antlers Club lunch today our friend Mr. Eubanks may just come out of obscurity and give us the benefit of owning an almost homegrown bush-league McCarthy. Cliff, I tell you, the way those chuckleheads cheered that Commies-under-the-bed shit was enough to curl my hair, and please don't point out the obvious."

PARIS

April 11, 1951: Ellen to Corinne: "Weird is the only word for it. I can laugh at it now, at myself, not at him, just at the whole thing, but it is evermore weird. It's not that it's an incommunicado situation, it's just that we go on talking day-to-day as though everything were absolutely normal. I mean, it's as though the reality of the marriage existed in some other world. Oh, during the first year, he got apologetic a few times. Never when he was sober and could talk about anything, only when he was drinking. Once or twice he got—well, maudlin and weepy, but without ever actually coming down on the point, you know, without ever coming right out and saying anything. And, frankly, I've long since been unable to bring it up, simply because I haven't wanted to, to tell the truth. Oh, yes, on our first anniversary he got all weepy about it. We went up to Mingo's in Carterville, it's a place run by a guy from Los Nubes, and he all but broke down during dinner. But, of course, without remembering a thing about it the next day. Or I more or less always assume he doesn't remember what's happening when he's in the bag, which is mostly every night. Oh, he doesn't stay out late. He comes home from the club around nine or so, say, and plop—sleeps like a baby. I've been reading up on that—the forgetting thing—and evidently it's not all that uncommon, at least with alcoholics. They call it a blackout. Except that I don't know that he's an alcoholic. Maybe he isn't, because he doesn't drink anything during the day. But from the very first, that liquor just seemed to wipe his memory clean off the map. Oh, I told you about our honeymoon. Down at St. Teresa'a. It was a riot in a way, but—oh, it's awfully sad, too. No, I can laugh at myself, but I can't laugh at him. I've often wondered whether when he drinks he remembers at least what happened when he was last drinking. But I don't know how it works. All I know, Corinne, is that it's weird, weird, weird. And that I don't really have a complaint coming, because—well, you know the truth. I married him to get the façade of legitimacy for Emily, and maybe there's some justice in the fact that that's all I got. Actually, I didn't envision it this way when I jumped into it. I actually was prepared to be a good wife to him—I mean in every way. And not in my wildest fantasy could I have imagined it would turn out this way. As to whether he's—well, as to whether he's the way Mr. Fielding was, I swear I just don't know. I don't really have any basis for thinking that he is. I mean, he just seems so utterly and absolutely strapped up that—well, I frankly don't see how he could let go with a man, either. Listen, is that Mark coming up? Well, let's drop it for now, I'd just as soon not—Anyway, I'm feeling so damn good. It's so marvelous being with you two at last. Listen, tomorrow let's you and I and all the kids drive down to Châteauroux. I just want to see. You know, I sort of need to."

May 12, 1952: Ellen to Claudette: "Do you know it was the first time I've *seen* a baby born—I felt Emily, but I mean seeing—and there I am delivering the thing. And not knowing a damn thing about it. Mary Kent called Florence when it started coming, and then Florence flipped out and called me, and I scooted down there and wound up bringing a baby into the world. And it was fantastic, although I thought I must be going out of my mind even to try it. And what do you think of a doctor going off to a damn medical convention and leaving his wife on the verge of childbirth. It was hours before we reached him in New Orleans, and, of course, by then half the county medical society had come in answer to the emergency call—but every damn one of them too late. Claudette, it was just the most fantastic experience. I remember a long time ago, that first summer, Henry saw a baby born—you remember—that migrant family. You know, I've often wondered if that boy I saw in the sheriff's office down in Tamerdes was from that same family. It could have been the same baby even, the one Henry saw, but—Well, anyhow, I wanted to call and tell you about my big adventure. Oh, goddam, I forgot the most exciting part. Mary's going to name her after me. Partly. Mary Ellen Kent. How about that?"

ELLEN'S NOTEBOOK

November 12, 1952: Portia Rust died. No way to get word.

December 18, 1953:
Dear Ole Horris:
All I can say is that you're not the only one I seem to write just when I am about to leave somewhere. And I am writing now to report that Henri and I are about to say farewell to Australia and sail off into the sunset or maybe the sunrise after a stay that has maybe gone on for too long for both of us. It's been a pretty good four years, however, with steady groceries from the crop dusting routine and a good climate for both of us. Actually, I suppose it's Henry more than Henri (we get some of our best sport confusing people with our names) that needs a change of scenery and pace. And, by chance, which seems to rule my existence, I ran into a connection from some old days who told me where I might be of service and enjoy a radical change of clime at the same time while also bringing in at least grocery money, which, frankly, is about all

the two of us need. I realize that you have no crying need to know all of these indefinite things about my meanderings, but I felt a distinct need to let you know that wherever I go I carry with me an enormous amount of affection for you, as for most of our mutual friends, and for one in particular, although I feel oddly constrained when I try to state it. In any event, say hello to anybody you see that you think might care to have a hello from me. And love, too, to Claudette. I am hungry for news about all of you, but I got no place to have it sent at the moment. C'est la vie.

Fondly,
Henry

May 20, 1954: Cliff to Horris: "Horris, with this goddam Brown decision, some of the decent folks around here better take the lead and settle the goddam thing before the Cecil Drums and the Jack Burcells and the Sonny Grindells and the—I may as well say it, the goddam John Eubankses—preempt the situation and fuck it all up. And since you and I can't count on the other decent folks jumping up in this particular situation, what I'm saying, I guess, is that you and I and whoever we can scrape up better take the goddam lead. Horris, you know that goddam cross is still in your backroom and nobody has come to claim it yet? Well, with this Brown thing, I wouldn't be a damn bit surprised if some semiliterate sheethead didn't come around asking for it. You reckon I ought to run another ad?"

ELLEN'S NOTEBOOK

July 16, 1955: Dropped Emily at Montaqua Camp this A.M. Dinner tonight at NYC with Paul Gans & editorial helper Gloria.

KEY WEST:

July 22, 1955: Horris to Henry: "What's he like? Well. I guess I could begin by saying that he's not like her. Or you or me either, for that matter. Not that we're all alike to a tee. But there is some certain kinship in our engagement with existence. So he is different. You'd have to look hard to find any kinship at all. It's not easy to guess exactly how the world must look from inside the man. And that's what we're really asking, isn't it?

"Of course, he hasn't been the same all along. Not that any of us are unchanging either. But the change in him has been, well, dramatic. On the outside, anyway. Although I would tend to guess that the thing that suddenly came out a few years ago was hidden away in him all the time. And no doubt took the form it did simply because of accident and circumstance.

"You see, when they first came back to McClung he was hardly noticeable. Oh, he was in evidence, there to be seen. But he was one of those men who tends to be almost invisible. Invisible even when they're around. Or maybe that word is too strong. Inconspicuous may be kinder. Anyway, he tended to remove himself from your thoughts. He led a kind of existence that was clear enough and yet became sort of blurred simply because it was so repetitive and without highlights.

"Now, in his physical appearance he didn't *seem* like that kind of man. At first glance you would have tended to get a favorable positive impression of him. Not handsome and yet good-looking. Even features. Maybe too even. Maybe that's one thing about him. Maybe there's some—some—Maybe he starts out with a lack of some quirky idiosyncratic thing about his face that makes it harder for the memory to hook onto it. But he's nice looking, as any matron would tend to put it. Big but not burly. Tall without being gangling or overpowering. Neat in his dress and all that. Maybe even too neat from my point of view, but then my prejudice against genteel sartorial conformity approaches certifiable derangement.

"In any event, if you had just glanced at him on the street you might well have gotten a good impression. But then pretty soon you would have noticed something. Within, say, ten or fifteen minutes, if you had stopped to get acquainted, you would have noticed a way that he has of almost disappearing while he's still there in your presence.

"It's an elusive thing, odd, but it's there. After awhile you would discover it in the movements of his face and eyes. A kind of withdrawing of himself from your vision, some habitual kind of furtiveness. I'm sure you get the picture. You've seen it in many men. It's only easier to recognize when it's a chronic thing in someone. It's chronic but still kind of subtle in Eubanks.

"But by the time you figured it out, your initial impression of him would have begun to erode. You would have sensed, whether you knew it or not, that inside that nice looking frame this fellow was fleeing you, or certainly fleeing something. Now don't misunderstand this. You wouldn't have wondered about his general courage, his primitive fortitude, if you will. You'd be aware that this impression of flight didn't suggest any common cringing or gutlessness.

"And, of course, you'd have at hand his history as an athlete, which in itself would tend to dispel the suggestion of physical cowardice. I don't know whether you paid much attention at the time, since you were busy with other things, but as a player this fellow's outstanding virtue was a certain extraordinary vehemence of action. His capacity for the violent and primitive commitment of his body to the play carried him far greater distances than his skill, although he had a lot of that, too.

"Mostly, if you were anything like me, you would soon have ceased to notice John Eubanks at all. That is, you would have during those first couple of years. Let's see, they came back the summer of '47. For the first three years, say.

"All that time, everybody would see him around, but he was about as distinct as a speck of dandruff on a Harris tweed. He plugged himself into a routine that just didn't seem to have even minor variations. And, of course, it was all there waiting for him—this routine he more or less disappeared into.

"Even before they got back Ellen had arranged for his office and even bought his legal library for him. You might be surprised how much law she picked up along the way, helping him out with his homework after they moved into the apartment down in New Orleans. Even after Emily came, Ellen was actually putting together most of his briefs and even outlining his arguments for the moot court. She'd do this while he'd tilt beers until it was time to go to sleep.

"Well, when it was time to come back she also arranged for his office. But try not to get the wrong notion about this. It wasn't gratuitous meddling. She didn't buy that library for him just to take command of his business. The truth is he had wound up almost incapable of getting himself started after his mother cut him off. Which she did with a vengeance, the very day he finally called her and said he had gotten married. That was the end of her support, financial and otherwise, too. Can you imagine a mother doing that? I can. So far as I know she never talked to him again, even though he kept trying to call. She did write him one long letter, some wretched bitter thing that only confirmed what she had already said more briefly on the phone.

"So Ellen wasn't trying to take charge. Actually, she was just trying to prime the pump, so to speak. So she not only had the office waiting for him but got the bank right away to put him on a retainer, and that gave him at least subsistence of his own as well as a little work, although they only had him write a few deeds and research some titles, things like that. I think the bank was his only client for most of the first year.

"Still, if you had clocked his hours—which I couldn't avoid doing, since his office and the stairway leading up to it are almost directly across the street from me—you'd think he was carrying a workload big enough to use up precisely eight hours a day. In at nine, out for a short lunch, back in until five. That sort of thing. Looking almost as neat at the end of the day as at the beginning.

"Leaving the office, he would take up a second phase of his routine that became just as predictable. He had plugged in right away at the country club. Percy sponsored his membership and helped introduce him around. And right from the start he was as much a regular at that club as he was at the office. At five he'd head out and shoot eighteen holes—weather permitting, of course—and then he'd sit at the bar and drink until about eight. Day after day. Then he'd go home, and the next day would be like the one before.

"Up at the club he didn't single out anybody for special friendship, but seemed friendly enough to anybody he would run into. You know, he'd latch onto whoever needed somebody to make out a foursome, or sometimes he'd go around by himself. Very good golfer, too. But there was something revealing perhaps even in the way he played that game. Watching him closely I'd get the impression that even though he could put the ball about as far as he wanted and where he wanted it, he fundamentally hated what he was doing. I mean, he's got this beautiful swing that somehow looks as though its primary purpose is not to propel the ball but to kill it. You detect that same vehemence he showed playing football.

"Well, at the bar he didn't seem at first to have any special drinking buddies, either. He would just drink with whoever was drinking. And if nobody was, he would sit and drink by himself. I suppose the general impression that all these acquaintances got was one of great shyness and modesty. I think everybody had expected a former sports celebrity to have a little more bull about him. After awhile, a few months, he did begin to get some kind of reputation for a sense of humor. Evidently he had remembered every locker room joke he was ever told, and he developed some knack at passing these around. When he had drunk a good deal he would reel those things off in mixed company, and I guess this added some slightly savory trace to his reputation.

"But with all this he never quite became a part of things that were going on. Up there, up at the club, he was almost always alone.

As you can imagine, Ellen never gave a damn for that kind of ma-
larkey and so seldom went out after the first few get-acquainted runs.
So. Because of this situation he also got some reputation for being
quote his own man unquote. You know, it was assumed that he felt
his marriage was solid enough to go his own way and keep his own
hours. To the best of my knowledge he never ventured any remark
that would have contradicted this impression.

"On the contrary, he was always at pains in any chat to tell
some ancedote about something that Emily had done or something
she had said to John-John—which is what Ellen taught her to call
him, and which evidently pleased him. Ellen herself always calls him
Mr. Eubanks. How he feels about that I haven't the faintest idea. All
of Ellen's friends just laughed at it as another more or less quaint
instance of her esoteric humor—or maybe her delight in the archaic.
As you can imagine, or as you know, people around McClung have
long since given up expecting Ellen to make any more than a nominal
gesture at the conventions. Either in her talk or her larger life.

"So, perhaps not surprisingly, there wasn't even any gossip
where there might well have been about that marriage. No serious
speculation even when Ellen plunged into her work, the paintings,
and doing the book and all that, and started traveling around by
herself. Not by herself, rather, but with Emily. She always took
Emily. In fact, until last year, when Ellen started taking Emily up
to a place in Vermont to begin giving her some time apart on her
own, where you saw Ellen you saw Emily, and vice versa. But their
gadding about didn't seem to alter his routine, either. Ordinarily, as
you know, if a wife constantly left her husband at home there'd be
a good deal of talk. Maybe his absolutely unvarying routine as well
as the general knowledge of Ellen's individual ways, maybe it all
simply left no room for speculation. I suppose catty women might
have wondered why she neglected her husband, but nobody could
fault her by even a hair in taking care of Emily.

"Would you believe she had that little girl swimming in that
wretched ice cold spring almost before she could walk? Not floating,
swimming. Fantastic. *They*'re fantastic. You ought to see heads pop
around when they're downtown. They'll be jabbering in English and
suddenly switch without a pause into French and then modulate like
a couple of improvising jazzmen into Spanish. Well, Emily learned
all three languages at once. Day after day, Ellen would bring her over
to my house and they'd sit with Claudette and switch back and forth
from one language to another while they gossiped, so—Well, I don't
know that she'd be a match for your boy. I've heard him in three

languages so far, and I gather from what you told me that he must speak some Chinese, too. Emily might give him a good race, though.

"But I've strayed, haven't I? John Eubanks. Mr. Eubanks. Frankly, I think that today—assuming you knew nothing about him, nothing about his activities—you'd still get a favorable impression at that first glance. He still looks like a clean-cut fellow. Well pressed. Still trim enough, maybe getting a little puffy about the face and middle. He puts away a good deal of liquor, but somehow it never seems to have run away with him. He's never turned into a daytime drinker, anyway, so far as I know. That is, you wouldn't find him in the Texas Cafe with Sid Fletcher starting on that first coffee cup full of bourbon at ten in the morning. But Eubanks still seems to get fogged out in the evenings. Nothing rowdy about him, just a lot of talk, or sometimes sullen silences that everybody accepts as moodiness.

"Come morning, though, he still pulls that car up to the curb in front of his office stairway right at nine on the dot. And, whoosh, sprightly as a chicken, there he goes charging up to that office. White shirts. Neat tie. Seersucker suits crisply done. If you glimpsed him just now you'd think of one of those insurance company ads that show a confident looking successful businessman who has just signed up for a policy that puts his worries about death to rest. Only at second glance you'd wonder whether this particular man—Eubanks—hadn't been turned down for a policy. Because now what you feel and see on closer inspection is this anger exuding from him. And it takes the form of a certain expression on his face and a certain arrogance and certitude in his way of talking.

"You see, today you wouldn't get that impression of someone who was furtive or in flight. You get the impression of something breaking into the open. And it's not fleeing but pursuing. It was astonishing how this change took shape. I don't mean that the fact that it took place is astonishing, I mean the swiftness of it.

"It was one of those overnight transformations. Though I guess I should be honest enough to say that probably it started brewing toward the surface long after I had stopped watching, long after I had assumed that John Eubanks was destined for some eternally blurred cipherhood. But in any event, to me, and to many others, it seemed like an overnight transformation.

"Now, this was, let's see, something under three years after they had come up to McClung. It was 1950. A vintage year in this country's history. Too bad you missed it. But, of course, you know all about the great witch hunt we enjoyed, courtesy of that fellow from the cheese country. Old patriotic Joe. Well, what happened to Mr. Eubanks in 1950 is that with a single speech he became our local facsimile of old patriotic Joe.

"Zaroom! He was off like a rocket. Suddenly the man I had come to think of as a cipher turned into the bold hunter. One little speech did it. Damnedest thing. His audience, naturally, didn't think it was a little speech. At the time everybody—or damn near everybody—seemed to think it was the most stirring utterance since give-me-liberty-or-give-me-death. Incidentally, are you aware that Patrick Henry never got nearly as close to a battle as Molly Pitcher?

"Mr. Eubanks, either, although he tried right hard or seemed to back then. Still, irony of ironies, it was his destiny to be turned into a great warrior at a luncheon meeting of the Antlers Club. Here was his first constituency. It hit them like a ton of bricks. You know that club, the usual fare they get at their weekly luncheon. Young lawyers stand up there and talk about progress and reform and blah-blah-blah. Hell, only young lawyers bother to accept their invitations to talk. They no doubt expected the same kind of blather from Eubanks, who, of course, had once or twice before done his part to bore them to death.

"I would suspect—hell, I know—they were sitting there lighting up their smokes and expecting more of the same, all of them straightening out their skivvies and preparing either to doze away or fantasize the day's receipts, among other spiritual matters, when what-do-you-know? *Wham!* All of a sudden this passionate and knowledgeable voice was telling them that there were enemies lurking all over the goddam town and countryside, enemies nobody was doing anything about. Enemies they didn't even know they had.

"Well, of course, they were more or less already primed for this stuff by old patriotic Joe. But after Mr. Eubanks brought the light to them directly they leaped to their feet and roared. Maybe it was basically a roar of gratitude. Maybe they were simply grateful for having been spared another half-hour of boredom. But no doubt they were also grateful for having been alerted to the grave danger into which the republic had fallen and probably were relieved to know that it looked as though the community were going down with it. Unless, of course.

"Anyway, we suddenly had a new Mr. Eubanks on our hands. Within days he and a few others had organized what they called the Council on Communism. And suddenly the witch hunt came home. They had a field day harassing librarians and school officials and, of course, managed to demoralize some of the more humane social and civic organizations. After they got onto the lady who had helped our mobile library get started, she had a heart attack. But, of course, she had been allowing dangerous materials to be transported among the people. It seemed more or less immaterial that most of the people among whom the dangerous matter was transported were at best semiliterate.

"Still, the thing took off like a kite in a hurricane. And a lot of people you would have thought might know better started chipping in. Some of his closest comrades in this weren't entirely savory to start with, of course. Sonny Grindell moved in very quick and became more or less his number two man. Mr. Eubanks, perhaps to his moral credit, seemed utterly unaware that in the legislature Grindell is nothing but a pure paid puppet for the loan sharks, the truckers, the liquor people—every avaricious element yet contrived by the greed of man. And, oh, he got—still gets—a lot of help from Cecil Drum. You remember Dynamite Drum. How could you forget him? He was still a town cop when you left. Well, he's a watchman now at the city hall. He's up to about two hundred and seventy pounds now, I would guess, but otherwise he's still pretty much what he always was, a one hundred percent good old country boy with an unfortunate tendency to homicide. Our Mr. Eubanks suddenly got to know some people he hadn't met out at the country club. And, of course, all of a sudden they were treating him with more respect than he was accustomed to, or maybe even with awe. I can't exaggerate the effect of that one speech of his.

"Anyway, while he was still the fresh hero they went around signing up merchants and professionals, practically anybody who could scratch an X in support of the council. And before it was done the damn thing had spread all over the state. Every time some pinheaded legislator passed into view down in Koppalouka one of them would jump out of the bushes and lobby him. What a charade! When they weren't lobbying against the red menace they'd get in a few licks against vivisection or fluoridation. It got to be almost magnificent. Sonny Grindell got enough signatures on a resolution to require the members of the house to take a loyalty oath every single day. Every day. Funny thing. Until this, treason had always been regarded as one of the least likely felonies to appeal to that bunch of pissants down there.

"Well. You can imagine what they did to anybody who wouldn't go along. Somebody brought it to my attention that Eubanks even began insinuating—privately, of course—that the fact Claudette and I have no children suggested certain things about my sexual propensities. Which—once I had ruled out murdering him—didn't bother me so much.

"You know what really sent me up the wall? It was when they started bad-mouthing Sumter Kent. Put one of their little pink stickers in his window, of course. Well, his offense was simply in not signing their original petition, the one supporting the Council on Communism. You remember Sumter Kent. Just possibly the most decent man in the county. Maybe in the state. Exquisitely naïve, but decent. Jesus, what else could you say of a feed-and-seed man who refunds the farmers when the seeds don't sprout or the hogs don't fatten?

"Sumter's trouble is that he has always believed what they taught him in Sunday school. He believes the commandments. Always did. You know, I don't think he's really had a woman yet, and—goddam, it's another story, but I think it had something to do with how strongly I felt when they started hard-timing Sumter. You see, Sumter Kent finally found himself a girl a few years back. Not too long after you left, I guess. Couple of years. Beautiful girl. Vivacious. Little younger than Sumter. Mary Edgerton. Came down from Carterville to work in the bank. And everybody was both surprised and delighted when Sumter took up with her. Unbelievable. Saintly Sumter was going to get married. In fact, what seemed unbelievable perhaps was the fact that she latched onto Sumter. Because Mary was—is—very earthy and very, very pretty. Lively, you know. One look at her and you begin to entertain grave questions about your fundamental scheme of morality. Anyway, she has a good deal of whatever it is that Ellen has in such excess. *Joie de vivre*. Why the hell don't I follow Claudette's advice and stick to rudimentary English?

"Anyway, not too long before Sumter and Mary were to be married, along comes his half-brother John, his younger brother —You know John, too. Different horse entirely. Lively. Personable. A man of the flesh, as we say. So he gets back from his internship, and he meets Mary Edgerton. Then the first thing everybody knows is that John Kent and Mary Edgerton are rolling back into town from St. Teresa's. Married. Well, as much as I liked both of them, I couldn't help suffering with Sumter.

"I guess I was surprised that they decided to stay in town. But they did, and everybody likes them. They bought that riverside house just below Percy's. They've already got a couple of children. Let's see, a boy came along first, then a girl. Little Mary. Mary Ellen, in fact. You know, the day that little girl came along—that was the spring of last year—well, John the doctor was off to some medical convention, and Mary Kent phoned Florence Ensley for help, since she was practically delivering this child without labor. And Florence got flustered and called Ellen. So it was Ellen who chased down the road and delivered that child. Had it all done up by the time any doctor got there. And, of course, once the word spread that a *physician's* wife needed a doctor, well, half the county medical society was at the door. So Ellen, anyway, got herself a namesake. Mary Ellen Kent.

"Oh. Sumter. What he got, of course, was a royal heartbreak. He tried not to let it show. Went about his business and all that. But, don't you know, it tested his power of forgiveness. In fact, I'm not sure he's ever been out to John's house, but he has received them in his house. He still lives in that brick mansion with the lovely garden behind it. You know the one. And he's still the most decent man in town.

"That crew, however—when that bunch of crusaders came to him and asked him to sign up, he was one of the very few merchants to say, no thanks. So they commenced to poor-mouth him. Imagine it. Sumter Kent a fellow traveler. My ass. Can't you just imagine what a heydey they would have had with *you*—if they had ever found out that you, a native son, had once been over there flying an airplane for that fellow in China. Whew! Well, they slapped that little pink sticker on Sumter's window, same as they did on mine. Incidentally, they also once gave me another nice Bible. Evidently they assumed that it had properties similar to those of light. In any event they tried to pass it right through the window. Did in fact, right onto my desk. Only it didn't leave the window entirely intact. Second time that's happened.

"But Sumter—he just let the damn sticker stay there. I don't think he lost much trade, if any. But, man, did I feel for him. One day I was standing around his place—I go over there, as you know, just to get the smell of the place, all those feeds and grains and seeds, good smelling—Anyway, I was trying to get a rise out of him, trying to joke it all away, but I was having no luck. So finally I said, 'Sumter, what do you really think about Mr. Eubanks and his big crusade?'

"Well, Sumter watched a little hill of seed run out of his palm through his fingers and said, just as mild, 'T.C., they don't know what they're doing.' Well, in a sense he was right. I don't know for a fact whether Eubanks, for one, is really aware of the consequences of all that shit. But I do know for a fact, because it was obvious, that he suddenly enjoyed being a *somebody*. Suddenly he began casting a shadow, and he plainly got some kind of relief out of it. Presumably it gave him a vent for all the crap he kept bottled up inside all those years. Maybe in the same way he enjoyed the façade of marriage. It must have been some sort of protection for him.

"And somewhere in every speech he would do the father-and-husband thing. Always tell some little story that would allow him to reveal this little girl who called him John-John. Well, Ellen didn't care for this much, although her feelings had begun one way and ended another. At first she said she felt almost relieved that he had found something that engrossed him even if it did seem like lunacy. But she soon soured on it, as soon as it became clear it was only hurting a few select victims, and eventually she asked him pointblank to leave her and Emily out of his public speeches. He did, too.

"So what's he like? Well, he's entirely different from what he seemed at first. I guess his new incarnation reached some kind of apex when his crowd persuaded old Joe himself to come down to Riverton and give a talk. Another shining hour in the on-going salvation of the republic. Old Joe came down and took the faculty of the state university to task while libeling one or two professors in particular. And then afterwards, so I hear, Joe and some of his asshole buddies got together with Mr. Eubanks and some of his, and they all got boisterously drunk together, and the Honorable Sonny Grindell got himself bitten on an immensely sensitive appendage, requiring some medical attention, although none of this was called to the attention of the journalists covering the event. I don't know for sure who bit Mr. Grindell, but the story I get is that it was an inadvertency committed by one of the young ladies he hires to help him out in Koppalouka. I am told that she was engaged in some coupling with her employer when another of the celebrants unexpectedly began trying to drag her away toward some other purpose. My informant assures me that the other celebrant was not Mr. Eubanks. By this time he had gone out for air and fallen asleep in an automobile where a surprised hardware salesman from Memphis found him next morning.

"In a way, after that, it all began to go downhill. The crusade and the Council, too. By 1953 the organization was sort of frazzled and spent. Which I suppose means only that everybody now was about as bored with the witch hunt as they had previously been with talks about progress and reform. Very likely, or at least possibly, Mr. Eubanks would have faded back into the shadows if 1954 hadn't come along as it did.

"The Brown decision resuscitated the whole mess of them. Mr. Eubanks discovered the black menace almost as fast as he had discovered the red one four years earlier. No doubt last year brought all of us to some sharper consciousness of the existence of these people we'd taken for granted or worse for a century or so. But for John Eubanks it brought not only the discovery of their existence and their threat but of the existence of constitutional law, too. Almost overnight he became an expert.

"Then the first thing we know is that he had picked up this idea that got started over in Mississippi or Alabama or somewhere and was organizing a white citizens council. And, of course, this one turned out to be pretty much the same old council under a new name and with a new purpose—though they didn't intend to let us forget that the reds were probably also behind the blacks as well as the Supreme Court.

"Lately he's started putting together what they call the White Brigade, which is a sort of subsidiary to the council and designed to appeal to the young. To some extent it has, but it also has a full quotient of old farts, too. As they put it, the purpose of the thing is to quote make a strong public witness unquote to constitutionalism and states' rights. Which they do by getting together every month or so out on Mount Oro and making speeches and reciting slogans around a big bonfire. They have a little drill team, too. And, man, everything about this new mutation burns Ellen up. What burns her more than the bonfire is the fact that this outfit meets on Mount Oro. As you know, that's where the Lomkubees used to conduct what they call the *bakana oro*—the birth of light or illumination. Ellen thinks it's a desecration for an outfit like this to meet there. One time she said, 'Horris, they might at least have the decency to wear sheets.'

"Well, it was after Mr. Eubanks got carried away with this business that Ellen in fact began to entertain the idea of asking him to leave the house. And frankly, some of her friends, including me, have in some ways encouraged her to do it. But, of course, she hasn't. As she says, she made a bargain with herself that she can't bring herself to break—yet.

"But who knows what'll happen? Hell, I certainly don't. I know that we've decided—I mean the school board and a few of us working very privately and quietly—have decided to get on ahead with the school thing. And if things come off as we've got them planned, we'll at least have made a beginning toward compliance when the schools open early in September. Funny thing, we got the real powers behind it not on principle but practicality. What's obvious is that we face a choice of either doing peacefully what's obviously right or else inherit a good deal of hell and fuss that will only hurt those who least expect and deserve to be hurt. So we don't talk constitutional law or morality to the bankers and businessmen on the board. Hell, we tell them trouble will be bad for business. They can see that kind of light.

"Well, I know you don't need to hear a whole lot about this, but I mention it because what's coming up is going to force Eubanks into the role of adversary to the prevailing power of the community. I would expect him and his crowd to chafe and holler and try to upset things, simply because if things don't get upset, they've no longer got a cause. But who the hell knows? Who knows what's going to happen anywhere? Anyway, that's more or less what he's like.

"And suddenly I realize why I feel so damn good about seeing you again. You always were the only friend in my life who would let me talk on indefinitely without either chastising me, walking out, or butting in. Hell, with Ellen sometimes I can't get a word in edgewise. And Claudette—she doesn't exactly butt in so much as she merely talks simultaneously.

"Well. Look. Here comes Henri again. Another message from Garcia, I presume. Henry, would you like another soda pop while I indulge my depravity with a bourbon and water? Key West always brings out the worst in me. I think it's these open-sided saloons."

1955

Midsummer

——— 5 ———

Horris said, "I would have given an arm to have had some way of getting in touch with you."

And Claudette said, "Ellen, he looked so—so—*très magnifique!*"

And Horris said, "He really did look great. Just great. Very browned. Lean. Maybe too lean."

And Claudette said, "No, no, no, no-no-no-no-no. He looked —Ellen, we went with him to the boat, and if he had just said to me, 'Come, Claudette,' I would have *leaped* onto the boat and waved goodbye to my beloved husband."

And Horris said, "We stood right there until the boat vanished at the horizon."

And Claudette said, "I don't think we made a motion. It was such a beautiful morning, and I had such an insane desire to swim out and pull him back, but—"

And Horris said, "You were the first thought out of his mouth and the last."

And Claudette said, "All his thoughts, Ellen. He was thinking of nothing else. I could tell. We talked the night through, without a single wink, and every minute he was thinking of you. I could tell from his eyes."

And Horris said, "He was guarded—no, contained, he was very contained in what he said. He didn't give vent to all that he might have said. But you could tell this was because he was more hungry to take in what we could tell him than to pass on what was inside him."

And Claudette said, "Yes, yes, and in some ways he was almost mysterious. We tried in a hundred ways without really finding out whether—"

And Horris broke in to say, "Well, now, we needn't stand up all night long. Why don't we—"

"Yes. Yes," Claudette said. "Ellen, would you like something to eat? Coffee? Did you drive all day? I think a trip from Vermont would simply put me out of operation. But you look so—the news is very exciting, eh?" Claudette impulsively hugged Ellen.

"To put it mildly," Ellen said. "What you say makes me feel like I'm drowning. I wish you could just start from the beginning and tell me everything. I just don't want to miss anything."

She had just got back from putting Emily Worth Eubanks in the camp in Vermont, and from a few days in New York where she had talked with her editor in the house that had published *Notes on the Lomkubees,* and from a stop in Washington where a gallery had included four of her works in an Americana exhibit.

In the early evening she had driven finally up to the house and had got the message to call Horris or Claudette, and so had fled to come see them as soon as Claudette had told her what had happened, had departed her house again without a proper hello or goodbye.

So now they were on Horris's long screened back porch that looked out on summer darkness that had covered over the daytime vista, the ridge of the river's bluff bank and, beyond the river, the myriad treetops arising from the vast swampy land of the west bank.

"Honestly, Horris, I don't want you to leave out *anything,*" Ellen said.

"Claudette!" Horris called out toward the kitchen. "You'd best make that two cups, *s'il vous plait.* Ellen—don't you realize it would take me longer to create an exact facsimile than the actual event took?"

"Horris, I don't give a damn if it takes the rest of the summer. Let's see, today is July 26, so I'll give you until Labor Day. No,

Thanksgiving. Because I also want to know everything you were thinking. Claudette, too."

Ellen kicked off her sandals and propped her feet on the low round rattan table around which they sat. She tugged her skirt of pale yellow cotton up to midthigh and jerked the tail of a sleeveless white blouse out of its mooring and let it hang free.

"By God, you do look like you're getting ready to make a night of it," Horris said.

"That's the only reason I'm drinking coffee," Ellen said. "It's insane to drink coffee in this heat."

"I think we may get some rain," Claudette said. "There's that smell in the air."

"Hospital," Horris said.

"What?" Ellen said.

"Is that the beginning? The accident? Michelle's death? Henry in the hospital with the baby? His call to you?"

"I know all of that, Horris, that's not what I mean."

"China, then."

"China? Begin there then," Ellen said.

"That's where he wound up after that call. Not immediately, but a couple of years later. Right after it, right after he heard that you had married, he plunged into—well, into what he only called a year of darkness. Maybe I can begin with that."

"Look, Claudette, he's torturing me on purpose. Horris, why don't you just begin with when you *saw* him. That's what I mean."

"Ellen, I'm not tormenting you. I'm just teasing. Hell, we've got all night."

"All summer."

From an extreme distance came a sudden plangent rumble of thunder, a sound as of the hammered bottom of a tub.

"I believe we're going to get it," Claudette said.

"Well, I hope. Anyway, it was raining in Key West when I got up that morning, just a fine mist. It cleared while I was fixing coffee. And so I went out for what I thought would be a short stretch and walk. Ellen, you know Key West, don't you?"

"A little."

"Well, then, you know it's a very pleasant place. Got sort of a humane geometry about it. Meandering roads, leafy streets that run through neighborhoods of mansions cheek-by-jowl with hovels. Houses squatting against the wind, and everywhere you see bougain-villea and banyans and open-sided saloons. And there are the people who call themselves Conchs. I suppose you do know their name is taken from a sea beast, a creature that lives in a shell shaped like a castle. Well, down there they cook these little critters into a delectable chowder, and of course they sell the shells. And, all told, it's a pleasant place to walk around. So I walked down toward the wharf that morning, and there was just a trifling breeze—"

"Horris, you are deliberately torturing me now," Ellen said. Her laugh had a mix of expectancy and exasperation.

"No. No, this time I'm not. I just want you to see it as I saw it."

Long before the sun came up she felt she did. She could even smell the tar and salt and oil and old timbers about the wharf. Horris in his baggy khakis and collarless shirt with the sleeves ripped off above the elbows, raveling. Glimpsing that intent distant figure sitting with feet and knees widespread, his head studiously bent over some busyness of his hands.

Peeling an orange. Its shell curls downward in a single lengthening spiral. He plucks it up from the wharf, holds the spiral before his eyes, makes it dance like a loose spring, then flings it to the water at his side. Behind him a pelican scutters toward the peel.

Then suddenly something sharply familiar in the profile and posture of the man. Horris feeling a tremor run through him. The man stands. He halves the orange with his fingers, stuffs a half into his mouth. Yes, it is. No, it couldn't be. Yes. He is wearing a blue workshirt with rolled up sleeves and army-type fatigue pants of faded forest green. Yes. No. His face is turned too much away. Horris preferring to be disappointed at a distance. The abrupt gravel-throw of his voice in the morning stillness, the rumbling voice calling out: "Henry!"

The face snapping about, keenly inquisitive, perplexed, perhaps alarmed.

Horris advancing, a rapid swing and thump, a march of two cannon across the timbers.

The squint and pierce of uncertain incredulous eyes of pale blue, translucent. The tenuous smile. Teeth skeptically crossed. The slow deliberate reciprocal advance of long springy legs. The sun-scored concavities of the face beneath an unruly, untended, unminded shock of dark brown hair.

Horris speaking before grasping the bony gripping hand.

And he at first speaking only with his eyes and face, incredulous, enormously pleased. He looking for a long, long moment, his nodding head saying, yes, good. And finally speaking, his voice soft, easy, and yet so controlled, so incongruously casual, the voice of someone who had been away perhaps a month or so.

"How's Ellen?"

"Great," Horris says. "Just great."

And Henry absently raises the other half of the orange toward his mouth but arrests the move and holds it out to Horris as though they met on this wharf each morning to share small talk and citrus.

"Piece of orange?"

It has a smudge of grease from his hands. Horris rips off two sections. Silently they chew. Gulls scatter cries above. Their mouths curve toward impulsive smiles.

A boat horn sounds. Henry snaps a look over his shoulder. He jerks his head toward the boat, a plain grubby fishing vessel. He puts a hand on Horris' shoulder.

"You mind?" he says.

They walk toward the boat but remain on the wharf close to where he had been sitting. Two men are working on the engine. Henry exchanges Spanish words with one of them.

"Your boat?" Horris says.

"More or less," Henry says. "You still close?"

"Close?"

"You and Ellen."

"Oh. Yes. Like that. You fish in this thing?"

"Some. She remember me?"

At that, a sharp laugh exploded out of Ellen. She asked, "What did you tell him?"

"I told him, 'Some,' " Horris said.

"You didn't!"

"Ellen, if you start butting in, I'm going to start skipping around."

"*Touché.*"

"I told him how you remember," Claudette said.

"*Merci.*"

Before the rain even, before the rain blew upon them in a swift prolific drenching that forced them to push their chairs further from the screen, before that Ellen felt she was there, *was* there on the wharf, a sentient and yearning ghost close by, her breath stopping and her heart pounding as she saw for the first time the rumpled miniature spit image of Henry Rust drowsily emerge shirtless from the cabin of the boat, trudging up at the call of his name:

"Henri!"

"*Bonjour, Papa.*"

Henry calling him down to meet *Monsieur* Horris, speaking to the blue-eyed boy first in French but passing into English and departing from this into phrases of Spanish. Then handing him Horris's address scrawled on a match cover.

"Come here when you are ready," Henry says. "Before you come check with Carlos to see if he needs me. Come in an hour no matter what, *si?*"

Horris leading him up the outside stairs of the old frame house and entering with him into their rented bedroom where Claudette wakes up and springs from bed naked to crush the man (by whom she stands as a ghost) with embraces and pats and kisses.

As Horris recalled this, Ellen stretched her bare foot over to give a playful shove against Claudette's knee. She whispered, "I hate you."

"*Je comprends*," Claudette whispered back.

Horris talked on. And in these moments Ellen was beset by the most extraordinary flux and mixture of feelings she had ever known. There was an eerie heating/chilling sensation, a sense of being buffeted by wildly contradictory forces, a sensation of spinning simultaneously downward/upward, spiraling pell-mell about some vortex engendered by tandem or inextricable rushing currents of ecstasy and anguish.

There was, yes, that undiluted joy of seeing him there alive, verified, still alive, eating a real orange with real juice squirting from the corner of his mouth. Soaring joy, yes, but with it, at once, there was that unutterable pain at knowing already that even as she stood ghostly within touch of him he would climb back onto the boat with his son and pass from sight, pass somewhere out into the Gulf leaving behind no clear sign that he would ever turn up again.

Ellen felt in some way that she was hearing not about reality, not about her own life and Horris's and Claudette's and Henry's and Henri's, but that she was strangely witnessing again some mere story or play whose end she knew but against whose end she would profoundly wish against all knowledge, hungering futilely for something other than an end that was inexorable, already written out, beyond amendment even. So, on the wharf, at Horris's vacation apartment, as they walked about the leafy streets, as they sat and talked through the afternoon in that breezy open-sided saloon, through all of this Ellen felt herself a presence perhaps like that of the girl in *Our Town* who as a spirit returns to her house and pleads, unheard, for her still living flesh and blood family to become something other than what they are: to truly talk to each other.

As the night passed, her feelings grew stronger still. Horris's voice, like the unseen river below them, flowed on in myriad currents and ripples as he tried to gift her with what she would have cherished most of all things: a presence there. His voice spun Henry's look and texture and the fabric of his life as it had been woven during the years of which he had seemed to wish to tell so little even as in a few casual hints he told so much.

So she was not only there in Key West, not only following him now to some destination of which she knew nothing except that it might be Cuba, not only where Horris and Claudette had been but where he had been before from the time they last knew, the time when he had ended in a hospital, his child with him, Michelle dead. Dead just after the three of them had driven away from the bureau where they had entered in the central registry the fact of his paternity, dead after no doubt hearing only the screaming screech of the taxi that rammed into the door beside her. Then, as soon as he was able, perhaps even before he should have, Henry had gotten out to call her, and she knew, of course, what he had heard: She's Mrs. John Eubanks.

He didn't say much about the detail of what happened then. He only said, 'I went insane, unless I was already insane. But I couldn't think.' He said, 'I had completely forgotten what I had done. All I felt was betrayal. Utterly incomprehensible, but that's what I felt. It's not worth remembering, what followed. It was a year of darkness. Then, somehow, I came out of it and—you know how these things happen—wound up in China. A flyboy again.' He grinned and said, after I had asked, 'Commercial? Not exactly.'

So she was there, too, now. China. Looking not for him now but only for his tracks, and Henri's, for the family who had helped him take care of the child and given him some of that language that he spoke along with the French and Spanish and English in which he had talked during that day when he had trotted back and forth between his Papa and the boat, running messages and instructions. China. Where her own trip around the world had really ended, its spirit gone after her mother had come down sick of the first devastations of what they thought then was some local disease but that never fully left and soon after they got home killed her. Matt saying, *Ellen, Mama just died. Ellen! Where are you going? Ellen! Papa! Ellen's running away!* In the spring the bitter cold encasement and life itself flinging her choking back to the surface, its placid ceaselessly moving stillness itself like the incessant and fathomless vastness of China. Henry. Flying for them.

Knowing, just knowing where the track had gone was like an immense unstrapping within Ellen's mind. It had long since ceased striving except in dreams, had striven all it could to know the unknowable, had striven without ever having imagined a path like the reality. Nor, even knowing him as she did, had she concretely imagined the boy continually at his side. He would have left him in the care of her family, some relative, visiting often, no doubt. Three times in the nine years she had gone to Paris, once for a showing of her work, and each time had, with Emily along, driven to the vicinity of the village and even to the town where Henry and Michelle and Henri had left the bus and borrowed a car from Michelle's friend, and had cruised about on an aimless reconnaissance that Emily always enjoyed but could never have comprehended.

It turned out that while they were in Australia your book fantastically enough found its way into his hands. How on earth a copy of Notes on the Lomkubees *found its way out there he didn't know, nor do I, nor, I suspect, do you or your publishers. But it did. He found it in a mountain of books in a second-hand store and bought it for thirty cents equivalent. He said Henri loved the illustrations and for awhile worked a few Lomkubee words into his small talk.*

Well, this was a couple of years after the book came out. He was flying a crop dusting plane, and when I asked how that went, he said, 'I'd rather plough.' But he said they loved the open country, and it was awhile yet before they gravitated back to this hemisphere. I ought to emphasize again that he was far more interested in listening than in talking.

I fell silent more or less hoping he would ask some further questions about Emily, but he didn't. He mentioned her at other times, though. Once Henri asked him who we were talking about so much, and Henry said, 'An old friend of mine.' He said, 'Henri, you know your book—the Lomkubees? We're talking about the person who wrote it.' Henri grew very excited, but also scolded. He said, 'Papa, you didn't tell me she was your friend.' Henry said, 'Henri, she has a daughter who is not quite so old as you.' Henri said, 'I know, it is in the book. Papa, will we see them sometime?' And Henry studied the boy's face very closely and tugged at his hair and said, 'In life we never know for sure what will happen. True? Otherwise, life would not be so much fun, eh?'

And, of course, when Claudette left us alone in the saloon he asked about—John Eubanks. He said, 'What's he like?' Henry didn't mention the name but didn't have to. I said, 'You mean Mr. Eubanks, I presume.' He nodded, and I went on, 'That's what Ellen began calling him after their legal marriage.' I wanted him to know more than he was ever likely to ask about. Here he said, 'Horris, you suddenly started picking your words very carefully. You could just tell me what you want me to know.' So I told him, Ellen.

I admit I wasn't sure that I should, but I did. I told him about him and about you and him. And then—if this was a crime all I ask is simple forgiveness—I told him about Emily. He was silenced by this, maybe even stunned. Henri came back just then—and by now it was getting dark—Henri came in with a message from Carlos saying that they had gotten the engine to working. So Henry told Henri he would walk with him back to the boat. I asked if this meant that now they wouldn't be able to come to supper, and he said, 'No, I'm going to tell them we'll be here overnight.' There was some strain in his voice as though it were a reluctant or, no, a difficult decision. And then Henri piped up and said, 'But, Papa, we're supposed to be in Santiago by—'

But Henry shushed him, and it seemed obvious Henri had spoken out of turn. So here, right here was the first and in truth the only hint that was to come out about their destination. I had probed around in both casual and facetious ways, but Henry had said nothing beyond, 'Oh, we just fish around for whatever we can catch.'

Well, they set out for the boat, and I went on back to the apartment. Claudette was fixing up some gumbo. And by then, somehow, as I said to her, I really wouldn't have been surprised if we had seen no more of them. No, not really. Still, I had a very distinct fear about it. So did Claudette. But they showed up on time, Henri gifting us with a bottle of good wine. Later the boy tried a glass of it, but Henry stuck to water and coffee. So we ate and then talked all night, and when it got late Henri sacked out on our bed.

Then just before sunrise we walked them down to the boat. Henri was walking along with his eyes closed, walking with Claudette behind us. On the way was the first time Henry alluded to what I had told him. His voice got very low and he said, 'I think you can see that I've killed myself a million times in the last few hours. But I can't undo anything, can I?' Then he stopped, stopped walking, and said, 'Horris, just suppose it became possible—a visit—how would she feel?'

And I said, 'What you're really asking is what she would do, and I can't tell you. And I don't have to tell you how she would feel any more than you had to tell me how you feel.'

And he said, 'Well, I don't know how things are going to go, anyway. I have some difficult commitments. Everything may be impossible, I don't know.'

We were walking again by now, crossing the wharf, in fact. And when we got to the boat he and Henri very swiftly said goodbye, went aboard, and vanished into the cabin. So fast it took me by surprise, I think. We lingered, of course. They stayed down out of sight until the engine was going, and then they came up and helped see to the lines. I don't know that he didn't somehow wish Claudette and I hadn't still been there as the boat got underway. I suppose Henry's one of those who find protracted farewells sort of tedious.

But there we were in any event. And there they were. And both of them waved. Henry cupped his hands and yelled, 'Adios. And gracias. Muchas gracias.'

And then Henri cupped his hands and yelled something, too—in Chinese. And after he had yelled he looked up at Henry and exploded in laughter. Which Henry did too.

So, soon the boat was quite far out. Henri stayed at the stern, but Henry was somewhere else. We stood there as they got smaller and smaller. And finally it was just a tiny speck on the horizon. One second it was there, and the next—poof. Gone.

It was past six o'clock when Claudette perked still another pot of coffee and hustled up omelettes for them all. They walked Ellen to her car, a recent low-slung car of European make. She had forgotten that the top was down. The seats were wet from last night's rain, and she felt foolish as she mindlessly sat down in the water. She grimaced, then turned to Horris and Claudette, a contemplative smile working about her mouth.

"*Adios,*" she said. "And *gracias. Muchas gracias.*"

They laughed.

And she said, "What do you suppose Henri yelled?"

"I don't have the faintest idea," Horris said, shrugging. "The sounds were very clear but, of course, they meant nothing to me. Some joke, I would guess, from the way they laughed."

She walked softly through the downstairs portion of her lifelong house. The door to Mr. Eubanks's room was closed. In the small kitchen a litter of beer cans in the garbage told of the nightcaps he would have had alone after his nightly stint at the country club.

Ellen went directly to her own room. She set aside the still unpacked bag of limp wine-colored leather that she had flung onto the bed on coming in the previous evening from the northern trip. She kicked off her sandals, closed the door. She stared for a moment at a framed picture of Emily on her dresser, and kissed the image, and half-smiled, and stretched out on the bed without turning down the cover.

She lay with the tail of her sleeveless blouse still tugged out and her pale yellow cotton skirt showing an infinitude of wrinkles.

She carried her steaming mug of coffee across the vast back porch and let the screen door slam behind her and went down the broad back steps where Cliff, at the bottom, sat leafing through the paper. An empty coffee cup sat on the step beside him.

They exchanged good-mornings, and after Ellen had sat down

on the step close by, Cliff handed her a section of the paper without looking away from the page he was scanning.

"Bottom of the front page," he said.

Ellen glanced at the story. Then abruptly she flung the folded paper with a loud flat thwack onto the old dark red bricks of the walk.

"Damn!" she said. And then she added, "Damn! Damn! Damn!" And then she took a loud gulp of her coffee and reiterated the string of damns, vehement and scowling.

"It's that bad?" Cliff said.

"Oh, that's horrible, Cliff. But it's not just that. It's everything. Everything's getting screwed up."

"It's going to be another scorcher, too," Cliff said.

August had come like the breath of a furnace. As its midpoint went by, it had already lasted an eternity.

She missed Emily awfully, and on top of this she had to endure this powerful new yearning for Henry. That and the strange and disconcerting struggle that went with it: a quenchless feeling that he would get in touch with her and also a growing and at moments almost bitter feeling that he would not. Hour by hour one intuition seethed up in ascendancy over the other.

And now this news, the news of the public protest meeting that Mr. Eubanks had announced. This awakened fresh rage along with a new struggle within. As she uttered her strings of damns she thought that, by God, now she *would* ask him to leave as Cliff had long ago suggested she do. But this resolve, which was not a resolve at all but a bitter whim—called up her other resolve: her private commitment to her privately made bargain. No, she would not do that, could not ask him to leave. Whatever life assessed of her she would yield, even if it was only complicity in the illusion of their marriage. But the fresh unsettling anger was there, and she hungered for a respite from inner tumult.

She profoundly missed Emily and began each day by scratching her a short note that she had taken to handing personally to the carrier. Through the end of July and now deep into August she had been going out each morning to meet the carrier. She would walk down the drive to the Trail and wait, and feel delighted if he brought a note or card from Emily. She would feel that along with some not quite admitted disappointment that nothing had yet come from Henry.

She had felt sure that he would send some word, but each day this certainty collapsed. Then it would restore itself and collapse again. She would walk down the pea-gravel drive feeling tiny under the tall reaching plumes of the quarter-mile line of oleanders, and as she walked the rising sense of expectancy would come, and she would say to herself, *It's foolish to expect anything. He's in another world somewhere.*

So the anticipation would be curbed only to break free and burgeon again the moment the carrier's decrepit old jeep rolled into view. Then she would *know* there would be some word, even if only that, even if only a single word. She imagined getting a mere card that would by something in its picture somehow convey some promise for the future. Perhaps it might even disclose a place to which she might go. The card would bear only his name.

Through the hot days of August she had struggled not only against this fresh moil of yearnings and conflicts but against time itself and her own conflicting plans. In New York she had committed herself to a new book. It would, like the first, be about the Lomkubees, but it would be almost entirely of pictures, sketches, and photographs, these to be presented with little text. She had planned to set to work at once, to fill her days with the task during the time Emily would be at Montaqua. She had hoped to begin selecting and editing from her enormous store of sketches and from a vast accumulation of photographs that she had taken over the years. And she had intended, as well, even before that to drive down to Temulca for a few days to talk to Bema about the new project, to see Kimo, if possible, if he were not still in his strange exile from Temulca as he had been early in the year. Or perhaps she would go see him wherever, assuming she could find out. Ellen had thus envisioned a busy month of clear directions.

But she had gotten to none of it, or scarcely any. At first the news about Henry had more than preoccupied her. It obsessed. Ellen had spent days at libraries trying to find out what was going on in Cuba. The library at McClung had left her unsatisfied, and so had the larger one in Carterville. So she had driven up to Riverton to the university library with its esoteric journals filled with articles by specialists. And from the speculations of journalists and advocates she wove her own speculations, conjuring circumstances into which she could place Henry.

As she read of this country to which she had paid little previous heed she came to detest its government. She found that the head of its government evoked Ellis Kelso in her thoughts, much as the handful of men who were evidently pressing militantly for change brought to her mind Kimo and his handful of followers.

Ellen would stare at a map of Cuba, at Santiago and the terrain arising about it, the highlands of the Sierra Maestra, and imagine

Henry's boat putting into the port, and imagine Henry and Henri—doing what? Going where? Bringing what to whom? Then, all over again, she would have to remind herself: *I don't know, I don't know anything. Maybe it really is only a fishing boat.* Then her mind would answer itself: *Just fishing he would have had no cause for mystery or reticence.* Hence she would know certain flashes of despair which she could neither believe nor quite permanently repress: *Unless he wanted to be, he could never be found.*

Once in the first days Ellen felt a powerful impulse to set out in search. She had even called the airlines to check schedules and the price of tickets to Cuba. Nor was it the essential folly of a wild-goose chase that held her in check. She refrained only because she could not rid herself of the belief that he would be in some way reaching out to her. So she was afraid to stray far from McClung for either a goose chase or for work in Temulca. She felt that she would no sooner depart than the letter would come, or the card, perhaps a wire.

August from its beginning had been a tumult of thrashing emotions and frustrations. She would get up early and dash off a note to Emily and go to the big kitchen to get coffee. Often she would join Cliff on the porch or the steps for a short visit during which their words would be mostly few and gentle. Then she would trudge up to her workroom wherein the flattened and impaled head of Henry Rust now had the look of a weird fixture that had been there forever. She would stare at the heaps of pictures and at the sheets of contact prints to which strips of 35-mm film were attached. She might make some headway or none, but never much.

Her mind would be listening for the midmorning moment when the mail carrier would be due. And first would always come the moment when she would hear the crunch of a heavy car going out the drive, and she would glance down through the tall windows and see Mr. Eubanks's big silver colored convertible receding toward the highway, its massive rear bumper displaying stickers that preached the gospel to which he had turned the previous year, the new crusade that had been born just as the other was petering out. His departure always meant that it was 8:50.

Now it meant as well that the carrier would be by in about an hour and ten minutes. Some days by 9:30, she would have turned away from her work and, with her note to Emily in hand or pocket, would have begun walking a winding circuitous way among the trees of the front grounds to find herself loitering by the mailbox fifteen minutes early, impatient, disgruntled even, at the traffic going by on the highway.

To her displeasure the Trail had been changed in the late 1940s from macadam to concrete, and its lanes widened, and now the flow of cars along the old road seemed to be crowding even that at certain hours of certain days, and during weekends, and now there was already talk of adding more lanes to the road. Often she would hear the mailman's old jeep before she would see it. Each time she would feel herself clutch up within, and each time she would simultaneously feel, yes, now there will be something, while telling herself: *No, he is still gone and if he were going to get in touch he would have said something definite to them.*

At the sight of a strange envelope in the packet her heart would catch. Once she audibly gasped at the glimpse of an obviously foreign stamp beneath the bulk mailed letter on top. But it turned out to be affixed to a card from a fellow artist and friend, a man who lived in New York but was vacationing in Chili.

After the mail she would go back to work with better concentration, but likely as not she would break off well before lunch to wander the grounds or drive downtown to gossip with Horris or go to his house to visit with Claudette or drive or walk over to Percy Ensley's vast old home where she would find Florence usually on her knees digging and ferreting weeds in endless flower beds.

Many days she felt that the only thing she really looked forward to was the afternoon downpour that would drench and cleanse the earth and cool it for a little while. It would come crashing down on her skylight with a sound that she relished. Yet, solitude that she had always cherished would on some days now become almost unbearable. She would drift downstairs to idle with Aunt Margaret in her room with its eternal jasminereek and watch her fingers flying at the interminable embroidering. She would gravitate to the front of the house and sit on the arm of the big leather chair where her Papa would sit alternately drowsing and watching the rain, his heavy stick making a light tapping on the heart-of-pine planking.

But even the reliable afternoon rain had failed to come down on several days in August. The great clouds up from the Gulf around St. Teresa's would blow over and shut out the baking sun for awhile and pass on, leaving the earth dry and more sweltering than before.

Today, as she heard the heavy crunch of Eubanks's car, Ellen in her workroom grappled with almost unmanageable irritation. She was still fuming at the news story, the account of his announced plan to stage a public meeting in early September on the eve of the opening of school. Even when his car had rolled from view and he had passed from her mind Ellen felt ill at ease with the diverse currents heaving within her.

Then the morning's mail brought a cheery one-sentence card from Emily that momentarily hoisted her spirits. It also brought a short note from her editor, Paul Gans, writing to applaud again the wish she had expressed in New York to plunge into the picture book at once. He also said that his colleagues now had tentatively approved the title she had suggested: *The Last of a Murdered Tribe*. But even his buoyant letter had a contrary effect. It sharpened her frustration at the way events had diverted her from sustained work. Then she thought, *No. Not events. Me. I've got to shake free and—*

And suddenly she wanted to talk to Horris about the strong feelings the morning's news had aroused in her. After phoning she went down to the *Mirror* to chat while sitting on his desk and having a sandwich from the drug store.

Horris, of course, shared her apprehensions about the protest Eubanks had announced. It could only cause needless trouble. But Horris didn't share her sense of frustration.

"We're just going to have to pull the rug out from under him one way or another," he said. "We've worked too hard to get this school thing decently set up to have it ripped up by a bunch of lunatics now."

"Who do you suppose the quote outstanding guest speaker unquote is going to be?" Ellen asked.

"Beats me," Horris said. "If we work it right there won't be any meeting or speaker, either. The truth is that if this bunch gets together that particular weekend it won't matter who talks, because they're going to hear only what they want to hear. Worse than that, they're also likely to go on to do what they really want to do. Ellen, let's face it, all that bunch are nightriders at heart, whether they know it or not. I don't know about Mr. Eubanks, he may not be, probably isn't. But the ones who would turn out for this, well—"

"Damn," Ellen said. "It even burns me that they'd be *allowed* to meet at Mount Oro. It's a damn desecration. The very word means *light*, and—oh, hell, what can I do?"

"Well, if they're going to meet we can't forbid them that. What we've got to do is find a way to make Mr. Eubanks deeply interested in calling off this particular meeting."

"But how?" she asked.

"Well, there are ways and ways," Horris said. "We'll see."

The afternoon rain bashed down as if to compensate for its few misses. She was back in her workroom when it began. It came in a flung drenching that showed no sign of blowing over in the usual twenty or thirty minutes. At the start of it Ellen was writing an acknowledgment to the editor Paul Gans. But she left the note unfinished to go downstairs and talk about the uncommon fury of the downpour.

The rain was forming almost a solid sheet of water that ran across the screen on one side of the back porch. Ellen looked through it toward the garage, glad that she had mindlessly broken her habit and driven her car into the shelter where the twins' roofless limousine still rested on blocks made of half-stumps, the cake of dust thickening year by year over its untouched surface. *Happy one nine four one, happy new year to—*

Cliff was soaping and oiling a bridle that he had spread out on newspaper on the kitchen table.

"I once had a Chinese cook who taught me what to do when it rains," he said. As he had said perhaps a hundred times to Ellen, maybe even a thousand. And she answered as she had whatever number of times it had been.

"What?"

"Let it rain," Cliff said.

"I never thought of that," Ellen said.

"Well, before this one's done you'll get to thinking about it. This one's got that smell about it."

"Really?"

"Yep. I don't know what it is exactly, but when they come to stay they bring a certain something with them. Can't you smell it?"

She was sitting astride a chair, leaning her chin over its back. She watched Cliff's hands patiently rubbing the leather, forming a brown sudsy muck, wiping it, rubbing more. The air of the kitchen was areek with saddle soap and neat's foot oil.

"I don't care if it never stops," she said.

"You don't, eh?"

Suddenly Ellen jumped as a hand lightly wacked down on top of her disheveled curls. Aunt Margaret.

"Didn't you hear Mrs. Pichon calling you? Western Union wants you on the telephone."

Ellen leaped backwards and was out of the door even before her chair finished falling sideways to the floor. In the reddened gloom of the back hallway she heard the piping voice of the spinster she knew who ran the Western Union office.

The voice went on explaining and re-explaining why she hadn't wanted to send a messenger boy out in the weather. Ellen felt her skull would explode if the voice said another word. This had to be from him, and so—

"Ellen, it was sent from New Orleans," the piping voice was saying, "and I don't know if there was a garble in transmission or what, but it doesn't read right to me."

New Orleans. Yes. He would fly in there and then fly up to Riverton. And this will say meet him up there and—

"Anyway," the friendly, familiar, and maddeningly discursive voice went on, "I can check it in a little bit, or maybe I can just check it with them when I close out my transmissions tonight, I'll be staying open until six, even though we don't get—"

"Could I—" Ellen began. Then the voice, as though it couldn't interrupt itself, went on.

"Anyway, Ellen, here's what it says. First, you have a pencil? Maybe you'll want to write it down."

Ellen scrounged in a tiny drawer on the phone table and found a pencil without a point.

"Yes, yes, I've got one. Go ahead."

"Well, it says—your name and everything, Route 1, McClung, et cetera, and then here's the message: Come if possible to Marilou . . . that's em ay are eye el oh you . . . Come if possible to Marilou stop Eye eye kay. End of message. Now, Ellen, did you get that signature? It was eye eye kay. Letter I letter I letter K."

"What?"

Frantically Ellen chewed away wood from the pencil to expose a bit of lead. "Can you read the whole thing to me again?"

"Well, that doesn't surprise me, Ellen, it doesn't make any sense to me, either. But here it is."

This time she read it even more slowly and emphatically. Ellen was utterly baffled, so perplexed that even her disappointment was for the moment forgotten. Then the familiar old spinster was telling her that later she would check the office of origin if Ellen needed the full name of the sender.

"Eye eye kay?" Ellen said. *Who on earth was Marilou?* IIK? Who? Who? Something had to be fantastically mixed up. Just then the voice broke in again.

"No, no, Ellen, I made a mistake. I made a mistake. But it still doesn't make any sense. That first eye isn't an eye. It's a one. It should be a one. Now that doesn't even make as much sense. One eye kay. Ellen, I'll just have to check the office of origin and—"

Now it came to her. Now she grasped the message. Now she made the connection that told her its meaning. Kimo. It was from Kimo, one-eyed Kimo. Last year he had lost an eye to a shotgun pellet fired into a meeting that he was leading to organize a protest against a fresh and brazen outrage perpetrated by Ellis Kelso. Kelso had personally stalked through the public schools of the county and ordered the expulsion of several Lomkubee students who manifested, in the sheriff's opinion, negroid features.

"Oh, listen, I get it now," Ellen said. "It's a sort of joke from an old friend. I get it, so thank you. Thank you."

Kimo. Yes, and Marilou was one of the innumerable islands of Los Nubes. Yes, he would be hiding there.

Ellen took the stairs three at a time to her workroom, which was twilight dark from the density of the storm. She switched on a brilliant photographic lamp that lit up a map of the state pinned to one wall of corkboard.

Los Nubes. Yes. Many, if not most, of the villages and a great many of the islands and islets of the section bore the names of women. Yes, Marilou: there, a dot deep in Los Nubes. It could be the name of the dot or of the tiny island it was on. She needed a larger scale map. Well, she could find it. But how find him? Some of the named places had only a single house, of course. Los Nubes: houses gaudily painted and usually built on stilts against tides and floods that often covered the lower islands.

Ellen packed a large leather camera equipment bag into which she also stuffed sketching materials. In her bedroom she changed into fresh tapered khaki pants and a dark wine-colored shirt that was tailored like a man's. From a dark wood chest under her window she took out the headband Bema had given her long ago. She adjusted it straight across her forehead.

She paused for a moment to stare in the mirror at an image that for an instant seemed very strange to her. She stared from her image to the picture of Emily on the dresser, Emily who powerfully resembled her even while looking unmistakably her father's daughter. Henry's pale blue eyes had been transplanted into Emily, but they peered out of faintly tilted housings that resembled her mother's, and she had Ellen's tumult of dark feathery curls about her face.

Now an indecisive moment drove Ellen to sit on the edge of her bed. She thought, *If I'm gone and he calls I'll kill myself.* And then, *I've got to learn all over again that he's gone.*

Downstairs Cliff was full of admonishments.

"Goddam, Ellen, you're going out in this mess?"

"Well, maybe I'll put up the top of the car," she said. She was on the back porch drawing on a voluminous yellow slicker.

"Well, now, don't do anything radical like that," Cliff said. "You don't want to suffocate. But why don't you wait 'til it stops?"

"Cliff," Ellen said, "I once had a Chinese cook who taught me what to do when it rains."

"All right. You gonna tell anybody where you're going, so we can fish for the body?"

"Temulca," Ellen said.

She started out the back door but turned back.

She said, "I'm going to Los Nubes, too. But don't mention it, will you not?"

"You going there alone?"

"I wouldn't want you to mention it to anyone, okay?"

"Don't worry about that. Just look out for yourself."

Ellen bussed him on the cheek.

He said, "How long you going to be down there?"

"A day or so, I think. I may come back tomorrow. It depends."

6

The dark green hood gleamed somberly under the crashing rain. It seemed to be coming down the length of the state. Here and there it let up only to resume as a demonic downpour.

Inside the car, under the furious drumming of water on the roof, Ellen would turn the radio loud when music was on and then switch it low or off to avoid the obnoxious voices of the announcers.

She had taken the bridge across the river just below McClung to drive down the still new highway that dropped southward a distance from the river, what she had supposed would be a faster trip through flat country until it began to grow hilly again around Koppalouka.

But the rain seriously curtailed her speed. At moments visibility closed down to a few feet. Once she sucked in her breath and jammed down on the brakes as suddenly the huge gray back of a van loomed just at the low nose of her car.

As she got further south the sodden afternoon began to grow even darker. She cut eastward onto the familiar road to St. Teresa's. In marshy places water in the ditches approached the level of the road. Northbound cars crawled by, lights on, passengers invisible behind the opaque blur of the water on the windows.

Soon the rain seemed to grow lighter, but now fog began to roll up from the marshes onto the road. Ellen almost passed by the cut-off to Los Nubes. It forked leftward from the road to St. Teresa's and wended thence to a single main artery that ran the length, north and south, of Los Nubes, a linkage of highway and causeway and bridges. The largest single uninterrupted stretch of solid land in Los Nubes was slightly more than three miles long and three-quarters of a mile wide.

In this vast sprawl of islands and islets the fog wrapped like great coils and loops of gauze about her car and windshield. At moments she was forced to come to a dead stop. A newscaster said rains were inundating the state from the Akana Mountains southward, as well as adjacent states. Some flash flooding had already been reported in certain low-lying communities located in the section west of the Bulomkubee.

Ellen snapped off the radio to free all of her concentration. In brief stretches the road would be free of fog, but then at a dip or turn her car again would enter a shroud that bounced her headlights back almost as a solid wall might.

(In the best of weather a mist or vapor of fog overlay all or most of Los Nubes twice a day. Often it would linger through much of the day in certain places, a cover that was not invariably blinding but often strangely translucent, creating the impression that the region was sprawled in a nest of gentle mist or a field of clouds. The phenomenon had given the region its name: Los Nubes. The Clouds.

(It had other no doubt older names which can still be heard in many corners. These evoke the far more remote time when Los Nubes first became inhabited by Mayans along with others thought to have stemmed from the same roots as the Aztecs. Migrating and probably fleeing groups of those Mexican civilizations had happened upon Los Nubes in the same broad epoch, between 800 and 1000, A.D., but modern scholars tended to accept that some group of Mayans from the Yucatan region had been the first. They had crossed the Gulf perhaps in that epoch when, one after the other, the great Mayan cities were being abandoned for causes that still have not been unraveled.

(Hard evidence drawn out of artifacts and rudimentary records point to the near certainty that the very first group to inhabit the region was predominantly female. The effects of this reality are to be found in the social customs and traditions that prevail in modern Los Nubes. Similarly the Los Nubian penchant for frequent festivals and ceremonials, as an important part of the lives of families and vague clans as well as communities, ostensibly echoes the Mayan obsession with religious ritual, and perhaps the Aztec as well.

(Although Los Nubes was from the beginning included as part of the principality of the state, the typical white inhabitant of mainland Nemisisipiana has ever looked upon the region as a separate realm. On the mainland those who lived there came to be called Nubes. And in the Anglo-Saxon argot, the word Nube came to carry a load of mixed distaste and envy as well as bewilderment, amazement, and disapproval. Such prevalent attitudes tended to be fed by rumor and legend, simply because not many genteel whites elected to investigate first-hand the idiosyncratic ways of Los Nubes.

(In the early days of the white man's conquest of America, Los Nubes had become a natural place of refuge for the illicit, and a natural home for certain of the dispossessed. It was a place, once the word of it had spread, to which the homicidal poet might be tempted to flee as might the preacher compromised by some discovered lechery. It appealed as well to the pirate, the slave fortunate enough to have broken his bond, the embezzler, the loose convict, the servant weary of indenture, the deserter, the fugitive traitor, and even a few adventurous housewives more fond of life than of the kitchen. Los Nubes over the generations had attracted as well its share of swashbucklers and speculators, including many of the same avaricious sort who founded the mainland society that they still controlled.

(To this pungent and racy history can be traced the popular conception of Los Nubes as the home of either desperadoes or godless barbarians. Thoughtful students, however, have tended to discover a contrary truth: With astonishing speed the culture of Los Nubes had always tended to assimilate the coarse and dangerous and desperate kind of men and women who were European civilization's primary contribution to the population. And far from being godless, the eventually polyglot Los Nubians, like their Mayan forebears, acknowledged numerous gods. To these they paid tribute not in disconnected and insulated ceremonies but in a way of life that included the earthy, frequent, and lively festivals during which mescalino was widely used, commonly dispensed in small cups of very rich, very bitter chocolate. Chocolate was and is the common habitual drink of Los Nubians. This, too, echoes the remote Mexican culture wherein the cacao bean was so revered as to be used for money.)

Slowly Ellen went on. She rolled down her window when the rain permitted. Now and then she stopped and backed to throw her headlights and yellow fog lamps on obscure road signs. Again and again she lost her sense of distance, of how far she had come, how far ahead lay her destination.

Approaching vehicles would loom up with astounding suddenness through the murk. She would see a great dazzle of light flattened and weirdly distorted within the fog. Some of them would pass by as though conditions were normal. Few cars overtook her from behind. But once a wildly brilliant set of headlamps rushed up to her rear, veered. A small truck shot past, several forms indistinctly huddled in its bed, forms filling the eerie night with spirited yells and laughter.

Ahead she saw a penetrating oasis of garish light within the murk: a gas station illumined by lamps of bluish or violet color. She could barely make out a small sign at its approach. It said: Last Gas.

Ellen pulled in and ordered her car filled. The station office was situated in a small stone room with a big frame for a window. No glass was in it. Inside she studied a detailed map of Los Nubes and took a closer reading of her destination. She turned away from the map to find the station attendant gazing at her from the doorway.

He seemed a man of indefinite middle years. His face had a caramel glisten. His eyes were dark, warm. His thumbs were hooked upon the pockets of orange trousers. A fresh receipt book of some sort was stuck in the pocket of his pale green shirt.

"It say $3.28," he said. "I give it you for three."

"Thank you," Ellen said, "but—"

She extracted four dollars from her large folded soft leather wallet in which she also kept her licenses, her passport, and other credentials. She said, "You can keep the change."

He smiled as she handed him the four. Then as she passed through the door he faintly and languidly bowed. She felt a brush of his hand, a touch at her pocket. She stuck her hand in and found a dollar bill.

Ellen laughed and, as she climbed back into her car, called out, *"Merci."*

He acknowledged not with a word but a slow regal nod. Then he burst into a laugh that shot upward into the lurid violet fog surrounding the station.

Marilou, so the map had disclosed, was not a settlement but a mere scrap of island. It would be reached by crossing over several other islands joined by one-lane bridges. The first bridge going in would be a pontoon bridge.

Some of the islands of Los Nubes could be reached only by boat. The pirogue and canoe and skiff were common in use. Even along the main road she could see, when the fog permitted, vehicles parked on the shoulders of causeways, left there by owners who would have paddled to their water-bound houses and villages. Even in the murk lights would sometimes disclose the vivid primary colors that were preferred for both dwellings and commercial structures of Los Nubes. It was common to see a house with its sides variously painted in glaring shades of blue and orange and green and purple. So was the sight of a wall daubed in fantastic forms and designs employing all colors of the spectrum. Los Nubians had been known to sink into grisly depression upon merely glimpsing the rat-gray drabness of typical mainland cities.

Suddenly she realized she was seeing no more lights, no more electric lights. There had been a new darkness the last half-hour of her drive. When she glimpsed the silhouette of a building there might be no lights inside or out. In a window or two she saw the faint golden lambency of lantern or candle light. The fog seemed to be clearing some, and now the rain was steady but no longer thrashing.

At a certain turn-off she was stopped more by intuition than recognition. She backed to fix her headlights on a difficult sign, a wooden plaque that had somehow split in half. Its legend was scarcely decipherable. Yet, it seemed the marker for her turn-off.

She swung left. Very soon a small sign identifying the pontoon bridge confirmed her direction. It said, *Por Margarita*. The floats of the bridge bobbed and wavered dizzily, yielding to the considerable weight of her car. It was one lane only. Ellen wondered what she would do if a car suddenly approached.

She kept her face pressed close to the windshield, straining to keep in sight the faint sheen of the cables that marked the edges of the bridge, cables at ankle and waist height. Then she was across. It exited onto a rutted road of crushed shell. The next two bridges were of rigid wood, but the timbers creaked and rattled as she crossed them.

A sign by the second said: *Marilou.*

Beyond it her lights at first disclosed only the narrow lane between squat, thick, wind-bent trees. At last to her right she made out the dark rectangular shape of a large house. It was elevated either on pillars or enormous timbers.

She decided to go on. Then suddenly she gasped as a flashlight beam cut into her eyes. At the left of the lane a form she could not make out was behind the light. The lance of light cut away from her face. The form approached.

Then bending close to her streaming window was Kimo's face,

grinning with its now habitually tautened mouth, its single warm/
cold eye, the narrow black ribbon from his left eye patch cutting
slightly into the skin of his forehead. She rolled the window down.

His hand reached to the wheel and touched hers.

"Follow me," he said.

Behind the house she had seen he signaled a stop. She got out.
Kimo nodded toward the house.

"This is where we are," he said. "But there are people in there.
We will go over there instead."

He led her to a smaller building behind the other. It was a
square structure also elevated on timber stilts. He swiftly went
before her up steps constructed simply like a tilted ladder. He lit
them with the flashlight as she followed up.

Inside he lit a small lamp.

"All the power is out," he said.

There was a great rustling of oilskin as he shucked off his dark
poncho and she her yellow slicker. He was wearing the pale blue
omanta shirt, its breast bearing symbols not of mourning but of
earthly death recognized in silence as the Lomkubees practiced
mourning. It had in recent years been his invariable costume, much
publicized in the stories about his activities.

For a moment Kimo clasped and unclasped his hands as though
full of agitation. And then, composed, he gazed steadily at her out
of a face that now seemed never to cease flexing beneath its dark gold
skin.

"You are so good," he said.

"I'm starved," Ellen said.

"I expected it," he said, grinning.

They ate at a small table near the corner of the room that
evidently had originally been constructed as a place for storage. From
a brown paper bag Kimo produced cooked fish and crabmeat, dried
figs, two ripe bananas, coarse flaky bread, a fruit jar of grapefruit
juice. They ate in close communicant silence. Again Kimo thanked
her for answering his plea, the wire he had had a contact in New
Orleans send off.

"You are so good to come," he said. "There are some things I
need to tell you, and ask you. Later."

"I've wanted to talk to you. I've been hungry to see you," Ellen
said.

While they were still eating the rain began thrashing down
again with a fury that filled the room. Its roof was heavy tin upon
which the water drummed with a violent plangent roar. In the closeness of the storm sound Kimo's face grew grave and harsh.

"I miss Puana bitterly," he said. Ellen reached and touched her fingertips to his. He went on, "I wish I were like Bema. I wish I had her wisdom. She has lost so many, but is still whole. But Kimo is not Bema. The foolish trout is not the mother whale, and since they killed her I am not whole. Part of me is gone that will never come back. Puana and I were truly each of one. I haven't been able to talk to anyone else of this. I—"

"I know what you feel," Ellen said. "Try not to feel alone. We are one, we are each of one, and—"

Kimo's face all at once seemed as open and vulnerable as a small boy's, and at the same time as distant and inscrutable as an old man's. His single eye brought Mark to mind.

"Us—yes," he said, "but—" He paused a moment. "Believe me, this is not what I most needed to speak about. It is only that you refilled me with warmth."

Above them thrummed and rumbled the rain sound, great fingers drumming on the tin. The thunderous roar of it encased them. For a long while they sat still, fingers merely touching.

Kimo's eye seemed sad but now calm. It stared at the low flame of the lamp. Ellen watched the slow heave of his breath beneath the shirt with its delicate flowing design of mergent red and green on the pale blue, the red in swirls and folds moving across the green and vanishing into it. A catch, a faint sigh, at the turn of each of his breaths disclosed a tension that no longer showed in his face. His mouth was trying to discover a smile. It called up the moment when his mouth had done the same thing while still swollen and split from Ellis Kelso's blows.

The time of that first meeting had joined them in a bond that had never been broken. Ellen now felt herself swarming with an overwhelming warmth and tenderness toward Kimo as with a seething detestation of the world that had become his enemy, the world that had insanely killed Puana in the same burst of gunfire that had taken Kimo's eye and left the flesh beneath it faintly pocked where other shot had penetrated. Ellen saw, in some way quite above thought, that this was the same malignant fold of the world that had carried Henry away from her and that perhaps even now was holding his mind and person captive, in a sense, holding him even though his only true place on earth had to be with her.

Ellen looked, as from a slight distance above them she looked, at Kimo, at herself, at the two of them, and at this remove her mind knew, *But for us I could not have endured.* Under the great dinning of the rain now her mouth moved to say what by now it had almost soundlessly said three or two or four times in each of the last nine years. She moved to say it now with some inexplicable unreasoned feeling that this would be the last time.

"Meshamantakubee," she said or knew she tried to say while knowing that once again she had not quite said it. But again he saw it, again almost imperceptibly nodded, a curveless mouth encircled by its tautened lines but nonetheless smiling.

His hand moved to the lamp. It went out but for a wild stubborn gasping flicker. He bent over the small sooty chimney and blew.

Galaxies exploded again, and her wild irrepressible gasping laugh arose trivially against the furious hammering of the rain on the metal roof. The laugh rose up as of its own volition out of a constricted throat. She could feel her collapsed face and eyes within it frantically rolling in the darkness with the startled scattered stars, stars rent and driven by the hot storm.

She knew this and then expected the slow lanquid descent of her spirit back to her flesh, the wafting of the constellations to their accustomed tracks, the cessation of the pounding soaring singular pulse they had become. But this time it was not happening. He was devouring her still, consuming her and absorbing her into himself, into them, and now impossibly filling her again and exploding her again into an almost unbearable seething of aliveness, of quaking gathering joy out of which his face emerged transmuted as ever into the other, into Henry. And then the subsiding, the ebbing did not come, either. And at last, with the cells of her mind molten into flesh, she shouted at a whisper, even as the rocketing volitionless laugh began to arise out of her gasps she cried out from behind melting unfocused unfocusable eyes, "Who *are* yoooooooou?"

Much later, when no word had yet been uttered, when her eyes stood open and wondering, when she lay with her right arm lost somewhere in the warmth between them, when her face rested on its side over the steadily slowly slowing beat of his heart: then she suddenly knew that what she had felt was true, knew that for reasons of which she had no knowledge at all that this would be the last time of their joining. And suddenly she knew that he, too, knew this, that this alone had so powerfully moved him to give to her all of his flesh and passion that could be given. So when he finally spoke she comprehended what he said far more deeply, she believed, than he could have imagined. His voice was a whisper at once close and distant like a subtle breeze.

"It is so important for me to know that you will remember me well," he said. Without speaking or looking up Ellen touched her fingertips to his face. She found his mouth and touched it, a seal. She felt very frightened, not of harm to herself nor even to him, frightened of something not fathomed. In the long silence she wondered what it was that she knew without knowing, what it was that he, too, knew.

Kimo pulled a blanket over the pallet on which they lay. The rain was subsiding again. Ellen could only dimly see her yellow slicker hanging on a nail, the pale ghost of his dark poncho hanging close by it.

She had been asleep, and the boat's engine was very loud, and then he was in the water, and she tried to reach him, but he was in the water far away, and she could not reach him, and why was he swimming away? She woke up with a shiver.

Kimo had gotten up. She saw him at the door. It closed behind him. Now the rain was falling demonically on the roof. Where was he going? Oh, yes. He had no clothes on.

Shortly he reentered. Yes, the lamp had been on when she woke up. He came back in dripping. He grinned.

"Two birds with one stone," he said. He wrapped himself in a blanket, drying.

"Two birds?" Ellen said.

"Relief and a shower."

Ellen burst into a laugh. She felt like snuggling in the blanket forever. But suddenly she threw it aside and jumped toward the door.

"The steps are slick. Be careful," Kimo said.

In the blackness the form of the big house was like black on navy blue. The rain hammered against her skull and skin. Her feet squished into soggy sandy earth. Ellen felt as though she were a Lilliputian under a gargantuan spigot, so dense was the fall of rain. She began giggling. The rain was cool but not cold.

Standing, she turned her face up into it and gathered a great mouthful. She squirted it upward in a thin stream, skeeting it between her teeth. She ran her fingers through soaked hair as though shampooing and rubbed her body as though in the shower. Only a very thin line of golden lambency shone from the small storehouse door.

Kimo was waiting with a blanket held open to her as she stepped back in the door. She was laughing. So was he as he rolled the blanket about her, furiously patting it against her. Her arms were trapped within the shroud of the fabric. Ellen began to lose her balance. She shrieked. Kimo caught her, raised her into his arms as though she were an infant. Kneeling, he placed her back on the pallet.

She lay with the tingle of exultant flesh, wrapped like a

mummy, watching him dress. His hands swiftly, sightlessly gathered his wet hair, divided it, braided it into a thick loose rope that dangled down to the bird-wing seam on the back of his shirt. He turned about.

"Now I'm starved," he said. He jerked his head toward the big house as he slipped under his poncho.

Ellen was dressed when he came back. He brought a block of cheese, two eggs boiled hard, and a small box of soda crackers.

"There's coffee over there," he said. "We'll go over in a little."

As they ate he began to talk. He was serious, intense, but not now solemn. He spoke of his efforts begun years before to organize the people of Temulca against the regular abuses of the white society about them. And of his other subsequent efforts to draw the laborers of the vicinity into some kind of union. And of his still more recent attempts to focus the protests of both his people and the Negroes upon the agencies of government, both within the county and at the state capital.

And at last he was saying, "I don't think I have been foolish in what I did. I think I was foolish only in what I expected it to achieve. It's strange. Each time I have grown too foolish, they have done something to open my eyes. Isn't it ironic that last fall when they shot out my eye they gave me my best vision of what I need to do? That when they killed Puana they at last taught me the value of my own life?

"What I see now is that its real value lies only in my exposing it to their worst. I have been thinking a long time about this. And I can no longer imagine myself working through long patient years at a game played by their rules. This is what I have been doing, and what I did not know before is that all such efforts are doomed, not only because the rules are theirs but theirs to change and change at will. So it is futile.

"As soon as we arouse enough pressure to change one despicable rule they reinstate it in some different guise. And even the law makes no difference to them. They don't really follow even their own rules. Kelso, last fall, what did he care what the Supreme Court had said. He not only ignored it but contemptuously reversed gains made long ago. What is clear is that it is because the Court had spoken that he went stalking through the classrooms. Can you imagine how those children felt? This lawman pointing to this one, that one. 'I don't like the shape of this one's nose,' he would say. 'This one's hair don't look right.' What could our children understand. Their hurt was direct. But there is a larger hurt. No one seemed to care, almost no one in that county. Some didn't even seem to realize that Kelso's message was not really aimed at us at all but at the Negroes. What was he saying? He was saying, 'Here's what the law here says about the Supreme Court. Try to become more than we wish you to be and you must deal with me—the great Ellis Kelso.' Argh!"

Kimo made a sound of immense disgust. He drew a deep breath and went on.

"Well, I am playing the game of rules no more. My purpose from now on will be very simple. It will be to strike them when they strike us, and to make it hurt more. It is the only protest they understand. And, yes, of course it is dangerous. It could bring prison or worse to us. But even this could serve a greater purpose than all I've done before. Even this could finally be good. The truth is that my life might in reality be of more value if I were in prison. Or even if I were dead."

Ellen swiftly placed her hand on his.

"I am not taking a sentimental view," he went on. "I mean as a practical thing, a thing that will bring change. What is needed ultimately is for more of them to be forced to see just what they are doing, to be forced to do openly what they do all the time covertly and by indirection. So many hide from the truth, so many are evil only in this passive way, this refusal to recognize their own complicity. To these, in a certain sense, any one of us would make a stronger witness in prison than out. When we are dead by their hand we suddenly speak in an unmistakable voice. I know this is true, it is true even of Puana's death. It tore me apart, but I know some whose eyes were opened for the first time by this. That is no small thing. Finally it may be that the most any of us can hope to do is reach a few, just a few.

"Right now, of course, there are only a few of us. And we are being watched. I know they are watching like hawks in Bienville County. If I had not left I would be in jail now, but not in a way that would matter. They were prepared to harass me to death by charging me with a thousand small crimes. I could spit and go to jail for it in Bienville County. The watch there is very close. It is hard to tell how close it is elsewhere. We know that they arrested one of our people who was bringing us some guns by boat. We know the papers carried nothing on it. We don't know how they knew. Perhaps the arrest was purely coincidental. But who knows? The immigration boat stopped him. And, of course, it is true that they spot-check routinely the traffic entering this bay or the river out of the Gulf. Sometimes they will wave a boat on and check it out later, and sometimes they will stop it at the moment. So it could have been coincidence.

"But, in any event, it's necessary for us to move with great care, and only when necessary, only when it counts, and to be prepared to defend ourselves. This is one thing I needed to talk to you about, and it is very hard for me to ask what I am going to ask. We are going to need some things, and so we need money. Sources that we had began turning away after last fall. You can't imagine how fast the fear spreads. Even a few hundred would help and—if you could consider any of it a loan to me personally—I—but now I'm being foolish again. Because I can promise nothing. I am only asking for help. I don't like to, but I must. You are the only one I trust enough to ask."

The rain had let up to a fine drizzle by the time they got into their oilskins and crossed the sandy soggy ground to the big house. Inside there was no one visibly about. It was almost dawn.

They walked stealthily into the kitchen, where Kimo poured coffee. Ellen had quickly said, yes, she would send money, and had memorized the name of the man in New Orleans to whom she was to send it by telegraph. Now, at the turn of things, ill-defined apprehensions welled up in her. As he had talked, Kimo's face had at times seemed as hard as stone, implacable. Anger and bitterness were clutching at his voice. Now in the kitchen he seemed calm.

"It is painful that your husband has become one of our enemies," he said.

"Let's don't speak of him," Ellen said. "I don't think he really knows what he's doing."

She felt some eagerness now to be gone. Once back, she would go to the bank and fulfill her pledge even though in the aftermath of making it she felt distinctly ambiguous. Finally she said to Kimo, "I will send it only as a gift to you personally. What you do with it is not for me to say."

The light of dawn was dull, leaden. The rain seemed in suspense for a moment as Ellen walked out to her car. Breezes were clearing some of the obscuring mists. For the first time she saw the green and red adobe of the small storage house and the same colors on the sides of the dwelling they had just left. Kimo climbed in the car with her.

"I'll just go check the bridge," he said.

The engine wheezed, sputtered, then roared into ignition. A lean curious brown face peered out of a back window of the dwelling as she began to back and turn the car. The face passed from her peripheral vision as she steered to the side of the house, curved left and reentered the shell-strewn lane whose ruts were now two small rivers.

Off to her right at a distance stood one other small dwelling, a hovel on stork-leg pilings. The stunted wind-twisted trees by the lane shut it from view now. A few yards from the bridge that joined Marilou to the next scrap of island she stopped. Fast water was washing onto its planking.

"It's painful to see you go," Kimo said.

"It's painful to go," Ellen said. She reached and took his hand in a clasp. "But I need to get back."

"Is there any news—that you haven't talked about?"

Ellen turned thoughtful. She said, "Well, I've learned that he's all right, alive. Henry. Horris saw him last month in Key West."

"I had the feeling something had happened. Is he still there, or—"

"No. He left. There's no telling where he is. Cuba, maybe. Or fishing. He was running a boat."

"It's very strange. I had a very strong feeling of his presence. If he's so close, he'll come back, true?"

"I don't know," Ellen said. "I have a hard time separating what I wish from what I know. Just knowing he's somewhere is good, but I—he has his son with him."

"When he comes back, what will you do?"

"You sound so certain, as though you know him."

"I only know what you've told me of him. But I know you, and this tells me he will be back. What about your—your Mr. Eubanks? You will leave him? Send him away?"

"Oh, God, Kimo, I don't know. I've been very confused. Some days I feel like telling him to go just because I don't want to be near what he's doing. When he announced this big protest rally—when was it?—yesterday, in yesterday's paper—it seemed like the last straw. But—I don't know. I made a bargain with myself. Or with life, in a sense. I accepted his name and decided I would give whatever was asked of me. It hasn't been much. Nothing, really, but the illusion of marriage. But if that's all, I still feel bound. But I don't know, I don't know. Actually, it's all out of my hands. Maybe I'll never hear anything more from him, or even about him. Who knows?"

"I think you will."

Ellen wearily grinned, her mouth wry, atilt. "I think so, too, but it's just another way of wishing."

Kimo opened the car door.

"Let me check the bridge," he said. But he stayed yet another moment in the seat. He said, "Ellen. I'm very grateful that you came. You will take good thoughts of me, true? The talk of money won't—"

"Oh, Kimo, it's nothing. I have nothing but good thoughts."

"So. We will keep in touch, true?"

Ellen fixed her gaze into his eye. "Kimo, are you telling me something? You sound—"

"Nothing that I haven't already told you," he said.

He stepped out to the road, into the water spilling over the planks. He walked the length of the short bridge, testing it with bounces of his body. Then he was back at her window.

"I think it is all right," he said. "But you've got the others, too. Keep a careful watch. Once you're back on the main road you'll have no trouble."

He touched his hand to her cheek. He said, *"Bumanta.* One of us. Goodbye."

He whirled and at a fast stride passed down the lane.

In her rearview she saw him turn and watch her crossing the bridge. Then he was beyond view.

Ellen paused at each of the next wooden bridges, scrutinizing closely the swirl of the buffeting water that seemed rapidly building. She crossed each slowly, prepared to reverse or spurt forward or jump out at any sign of sudden yielding. Each of the islands in this connected chain was perhaps half a mile wide, perhaps less, the dividing channels of varying widths.

The main road could be seen when she came at last to the narrow pontoon bridge. The sections of its forty-yard length were bobbing and bucking in the racing water's growing turbulence.

Ellen eased the car onto it only a few feet and then observed the bridge closely again. The waist-high cables on either side seemed taut and sound, but the bridge itself called to mind some gigantic aquatic beast writhing in torment. Ellen, tensed at the wheel, eased forward.

Instantly she stopped. At the other end an old pickup truck whipped off the main road and came bouncing onto the bridge at a preposterous speed, its horn tooting frantically, no doubt to warn her back. She reversed, backed off the bridge, came to a stop a few car lengths back on the lane, half off of it, watching the truck.

It had slowed, perhaps, but was itself bobbing and swaying with the bridge. In it Ellen could see the youthful, wildly laughing faces of a man at the wheel and a woman in the seat close beside him. Then suddenly her eyes saw something else, something they perceived without instantly comprehending or even quite believing. It was the rushing approach toward the bridge not merely of the flowing body of water but of what appeared to be a distinct body of water riding on top of it, stretching at an angle the whole width of the channel, racing along somehow at a rate faster than the main body. At a glimpse it looked like a marvelous step or shelf of water upon water, the higher surface a foot or two above the main surface, higher and surging at a greater velocity as though urgently, maniacally seeking to thin itself to the level of the water beneath it.

It was still a sort of rushing wall when with astonishing impact it smashed into the already bucking and bobbing pontoon bridge. There was a weird mushy kind of resonance as it battered the bridge. The impact came as the truck was perhaps thirty feet from her side.

Ellen saw not the rising of one side of the bridge but the slow sliding of the truck. Even as it seemed to maintain some headway it slowly slid to the side until its two right hand wheels had slipped off the bridgeway. The cable on that side stretched far out against the weight of the vehicle. Strange: the faces of the occupants were still wildly laughing as this happened. Ellen felt she could almost hear them.

She was jumping out of her car and did hear the scream of the single rear tire of the truck against the bridge boards as the driver raced in a desperate effort to regain traction. She heard that, and now she saw that the new onrush of water was still thrusting the side of the bridge into the air. As she stepped onto the ground a swiftly racing inch of water about her feet grew to two inches before she had reached the bridge.

The driver had swung open his door and was standing in an impossibly awkward attitude, holding it while with his free hand he held to and pulled the woman up the front seat toward him. Now she was out and bending low to get under the outheld door. As she emerged from underneath it the man let the truck door fall shut of its own weight. And now the woman began to struggle for a footing on the slick, tilted boards, and her companion was precariously clinging to the higher cable trying to work his way to her.

Suddenly with a hysterical shriek that Ellen would have sworn was still another laugh the young woman seemed to dissolve into a blur of gold-and-green skirting, she dissolved, became a part of some frictionless world. She skidded across the bridge boards and underneath the cable on the downstream side, flailing in a wild clutch to grasp the cable. She spilled or spewed into the channel that was now a seething tumult of multilevel waves and ripping currents.

Ellen sprinted to her left, her feet splashing through shallow running water, down and along the bank of the island. Some ten feet from the bank the young woman seemed to see her. Her arms were flailing futilely in the bucking current as though she did not know how to swim. Ellen looked wildly about for—what? a line, a stick, a pole, a vine, a plank, anything. She saw nothing and ran on, trying to stay abreast of the flood-borne woman. Suddenly a quirky current swept the woman to within perhaps six or eight feet of the bank and—just as Ellen leaped—hurled her outward again.

Ellen landed clutching for whatever could be clutched, her furious swimming strokes seeming puny in the heaving mass of water. Finally she felt her hand grasp some fabric, and then she had pulled herself closer, and finally she had the young woman's chin in the crook of her right arm. She furiously kicked and stroked against the wild water, battling for inches, struggling to get close enough to shore to gain some kind of footing. Full of terror she saw the neck of the island approaching. Just before they would have swept past it she felt her thrashing feet strike sludge on the bottom, and then with a demonic final effort she gained a purchase and slogged and fought to a shallower bottom just at the bank. Her lungs were about to explode, and into the final exertion of dragging the young woman up so that her head was on the bank beyond the deeper water Ellen felt she was using strength she no longer possessed. Both their bodies were still sagging into waist-deep water as she lay the young woman's head down.

Now her lungs were exploding. Now they were being pierced by a million needles. Now an immense nauseous pounding filled her stomach and chest, and an immense hot/cold flash seared her lungs and encompassed her head. Fleetingly, dimly she became aware of arriving feet, of the man's feet, of the very bottom of his wet green trousers. Breaths of fire were tearing in and out of her flaming throat and chest. With each breath she strained to look up at his face. There. It seemed to be insanely smiling through a veil of speckled heat waves. There was the girl's head still limply resting in the inches-deep water on the bank. She seemed to be laughing. They were insane.

Suddenly the flaming pain of her chest did not so much ease as simply grow dark. The darkness arose out of her chest. She felt her neck muscles evaporate. Her head was falling off. She thought she heard a subtle splash as her head fell to the bank.

An impenetrable shroud descended upon her, over her eyes and ears, darkness, silence. Nothing.

First she smelled some fragrance. It was sweet, sharp, pleasant. Then she heard the music, then many voices. They came murmurously as from a distant closed off room. Then she heard the rustle and felt the smooth slickness of the fabric that was covering her. Then it occurred to her: it was Papa's birthday again, and all of his children and their progeny had come home as usual, and they were in the front rooms babbling, and she was taking her nap in Aunt Margaret's room on the daybed under the satin coverlet, and:

Ellen opened her eyes without knowing whether she had felt the hand on her forehead first or merely at the same time that she knew that wherever she was it was somewhere she had never before been and it was not Aunt Margaret's room because the fragrance was not jasmine but something else that was on the hand that was so gently feeling her forehead, the hand of someone half-dressed sitting on the side of the bed. No, sitting on the floor: she was not in a bed but on a downy pallet on the floor covered by this vivid quilting of variegated silks, and:

Her eyes slowly tracked upward along the unbloused woman touching her forehead. Yes, she had seen that person somewhere, but where? When? How had—

Then she saw the strangely familiar face smile with pleasure at the sight of her eyes. The wide mouth smiled and said something in French strangely accented, something whose words she grasped but whose import baffled her.

"Ah, you are all right, no?"

And this she grasped, but then the voice, a musical voice said, "So, open your eyes and look at your new possession. I am yours to bid as you please."

This baffled her immensely. It was as mysterious as the moment, which was unfathomable, both like and unlike a dream, disconnected from all time as from all familiar sense of place. Where was she? How did she get here?

The voice was musical, like crystal. Now it shattered into spirited laughter. The wide mouth flew open and the eyes glittered with elated spirits. Laughter.

At that, it came back, came back in a rush: the bridge, the flood surge, the girl, the channel, the pickup, diving in, the terror, the sludge that wouldn't stay under her feet, the bank, and her lungs exploding and her body turning to immovable stone at some incredible moment.

"I am Lucienne," the girl said.

Ellen smiled, and Lucienne sprang to her feet. She opened the door to the room, and from beyond it the sound of babbling voices became louder as Lucienne shouted out to someone and then closed the door again.

Very soon an older but not old woman came in bearing a steaming bowl of soup thick with seaflesh and vegetables. For the first time Ellen spoke, asking a question in French.

Lucienne laughed wildly again as in delight over something she had not expected.

"You speak French, but you are not from here?" Lucienne said.

"No, no. I got lost in the fog and was trying to find my way out," Ellen said.

"And so now you have only found your way in again," Lucienne said. She appeared to be perhaps twenty, maybe younger.

Several times while Ellen ate the soup ravenously, Lucienne expressed gratitude that was evidently boundless but scarcely somber. Her chattering seemed to be carried along on a surf of recurring laughter. So it was with both mirth and seriousness that she explained an earlier remark.

"You saved my life, and so now it belongs to you. You understand?"

Before Ellen finished the soup a stream of visitors began coming into the room. They came one at a time, perhaps ten or twelve in all, men and women, and each with immense cheerfulness expressed gratitude to her and paid tribute in grave words that came forth, like Lucienne's, in festive voices. As each came in, Lucienne stood and made a ceremonious introduction. She would mention only the first name of the visitor—Donante or Bethena or Robertalio—pungent names with an admixture of cultural roots. Ellen gathered without being quite certain that they were all of a family.

During this Ellen saw other women coming in wearing only long skirts with nothing above the waist except perhaps flat and intricate metal necklaces. One aged woman was covered by a brilliant shawl. Soon Ellen realized that Lucienne was not, as she had at first thought, half-dressed. She was fully dressed for some festive gathering. She wore a long scarlet skirt that glimmered with a protean iridescence arising from brilliant interwoven threads. The men who came in wore pants of vivid hue and sometimes screaming patterns. They wore gaudy buttonless shirts that opened in a wide V to the waist.

Somehow the last to come in looked familiar to Ellen. Lucienne called out his name with a special caress.

"Beaumonte," she said. Yes, Beaumonte had been driving the truck.

Unlike the other visitors, he kneeled beside Ellen's pallet and took her hand, and kissed not its fingers but its palm. Then with a smile at once grave and tender he pressed into her palm a ring of gold that was a wide braided band inset with a perfectly clear red stone. He spoke in a pleasant resonant voice and a singsong manner that made her feel oddly like laughing.

"This trivial token is yours, Lucienne's life is yours, and I am yours, in eternal gratitude," Beaumonte said. He seemed about Lucienne's age, perhaps older.

Suddenly Ellen realized why she had felt like laughing. She had expected him to speak in French. He spoke in Spanish.

Now he arose, and bowed, and glided backward, smiling, as though to withdraw, and did, but only after he and Lucienne had exchanged some remarks, she speaking in French and he in Spanish.

Now Ellen did laugh and called out after him, *"Gracias, merci, gracias, merci."*

For awhile she remained alone with Lucienne, in whose room she was and where she had been placed after they had brought her to this house. Ellen looked closely at the ring. The stone cast its luminous redness into her eyes and evoked the red windows of the back hall doors of home.

"It is too much," she said to Lucienne, "too much for me to accept." Lucienne sat down beside her again.

"It is not necessary for you to accept it," Lucienne said. "It is yours. It was made for you long ago."

Puzzlement widened Ellen's eyes, her whole face. Bafflement again. Lucienne laughed and said, "It was made for the girl who saved my life, and so it was made for you."

"I don't really understand what you are saying," Ellen said. "I've never been here before today."

"Ah!" Lucienne laughed wildly. "But you were here yesterday. It was yesterday you saved my life, and we brought you here."

"Yesterday? Yesterday? Isn't today Thursday?"

"No, no, no. It is Friday. It is the day of the rain festival. This is the noise you hear beginning downstairs."

"It's *Friday?*" Ellen felt her thoughts spiraling into darknesses.

"Oui, oui. It is Friday. It has got to be Friday. It is the day we set for the rain festival, and if it is not Friday then everyone in our family has made a great mistake."

"And the bridge? The flood? That was yesterday? Yesterday was Thursday, true?"

"Ah! You are puzzled by your long sleep. Yes. It was exhaustion you had, so we gave you a draught to make you sleep good and long." Lucienne laughed. "And you did, you did. All through the day and the night. But, ah, the ring—it was made for you long before yesterday. It was made by my father when Ramos foretold that the water would try to kill me and that a strange girl would be sent to save me. As soon as the water carried me off the bridge I looked over and knew that you were the one. No, it is not quite true. When I first saw you running, you were wearing the pants and the burgundy shirt, like a man's, no? And so at first I thought you were a boy, and I thought, well, perhaps I must die in spite of Ramos, and then suddenly I saw *you*—" Lucienne with cupped hands hammocked her breasts. "—and at once I knew that Ramos was right and felt secure again."

A fury of fears had begun spinning up into Ellen's thoughts. She felt she were suspended by some fragile thread above a dark chasm of timelessness. The sense of lost time severely shook her. She felt an urgent wish to call her home, to call Emily.

"A telephone—is there a telephone in the house?"

Lucienne laughed and said that the only phones were on the main road. Even those were out, even parts of the main road were out with the flood, parts in either direction. Lucienne studied the expressions crossing Ellen's face.

"Still, it is not so bad," Lucienne said. "Look, look." She scampered across the pallet and drew back a curtain at the window. Ellen drew out from under the cover to go see. Lucienne said, "Ah, let me get you something." Lucienne skipped to a wall on which innumerable skirts of variegated colors and cuts were hanging, one on top of the other, bunch alongside bunch. She held up one, a fabric of yellow and green and brown. "So?" She tossed the skirt to Ellen and herself skipped back to the window. "You will not need your other clothes until the festival is over," Lucienne said.

Ellen climbed into the skirt and tied its cloth belt in a bow at her waist. She set aside for the moment her temptation to ask for a blouse. At the window Lucienne stood beside her.

"Your car, see? It is all right," Lucienne said. "We brought all of your things in. They're in a safe place downstairs."

In the yard below, close by the house, Ellen saw her dark green roadster parked with water flowing about it just above the hubs. Nearby bobbed a small flotilla of pirogues and canoes and skiffs, their lines tied to various appurtenances of the house front.

"See? They have come to the festival." Lucienne was pointing to the pirogues and other boats. "It is beginning, but it will not truly begin until you feel like going down. Anna-lia has ordered that you must be the guest of honor. So they are not supposed to begin until you are there. But they are beginning, anyway, eh? They always do."

"Did I meet Anna-lia? I did, didn't I?"

"Yes. Anna-lia brought you the soup. Anna-lia is my mama."

Ellen could feel warmth emanating from Lucienne's body close by her arm. Outside the sky was overcast, the horizon leaden, indistinct. Ellen could not guess the time of day. It might have been morning, perhaps afternoon. Evening might have been about to descend. The hard rain had ceased, but a fine mist seemed almost suspended in the air, a transparent veil.

She felt oddly reluctant to ask the time, as though the question might suggest disapproval of the festival plans Lucienne continued to chatter about with excitement. Ellen supposed that with so many already assembled for a party it must be at least late afternoon.

Friday. She still could not absorb the fact that she had slept through all of Thursday and perhaps most of this day. Around the corner of a distant dwelling another pirogue veered into view. Under the weight of several passengers it seemed to be floating with no freeboard at all. A child was among the adults in the craft. It began cutting through the water in the direction of this house, a bizarre floating island of life in a vista that appeared endless, directionless, horizonless, timeless, a vista of moiling water. Ellen developed a feeling of almost dizzy disorientation.

"It is subsiding faster than we can see," Lucienne said. "In a day or so it will be down. Unless the rain begins again above us."

Far away Ellen saw the myriad tops of an expanse of mangrove limbs. They raised the illusion that the vast expanse of water existed at a plane in the very tops of some forest.

"You are all right now?" Lucienne said.

"I think so," Ellen said. "We are on the same island?"

"Margarita, *oui*. We could not have left it. The bridge on the other side has tilted dangerously, too. Do you worry?"

"Oh, I only wish my family knew I was all right."

"Ah, yes, I understand. But do they have any reason to believe you are not?"

"No. You are right. Anyway, my daughter is away at a place in New England."

"You? You have a daughter?" Lucienne sounded incredulous.

"Oh, yes. Emily. She is eight."

Lucienne touched her cheek with what seemed to Ellen almost satiric awe. "It is hard to believe," she said. "You must have been very young when you gave birth."

Ellen smiled wryly, pleased. She said, "Don't be too sure."

"But we look the same age, and I am nineteen."

"And I'm thirty," Ellen said.

"No, no. It can't be. Look at you. You are so—so young, so beautiful, so—so—so—When I first see your body I cannot believe that even for a moment you looked like a boy running on the bank. And now I am asked to believe that you are thirty years. No. I refuse." Lucienne laughed and then screwed her face into a whimsical grotesque mock pout. She said, "I wanted to be your sister, not your daughter. Do you like the skirt? You can pick another if you do not. Any of them. Even this one." Lucienne raised up the brilliant fabric of the skirt she was wearing and let it fall again to its midshin length. She said, "Since I am now yours, so is everything that is mine. So are my friends. Will you like them? You like Beaumonte? He is yours, too. Ha! What a gift I make you. Do you feel almost ready to go down to the festival? Come, come to the mirror, and let me decorate you properly. And tell me, how do you think I look?"

"You look beautiful," Ellen said.

Lucienne closed her eyes and enjoyed the words not only with her ears but her mouth. She smiled and smacked her lips as though the compliment were palpable, a morsel to be chewed or sucked. Like the others who had come in, she had a skin of deep golden brown, a glistening skin that shone even in the small light of the room. She had very dark hair loosely coiled and interwoven into a great soft nest on top of her head. From her pierced lobes hung large thin rings, circles of woven gold and silver.

Lucienne's form, her dress, her unassuming poise in the candid display of her body suddenly recalled to Ellen's thoughts a depiction of young Mayan women that she had scrutinized with pleasure and ambiguous wonder as a child long ago in some large room in Mexico, a room that might have been in a museum or perhaps in one of the great houses they had visited. She remembered the sharp puzzlement and delight she had gotten at this first view of bared women shown in the presence of their men. She had wondered either why it was so or why it was not so everywhere. *Wouldn't it be comfortable,* her mother had said. *Except on very cold mornings,* Ellen had said. Her Mama had laughed and said, *Yes, we would never want the men to see our goose bumps.* Ellen had giggled, suddenly conscious of her rosebuds and how they would pop out when rubbed. Embarrassed, she had stood close with the top of her head pressed against her Mama's breasts that looked so firm but felt so yielding and reassuring. In the stillness of that great room she had prayed that hers would be like that when the time came. The Mayans. The mural. The vivid primary colors. Mama. Where had Papa been? Where the twins? Where? Where was the room? Where were they? Where?

In the mirror Ellen saw that her hair looked like a tangled seethe of seaweed. She raised her hands to straighten it.

"No, no," Lucienne said. "Let me finish this, and then I will brush it."

She was standing close behind Ellen. Ellen could feel her warmth flowing to her own flesh. Lucienne's hands reached over each of her shoulders, the slender hands were adjusting a neck decoration of flat thin gold-colored metal, a smooth plating into which had been carved or stamped an intricate geometric pattern of circles, squares, triangles. Its smooth undersurface hung snug against her upper chest and the two curves of its lower edge fitted, still pendant, over the upper curves of her breasts. From its center dropped a chain of long thin links suspending in her incleft a drop-shaped red stone of the same clear lustre as that in the ring Beaumonte had given her.

"It pleases you, eh?" said Lucienne when she had fastened the piece behind Ellen's neck.

Yes, it did. And yet Ellen realized that she was not yet comfortable at the prospect of actually emerging into view in the costume. Lucienne said, "So—now—sit down again."

Ellen sat leaning back on her arms as Lucienne brushed and straightened the tousled thicket of loose tangled curls that she wore still cropped although at much greater length then years before.

"It is not brown, and it is not black," Lucienne said. "It is so beautiful. Why do you not let it grow—so—" She ran a light indicating finger across the small of Ellen's back.

"Because," Ellen said, drawing a disorderly zig-zag line in the air. "Because it grows so when I let it."

"Ah, Ellen—" Lucienne made it sound more like "El-laine." "Ah, Ellen, you have almost the same skin as ours except—" Here she ran her fingertips across the lowest part of Ellen's back where the skin was left pale from sunning in a swim suit. "Except down here."

As the brushing went on Ellen closed her eyes and yielded to a deep sense of warmth and well-being. It was not diminished but strangely enhanced by a sudden pang to have Emily at hand. Then Henry came into her wistful thoughts, and she was transmitting to him the gentle caring that she was now receiving. Lucienne hummed brightly as she busied herself, echoing the tune that was being played by unseen guitars beyond the door. Now Lucienne began rubbing Ellen's back with some oil of the same sharp/sweet fragrance she had discovered on waking up. Lucienne raised Ellen's arms and spread the savory oil all over each in turn. She knelt then on the bright green and brown and yellow fabric of Ellen's skirt, which was spread wide by spraddled legs, and leaning close she daubed and rubbed the oil over the surface of Ellen's face and sides and breasts and stomach.

Ellen felt a great answering warmth arise within her. The flood, the recent days, Kimo, her yearning expectation of some word from Henry—everything seemed very far away. Her mind argued briefly with her surrender to good feelings. But then she thought, *Even if I tried there is no way to get out.*

"So! Finished!" Lucienne shouted, triumphant.

Ellen was up and shaking out her skirt as a knocking came at the door. Lucienne yelled in answer. Beaumonte's face stuck in and delivered a rapid message.

"Anna-lia and everybody wonders if you two are ever coming down," he said.

"We're ready," Lucienne said. Beaumonte's face lingered upon Ellen with an expression of exaggerated adoration. Then it withdrew, and the door clicked shut again.

Ellen felt almost paralyzed by a great reluctance as Lucienne reached to open it again. Her feet held fast perhaps against her conscious will. Lucienne was beckoning, but she didn't move. Suddenly her new friend's face grew bright with dawning comprehension.

"Ah! I see," Lucienne said. "It is the first time you have dressed like us, no? This is your worry, no? Ah. You will forget it in a minute. In a second. Believe me. You will make everyone happy. So happy you will not even notice them noticing you."

Lucienne took her hand.

The door opened onto what Ellen, of course, had not previously seen. They exited from the room onto a narrow banistered mezzanine. It looked down from four quadrants upon the center of a much larger room below. At Ellen's first glance the babbling milling crowd looked enormous. A fantastic emanation of vivid chaotic color came up from the swirl of clothing. A soaring feeling of exultant festive energy arose from the buzz and thrum of the multilingual babble. She could hear French, Spanish, English, and an argot resembling that of the Cajuns. The crowd was aseethe already but only beginning to gather its strength.

A hush of almost explosive suddenness fell over the gathering as they paused at the banister staring down. Suddenly every face turned up toward them. Ellen felt almost physically jarred. Then almost at once the unnerving silence ended, and Ellen saw a sea of waving arms and hands and grins and heard a tumultuous muddle of hellos and salutes and acclamations and wild innocent laughter. The exalted hubbub at once astonished and frightened her, and also melted her with its warmth.

"You'd better stay with me," she said to Lucienne.

"Remember, I belong to you," Lucienne said. "And remember you are the guest of honor. Come."

Now Ellen almost had to yell to be heard by the friend at her side. She said, "Tell me, what is the guest of honor supposed to do?"

Lucienne laughed jubilantly, and with her free hand she playfully patted Ellen's stomach. She said, "You can do anything on earth that you like." With immense zest and warmth she quickly added, "With anybody that you like."

Suddenly Ellen felt her strapped apprehensions fly away. She expelled a rocketing explosion of laughter.

On the floor of the large room the number of people seemed fewer. There were perhaps forty or fifty, a number increased and diminished from moment to moment. Children would wander through the crowd soon to gravitate or be shooed back to some other part of the large house. It was a place of vast but not immediately evident spaces.

Here the interior raised the illusion of being caught oddly within a not quite orderly set of brilliantly enameled Chinese boxes. Each different plane and recess of the room was painted a distinct color. Even the ceiling occurred at different levels, each glaring with its own shade of paint.

As she moved about Ellen had a sense of experiencing an almost physical shift of the very structure as, one after the other, garish orange or purple or cobalt or rich deep green impacted into her vision. Her eyes after awhile grew almost maddened with a peculiar hunger, a compulsion to search out and fix the rectangular limits of each particular color. Thus her eyes would toil to fix upon one but at some point would be torn aside by some smashing red or azure or gold in still another horizontal or vertical plane to the side or above. Ceaseless flickerings of candles and lamps rendered it all the more chimerical and shattering.

She and Lucienne did not so much enter the fluid stir of people as get drawn in among them. Ellen at one moment felt herself a child being led by Lucienne and at the next that she was indeed a strangely new mother leading her own daughter about in some bizarre debut of introductions and incessant flirtations.

Golden glistening faces passed before her, at once languid and intense. Each during the fleet introductions would seem warmly engaged and yet somehow detached as though each were also a spectator to his own engagement. The murmurous hubbub about them was incessant but not shrill. Lucienne's voice babbled on, her sentences hooked together by some seemingly irrepressible mirth, some inextinguishable playfulness. The names of men and women sprinkled from her mouth almost as though she were making jokes about them. And the names themselves spoke of long and diligent meldings of many cultures. To one name Lucienne would lend a seemingly gratuitous Spanish ring and to another a French inflection. There was an Adamalia and an Adamano and an Adamito among the men.

Beaumonte would suddenly materialize at their sides, or he would squeeze between them, grinning and laughing, and then he would vanish as though suddenly sucked away by the tidal flow of the crowd, and soon Ellen would see him beholding another woman with the same adoration with which he looked upon Lucienne and even upon her. Ellen discovered that at the moment of introduction all the men seemed to be insanely in love with Lucienne, and she with them. Only after awhile did she become conscious that they as well seemed insanely in love with her too. She felt free of the law of gravity. Once she felt inordinate terror when she lost touch with Lucienne's guiding hand. Quickly she reached to clutch it, and did.

Ellen saw a strange and glistening woman staring directly at her, staring at her with eyes flickering with light, staring at her out of an obscure lambent dimness between and beyond another couple, a man in a dazzling shirt of scarlet and yellow and a young woman swaying within a loose skirt of cream fabric splashed with garish zigzags of colors. Ellen tried to turn her gaze away from the staring woman. But she was riveted by something profoundly knowing and devastatingly familiar in the widening naïve flickering eyes. Now Lucienne's hand tightened on hers, she heard her friend's voice.

"Ah, yes, so now you like yourself at last!"

Ellen gasped, dumfounded. Then exploded into a laugh. Then gazed once again past the scarlet and yellow and the garish zigzags into the obscure mirror. To her surprise she saw that her torso had taken on the slightly tilted languid swaying of the other women. She could hardly believe she was seeing her breasts in full view below the intricate geometric gleamings of the neck piece. The lustrous red gem pendant within her incleft picked up a gleam of lambency and sent it like an arrow into her eyes.

The sound of the music—guitars and mandolins and other unfamiliar stringed instruments—would swell and recede, but the pace of it grew slowly and steadily faster. Ellen found herself moving and swaying to it as they drifted about. One recessed wall was distinctly different from all the rest. Working on it was a striking boy Ellen took to be thirteen or fourteen.

"This is Ramos," Lucienne was saying.

Ramos was—had been—painting on the wall, drawing and painting, his concentration as close and detached as though the house had been empty of other human beings. At first glance Ellen thought he was extending a vast and intricate abstract design. She thought him extraordinarily beautiful of face and body, a face perhaps thin for one still so young and a slender physique that showed yet well muscled arms and hands, hands that paused as they stopped but that did not quite cease the toil that had been engaging them.

Ramos turned to Ellen with large calm black eyes that picked up the gleams and highlights and even the figures within the room. He was almost exactly Ellen's height.

"Ramos," Lucienne said, "here is the one you said would save my life. And of everyone at the festival only you have not thanked her."

Ellen felt vague discomfort that was dispelled when Ramos turned his eyes calmly upon her.

"It is good to see you again," he said. His French had a slightly different accent from that of Lucienne's. His voice came more softly with greater detachment. Ellen was baffled by his remark.

"You see, he remembers," Lucienne said. "Ellen, he remembers seeing you when he remembered seeing me about to be killed. He is a strange one, eh? He remembers these things. This is how he knows our story, our history. This is what he has been painting on the wall all of his life."

Ellen suddenly glanced back at the wall. She looked very close and saw that what she had thought was a mere geometric abstraction consisted of hundreds of depictions of tiny human figures—no, thousands, tens of thousands, figures in innumerable costumes and attitudes and poses, depictions of episodes and events, of ideas and ideals. Her eyes swept over the whole vast wall, which was perhaps three-quarters full of his work. She thought, *Hundreds of thousands.* She looked with amazement at Ramos, who was calmly studying her.

"You see," Lucienne said, "it begins at the bottom, down there, and the story goes along to the other end and then turns back in the next line of figures and proceeds. So. Centuries. Centuries. Ramos remembers them all. Can you believe it? Ah, my Ramos. He is stranger than his mother. His mama is my cousin, Annamelio, and she is gone. She lives on the mainland and makes money that she brings back."

Ellen thought to mention that she knew Annamelio. But the thought was immediately lost in the furious flight of Lucienne's words.

"Ah, Ramos. Busy Ramos. Ellen, he paints tiny pictures of love that quickly make you need to go to bed. But I try and try and try but I cannot get Ramos to go to bed with me. Ramos, you still have not thanked Ellen for saving my life."

"Lucienne," he said, a smile barely visible on his almost exquisitely perfect mouth, "perhaps I should save my thanks for the time when she will save my life."

"Ah, Ramos, you are joking. Your life is not in danger. You cannot die!" Lucienne began laughing. "You must not die until you give me your love." She turned to Ellen. "It is so sad, Ellen. I have pined for him since I was a little girl. Ramos is older than you, but he still acts like a shy little boy."

"I am the same age as Ellen," Ramos said.

Ellen felt vast astonishment, both at the intimation of his age and of his claim to know hers.

"You know my age?"

"I cannot help but know your age."

"Well?"

The barely visible smile quivered over Ramos's lips. He said, "You are thirty, of course. So am I. We were born the same month."

Ellen felt fantastically removed from the demands of reason that nonetheless pressed up in her mind.

"And you *remember* this?" she said.

Ramos smiled more broadly. "That is not it exactly. It is not really remembering, but I have no other word to describe it. I do not even truly understand it. It is some peculiarity that Annamelio passed on to me."

"Ah," Lucienne said, fondly clasping his arm now. "If Annamelio had only passed you on to me, Ramos. One day I will sneak some potion into your soup and then you will hunger for me more than for your soup."

"And that is the day my life will be in danger," Ramos said. He shrugged and grimaced sardonically as though in proof of his assertion.

"Not so, not so," Lucienne said. "Loving Lucienne could not put your life in danger."

"Beaumonte would kill me as soon as he found out."

"Beaumonte! Beaumonte! Ooof! Beaumonte would never find out. How would Beaumonte find out?"

"Lucienne, you are silly. You would tell Beaumonte. You tell him everything. If not in words, then—" Ramos trailed off, shrugging. But then he looked across the room and went on. "Only Beaumonte would do far worse to me than he did to Juantama. Juantama he was satisfied to mark."

Ramos gestured toward the man with the scarlet and yellow shirt. Now Ellen saw the side of the face that had been concealed when he had been standing by the mirror. Across his cheek glistened a subdued but distinct ridge of scar tissue.

"Beaumonte would go—" Ramos drew a finger across his throat. Then he softly added, "Unless, of course, I was the first to go—" Again the lethal finger severed his throat. He laughed and said, "But, after all, I am not a violent man."

"Ramos, shhh, you will frighten Ellen," Lucienne broke in, laughing. "Ellen, there is nothing to fear. In our family the woman need fear nothing. It is hers to ask and hers to receive love. It is the silliness of the men to go insane over such things, but they cannot—Beaumonte, none of them—they cannot touch a hair of us without our permission. So there is nothing to fear. If they behave like savages among themselves, it is too bad, too sad, but—oof. Ah, Ramos. You are impossible. Ellen, let's leave him to his endless work."

Now Ramos gazed calmly at Ellen and nodded and said, "I am grateful for what you did. I will come talk to you when there is a chance."

Something in his smooth boy's face called up memories of the faces of the twins when they had been twelve or thirteen, when she had thought to marry them both. *But you're our sister. I don't care, what difference does that make?*

The room had grown reverberant, tinkling, plangent. It shimmered with splashes of candlelight and arcane shadows. Lucienne snatched a great handful of smoked shrimp off one passing tray and a handful of small cookies or wafers with a seed topping off a table. They wolfed the refreshments while drifting fluidly through the moil of celebrants. The wafers gave off some sweetish pungent reek.

Ellen felt all cares flee. Some new buffeting wind began blowing within her. Lucienne suddenly laughed with greater abandon than ever as though at some secret joke. Anna-lia broached and embraced them in the middle of the room. Lucienne's mother was also full of inexplicable mirth. Each time she threw her head back and laughed the shaking of her body tore apart the gold and purple shawl that partly covered her melonheavy breasts. Couples standing at the rail of the mezzanine gazed down, distantly smiling.

Anna-lia shepherded Lucienne and Ellen to a broad bench along the front wall of the room. The bench looked toward the wall on which Ramos was working. With insistent motherly gestures Anna-lia sat them down and even pushed them back against the numerous cushions piled at the back of the bench. She commanded, "Now. So. Sit still and rest and I will get you something to eat."

She vanished through the stir but soon returned with more refreshments. Two guitarists played standing at the end of the long bench to Ellen's left. Lucienne, leaning back against the cushions, kicked her straightened legs high. Ellen resisted a temptation to do the same.

"You enjoy, yes? It is a good festival, eh?" Lucienne said.

"It's the only celebration of rain I've been to," Ellen said.

"The Trussante festival is always the best," Lucienne said, "except when the men grow insane. And then—poof."

"Trussante is the name of everyone here?" she asked.

"No, not everyone, but it is still all Trussante, all the same clan."

"Everyone is kin?"

"*Oui, oui,*" Lucienne said. "Even if it is only just this much—" She held thumb and forefinger close. "Ha! Now here comes a real Trussante man." Lucienne was laughing as she pointed.

A stocky, dark-haired beautifully shaped boy of about ten swaggered through the crowd, arousing a mixture of laughter and gentle obscenity and admonishments. His shoulders and head were tilted back in an exaggerated strut. His belly and pelvis jutted forward in front of him. His deep glistening gold face seemed serious, aloof, in spite of the uproar that followed him about. He strutted to within a foot of Lucienne's knees and jutted his pelvis even further toward her. She shrieked with laughter. She said, "Ah, Tomas, you tempt me, but run back now to your sisters, who need you. We are waiting for the real men to discover themselves."

The boy called Tomas Trussante now turned toward Ellen. She felt as though she were coloring over with a blush even though, like Lucienne, she compulsively laughed in an abrupt series of shrieks. Tomas's eyes gravely engaged hers as he thrust his pelvis forward again in pronounced and provocative movements. He was naked, stitchless except for a single long feather of brilliant orange with black markings. It was attached, longitudinally, either as nominal covering or brazen decoration to his male organ, which, from the moment of his entry into the room, stood protruding in a state of gleaming rigidity.

"Ah!" Lucienne spoke in a stagey whisper to Ellen. "Lucienne knows how to make Tomas behave."

Lucienne leaned over close and whispered to Tomas. A wild and fearful look overcame his face. He abruptly fled through the crowd and from the room as Lucienne's laughter split the murmur of the crowd. She said, "A true Trussante. I told him that I would cast a spell that would turn it into mush forever."

Ellen laughed hysterically and Lucienne went on: "He is my older sister's son, but we do not know for sure if the father is a Trussante. Tomas resembles Beaumonte, eh? I have always thought Beaumonte was his father, but my sister protests. She says, 'Ah, Lucienne, but Beaumonte would have been only fifteen years when Tomas father was in me.' But I say fifteen is old enough in such a thing. I believe little Tomas could become a father himself right now at ten. Ha. Probably all of his sisters would be pregnant now if their wombs were only ready. They adore Tomas, and after seeing him it is no wonder, eh? Hmmmmm. Ellen, perhaps I will test his man-hood myself some rainy day when Beaumonte is fishing and my sister is on the mainland. Ha! Ellen, you look beautiful but strange. Do you like to talk of such things as I?"

Ellen grinned and squeezed Lucienne's hand. She said, "I am glad you are staying with me. I might lose myself without you."

"So," Lucienne said, "So I am the mother again now." She embraced Ellen with an arm about her shoulders. "*L'enfant.*"

Now a few men and women were passing about the room bearing trays full of tiny silver cups and baskets of the wafers that were seeded on top. When each person had taken one of each, a cup and a wafer, a silence fell over the crowd, although the guitarists continued playing a very soft strain. Now suddenly Anna-lia was standing conspicuously before the wall of Ramos's mural, and she was making an announcement that seemed to be ending even before Ellen had realized it was beginning.

"Out of the rain comes the sea and out of the sea, life, and out of life, life and life within life, and all Trussantes rejoice in rain and life and our beloved friend Ellen."

Everywhere in the candlelight she saw the quick precipitate tilting of the silver cups. It was a movement that flashed about the room like sudden quick ripples in a pond. The small amount of dark liquid chocolate in the silver cup was very bitter. But it was very good, and it brought an immense and almost instantaneous sense of calm to the flighty excitements of her stomach.

She first noticed it in the music, first noticed her new perception. It seemed it had not just begun but had been there all along. She could see the music.

She could see the sounds. Each sound had a tiny distinct body, vaguely spherical, no, shaped more like a tiny tadpole, but distinct, demarked not by material borders but in the way a heat wave is marked, by the refraction of light about it. They were skeetering out into the crowd like some infinitude of shimmering skimming tiny phantasmal tadpoles. They skeetered out and then made an elegant racing turn and skeetered directly into her.

Ellen shouted with delight at the rediscovery of something she had not noticed in a long time. She laughed. After she had laughed for about a year she clasped Lucienne's arm and told her about the rediscovery.

"Oh, oh, oh, I can feel them again, I can feel them," she said.

After they skimmed out and curved back she could feel their impact against her. They pummeled her breasts and tickled almost unbearably. She looked at the guitar. The guitarist was very tall, his fingers invisible. The wind from his invisible hand made the sounds go much faster. She followed the path of a single sound that raced out and curved back and struck her directly in the navel. It awakened a path of nerves that ran a thousand miles up into her brain. The impact knocked her backwards.

She sank forty or fifty feet into the cushions. Now her mouth was wide open and the sounds were pouring into it like rain and tickling her throat. She laughed. The more she laughed, the more sounds poured in, and the more sounds poured in the more she laughed.

Then she opened her eyes. It took a day or so for the lids to raise and another day or so for the pupils to focus. Sure, she remembered this, now that she thought about it: She could see her laughter, too. It was rising right up to the ceiling, scattering upward and then blowing about like ten million tiny leaflets off of the mimosa tree.

The music sounds began sticking to the laughter. The sounds were skeetering into her mouth and getting caught in the laughter which was shooting up to the ceiling and spreading outward and gently falling upon the crowd. She followed the path of a single piece of laughter. It took about a month for a piece to float down from the ceiling.

The ceiling got low. Ellen reached up with an arm and almost touched it. She almost touched the faces along the banister of the mezzanine. Just as she would get her fingers close to them they would drift away. Wind from her hand. She held her hand back and faces began drifting down from the banister, drifting amidst the wafting laughter and the skeetering sounds. Faces with gorgeous smiles ten miles long and eyes the size of moons.

Ellen blew hard. She saw her breath lightly catch upon the faces and loft them like thistle back up to the banister. Her breath was sky blue. The air was gold and chocolate. As soon as she got up she would peel some of the chocolate off of the gold and eat it. It would take about ten years to get up. The wall behind the bench was leaning down over her. Little tiny silvery lines were spilling out from the stunning gorgeous blue wall trying to touch her face.

Her laughter intertwined around Lucienne's. Beaumonte's laughter was winding around them both. She wondered if he knew. He looked as though he knew. Some sounds were going right into his nose. That was why he was laughing so hard.

She discovered that she could let the sounds race into her mouth and pour out of her nose. Then she found out she could let them come in her ears and spew out of her mouth upon Lucienne and Beaumonte. When she pummeled them with the spew of sounds they laughed for a few years.

Finally Ellen discovered she could let the sounds in her navel rise like bubbles within her and squirt out of her ears. Only she had to look very fast to see where they went then. She wiggled her head back and forth. Lucienne asked her something, and she said, "I'm watching them."

Right after that, she made the greatest discovery of all. As the stream of tiny sounds raced toward her she could make them focus and enter her nipples and shoot out of her navel. She stood up so she could fire a long stream of them out of her navel into the wafting mimosa laughlets. This made the laughlets scoot back up into the air.

Suddenly she sprayed sounds across the gorgeous glistening faces of everybody who was watching. If they were quicker, they would duck, she thought. But they only opened their mouths and swallowed the sounds.

And this was when she got the most brilliant idea so far. She guided the sounds simultaneously into her mouth and ears and navel and fired them out of both nipples at once. By twisting about she sprayed the entire room with music. As it pummeled them everybody laughed.

Ellen tried to fix a candle in a convergence of both streams of fire. But it was no use. Even though the candle was a hundred miles away the streams did not converge but got further apart. Now the candle turned into a tiny glistening head and floated away. Ellen thought, This won't do. She decided to draw all of the sounds back into her nipples. This was the first time she remembered she could do this.

Lucienne and Beaumonte were very pleased with the trick. They laughed for four or five years. Now she set the sounds on a grand circular course, out of her navel and into her mouth, around and around, faster and faster until the tickling inside caused her to dive a mile or so down into the cushions to get away from it.

Now she was under a green and brown and yellow tent that she could not blow back into the air. A magic tent. It vanished when she stood up on the bench.

She leaned over to pick it up, but it vanished. She saw that the guitar player was growing out of his guitar. Or maybe the guitar was growing out of the guitar player. Only it was the player growing out of the guitar because he was getting larger and larger and larger. She called out for a long time to draw attention to his immense size and then fell forward for half a mile. Or maybe it was backward. The ceiling again was just beyond the reach of her hands. Maybe she could touch it with her feet. The magic tent again, the green/yellow/brown tent, they had dropped the tent over her.

She could hear them laughing through the tent and called to Lucienne and Beaumonte to come in. They couldn't find the door. She would have to blow the tent away again. Now someone had taken the tent away. They were holding her hands so that she could not look for it. They were trying to laugh without making a sound, but she could see the laughter coming out in little gusts of tiny clover petals. She could see through the petals. They were translucent green like the green of the tent. If she let go of their hands they might be carried away like the clover laughlets. Already they were drifting. She pulled them back.

Through their eyelids she could see their thoughts. She could see herself in their thoughts, flowing into and out of their thoughts. She went in and out of them, drifting like laughter. They were growing out of her or she out of them like the guitar player and his guitar.

Remember, remember. Ramos would remember. Her eyes would open and she would see Ramos and he would remember. For several days her eyes opened, she could feel them opening. Now they would find Ramos by the beautiful wall. Yes, everyone was sitting down so that her eyes could find the beautiful wall. Everyone was closing their eyes so that the little rivers of vision would not interfere with hers. Her rivers of vision were beautiful and made of the same vaporous stuff as the sounds only it was in a continuous flowing stream that flowed straight out, shimmering, and splashed against the wall and then over it, covering it as a heat wave covers a patch of sand or a street. Even though the wall was as far away as the stars the rivers of vision got to it at once and spread over it and kept it from going any further away.

Each figure on the wall was perfectly distinct. All of them together were perfectly distinct. Thousands of them, tens of thousands, were there in lines that went back and forth across the wall, across the surface that seemed creamy and luminous. Her rivers of vision spread over it all, over things she suddenly remembered she had known for a long long time. Events, tableaus.

Seven large boats filled with many Mayan women and a few men landed at an island. A man with golden skin crawled through a marsh and grabbed the legs of a crane and bit into its white neck, and blood squirted from the white neck across his mouth. Three old women squatted about a large flat stone grinding cocoa beans. She could see the creases in their faces, the hair in the creases, the particles of the hair.

The wall was coming closer. No, it was still the distance of the stars. The rivers of vision were running very strong and entering into the figures. She could see and smell the odor of salt blowing across the shining faces of the women in the boats, salty wind. They are departing. Their backs are turned to clamoring men amidst the rubble of a city on a dark green coast under an almost red sky.

At sea their boats form a close circle. The women bring forth the few men and display to them a man wearing the symbols of priest and executioner. All the men are bound. So is the executioner, and now a line is tied about him, and he is commanded to jump into the sea encircled by the boats. He leaps. A silver shark appears. The shark bites away his groin. Blood billows and covers the circle of water amidst the boats. They haul the executioner aboard the first boat. They bandage him and install him in a cage on a stone dais. Later the women anoint themselves for mating. They bring forth the bound men with fear-stricken faces. A woman with a sternly pointing arm commands them to behold the executioner in his cage. The men see and grovel pliantly and are unbound. They are caressed and aroused by the women awaiting union. Two times each day of the voyage the men are brought forth to plant more seed. Soon the rite is enacted with pleasure. Before they land on the island the voyagers anchor, and the men are joined to many women in a festival of unions.

Her rivers of vision flowed into them and brought her in sudden hot waves the texture and taste and smell of the flesh reek. It rushed upon her, permeating, as though the lovers themselves had entered into her. It overswept her, a startlement. She heard/felt as though from some immense distance a gasping laugh arise within her and erupt into the room.

Yes, the warm waters of the sea had coursed up her vision and drenched her within. Now through closed eyes it ebbed, returned to the wall. She was very still for a very long time. Her eyes opened again. The executioner was not in a boat. He was in the temple and in his hand gleamed the blade of the obsidian knife. She had seen him many times in many places.

His glittering eyes were shrieking terror and rage. They shrieked as they looked upward and then downward at the girl stretched taut across the altar. The gazes of several other waiting girls were baffled. Their eyes were dry but they made the sound of weeping. His golden arm was raised to bring the knife down. Her vision washed through his ceremonial robes. She saw his maleness erect, aseethe, pounding and beginning to ejaculate as he held the knife ready. Who? Her vision encompassed the doomed girl's face, moved on: There, the golden arm thrust the glass knife in. She was open, her heart was being lifted out. The wall rushed toward her.

The wall, the face: Oh, God, it was Ellen. No, she was here, no, she was there, there. The walls rushed, the face, the face and heart severed from the wall and rushed up the rivers of vision, the face and the pounding dripping heart, up the rivers and into her head: the face beholding its heart, the face scalded blank and vaporized by the unbearable sight: the heart, bleeding, filling her head, pounding, swelling.

Inside her the heart exploded. Its surging screaming red was driven into every cell of her being. The red was screaming, the red heart, the dying heart, dead heart screaming to a pitch that roared up like a blind rocket, soared up to a pitch beyond sound. It soared up and became the sky, and then shrank and became a dot.

It was an exquisitely tiny dot at an incredible distance across a mercurial vaporous sea of faint flue. It was receding. Then poof—it was gone. She was a faint chill wind moving into the darkness, gone, darkness.

A gentle hand clasped each of her feet.

"Oh," Ellen said. "You startled me. I must have dozed off." She was on the bench nestled back amidst the cushions. She sat up. Ramos was sitting cross-legged on the floor, regarding her with a calm faint smile.

"It seemed a good time for us to talk," he said.

Ellen gazed about the room, puzzled. Everyone seemed to have dozed off. Some sat on the floor with knees raised, heads nodding between. Others sat in chairs, eyes closed, heads atilt, or on other benches along the walls. Two were simply leaning in corners, knees bent but somehow locked. Through the banisters she could see forms on the floor of the mezzanine.

"It will take awhile for it to wear off," Ramos said.

"For what to wear off?" Ellen said. She felt very refreshed but still puzzled. She was surprised to find her hands loosely clasped to those of Lucienne on one side and Beaumonte on the other. Each of them was tipped over, dozing, like everyone else.

"The mescalino," Ramos said.

"Did I have some?"

"Did you drink the little chocolate?"

"Oh. Yes. Was it—"

Ramos smiled. He said, "Do you remember last night?"

"Last night? Is it morning? Did I sleep that long?"

Ramos shrugged and smiled. "Sometimes when I saw you you did not appear to be asleep. You were like a bird."

"I was?"

"Sometimes it comes back. The memory of it. Sometimes years after. Sometimes never. In this it is just like memory."

"Was it in all the cups?"

"You are not worried? I loved the sight of you. So did the others. My advantage is that I remember. Are you all right?"

Ellen struggled to reflect. She had a deep sense of well-being in spite of the teasing awareness of some gap in the recent scheme of time. Her mind strived as though to rise back into some dream that had come and fled. It was not a stressful striving.

Nor did she feel dismayed by the general situation which came clearly to her thoughts. Outside was the flood, she was marooned, and perhaps there was some worry about her at home, and conceivably if not probably she had been absent at the receipt of some word or signal from Henry. Yes, she still wished that she could call her house, and yet she felt somehow perfectly reconciled to the simple reality that she could not. She accepted that she had no sound reason to suppose that Emily was not in usual good health and enjoying herself. Yes, there was the favor to do for Kimo, but it could be done as well in a day or so when the flood had subsided.

"I think so, yes," she said. "In fact, I feel very good. I like you." The assertion came out seemingly of its own volition. But it was true. Ellen felt a distinct liking for Ramos, a warmth toward the calm young boy's face that even now she found it hard to accept as the face of a man of thirty. Except that his eyes might be that age, the placid dark eyes that were turned up to her. They seemed like the eyes of certain children who somehow manage to appear to be at once fresh and innocent and ancient and knowing. His clothing was colorful—an azure shirt, green trousers—but without the rococo complexity of decoration common to the clothes of the other men.

"That pleases me," Ramos said. "I like you. In truth, I love you passionately."

Ellen's warmth became something more. She sat silent. She felt a trace of alarm along with the flash of excitement. Still, Ramos had said it in the way he might have said, after glancing out of a window and noticing the reality, that it was raining very hard. His eyes seemed amused, detached. In the slight movement of their gaze they caught some flicker from a lamp or candle somewhere on the wall behind her. His clasp on her feet had been so light that she had lost awareness of it until now when he released them. She tucked her legs under her on the broad bench, her green and yellow and brown skirt spread wide, tenting her from the waist. Suddenly her hand moved to her neck and discovered that the decoration was missing. She looked about. It was resting on a cushion behind Lucienne. Ellen could not recall taking it off.

"Do you love me passionately?" Ramos said in the same gentle inconsequential tone. A smile impelled itself across Ellen's face, but still she said nothing. After a long silence Ramos spoke again: "Can you imagine us as lovers?"

Ellen thought there was a faint smile on Ramos's beautifully defined mouth. She studied the room, shivered. "I imagined it for at least that long—" Ellen silently snapped her fingers.

"Your heart is committed to someone," Ramos said. Again he might have been observing, the wind is blowing.

"How do you know?"

"It shows."

"Just now?"

"Ever since you first came down from Lucienne's room. It shows whenever you meet another man who attracts you. It is there now."

"How do you tell this? What do you see?"

"It's your eyes. They reveal you. This is how I knew you have met my mother Annamelio."

Ellen drew in her breath, astonished again. "You amaze me. I've been to her a number of times."

"This showed in your eyes when Lucienne mentioned her name."

"I'd love to have your powers. Or maybe I wouldn't. Perhaps it's frightening. What is it like?"

Ramos crossed his legs and drew his knees up under his chin, embracing his legs. His eyes grew thoughtful, even grave. Someone in the middle of the room groaned and abruptly muttered an incomprehensible word. Ramos shrugged at the sound.

"In reality, it is not a power," he said. "You understand? It is almost the opposite. If you see power as a positive exercise, it is the opposite. It is not perfectly clear, not even to Annamelio, but it is as though the mind ceases to strive to discover things and instead simply lets go and begins to receive them. I can see that I have not made it clear."

Ellen was rapt, waiting. Ramos went on: "Perhaps it can only be seen in terms of these opposites. Perhaps you will get the notion if you will first think of the mind struggling to reach out and penetrate reality and then giving up this struggle and allowing reality simply to flow in. Annamelio taught me that the world's secrets behave like a flock of geese. When you charge among them they fly in all directions. When you grow still they assemble again. This is all more difficult for me because I am a man. A woman can achieve the right frame of mind more naturally, because she is made simply to open herself and receive. But the man is made to thrust and penetrate. Unfortunately, his mind tends to work in the same way as his body. Does this make sense to you?"

"Tell me something particular," Ellen said. "Did my age, my birth month simply flow to you in this way?"

Ramos broke into a larger smile. "I would like to tell you," he said, "but I enjoy being mysterious. Do you love me passionately yet?"

"I love you, but—" Ellen smiled. "—Lucienne loves you passionately."

"I know. She loves every man passionately."

"But she says that you won't have her."

"Well, this is no longer so, but then you do not remember, do you?"

Ellen glanced at her dozing companions again. She remembered nothing that illuminated his vague allusions.

"You look very puzzled," Ramos said. "Nothing comes back to you, eh?"

Ellen decided to ask nothing about what she could not remember.

"Ellenita, you suffer the absence of your love," Ramos said.

"This shows, too?"

"This and something else—that your wait is coming to an end."

Ellen hugged her knees, upraised and tented over by her skirt, her face propped, gazing down into his young/old eyes. She said, "Ramos, I wish you truly *knew* what you just said."

"We never know for sure. But sometimes we can perceive certain invisible realities with exceptional clarity. It is like—Tell me, have you ever see the sounds of music in the air?"

Ellen laughed, a sharp yawp, delighted at the absurdity. "Oh, I never heard of such a thing!" she said.

"Well, it is very beautiful—the sight of music racing in the air."

"Ramos, you're teasing me."

"No, I have seen it. Others, too. Our perception of unseen realities can become very sensitive, Ellenita. You like your new name?"

Ellen nodded. She said, "It is your invention?"

"Mine? No, of course not, it is yours. Rather, it is what you remembered your name to be at some beautiful moment last night." From his expression Ellen took the feeling that Ramos was getting immense enjoyment out of tantalizing her. Suddenly from beside her she heard Lucienne's voice, heard her rouse up and awaken laughing, and then speak.

"Ellenita," she said. *"Bon jour.* What a beautiful way to come back." Lucienne's eyes found her cousin Ramos now, his face still placidly at rest on his raised knees. She said, "Ah!" She nodded toward Beaumonte and said, "Ramos, quickly, before he comes back let us sneak up to my bed."

"He is back," Beaumonte said. He was raising himself and stretching, his hair an abrupt explosion of black. A grin came over his face in contradiction to some searching glitter in eyes that now looked back and forth from Lucienne, who was laughing, to Ramos, who shrugged. Ramos said, "If you sneak away do not forget to take me with you." Then he exploded in mirth.

Ramos rose. With a half-smile and a courtly nod he turned and receded toward the other end of the room. He stepped amidst the gaudy figures about the room. Wakefulness was spreading among them rapidly like a gust. Suddenly the big room was astir with the life of vividly colored shirts and skirts. A low babble began to arise. Somewhere beyond her view one of the odd stringed instruments came to life with a tune as bright as the first sun. At the end of the long bench the guitarist woke up, and his guitar became part of him again as he wrapped his torso about it. His music began echoing that of the other instrument.

Anna-lia emerged through the far door of the kitchen. She was bearing a small tray and glided amidst the festival guests toward Ellen.

"Bon jour, buenas dias, good morning," she said. "Ellenita must take the first breakfast." She handed the try to Ellen.

Ellen shared the breads and jams on the tray with Lucienne and Beaumonte, who stared at both her and Lucienne as though he were insanely in love with them. Ramos was still slowly threading his way across the room, stopping to talk here and there. Now several men and women emerged from the kitchen once again bearing trays laden with the small silver cups and baskets of breads. As a tray floated by Ramos he smoothly snatched off a cup and in an unbroken motion tilted and drained it. He set the empty cup down on a second tray that passed by and from it took up another full cup and drank it down, too.

"So!" Lucienne said, placing a hand on each of Ellen's cheeks and turning her gaze into her own. "Tell me how you like your first festival. It is marvelous, is it not?"

Ellen smiled. "I feel very good," she said.

Beaumonte with a rich laugh leaned across her so that his face was close to both of theirs. His body pressed against her breasts as he reached and captured Lucienne's face between his hands and kissed her. He said, "Yes, let us do what we are thinking." They got up. Ellen remained seated, and Beaumonte and Lucienne looked warmly at her. Lucienne said, "Come play?"

"I think I'll finish breakfast," Ellen said. Beaumonte turned his mouth into a mock pout. He brushed her cheek with his hand.

Ellen saw them for another moment on the narrow mezzanine walking close with arms encircling waists. As they passed from her view the numerous rectangles of garish color about the room suddenly smashed into her vision, freshly, all at once, raising a great giddiness in her, an elation and a yearning to capture the effect in a painting or on film. She also had a wish to photograph Ramos's mural, to take color slides of it and show them to Paul Gans or perhaps to one of the magazines. She thought that perhaps she could do this today if the light improved. Then she was smitten with primitive wonder and astonishment, and she shook her head vigorously to dispel an uncanny feeling. She thought, *Today?*

At a front window she drew aside a heavy curtain. Brown trash-strewn water still flowed about the tires of her squat dark green car, but its level was not so high as before. The atmosphere was still dull but in small places seemed clearing.

Gulls looked silvery black against the low sky. As she watched the curving gulls the vibrations of the pulsing music began to enter her body, and it began swaying to the sound. Within the music she could hear echoes of gypsies, Indians, Spaniards, peasant French. The gulls outside seemed far away as the babble of the reawakening festival of the rain took on a certain irresistible resonance.

8

NEW YORK:

She was sitting back down.

"Ellen, was it the phone call or did you suddenly get drunk on half a martini?" It was the question of Paul Gans, a gray-haired man whose thin body was lost somewhere beneath the gentle folds of a navy blue blazer and wide-collared gray shirt. His eyes were recurringly obscured by light glancing off his large horn-rimmed glasses. Now his eyes seemed bewildered or amazed.

"No, but I think I'll have the other half," Ellen said. Some irrepressible delight disrupted her words with sounds resembling either gurgles or giggles. She was sitting back down in one of the two upholstered wing chairs flanking their tiny low table in the lobby of the idiosyncratic old hotel whose motley clientele sat or strolled chattering all about them.

"Now what kind of an answer is that?" said Paul Gans.

"In fact, I think I definitely will," Ellen said, the sudden seethe of good spirits still sputtering inchoately somewhere in her throat.

"You think you will *what*, for heaven's sake?"

"Have another," she said.

"Another martini?"

Ellen drained the last half of the contents of her glass and flamboyantly signaled a waiter.

"Maestro!" she said.

"You *are* getting drunk," Paul said. "You *never* have two martinis."

Ellen was aware that she was breathing fast. Her heart felt as though it were rising and trying to fly within her. She half-giggled again, and then furiously shook her head, no.

"It had to be the phone call, then," he said. He whipped off his glasses and inspected her as though for the first time. "Yes, that has to be it. That accounts for the dress *and* the call. You've just taken a new lover."

Ellen exploded with a wild laugh that caused eyes to pop around in their direction. It even touched off a small epidemic of sympathetic laughter around the murmurous lobby.

He couldn't get over the dress. She was wearing a sleek sleeveless melon-colored frock with an enormous string of huge brilliantly colored beads, had in fact bought it just that afternoon, the dress and the beads, at a price that was preposterous, had got them in one of those extravagant shops that she fundamentally detested, had deliberately decided on the extravagance that might, along with a radical change of style, just raise her spirits before the dinner with her editor, which of course was now underway.

"Maybe that explains the ring, too," he said. "Maybe it wasn't given to you down there at all." Ellen held up her right hand and examined the braided gold ring with its lustrous clear red stone.

"No," she said, subduing an impulse to laugh. "I just found out what it meant."

Paul Gans now looked a man whose patience was being too

much tested. He also seemed close to laughing at his own exasperation.

"Ellen, you found out what what meant?"

She had the feeling that anyone would know what she was talking about. Ever since Horris had said it just a few minutes ago it had seemed to be a possession of the very air around her. Now at his question she realized that her elation was undoubtedly inordinate, and that her intuitions were not in the public domain.

"Oh, that's right. It was something you wouldn't know," she said. "Something I haven't mentioned. It was just some good news."

"That you just got on the phone, right?"

"Yes. That was Horris calling me."

"Well, you would hardly be taking him as a lover. Or would you?"

More laughter. She said, "No, it was a translation of something."

"A translation," Gans said. His long equine face was all perplexity now. "Only a damned editor is entitled to get that excited over a translation. You go to the phone all depressed and hang-dog and a translation sends you into ecstasy? I give up."

"No, wait. It was, it was a translation. He found out what somebody said."

"Well," he said, "that makes it perfectly clear. You won't mind if I have one of these with you, eh?" Paul held up his empty crystal as a signal to the waiter. "How would I ever have guessed that a translation might relate to something somebody had said."

Ellen lost control of another laugh and tried to muffle it in the large linen napkin. She tried to say something, but Paul went on.

"Ellen, in five years now—or is it six—I have never seen you so volatile. You make one phone call from your room and it turns you to fuming raging gloom. And then an hour later you get one call and come back as giddy as a school girl. Skipping, for crying out loud, skipping across the lobby of this sophisticated old mausoleum. Now—"

"I haven't embarrassed you?"

"Oh, God, no, love. Don't take this that seriously. Don't take me that seriously. No, no, no, don't think of that. And don't hesitate to tell me to shut up if I start prying into something personal." Paul Gans took a gulp of his drink. He peered over the rim of the glass. He said, "I'm just a friend. Granted, if I were twenty years younger I'd try to be more, but—so goes the story of my life."

Ellen sipped her second drink. "I do feel very good," she said.

"Better than I should, really. I'm making too much of very little, and I know it. I shouldn't, but I can't help it."

Paul Gans sighed. In his habitual way he took his glasses off again, nibbled the earpiece, and then returned them immediately into place. Now he would take up his long straight pipe and rap the bowl against his hand and set it back again while searching for a book of matches.

"It won't seem nearly as exciting to you, I'm afraid," Ellen said,

"Ellen, I'm not expecting some shameless scandal out of you even if I might enjoy one. In fact, I would be astounded if you topped the story of being marooned in Los Nubes with—whataretheir-names—Lucienne, Ramos, Dumonty—"

"Beaumonte."

"Whatever. So you've already given me more vicarious excitement than I deserve. When the hell did I ever have a government helicopter land in a gypsy camp to bring me a message to call home as soon as possible. But—No, honestly, don't let me pry. But I really have wondered what's gotten you so—so—what do I mean?—so down and up and up and down."

"Well," Ellen said. She was taking very small sips from the martini. "Did you ever notice that martinis are smooth on the outside and fuzzy on the inside?"

"I see. Ellen, did Dumonty or Ramos put you onto that, too? Or the same fellow who told you about seeing sounds flying through the air? I'm about to go back to my first diagnosis. Are you tight?"

"No, really I'm not. It's just such a long story I'm stalling for time."

"Look, Ellen. Just awhile ago you described an entire book for me in two or three sentences."

"Hmmm. Well. I'll try. But it may sound silly to you."

"Try me."

"Well." Ellen suddenly cut her eyes away from the predatory stare of a man hidden from Paul Gans view by a column situated in mid-lobby. She said, "There is a very good friend of mine who went away a long time ago and is still away somewhere. And just a few weeks ago Horris saw him, saw him and his little boy, down in Key West. And they talked for a long time. And then they got on his boat and sailed away to nobody knows where. Just as the boat was pulling away he yelled *adios* and many thanks to Horris and Claudette, I've told you about her, and so he left without saying whether he would ever be coming back. You see?"

Paul Gans solemnly nodded.

"Then," she went on "as they were pulling away, Henri, the boy, also yelled something. Henri's nine—Henri yelled something that nobody could understand, you see, because it was in Chinese. So he shouted this out and then he looked up at his Papa, my friend, and laughed. And his Papa laughed, too. And then they were gone. Now, what Horris just told me is that he has been tracking around trying to find out what Henri said. He hadn't at first thought to try it, but then he just got the idea. So he was going to the few Chinese around McClung and trying to reproduce the sounds that Henri had made, you see? Well, he called to tell me he had happened to be in a certain restaurant up in Carterville and asked the Chinese chef there, and this chef felt sure that what Henri had said was, 'We'll see you soon, but it's a secret.' "

She felt her lips and chin rebelling. She tried to bring them under command, and then said, "See, I told you it would seem silly." Paul Gans unobtrusively slipped a handkerchief across the arm of his chair to her. He sat silent while she caught her breath and took first a sip from her martini and then several large gulps from a glass of iced water. With his long bony hand simply resting available on the low winglike arm of her chair, he sat silent as she said, "You know, they'll never improve on water." And remained silent still when she reached over and put her hand under his and let him clasp it as she said, "Unless I'm mistaken there's a man you can't see who wants to pick me up."

Then he finally spoke up in that strong exuberant way he indulged when he was talking about important things like writing or friends, but seldom otherwise. "Well, you're mistaken if you don't think this place is crawling with men who would give an arm to pick you up."

She accepted the flimsy springboard to a laugh, and then was all right again, which he recognized and acknowledged by withdrawing his hand and making a big fuss about studying the menu. She was all right still as they were finishing up their red snapper and he elected to return to the subject.

"Ellen, you've given me a memorable evening," he said. "Where I expected only some shop talk you've given me something I've wanted ever since your first letter popped up in my mail. Now and then I've thought I had it, but tonight I realize I didn't before but do now. Somewhat, anyway. What I'm saying is that I finally feel that I'm getting to know you."

"Really?"

"It's the nicest thing that's happened to me in a long time."

"Are you through with your snapper?"

"Would you like it?"

"Only if. I've suddenly gotten hungry again."

"Are you aware that until this evening you had never—of your own volition—mentioned your husband to me. In all these years. After you talked to your brother on the phone upstairs, when you were fuming about this off again-on again protest meeting or whatever, the thing he's sponsoring, that was the first time you had ever brought him into our conversation. It's mystified me for a long time."

"I guess I've never felt a need to. He sort of mystifies me. And maybe even himself. Nothings binds us, really, except his name. Probably if I had ever talked about it somebody might have gotten the wrong impression."

"Somebody like me?"

"You know what I mean. It sort of gives off the idea of unhappiness. But my life hasn't been that way."

"May I ask you one utterly presumptuous question?"

"Yes, but I won't promise to answer."

"Fair enough. I was wondering if it was your husband you were talking about all the time on the phone."

"Well, yes. You heard everything I said. Probably I should have excused myself to make the call, but—Anyway, I didn't expect any of that. What happened was Cliff told me that Mr. Eubanks had just announced again that this meeting or rally would still be held. Of course, he had announced it about a week ago, but some of the men in town had gotten him to cancel or postpone it. Well, he had, he announced a postponement, but the new thing was his going back on that. Now he's going to have it, anyway."

"No, I understood that, more or less. I meant when you said something like, 'He's such an evil bastard, he almost broke my jaw down there.' You were talking about him then?"

"Oh, no, no, no. That wasn't Mr. Eubanks I was talking about. That was a sheriff down there. No, God, don't carry away the idea Mr. Eubanks ever hit me. He's never touched me or anything like that. But what that was about—Well, he announced that this sheriff, who is a really awful man named Ellis Kelso, is going to be the big speaker at this rally. Next Saturday. You see? And it was when I heard that that I just sank, because he's such a hateful S.O.B., so cruel. If I told you about him you wouldn't believe it. But it was him I was talking about. And, damn!" Ellen raised helpless hands into the air and threw her eyes up toward the ceiling. "Damn! Did my brother sound furious when I said that. I really do wish I hadn't thought of it. Cliff said, *'He hit you?'* And that's when I said he almost broke my jaw. This was a long time ago, actually. But tonight as soon as I heard Cliff I remembered that when he came down there—you see, I was in this bastard's *jail*—and when Cliff came down to get me out I took one look at him and decided not to mention anything about what Kelso had done. About hitting me."

"Why wouldn't you tell him?"

"Oh, you just can't imagine the fury he was in. I think he would have killed him right on the spot. Or as soon as he saw him. And maybe the deputies, too. Oh, I know he would have killed one deputy if I had told him everything."

"I don't guess I would dare ask what the hell you were doing in jail?"

"Well—" Ellen said. And laughed. And told him.

After dinner they walked for miles, walked downtown and talked as the nervous traffic of Manhattan screeched and honked its way past them, walked through garish neon into a cooling evening that brought some intimation of a break in summer's harsh heat. She told him about Ellis Kelso. Paul Gans was, as expected, incredulous.

"I can hardly imagine you amidst people like that," he said. "You must love something there very much to stay."

"Well, of course," she said. "But I'll tell you something. Horris is always telling people that of course the place is full of evil and violence. Then he says if you ever find a better place, let him know. I sort of believe that."

"I'm not sure," Paul Gans said. "New York can get pretty rough, but I don't think we have any Ellis Kelsos—currently."

Paul finally turned the talk back to the story of the translation. He said. "I gather your friend is something more than a friend, or am I threatening to open an old wound again?"

"No, I'm all right, Paul. Actually, back at the hotel I was so happy I couldn't contain myself. But it was silly, in a way. I mean, for me to take so much hope from the shouted words of a child. Who might not even have shouted what we think he did. Still, I did, and—"

"It would be that important, if he came back."

"Yes. It would be the most important thing that could happen. For me."

"I think I see. He's been gone a long time?"

"Nine years. Nine years this month."

"Any communications?"

"Not direct. Until Horris ran into him."

"Ellen, did he just up and—"

"Oh, God, Paul, really, it is all so complicated, how it happened. But there was no breach between us, if that's what you wonder. There was no betrayal, really. It was just a complicated set of strange circumstances. All one after the other."

"Destiny?"

"Why not?"

"Do you really think he's going to be back?"

"What do I really know? I don't know, I don't know. All I really know is that learning he was still alive made me very happy. And very hungry to see him. And then I guess tonight I leaped wildly after a straw. Paul, I don't have the faintest idea what will happen."

"If he does, what happens to Mr. Eubanks?"

"I don't know that either. I don't know what will happen. I don't even know what I would do if he actually came back now. Maybe just go crazy. Maybe I'd just start circling the earth like that sputnik thing up there going beep-beep-beep."

They walked a bit in the lost sound of their footfalls.

"Really," Ellen said, "I guess the up and down thing you see in me is from both of these things. In honesty, I suppose I'm running out of staying power as far as Mr. Eubanks goes. He's turned into such a—something. Actually, he's just sort of lost and very unhappy and all screwed up inside, so much that he doesn't really know what he's doing. I think I could probably go on sweating out all the—well, all I have to sweat out really in his existence. But I think I could stand up under anything alone. It's Emily I worry about. She's very perceptive, and very wise, and she doesn't like what he's doing, either. Well, the conflict of feelings can only damage her. I've actually thought of just picking her up this Saturday and just skipping right out with her, maybe to Europe, maybe to Switzerland, anywhere. You know, for good. But—I don't know."

"I thought you said you were going to get her tomorrow."

"Oh, I said I'm driving up to Vermont tomorrow. I don't pick her up until Saturday."

"And what happens to Thursday and Friday?"

"Well, I'm sort of hungry for some solitude, to tell the truth. It's really the reason I came up here on the spur of the moment. When I got back from Los Nubes last Sunday I thought I would be able to get into the work on Monday. But Monday rolled by and Tuesday, and I finally realized all I would do down there would be sit around and wait for that damned word that probably wouldn't ever come. So there you are. I drove up to Riverton this morning and climbed on a plane, and here I am."

"You have a place to stay up there?"

"No, I always take potluck with a motel or hotel. I'll find something a little out of the way, I don't know. I never make very good plans."

"Would you like a place that's not close to anything?"

"I'd love it."

"I've got a friend with a lovely cottage out in the mountains, not too far from Brattleboro. He was planning to use it this week but had to cancel out and was offering it around. Of course, it's not even close to a telephone. Can you take that kind of solitude?"

"Oh, heavens, yes."

"Eighteen or twenty miles to a country store?"

"So long as I'm close enough to check in with home once a day. I'm not liberated from my vigil. But that sounds great."

"Listen, there's a good little Italian restaurant about four blocks further. Why don't we stop in there and have an espresso and I'll call him and maybe save you some rent money. But I warn you this place will offer you nothing but solitude. And landscape."

"Sounds perfect. I love Vermont."

After he had called, and as they sipped the strong coffee, he was saying, "Well, Ellen, I'll have to confess that as of this moment I'd ask for your hand if it weren't for Mr. Eubanks, and the fact that your heart belongs to some wandering wretch, and the perhaps predominant fact that I'm about fifteen years too old for that sort of thing."

"Paul, would you be offended if I said bullshit?"

"It would depend on what you were referring to."

"Your obsession with age."

"Obsession, hell, I'm fifty-seven."

"That makes you at this moment exactly ten years younger than Papa was when he begat me."

"One other thing I love about you is the way you call your husband Mr. Eubanks and work words like begat into a sentence when I'm least expecting it. But you're pulling my leg, of course."

"And let's see, you're fifteen years younger than my brother is right now, and he's still wondering whether to betray a love he's carried for about thirty or so years and get married. Not *when* but whether. He still assumes he's got plenty of time to decide when if he can only make up his mind whether."

"Your brother is how old?"

"Seventy-two. Half-brother."

"Now I'm afraid to ask about your father."

"You assume he's no longer with us."

"I may as well admit it."

"He's ninety-seven. And still makes Mrs. Pichon giggle nervously when he walks by her."

"And Mrs. Pichon?"

"She just sort of lives with us. She came a long time ago as a nurse when mama was ill."

"And she?"

"I love the espresso. Will you treat me to another?"

"You'll never sleep."

"Nothing will keep me awake tonight. It's been so good talking." Ellen suddenly lowered her voice. "Paul, look at the people at the corner table. Now, those two men, and the girls, too, would fit right into the Trussante house if they only looked happy. They have that same tawny olive sort of skin that looks like everything Mediterranean and Spanish and Mexican-Indian rolled into one. But why do they look so unhappy?"

The coffee came, and they silently stirred with tiny spoons. Ellen was still staring into her cup when she felt Paul's hand severely clench her upper arm. He was whispering vehemently, almost viciously.

"Sit very still, and don't look up!"

Ellen glanced first at Paul and then instantly in the direction that he was looking, toward the table where the tawny skinned people were sitting. Her eyes fell upon the table just as the face of one of the men became an explosion of blood.

Only then did she see the pistol that a standing man was holding, saw it turn to one of the women, saw a hole under her eye spurt blood, saw without comprehending that the other man was not at the table, and wondered confusedly whether the one standing with the pistol was he. Again she tried to rise, but Paul's vehemently clenching hand held her in place.

Now the standing man was swinging his eyes and weapon about the room. He was backing slowly toward them, no, toward the door by them. Now he was right there, right by them in this strange silence, this pounding silence, and now his eyes were there, his moist brown glittering eyes were suddenly looking right into hers, caught by them, and his mouth was pinched in on itself, and he seemed to have stopped backing, and now his arm and hand had brought up the pistol and it was pointing directly at her and the scream she felt was not coming out, nothing was coming out, and there was a sound like scraping close by, and suddenly she knew she was about to die, too, and tried to say something but couldn't with her mouth but within her in a filling beseechment she said, *Help me.*

And then, just then, saw the side of his head explode in blood, too, and then saw that the other man had come back from wherever he had been and had fired and now was firing again and again into the man who was going to kill her, was firing several times and then rushed to the table where one girl was still in a chair and grabbed her arm, and they were running out, and—

She still saw the blood, and now saw only the blood, and it became an exploding heart that entered into her eyes and filled her mind and then within her exploded again and drenched through her, permeating her with screaming red that became impenetrable darkness, a darkness that shrank and shrank until it became an infinitesimal circle, a speck on an immensely distant horizon across a vaporous translucent sea of blue, a speck: now there, now gone: darkness.

VERMONT:

Now it might break her in two. Now would be the time, wouldn't it? Now with him back. Him back and she invisibly dismembered, pulled apart like a snapped thread. Or a cable, yes, like that bridge cable before the invisible force of that sudden flood. A woven cable drawn suddenly taut by two irresistible rockets. Snapping with a shrill twanging fray, with a monstrous raveling at just that instant: that instant when simultaneously this ecstatic anticipation snatched her being up toward infinity again while that shrieking ineludible horror dragged it plummeting into the abyss.

It would happen, could happen, now in this silent shrill dark tumult: now on the one day out of millions when he is there alive waiting untouchable. And tomorrow, if tomorrow should ever come, if it should come and she should know it, tomorrow she might be unable even to call, or even to remember to try to call, or even to remember why she yearned to call, or if she called unable to utter it, unable perhaps to hear, to receive, to gather in his words, or to comprehend them with a mind disordered, a being rent, tangled and inextricable like snarled thread out of a raveled fabric, like the underside of Aunt Margaret's embroidery which was the only part of which she would show any area: an incomprehensible snarl of threads.

Maybe it was already tomorrow. How long had she been lying here, catapulting, plummeting, unable to fasten upon these fleeting stillnesses in between. What time had she got back? Minutes had become days from the instant Cliff had uttered his name. Before. She had known he was going to. Oh, shit, she should never have asked permission to make another call, should simply have made it and never have suffered the storekeeper's insufferably polite stubbornness: *Sorry, mam, it's closing time for sure. Filling station down the Duck Hill Road's got a phone. Sometimes he's open late. Sorry, mam.*

Closed station. Closed store. A road to nowhere. A flat tire. That goddam flat tire on a rented car with brand new tires. And then, oh, shit, the phone dead in the one house with a light. She: *Isn't there another phone somewhere around here? I've got to find one.* And he in his twanging drawl not only insufferably patient but maddeningly sanctimonious: *Miss, I'd be the last one to discourage you from looking, but I can almost promise you ain't going to find one very close by unless some strange things have been going on. Now, could you possibly take kindly to the thought that maybe providence doesn't intend for you to make this call of yours at just this time of night?*

Yes, probably already it was Saturday. Should she go turn on the car radio? No, it wouldn't do any good to know. Maybe it had not even been today, maybe she had already been severed, mind out of time, maybe it was still yesterday and the nightmare search for a phone was only a strange waking hallucination, the call to Cliff simply a delusion, sheer delusion, one dazzling delusory respite begat by intolerable horror, a delusion designed only to refresh her and condition her for more: shattered heads, exploding hearts, and that strange awesome chilling waking dream: a sacrificial execution enacted like a languid vivid mirage across the sunny shimmering verdant slope of the mountain. *Help me.*

Madness. Was it madness? Derangement born of exhaustion, born out of that interminable night that would not let go of the interminable day that followed, a day that was like darkness under the sun. In this lovely solitary stillness, predatory terrors, doom hungry guns and whistling knives, life drowning in the sweet screaming blood of life itself: the butchered heart of that golden girl in the clutch of some priest of death.

Oh help me what was I seeing what put it in my mind?

Yesterday? Yes, today was Friday, and this morning she had crept out to the little porch of the cottage, and it had been still again, it had been all right. The faces had been dispelled and again she could hear Henri calling from the boat in those falsetto syllables that she did not even know but that meant had to mean they would be coming sometime, and now, oh, now, oh, soon, tomorrow, she would hear his voice, and tomorrow, if they could get on a plane, tomorrow night, if they could get seats, damn, it would be a holiday weekend with a glut of travel, the goddam Labor Day run-to-the-sun, but: yes, she would bribe the damn ticket agent if she had to, she would charter a damn plane, she, and tomorrow night he would be right there, alive, and they wouldn't stop they would just go and it wouldn't matter she and Emily and he and Henri they would go they would go they.

Help me not get killed help him help us help us together together omanta omanta *we are one have been one are one and he's there and was almost there when that man with the gun was about to ooooooooooooooooooooooh. Help me.*

Yes. Yes, this child is safe, this child is safe, alive, this child of life, of this body, this mind, animated by this life of all life, grateful to life for life. Yes, this mind must be still, still, still, must cease, withdraw from striving, not strive, be still, listen, listen, listen to the silent singing, silent stars: you are nothing, you are everything. Out of nothing this mind by these eyes contains the stars. Be still. Stillness. Stillness. Providence doesn't intend for you to make this call. Yes. Nor die. I died but did not die. How strange to die and return and die again a million times as of some narcotic enamorment. Of this child is grateful, grateful.

Paul: Oh, God, Ellen, you were incredibly lucky.

She: Why didn't any of us move? Why didn't we do anything?

He: There was nothing we could do, and we knew it. To move would have been to get it for sure. It was just catching his eye that almost got you killed. Oh, Christ! If that other hood hadn't come out of the john when he did! God, it's weird the things you notice at a time like that. You know, even before I saw his pistol I noticed that the tail of his pink shirt was sticking a little bit out of his fly. Do you realize that if that bastard had suffered a slightly different call of nature you'd be—

She: Paul, I'm going to go ahead and pick up a car right now and get out of this place. It's daylight and—

He: You think you should drive without any rest at all?

She: I'll rest when I get up there. There's not much danger I'll go to sleep at the wheel. But I know I'm going to pieces if I don't get out of this city quick.

He: Well, I guess I'm concerned. But the truth is you seem to have yourself together better than I.

She: Don't be fooled. It's just an old bad habit of mine. I prefer to be alone when I go crazy.

So had driven up while her mind disgorged seemingly all of the violent blood of her experience and knowledge. They, the disgorgements, seemed to be trailing out behind her in a malignant wake or, no, like some malevolent tide ripping after her, in pursuit, chasing, so that finally she was making the car shoot through the countryside like a cartidge, fleeing.

Her eyes became Kimo's, and she saw as he had, staggering up with one eye gone and bleeding to stare with the other at the jagged hole in Puana's tender neck, lethally rent by the guns of nightriders firing blindly into the warehouse where Kimo had called together a handful of people merely to talk of their kindred outrage. She thought of the savagery aseethe beneath Beaumonte's glistening skin, there in some murky and inextinguishable passion, savagery that had impelled him to slice the face of a friend, mayhem behind the mask of outraged love. Even a vision of Ellis Kelso's father loomed up: he whom she had never seen, would never see, he with his head spouting blood where his ear had been, his wife gaunt and furious, laying aside the bloodied butcher knife to bandage and tend his wound while in the hidden distance of the woods her not lover but—what?—her appeaser, consoler, he standing in his fearful vulnerable blackness watching, wondering. She had thought of Kelso himself and his chronic abuse of the helpless, of men and women, of the recurring stories of prisoners beaten and maimed in his jail, of the incomprehensible complicity and silence of the people he ostensibly served. *Why didn't any of us move? Why didn't we do anything?*

Her mind called up, too, her own ferocious yearning to kill Kelso herself during that moment of black and inarticulate rage in the detention room. Connecticut and then Massachusetts had unfolded alongside her but she almost all along the way had inhabited those pursuing bloodscapes out of memory. They seemed to arise from every corner. There was her Papa as a man-boy of sixteen running up just as the militia fired its cannon into the central corridor of the old Spanish-style courthouse, killing her grandfather Worth and, God, how many others of the Rooters, those gaunt and hungry and desperate farmers and croppers who had been unable to make their voices heard and so had spoken their protest by capturing the citadel of the law, that facade of power: They demanding, in truth, only the wherewithal to live, desperate at the end of three successive crops so bad that the banks were pushing them off their land, the banks demanding payment while by repossession depriving them of the land and equipment to make it to pay. The Rooters: they, too, resorting to savagery, some unknown cutting the throats of two of their number who wanted to give in. Papa *seeing* it and knowing at once, knowing even then: *What I knew is that I either had to kill them or bring them to heel like dogs. I guess God put me on the better path. He sure let me get on top of them and let me run the worst of them into the dirt where they belonged. But I'll tell you this, every time I think about the sons of bitches I still wonder if I shouldn't have done it the other way. Funny, I didn't feel much at all about those stupid soldiers. They didn't really do it. They didn't call themselves to duty against a bunch of Rooters armed with knives and hatchets and maybe three or four guns. It was the goddam bankers of McClung and Carterville that put that cannon there, and they as good as aimed and fired it. Now that I think of it again I do wish I had just gone ahead and killed the sons of bitches.* She had shivered at the wheel recalling, recalling the way her Papa had at that smashed the end of his stick to the floor of the front porch where on a summer evening long ago he had been sitting in the swing with her mother Emily beside him, she and Matt and Mark not sitting but squatting in the old web-seated rockers. His stick had smashed down and then her mother had said, *Oh, Papa, you don't mean that, you wouldn't hurt a damn fly. Children, your Papa is the gentlest man in McClung.*

McClung. McClung. Even the town seemed to have arisen from a well of blood. There was the brooding Mississippian for whom it was named, Alexander Keith McClung, and the stories about him, the account of his having killed six brothers in a succession of duels. A duelist and melancholy poet winning practically the whole region at the end of some marathon card game from the preacher Winston Carter, who had been given it as payment for his murderous betrayal of the Lomkubees. Old Bema still seething at the recollection of blood she could not have seen and yet sees still because it was of her and she of it. Of Ellen, too, this child, who had also dreamed of murder in the jail at Tamerdes. And, of course, of self-murder at the loss of her mother. That strangling terror and rage at loss that always seems somehow a betrayal.

As when Henry left, when she first knew he was gone, those bitter boiling passions surging up with demonic concussions. Blood and some errand of killing even taking him away in a sense twice: Henry in a plane flinging bullets impossible distances at unseen men in other planes and shooting down fourteen that became the coffins of beings he had never seen. Himself downed by the betrayal of his own machine. Hence passing down, parachuting into the woods to be taken in hand by Michelle, herself at war, herself destined to survive it but doomed to die in the fury of civilized traffic, and Henry gone: Cliff by the river shooting bottles out of the air. *I didn't violate my love for her.* Gentle Cliff, waiting forever to outlive the husband of his one true love who did not even know that he was waiting. Cliff, who also had taken life with no doubt some fury hard to guess from his soft way of telling it: How two spokesmen for the crew came to say they couldn't take the ship into that certain West African river. *Cliff: Well, I didn't say anything. I just shot. She: You killed them? Cliff: Only one of them, but it made the other one think. Ellen, you look horrified.*

*But at sea you can't tolerate that sort of thing. You can't even let it be
discussed. If I had let it go I'd probably be the dead man today. She: Why
were you going up the river? Cliff: Had a cargo of cloth. Couple of tons of
it.*

*Paul Gans: No, I doubt that the killer had any personal feelings at all.
With those guys it's strictly business. That's why they almost never get caught.
They don't leave any of the usual traces because they don't have any of the
usual human motives. You know, Ellen, except for a very few, the only
murders that ever get solved and punished are murders among friends and
families. Just check the statistics and you can't be surprised to reflect that our
most ancient murder myth involves brothers. Maybe the Cain and Abel myth
is the oldest of all. She: Except that the Eden myth would have to come first.*

So she had fled, driving faster and faster, faster without knowing it than even her usual abandoned speed. Once in Connecticut
hearing the brief purring siren and having the towering trooper bend
into her window shaking a young paternal head: *Miss, I know there's
no fire ahead or I would have heard about it.* Then letting her go with a
lecture. Which had passed from her mind, displaced by the horrors
again by the time she had crossed over the river at Springfield and
heard another siren. This time a squinty deputy who had insisted on
issuing a ticket and obliged her to detour to the magistrate's office
and put up thirty-two dollars. Then onward.

At the store she had handed Paul's note to the skinny slumped
proprietor and gotten the keys in return. She had seen the phone and
been tempted to call home at once—it was then noon—but had suddenly felt a biting impatience to buy a few things and get on out to
the solitude of the cottage. She would call tonight, and had been
about to ask the store hours when she saw the sign printed on a gray
cardboard shirt blocker: "Open til 10 through Labor Day Weekend."
Night, but, exhausted, she had slept from afternoon into Friday, had
slept again that afternoon and had not gone back to the store until
barely before closing.

Cliff: Ellen! I wish there'd been some way to get you on the
damn phone.

Even when he said that, she knew without quite knowing.

She: Well, I'm sorry, but I'm miles and miles back up in the
mountains.

He: Can you hear me? I'm getting a lot of racket from up there.

The impatience and solicitude of his voice confirmed what she
already knew without quite knowing.

She: It's a party line, Cliff. I can hear you, but talk loud, okay?
What's happened?

Already the horrors were out of her mind, and somehow she didn't sense doom in what he was eager to tell her, and already she had forgotten that right off she would tell him about last night's ghastly adventure in the Italian restaurant.

He: Henry's back! He was by here!

So then she began to tremble and feel hysterical, not wanting to feel so much that way because she had to listen now, hear, remember, find out. And she tried to ask something but couldn't say anything.

Cliff: He and his boy came by this morning. Listen, you can get him at Percy's house. You hearing this? They're staying over at Percy's. They pulled in late last night. Or early this morning, I think. Came right up the river and tied up right there at the Ensley tie-up. Ellen, you got that?

She: Uh-huh. Can you speak louder, Cliff?

He: He and the boy just popped in right around noon. He already knew you were out of town but he wanted to say hello and get your number. He tried to call you from here at that hotel in New York. And then when they said you had gone he tried that camp up there, Montaqua, but they said you hadn't gotten there yet. Ellen, you ought to be able to get him at Percy's. Or if you can't tonight, don't worry, because he's going to be around. You know Percy's number?

She: Uh-huh. Cliff? How did he look? They?

He: Well, he looks like himself. What do you mean how did he look? And his boy looks just like him.

She: Did he see—was—did—?

He: No, he wasn't around. He left at his usual 8:52. But I'm already wondering what he's going to think when he does see him. Ellen? You want me to tell him to go ahead and start packing?

She: Cliff.

He: Well, you're the doctor. Anyway, Mr. Eubanks is all busy getting everything ready for the honorable Ellis Kelso. I may just have to go take a look at him myself. In fact, Henry said he might go out himself in what he called his role as a connoisseur of rare sons of bitches.

She: Let's don't talk about that. Listen, Cliff, I'm going to hang up and see if I can call. Just in case, will you get him and tell him, tell him Emily and I will be flying in Sunday morning or maybe Saturday night if I can get reservations and get to New York on time.

She had signed off hurriedly only to suffer the multiple deaths of the nightmarish search: no phone, no phone. That and the interminable labor of changing the damn tire on a lonely road where suddenly she knew this would have to be just the moment for her to be accosted and killed.

But it had passed, and, yes, the horrors now had even receded, waned, and, no, she had not yet broken, and, yes, he was there, and this was today even if Saturday was technically here. Probably the sanctimonious householder was right: It, providence, life, whatever —it did not for some obscure reason want them yet to talk. But anxiety was folly. He was there, alive. In the morning on the way to Montaqua she could stop along the road and call, and then: His voice, being, flesh. This child with that on this earth.

Now in the suddenly hospitable bed she lay still and heard the distant bark of a dog, and an answer, and a faintly stirring breeze whose passage by the curtains close by brought the aroma of evergreen, not resinous but dry, bittersweet, dry but pleasant, an aroma that, like the tremulous swelling of the nervous insect chorus outside, was evocative and consoling, speaking in a mysterious language of some home more dear than home, of a vast life within which her own burgeoned, infinitesimal, incomprehensibly vast. In the recession of yesterday the bloodreek was gone. Soon:

in the pines i seem what he says of me: my thoughts resemble him i am his words his mouth evokes me dispels me conjures me consumes me ellen blindly i-less in the pines impaled on henry's tender wit ellen/henry henry/ellen miming oneness beneath the moon in complicity with all creation: discovering as it was a million years ago lust transformed to startling love that drives us on feverish odysseys among the soaring trees jabbering in search of a way to utter it

It woke her up.

At least it was there the instant she awoke, a smell not thick and immediate but thin and sharp and acrid and, though from a distance, unmistakable: fire.

It was only a trace, a hint in the breeze, but along with the other urgency it impelled her to haste and awakened some alarm within her, an apprehension that was amorphous but certain, distinct enough to make her wonder whether the pursuing horrors were about to surge up again.

Then she thought, *No, it's not that.* She dressed swiftly and almost lost her balance after getting a leg partly into the tapered white ducks. Then she did, teetered and flopped back onto the bed, there hoisting her legs high as she jerked the pants on and up. She flung her few things into the limp leather bag and checked the kitchen and then was out to the car, where she muttered *damn* and rushed back to the cottage to retrieve the ancient briefcase of cracked leather that contained the photographs and other materials for the projected book, stuff she had anticipated going over in the stillness and solitude. She had not touched or even reached for it during the two days just gone by.

It was on leaving the drive and entering the road that she looked leftward and saw the sky: great billows of nasty smoke rising and spreading against the dry morning blue. It was there in the direction she would be taking. She was surprised at the traffic on the back road. It was not thick, but the few vehicles, a truck and a couple of jeeps, seemed to be scurrying.

At the store the skinny slumped proprietor looked at her as though she were out of her mind.

"*Phone?*" he said. "Miss, nobody can use this phone but the precinct warden until they've got that fire under control." Then he turned to a bystander and, in a voice not sardonic but insufferably self-important, said, "Now how about this? This young lady wants to make a personal call while half of the wood on Montaqua goes up in smoke."

"Montaqua!" she said.

"Why, sure, mam, where did you think it was?"

"Listen," she said, "my daughter's at the camp up there. Is the fire around there?"

"Well, now, I don't think so, lady. It's all on this side, last we heard. But you never can tell about these things unless you're right there. A little change of wind and—"

"Can't I phone up there and—"

"Lady, the thing is if that fellow over there don't stay on that phone turning out folks to help, well, that camp and all of us will be in worse trouble than we are right now."

So all else was forgotten. With a sharply tooting horn she was pushing the rented sedan around the scurrying local traffic and careening around curves, racing on, annoyingly disconcerted at the sight of an outdoor public phone at one service station. She was through the city and then stopped by the traffic light where its main thoroughfare joined the highway again. She yelled to the driver of a car beside her.

"Do you know whether the fire has gotten to the camp up there?"

"I don't know, lady. We're just heading up there ourselves now. You got a kid at the camp?"

She nodded.

"Well, I speck she'll be all right. Don't get to rushin' and hurt yourself now."

Ellen thought, *don't get to rushin'.* At the light change she bolted across and around the intersection, leaving behind a scream of tires. Now the insane music on the radio stopped and an announcer's voice delivered a report on the fire that told her no more than the man at the store had. She thought, *Nobody knows a damn thing, but everybody's so goddam smug and sure.* For twenty minutes she shot along a two-lane road, leapfrogging around cars that seemed to be full of people heading, insanely enough, on picnics and other outings.

Now down the road was the cutoff that would take her through the woods and thence winding up to the camp on the mountain top. A cluster of men stood about the joining of the road. She could see smoke billowing up from flames out of sight beyond a knob of land but none close to the road, and smoke seemed to be blowing over the closer side of the mountain, but only blowing there. Now a trooper was standing in the middle of the road, flagging, and now he was at her window, voices squawking out of a walkie-talkie he held in a hand at his side.

"All traffic on this road's cut off right now, mam," he said. His voice was full of calm authority.

"It looks okay," she said.

"Well, what you can see looks okay, but it's getting close a little further in. I'm sorry. You got a kid up at the camp, too?"

Ellen nodded.

"Well—" He held up the walkie-talkie. "No danger up there so far. They've got it fairly well contained on this closer slope. I can only tell you what I've told these other parents coming along. Best thing to do is go on back to town and wait it out. It might not be too long before we get an all clear. I suspect it'll be under control before the day's over."

"What's that rumbling?" Ellen said.

"Well, they're dynamiting in some places and running a back-fire in others. Would you like to back around here, now, and let me get to—"

"Well," Ellen said. Then she thought, *Wait it out, hell!* Her foot slammed down and the car rocketed away from an astonished and swiftly receding voice that yelled, "Hey! Hey! Hey, lady! You can't do that!"

With trees flashing by her and the car bucking and knocking up dirt at each turn, Ellen said, "Hey, hey, hey, yourself. Who can't do that?"

One rutted root-strewn bump in the ascending trail made the car rattle like a breadbox hurled down a flight of stairs. She kept checking her rearview to see whether there was any pursuit. Now as she glanced into it again, the mirror absurdly fell from its mooring.

A straggle of men with shovels and other tools were walking along the road ahead. She leaned steadily on her horn. They gaped, looking back, gaped as though she and the car were an apparition. The foremost of them stepped into a track of the road as though to flag her. Yes, he wanted her to stop. She hit the horn again and plunged her foot to the floorboard, throwing the car into a convulsive overdrive spurt. The man with the raised arm leaped wildly backward into the brush.

At a sharply tilted segment of the road she saw thick smoke encroaching directly into her path. Then around another sharp turn she got her first glimpse of flames. She could feel a sudden blast of heat as she hurtled past, bouncing wildly. She heard a monstrous insucking sound over in the woods, heard the sound and then glimpsed some falling timber to one side. A thick tangled mass of flaming branches or vines blew onto the hood of the car and then off.

Then it was all behind her. Suddenly the air was strangely clear. She slowed at an overlook and peered back, and could see the area of the blaze and the wind-carried smoke. Not far ahead was the split cedar gateway that was the entrance of Montaqua Camp.

Even from the entrance she could glimpse the flash of the high lovely lake between the trees and thickets. She stopped and sighed, breathing hard. She almost laughed, and then did. Out on the lake around a large white raft she could see the figures of girls swimming.

"How on earth did you get through?" the camp director, Mrs. McCormick, was saying.

"I just came the usual way," Ellen said. "The trooper suggested I ought to wait, but I decided to come on. I hadn't expected to get here until this afternoon, but—"

"Well, we're in no real danger, as you can see. But we are—prisoners, so to speak. All the girls have been talking about how they'll all swim out to the rafts when the fire gets up here, but—Can you spot Emily out there?"

"Lord, yes," Ellen said.

"Well, Mrs. Eubanks, she's a true fish. She's won almost every water activity medal there is this year. And she's, since last year she's become so—Oh, let me tell you. When we first got word about the fire, and first found out that the phone lines were out, well, as you can imagine, two or three of the girls got a little hysterical. And guess who was talking one of them out of it. Oh, yes, little old Emily. Squatting there by this girl's cot, big as a minute."

They were sitting in canvas chairs outside the camp office.

"The phones are still out?" Ellen said.

"Oh, completely. Ours are burned out. But, of course, even if they were working they'd be preempted for the emergency. It works that way around here. That's what I meant. Like it or not we're true prisoners. I still don't see how you managed to get through. I thought they were turning away all traffic. It'll be tomorrow, I imagine, before any of the other parents can get in. But, of course, we never can tell. We'll be monitoring the radio, of course. It's our only link right now. Listen, would you like me to whistle up Emily for you?"

"Let's just wait'll she comes in."

"All right, but if she's not in soon I'll whistle her anyway. I assume you swim, Mrs. Eubanks. You must, to have a daughter like her. So maybe this afternoon you'd enjoy a dip. Anyway, we're awfully glad you joined us for the crisis. You know, the fire's tragic, of course, but can't you just imagine being eight or nine and having an adventure like this to top off the summer?"

From a distance came the muffled thumping rumble of detonating dynamite. Jays squawked feverishly in the trees about the helter-skelter sprawl of paintless cabins.

"Mama, do you like forest fires?"

Laughing, Ellen's chin abruptly reared up from the stacked hands on which it was resting close and opposite to Emily's face similarly propped on pillowing hands. She had come not trotting but sprinting, a tanned gleaming flash of skinny wet body and sodden flying hair, sprinting and then becoming airborne an incredible distance away to impact against Ellen's breast, to impact like a flung missile and to spraddle about her waist upon landing, clutching her mother's waist with her legs the way she might (as she often had) a barebacked horse. In that moment, in the impact and the strangling clinging strong skinny arms that encircled her like hot wires Ellen was restored: The world might crumble or even burn away but it had given her its best already.

So they had lunched, and with mutual jabber exulted over the medals and trophies, and Ellen had met the new friends, and Emily had said, "How is John-John?" and Ellen had said, "He was all right when I left," and Emily had said, "Is he still busy all the time?" and Ellen had said, "Yes, he's still working very hard."

They had passed news back and forth as, at the center of a gaggle of spirited chattering girls, they had walked down to a knoll from which the fire could best be seen. And then they had sat on a stone retaining wall at a magnificent overlook and talked some more. Ellen said, "And while I was in Los Nubes, Tina Beagle delivered." And Emily said, "Oh, how many?" And Ellen said, "Five." And Emily said, "Boys or girls?" And Ellen said, "Four girls, one boy." And Emily bounced with excitement. "Mama, can we train 'em as a pack?"

Then they had changed and swum out in a wide arc around the lake, easing along side by side with a back stroke for a long time, both of them feeling they were in some miracle pool in the sky. And now they lay belly-down and face-to-face on a float, a raft, and Ellen was laughing at the sudden question.

"No," she said, "I hate forest fires. Why do you think I might like them?"

"I don't know. You just seem something. You seem so happy about something."

"Goose, I'm happy to see you."

"Oh, I know that, but you're happy in some other way, I can tell. I thought you might like forest fires. I bet some people do. Don't you think? Well, if they weren't so bad, if they were only to look at, I'd like them."

"Well, I don't."

"Then what is it?"

"Well. Let me tell you. You were right. It's something I heard, something about a very dear friend of mine."

"Do I know him?"

"How do you know it's a him, smarty?"

"If it was a her, you would say *girlfriend*, wouldn't you? When you say *dear friend* it's always a him. Isn't it?"

"If you say so. Anyway, when I talked to your Uncle Cliff last night he told me that this friend was back in McClung, and it just made me feel good to think that we might see him when we get back."

"Have I ever seen him?"

"No, he's been gone for a long time. He has a little boy who's just a little bit older than you."

"He *has?* Are they going to visit us?"

"They're staying at the Ensleys. But we'll go over there and see them."

"Do they have any other children?"

"Well, it's not they any more. The little boy's mother got killed in a car wreck."

Emily glanced around the lake for a moment. She said, "Is he sad?"

"No, I don't think so any more. His name's Henri, and your Papa Horris and Claudette said he was very happy when they saw him down in Key West last month. You see, I've never met Henri either?"

"Henri. Henri. Does he say it like that?"

"Yes. Henri. His mother was French."

"Is your friend, too?"

"No, he grew up right in McClung."

"You mean you knew him when you were a little girl?"

"Yes, we were very good friends."

Emily giggled. "Were you *sweet*hearts?"

"Oh, *you* might have said so."

"Mama, why did he go away?"

"Oh, come on, you'll have to ask him all these silly questions." Ellen scrambled to her feet. She forgot she had unhooked the top of her suit, and the bra remained below her on the float. Emily suddenly grabbed it up and like a flash sailed into the water.

"You'll never catch me," she yelled, and scooted off at a furious pace with the yellow swimsuit fabric flashing up into the air with every other stroke. Ellen bolted into a sprinting dive and in about three strokes had Emily in her clasp, wildly giggling.

On the radio after supper they learned that the camp would be incommunicado at least until Sunday morning, perhaps into the afternoon, even though it was expected that the fire would soon be contained. For a long while after the meal everyone sat around the dining hall listening to the emergency bulletins. At each mention of the name Montaqua the girls would raise a hysterical cheer, even though it was the name of the mountain and a hamlet below as well as of the camp. Once an announcer disclosed that a providential rain appeared to be moving toward the area. The forecast triggered a deafening peal of boos from the campers.

Ellen bedded down on a cot brought in and squeezed into the row alongside her daughter's. After the lights were out their hands joined in the narrow space between the cots. Soon Ellen felt Emily's hand go limp, fall away, and she saw it withdraw itself up to the lean little chest that was suddenly breathing in utter peace. Ellen felt very tired, and yet serene, too, now. She soon fell asleep.

It looked as though bouncy Mrs. McCormick had been waiting just for some glimpse of them. As soon as they stepped out onto the grounds Mrs. McCormick popped out of the dining hall's screen door and at a fast stride came to intercept them. Now in her khaki shorts and stenciled windbreaker she was at their side, saying good morning as though in haste. Then in an excited rhythm she went on.

"Listen, Mrs. Eubanks, there's been something on the radio news the last couple of hours about your town. Some disturbance or outbreak at a big outdoor meeting. Do you know anything about it?"

"Yes, I think so, but what happened?"

"You can hardly tell from the news except that there was a lot of shooting, and four men got killed, and some others are in the hospital, they didn't seem to be sure how many. But it sounds awful, there must have been a riot or something. It says one boy who was with one of the men was badly injured."

"Do you—did they give any names? Do you know who?"

"Yes—it ought to be coming on again when they give the next news—but the last report mentioned some sheriff who evidently got killed, Ellis or something like that. Is he—would he be the local sheriff? Well, there was that, and they gave the name of some state legislator or something, Grindell, I believe, and then—well, I was listening because—but it just didn't make a clear picture to me—oh, they said some well-known Indian leader from down there some-where, he got killed, but I didn't catch his name, I mean, I heard it, they gave it, but I don't remember, it'll all be on again, so—"

"Mrs. McCormick, did they say who else got killed?"

"Mrs. Eubanks, are these people you know personally? You seem more shaken than I—"

"Did you *hear* any other names?"

"Mama, are you all right?"

"Mrs. McCormick! Did—you—get—any—idea—of—who else —got *killed?*"

"No, no, I don't, I didn't, they haven't broadcast any other name that I heard. Let's find a place and sit down, Mrs. Eubanks, Emily. Mrs. Eubanks, I'm awfully sorry if—if something—if I—Why don't we sit down and try to listen and—All they said about the other person was that he—he was killed instantly, I believe."

"And the boy?"

"Nothing, no, I don't know, they didn't say."

"Mrs. McCormick, I'm sorry I—that I shouted—that I lost my composure."

"Oh, don't you worry about that. I can understand. I can certainly understand if you had some friends there. I should have thought of—"

"Mama, sit down here, let's sit down here."

Help me help me once again help me.

9

Maybe it would circle forever.

Or maybe their flight had already been circling forever, spiraling round and round far above the sprawling luminous miasma below.

Maybe the very logistics of the flight had been calculated with the purpose of drawing her tensions ever tighter.

Already their flight out of New York had carried them once over Riverton and the lesser twinklings of Carterville and McClung just so they could get to New Orleans and climb on another flight and ride for an hour or so all the way back up to Riverton, thence to drive southward once again to McClung.

Now conceivably they could miss the evening's last direct flight to Riverton, could if they didn't stop circling and land the damn thing.

Ellen felt that perhaps the only sustaining strength she now had was flowing into her from that strong small hand that was clasping hers as the plane circled. Together she and Emily shared some sense of being on a tiny island within the jocular mood of the holiday weekend crowd. She felt that she and Emily were a million miles away from all the others, all the jovial sports and good ole boys who kept laughing and making grisly jokes and calling out for additional bonus drinks from the stewardesses. Them. And the captain on the intercom in that dry paternal but remote voice that kept insistently injecting drolleries into the situation.

"The, uh, New Orleans, uh, Chamber of Commerce, uh, reports that our, uh, visibility difficulties are due to, uh, some amount of Los Nubes fog that, uh, should not be mistaken for a, uh, a native product. Ladies and gentlemen, we, uh, should be getting a clearance, uh, very shortly. And, uh, on behalf of the crew, I, uh, want to thank you for, uh, sticking with us, uh, through this, uh, slight delay."

She tried simply to endure it, to hold that small hand and wait for the landing silently, wordlessly, trying to shore herself against the buffetings within of some inextricable mixture of grief and anguish and mystification. Grief for Kimo Bumanta, who had so quickly found the martyrdom he had so clearly begun to cherish when she had last seen him a million years ago, no, a dozen days, eleven, a week and a half. Grief for poor beautiful Kimo, yes, but what for Sonny Grindell except pity and some unanswerable wonder that he had been sitting where he was instead of the one who was supposed to be there. And some stranger than strange anguish for the unnamed man on crutches who had toppled dead before the furious random hail of deputies bullets, caught in the violent storm after Kimo had leaped to the dais with his knife already diving plunging for Ellis Kelso's chest. And what toward Kelso, first thought dead but now still alive and in a way also martyred among his following, stabbed in the presence of perhaps a thousand witnesses and yet also wounded by some bullet that no one could account for, not a pistol but a rifle that no one saw before or during or after.

On the road she had first called not home but Horris, knowing that he would know everything knowable. But his knowledge had only dispelled morbidly imagined certainties to replace them with anxious uncertainties.

He: No, Ellen, neither one of them were even in the vicinity. Nobody knows where Mr. Eubanks is, but there's something I need to tell you about him when you get here, so I'll meet your plane.

She: I left my car at the airport.

He: Well, Claudette and I'll drive up and I'll keep you and Emily company on the way down. Now, for better or worse, we do know where Henry is. And Henri. They're under arrest. But don't panic. I'll give you the details when you get here. Briefly, though, they got picked up by immigration authorities and hauled down to St. Teresa's, and they're under detention there pending some sort of hearing.

She: But *why?*

He: Well, it's just one of those things. After that boat of his entered the river but never reappeared down at the harbor checkpoint they put out a patrol to check it out and spotted it tied up at Percy's, and so—

She: But what the hell have they done?

He: All that's alleged is illegal entry.

She: Illegal entry! Hell, isn't he an American! Traveling with his own son!

He: Well, maybe I neglected to tell you. Before he went to

China, way back then, he became a Swiss citizen, along with Henri. I'm not even sure just how legal a Swiss citizen either one of them is, but, anyway, they've been traveling on the Swiss passport ever since. Ellen?

She: I'm here. Is there any reason to think anything's happened to Mr. Eubanks?

He: I don't know. All we do know is that he's gone—somewhere —in his car. I'll talk to you more about it.

She: Horris? Is Henry in serious trouble?

He: Well, I'd be lying if I said no. The outcome depends on a lot of things. But we've got the right people working on it.

So she and Emily had gotten seats on a direct flight to New Orleans, and now, still in a skirting of scattering mist, the city was coming up beneath them. They had to run to make the flight to Riverton. Once they were airborne again somehow her freight of moiling emotions lightened. Suddenly they were peering down again at the now fewer twinklings of McClung, then Carterville. Then there was the larger brighter city sprawl of Riverton.

Horris drove, and Ellen sank back in the enfolding contoured leather seat of her dark green roadster, holding sleepy Emily in her lap. Claudette followed behind them. Late Sunday traffic on the Trail held them under the speed limit. They rode mostly in silence.

At last they rolled past the soaring oleanders, the tires crunching on the pea-gravel of the drive.

"Listen," Ellen said, "you and Claudette have just got to sit with me awhile. I've just got to talk or I'll explode."

"One condition," Horris said.

"Name it," she said.

"You'll fix me a toddy and have one with me."

"I think it's the first time in my life I've ever said it, but I need one. I'll fix 'em as soon as I get Emily in bed."

"I'll fix 'em while you're doing that."

"I hope Papa's got some whisky in the house."

"Don't worry. I didn't take a chance. Claudette's sitting on a brand new bottle of the best."

They sat on the front porch in a row of three of the old high-backed web-seated rockers. They were pulled close together and close to the front banister so that they could prop their feet up. Horris's legs rose up like two stubby cannon from the middle chair. Their legs, their feet, and the lines of vision that passed along them aimed out into the constellations then wheeling in the eastern heavens.

All of them sipped from the strong sugared toddies, and all of them unconsciously fiddled and adjusted themselves against the warmth that was still of summer, McClung-style, even though it had eased up with the coming of deep night. Claudette sat with the hem of her loose shift lying across the very seam of thigh and torso. Ellen, in ducks that lost all definition in the dimness, sat with her shirt out, its front unbuttoned to her waist. Horris from time to time would raise his free hand to his habitual tugging of the neck of his collarless shirt, or he would pass it in slow ruminative motions across the perspiring surface of his hairless globelike head.

Across the vast tree-looming darkness of the grounds, an unending shrill trilling of insects arose like swells of some desperate surf. Horris's voice rumbled gently out. Even when it seemed to know everything it was constrained by some constant wonder at what it did not and could not know.

Horris said:

"I saw him twice that afternoon, Friday. The first time he exploded out of that doorway in a livid rage, the origin of which I could then only guess at. But the second time—that was the time I felt that I saw that man almost literally die and descend into hell. And then come back, at least to earth, but I wouldn't swear that he actually came back to life, if only because of what I don't know right now. Of course, this second time the cause was very clear. And I guess watching it happen gave me some feeling of complicity, even though in reality I was innocent enough, as we all are. Both times, of course, I was sitting there at my front desk.

"I spent the whole afternoon sitting there talking on the phone, as usual, and staring out of the window, as usual. As a matter of fact talking with first one and then another about that damned rally, trying to stay on top of that situation. Well, earlier in the afternoon I saw Cecil Drum lumber up into that stairway, and saw him come out I guess about fifteen or twenty minutes later. Well, that interested me, because I assumed that since he's their sergeant-at-arms, so-called, he wouldn't have been visiting except for some talk about the rally. So just a minute or so after Drum comes out so does our Mr. Eubanks.

"Only he comes bolting out of that stairway onto the sidewalk looking furious. Came out like he had been flung by a catapult. Necktie flying. In his shirtsleeves, which was itself odd. At least I've never seen him come out even for a drugstore lunch without putting his jacket on. Well, as he came out of the stair he hit Baptiste, his foot did, and he just almost went sprawling. Baptiste had just trotted down from in front of the Texas Cafe, where, of course, he sleeps and scratches and waits while Sid Fletcher is inside medicating himself, which ordinarily is from about ten or eleven in the morning on. Anyway, Baptiste had decided to trot down the sidewalk, and now Mr. Eubanks almost trips over him. But he recovers very fast—Mr. Eubanks—and all of a sudden plants a kick right in the underside of that dog. After the first brush, Baptiste had cringed and froze, but now he sails a few feet through the air and then turns into a black and tan blur, his yipes shooting up in the air like splinters of glass. He streaks back toward the cafe and past it, still yiping. Well, his racket all of a sudden draws Sid Fletcher out onto the sidewalk. Mr. Eubanks has just sort of frozen as though either in a raging daze or maybe astounded at himself. But now everybody's favorite erstwhile preacher Sid Fletcher comes out onto the sidewalk with the sun glancing off of that wild yellow-gray hair and that wild-looking Hawaiian sports shirt he wears a lot. And he stands there with his face squinched looking in the direction that Baptiste has taken to flight. Then with a good deal of puzzlement showing, Sid looks to his left and all of a sudden sees Mr. Eubanks standing there with this furious glare on his face, although I'm not certain Mr. Eubanks was actually seeing anything just then.

"Well, by this time, Peggy has waddled out from behind the counter of the cafe and is standing with her hands on her hips behind Sid Fletcher. And just then one of the loiterers there tells Sid what just happened to his dog. So I see Sid's mouth say, "That son of a bitch." And then he rushes over to the curb and hoists up that little chest-high Reserved-for-Trailways sign—picks it up like a feather and holds the damn thing with the heavy round base to his shoulder with the sign pointing down like a canoe paddle. Then he starts to rush Mr. Eubanks. Only he doesn't actually get going, because Peggy grabs his arm. Well, Sid struggled a little, but then he yielded to Peggy's superior strength—I would guess his cadaver weighs about a hundred and thirty-seven now against her hundred and seventy—but then for a long moment he and Mr. Eubanks glare at one another like a couple of bad cases from the cowboy movies.

"Sid's still holding the damn sign, and his face is all dark and colored over. As you know it's almost purple ordinarily, but now it was purple and blood red. And then I can see his mouth say what I was later told he did say. He says, "God damn the man that would kick a little dog." Then tears began to run down across the ruts and ridges of his face and through his stubble to splash down onto that gaudy shirt. Then all of a sudden he sets the sign back down. And even though he had picked it up as though it were light as a feather, the thing almost capsized him as he tried to ease it back to the curb. Well, then, with Peggy's hand still on his arm he goes back into the cafe, stopping at the door to take one last look east where Baptiste is, of course, by now long gone, no doubt somewhere out there where the street turns into the highway.

"Well. I saw all of this, and so did maybe a score of loafers and shoppers who happened to be around during that part of the afternoon. But I wouldn't testify that Mr. Eubanks saw it. While Sid was still standing there, just after he had uttered that imprecation—and I couldn't call it anything else, coming as it did from a man raised in the ministry even though he has long been out of it—anyway, right after that Mr. Eubanks suddenly looked all about him at the frozen stares, scowling and even showing some surprise, as though he had just discovered he was out there in broad daylight being observed, and then he spat and very abruptly whirled and went back to those stairs as though he had been pulled by some immense suction.

"And so ended the first chapter. Mainly significant—to me— because it shows how deeply something had shaken up Mr. Eubanks even before chapter two. It was only later, of course, that I found out why Cecil Drum's visit so disturbed him. The word that Drum brought cut Mr. Eubanks pretty effectively out of the leadership of his council, you see, and of the brigade, and even of the rally that he had at first taken the initiative to organize. Drum brought the word from Sonny Grindell, who got it from Ellis Kelso, that the rally was to be in effect merely a launching pad for Kelso's campaign for the governorship next year. Assuming his survival, I suspect Kelso was launched better than he could ever have hoped to be. Of course, it was some heat cooked up by Kelso and Grindell that had caused Mr. Eubanks to reschedule the protest thing for last Saturday over all the local objections that had caused him to postpone it. But he was very slow realizing that those characters were playing a new game. They were turning the whole thing into a campaign machine, and it just didn't include him as one of the big wheels. All of a sudden he had become competition, and all of a sudden he was out. Of course, he was still welcome at the protest he had organized, he was still expected to sit on the dais, but now it would be Grindell who would give the big warmup speech, and this would be the introduction of Ellis Kelso as the next governor, et cetera, et cetera.

"As we can imagine, it must have been quite a shock. Or we don't have to imagine. I could see the effect. What I couldn't have imagined was something even more devastating happening within the next few minutes—when Mr. Eubanks came out again, popped back out of his stairway.

"Meanwhile, you see, Henry and Henri had come walking toward his office on that side of the street. I wasn't surprised to see them come into view, because Henry had called and said they were going to stroll around and drop by to see me. Henry had got on some fresh khakis and what might well have been that same blue workshirt he had on down in Key West. And Henri's got on some blue jeans cut off short and raveling around the legs, and a common pullover polo type shirt. And they are just ambling along the sidewalk, right? Gossiping as they go, Henry gesturing, pointing out things here and there, no doubt giving Henri a guided tour to some childhood recollections of his own. And then they come to that doorway.

"And they happen to be right in front of it, just like Baptiste had been a few minutes before, when Mr. Eubanks comes barging out. This time he still looks furious but somehow not as abandoned. In the meantime he's put on his jacket and his tie is pulled up, and when he appears I get the impression from across the street—and, after the first episode, I had left my desk and was standing outside on the sidewalk, still puzzling—so from there I got the impression he was coming out this time to head for his car at the curb. Pure guess.

"But as he exits, there they are, Henry and Henri, and I was forced to recollect at once—or at least when I saw what happened I recollected—that Mr. Eubanks is suddenly looking at two people he has never seen before either in the flesh or in pictures. I, of course, recalled that all signs of him in this house had been filed away for good reason, et cetera. So—

"There they were. Mr. Eubanks at the threshold of his stairway, and Henry and Henri blocking his path. Well, those two stepped back to make way. But Mr. Eubanks, who at first had glared at them, is suddenly not glaring but staring. Henri looks a trifle nervous and glances up at his Papa. And Henry at that instant glances at the shingles by the door and among them sees the name of the man he now presumes is staring at him. I could see Henry say what he later told me he said. 'You must be Ellen's husband,' he said, 'I'm Henry Rust, I'm an old friend.' And he started to extend his hand but quickly let it fall back to his side as it became evident there would be no reciprocal response.

"Again, it was as though Mr. Eubanks didn't actually hear him. He suddenly was rooted like a fixture in the doorway, an automaton with eyes that first stared hypnotically at Henry and then at Henri. Then his eyes finally fixed themselves on Henry's. Transfixed. I use the word thoughtfully. He was transfixed. Then his own eyes closed. Then his color drained away. His face, which had been flushed and red, grew as pale as ivory, and so help me it finally took on the waxy pallor of a corpse. Then, after some space of time that must have been brief but that seemed eternal, his color returned in just a flaming bloody surge. His color came back and his eyes popped open and he stared for another second or two at Henry and once again at Henri, and then he sort of ripped his gaze away from both of them and glanced frantically toward his car. But then he turned about and very very slowly began climbing back up the stairs.

"Henry and Henri walked on, of course, gravitating over to my side of the street and shaking their heads and exchanging comments as they came. It was while I was standing waiting that I got the very clear feeling, a whim no doubt, that I had seen that man literally descend into hell. Well, Henry and Henri and I had a good talk, and I didn't see Mr. Eubanks again until a bit later. Henri had gone into the back shop to watch the linotype man, and Henry and I were sitting there at the front desk when, not long after he had climbed back up to his office, I saw his secretary, Edna Sands, come out carrying her bag and some parcel as though leaving for the day. By then, I remember, the rain had started, not hard yet, but by the time it was really pouring, well, there he came looking very gray and drawn about the face. He stood by the door of his car for a little bit before he got in, just stood there as though he couldn't care less that the rain was soaking his seersucker, or maybe as though he were unaware that it was. And then, in a sudden decisive sort of movement, he snatched open the door of the car and ducked in.

"Then he backed out very fast. I'd say heedless except that I don't know, and there wasn't much traffic anyway. But instead of driving away as usual, instead of heading westward, he whipped about in a sudden U-turn right there and headed east, his head bent over the wheel like someone who intends to go fast wherever he's going. I'd say he also had the look of a man who had already decided on some place to go, but this, of course, is pure guess.

"So, since that moment, I haven't run into anybody who saw him subsequently. There was a good deal of calling around by the other people involved in the rally. Edna Sands was saying that she had no idea where he was, that he had just all of a sudden told her to take the rest of the day off because he had some personal business he wanted to take care of. So far as we know—so far as *I* know—he didn't talk to anybody else in town after that conversation with her. Edna said he sounded tense, as though he were trying to control some irritation, but that she didn't make too much of it because it wasn't so out of the ordinary. She said she didn't have any idea what was on his mind unless it had something to do with the rally and all that.

"Well, it's likely that any one of the three of us can make a much closer guess about what was on his mind than Edna Sands or anybody else. I personally am forced to suspect that he must have been in a devastating state of shock, that some critical fabric in him had just unraveled. I would suspect that in the moment he saw Henry and Henri—and, therefore, it goes without saying, Emily—in that moment there might have been simply the evaporation of that one essential delusion that he had been hoarding by willful blindness. At the sight of them, it simply could not have survived any longer, if my guess as to its existence is right. Maybe he saw that even if he had been able to preserve it longer it would now be useless, because it could never again be taken as anything but counterfeit in a town in which Henry Rust and Henri had been recently seen. After all, after what Mr. Eubanks had just seen, had just been finally obliged to see, how could he imagine that anyone with eyes could fail to see the same?

"Well, certainly I'm only guessing. None of us know. Just as none of us know where he went or what he's doing or what he had in mind to do. I guess we'll know in due time. I guess we know he couldn't be any worse off wherever he is than he would have been had he remained for that protest. He would have been sitting right where Sonny Grindell was when he got that deputy's bullet. Incidentally, they're still utterly mystified by that bullet they found in Ellis Kelso. The doctors say that it's the thing that almost put him under and not the knife wound he got from Kimo. But they still can't imagine where it came from except that it had to come a hell of a long distance since nobody in the immediate vicinity even remembers seeing a rifle. Our sheriff says it conceivably could have been fired from somebody in the trees on that little hill just below and to the side of Mount Oro. But he says it would have taken a hell of a marksman. So far, I haven't heard even a guess as to who that marksman might be. In any event, it looks as though two people were stalking Kelso simultaneously. Two near misses. I suppose it could have been somebody that Kimo brought with him, but who knows. All they've got to go on is one .22 extra long rifle hollow point that they dug out of Kelso's chest. Well, I didn't mean to ramble on into other things."

Horris got up, stretching and tugging at his shirt, and without a word collected their glasses and vanished into the house, and returned bearing three more toddies.

For a long while they sat without talking, washed in the insect cry and watching the eastern constellations. From far behind the house, from across the river, out of the swamp and marsh, they could hear from time to time the wail of hoot owls. *Who-who-ah, who-who-ah, who-who-eeee.*

1955

End of Summer

---IO---

LABOR DAY:

In the morning, conscious of a certain morbidity in the act, Ellen drove out to the cemetery and looked at her mother's grave and others in the Worth plot, and paused at the other plot and stood for a thoughtful moment by the grave of Portia Rust (1884–1952), wondered where poor Polly Rust might be, and then wheeled through the desertion that was downtown McClung before going on back to the house.

By then Emily was up, and she and Ellen after breakfast walked down the river path to the Ensley tie-up to look at the boat. A legal notice on its windshield and instrument panel warned against trespassing and declared the craft to be temporarily in the custody of the U.S. government, the immigration service. Emily was hungry to steal aboard, but Ellen forbade it, not so much out of regard for the official prohibition as out of some superstition that counseled against taking any hazardous step at the moment. She had that feeling of walking on a very thin crust.

They strolled up to the Ensley house and found Percy and Florence still in the kitchen drinking coffee. Once in, Emily quickly vanished in the direction of a racket arising from the Ensley children elsewhere in the house. Ellen swung herself astride a wooden chair.

"He won't even let me put sugar in my coffee," Florence was saying. She was a good-natured woman of curvy prettiness who during the last couple of years had taken up a ceaseless battle against encroaching chubbiness, urged on in the effort by a husband who was himself so lean as to seem fashioned entirely of bone or springy wire.

"Any word on—" Percy began but ceased, frowning sympathetically as Ellen anticipated him.

"No. Nothing," she said.

"You worried about this other thing?" Percy jerked his head in a vague southerly direction where lay St. Teresa's and the immigration offices where Henry and Henri were being detained pending a hearing set for Wednesday morning.

Ellen wanly smiled. She had thought of it too much to talk of it. She said, "Right now my mind's on getting down to Temulca. I ought to—I want to see Bema and the others before—Well, I was thinking of driving down in a little while and back this afternoon. Only I've got such a damn conflict. Somehow I—You know, even with things as they are, if anything has happened, I—"

"How about this—Let me fly you down and back," Percy said. "No Labor Day traffic, no pain, no strain. Half an hour each way instead of three."

"Well, thank you, Percy, but that would shoot your holiday, and—"

"Shoot his holiday?" Florence said. "Hon, I can't get the scoundrel to go out of the yard on one of these great holiday weekends. Or if he does it's only to go down to the damn lumber mill and smell sawdust. Honey, tell us the truth, isn't that what your job actually is? Smelling sawdust?"

"No, I am only queer for sawdust. I am queer for sawdust and thin women."

"Oh," Florence said, "so it's assassination time. Now will you tell me why, after that—why I should let you fly off by yourself with Ellen?"

"Discussion closed. Ellen, let's do it." Ellen nodded, yes, and Percy went on: "Flo, if you want to go along and chaperone—"

"Hon, frankly I can bear the thought of your infidelity better than I can the thought of your flying. The former will only give me relief, the latter could kill me."

"By God, it is assassination time, isn't it?"

"Hon," Florence said, now to Ellen, "why don't you leave Emily here. Percy just got these kids a pinball machine, and they think it's the greatest invention since television. For at least a week it'll probably be a good babysitter. Percy has a theory that if we provide sufficient evil in the house they won't get in trouble on the outside."

"But you don't concur entirely?" Ellen said.

"I go along with everything except his plan to rent a prostitute when the boys get older."

"Now, Flo, that was supposed to be a family secret," Percy said. He was up and heading out of the room but lingered in the doorway for a rejoinder.

"I asked him," Florence said, "how we could raise 'em as good Catholics with a rented whore on the premises. He said, 'Well, we'll give her Fridays off.'"

Ellen laughed from her stomach for the first time since early Sunday.

Temulca was quiet, her visit almost wordless. Bema began rising at her approach to the center shelter, but now the matriarch's movement was slow and probably painful though she would never have said so. Her face looked ancient, a maze of wrinkles and creases, ancient and yet oddly timeless.

Ellen embraced her, gently clasping a body reduced now to its skeletal essence. They held each other in embrace for a long time, pressing their faces close. Others of the village were passing about as though nothing had happened, though some of the men, primarily the older ones, wore the pale blue *omanta* shirt that was the sign of a member passing on.

The name of Kimo was never mentioned, as was the custom. Already his body had been reduced to dust, cremated, and the remains cast without a word into the river. Until a full cycle of the moon had gone by his name would not be spoken.

Ellen had often wondered about this custom of silence. Now as she moved about the village, embracing many of those she had come to know, she marveled at the powerful effect of the custom. Every urge within her was to speak of Kimo, to utter some of the powerful things she felt about this being whose life had become so deeply mingled with hers, this man whom she clearly had loved and yet of whom she had never spoken or even thought in the conventional language and metaphors of love and passion. Now in the constraint of silence she found a strangely moving thing happening within her, this which was the intent of the custom whose origins Bema had long ago recounted for her.

In the very struggle of countering the impulse to utter the name of Kimo, Ellen came to see more clearly than ever she might have that he was not in truth gone, that he was alive yet within her, that it was he therein struggling to speak now. So it would be the same with the others. Again and again the name of the cherished man would rise to her lips, and she would remember, and fall silent, and in the silence his voice would speak, and his very body and substance, his warmth and his breath, all of him would pulse within her. She saw him get up from their pallet and go out into the rain in the dark night on Marilou. She felt the rain on his skin and then on hers. As she came in he wrapped a blanket about her and lifted her from the floor.

Ellen stayed only a short while.

"Henry is back," Ellen told Bema. "He and his son Henri. But I haven't been able to see him yet. They are being detained. He's in trouble with the immigration authorities."

Bema's old head nodded as she listened.

"You be patient," she said. "Life will go your way. There is only one way to defeat the enemies of life. That is to outlive them. It is not a lesson that is always learned in time. But Ellen knows, Ellen knows."

They fell silent. As Ellen was about to go, Bema spoke again.

"Our child Ellen will come back before it is Bema's time?"

Ellen laughed, but inside she shivered. "Hush, hush," she said. "Bema's time will not come until long after Ellen's."

Bema embraced her.

"Beloved *bumanta*," the old matriarch said.

Through Monday night there was no word, no news of anything. And within her came a gathering sense of foreboding, a disconcerting conflict. It arose from an overpowering yearning against what she now expected without knowledge or articulation.

Tuesday morning when his letter came she felt a wracking chill even before she clearly recognized that it was from him. So strange. Its envelope bore only her maiden name—Ellen Worth—and the address. She did not distinctly recognize his handwriting at first, not incontrovertibly. In fact she was certain of it only after she saw the postmark: Natchez.

His letter came in an accumulation of mail from the weekend and the holiday, a delivery that brought two other letters that struck her at first sight, each arousing some new strong feelings in a different grotto of her being.

Ellen clasped them all in her hand and walked back to the house and to her bedroom before reading any. Along the way, walking down the pea-gravel drive beneath the tall oleanders, she shivered. She waved to Emily who was with one of the Ensley children at a swing suspended on a distant tree. In a few hectic minutes at eight they had accomplished Emily's school registration. At the school the atmosphere had been suspenseful as the board's plan began going into effect. Evidently the bloody events of Saturday night had chastened everyone.

Before she opened any of them, Ellen stared at the three envelopes again and again. Only the one from Paul Gans bore the name of the sender, although the second had the small printed initial K in the upper left hand corner. So she knew, she knew, the origin of them all. Finally she set aside the one from Mississippi to read last. First she opened the letter from her editor.

It was brief, written on a typewriter, dated the day she had driven away from New York at dawn after talking with Paul the whole night up in her room where they had gone after the—Ellen wrenched her mind away from any recollection of the Italian restaurant. She read:

Dear, dear Ellen:

After you pulled away this morning I felt such an enormous tug that I feel some need to tell you of it.

After the few hours—what? 12? yes—that we were together I came away with the feeling that something in my life had changed.

And I feel sure that it was—is—something that I took from you—no, that you gave me whether you knew it was happening or not. Earlier in the evening I said that I felt I had come to know you for the first time. By the time you went away I felt this still, but something more, something mysterious, a sort of thing that certainly yesterday I would have scoffed at.

It is not easily defined, perhaps not definable. But what I felt as you drove off was a sense that you had somehow imparted to me a terribly important secret. Something you have. Something that seemed so close at hand that if I just tried hard enough I would possess it, too. Perhaps

I had it for a bit, walking back to the early morning emptiness of this office, because on the way—and now, too—I felt, so help me, as though I were actually glad to be alive for the first time literally since my childhood. Strange? The God's truth is that through most if not all of my adult years I have looked on life as a burden. But suddenly I saw it differently.

Suddenly all the great stone and steel canyons of Manhattan where I have burned up my life chasing after—what?—all of it seemed as nothing. The chase of the traffic seemed suddenly utterly futile, insane. Perhaps this feeling came somehow out of the nearness of what we witnessed together. But I don't think so, because I have closely witnessed death in this city many times and in glutting numbers in World War I (show me a man who was in that who does not feel as old as I do). New York, after all, is a place where on any morning you can see crowds flowing by some gray corpse on the floor of Grand Central, where any afternoon might turn out to be the one on which a screaming body plummets out of some window to the sidewalk where you are walking. So it could not, for me, have been only the vision of grisly death that had this effect.

It somehow came from you. I know this in my heart. And I am only writing to say thank you. I cherish your friendship, and I hope that life turns your way. Strangely, too, I more than hope this: As I was walking back here, for the first time since my childhood, I prayed even though I don't even know to what I was praying, since I think I am hopelessly over the hill on that score. And yet, that's unmistakably what I was doing, praying, and I prayed for you and for the dream that you shared with me to come true.

Warmly,
Paul

Ellen opened the letter marked K. It was very short, a printed note that had been mailed in Taliaferro, no doubt as Kimo had been en route from his seclusion on Marilou to his destiny in McClung. She read:

Our Ellen,

No matter what is said, no matter how it turns out, only you of all of us will fully understand. Perhaps you will wonder why now, why here. I answer, if not, then where, when. The answer came with the news that this man was to take his evil to our Mount Oro. The vision of it was unbearable to me. Could there be a better place to take a stand against darkness than at our place of illumination? I do not know what will happen, but I feel determined and feel I am doing what is right for me. Whatever happens, Kimo is with you. We are together always cherished Bumanta. K.

And then she read the letter written in script that was very large and very neat. She read:

Dear Ellen Worth,

By now you know, and this is just to try to say why. Today I saw something about myself that I had never seen, never allowed myself to see. Perhaps you will even hear of the encounter that caused me to see it. But that doesn't matter, not really. What matters to me is the burden inside me that I have been carrying so long without even knowing it. Now I simply need to lay it down. Just deciding this may be the only good thing I have ever done. The rest has been a mess. So now I am going where I belong. What I am doing, in point of fact, is only completing what somehow happened a long time ago. The truth is I have never been really alive, never really been able to be alive, as you and most other people are.

There are one or two other things I would like for you to know. At times in the last few years I have often felt angry toward you and, in my mind, blamed you for everything. But I know, and now I know for sure, that you have not been to blame for anything. From the beginning, I realize, you have been ready, willing, and able to give me everything a wife should give, and could. I am the one who could never ask. In the beginning I saw this and then I forgot somehow but now I see it very clearly. Something in me is just hopelessly dead or locked up, and it is no use.

All that I can say in my defense is that I see these things now but didn't before. One other thing, I have no bitterness. Emily is such a beautiful girl, and you, that just being around you two was the best thing that ever happened to me. I only wish that I had been different. If only I had been able to love you as you deserved, both of you. Please do me a big favor, please tell Emily that John-John did love her and showed it the best he could.

Sincerely yours,
John Eubanks

P.S. Mother will take care of the arrangements.

When Mrs. Pichon called her to the phone, Ellen had just lain back on her bed, the letter still clutched in her hand. She was clutching it still as Horris's very gentle rumble came to her.

"Ellen, I just wanted to make sure you were there. I've heard something and I'll be right over. Okay?"

"I just got a letter," Ellen said.

"Well, look, I'll be right there, okay?"

Claudette got there even before Horris, and just behind Horris Florence Ensley pulled down the drive. And a few minutes later Mary Kent piled out of her car and was walking across the grounds with three-year-old Mary Ellen spraddled on her hip. So the plummeting began to stop even though the puzzled and ambiguous and murky sadnesses were spinning on within her.

Somehow they all gravitated to the big sitting porch in back, and there Cliff just sort of materialized beside her on the creaky metal glider, and Aunt Margaret on the other side sat stitching furiously on a circled patch of the light silk, stitching even while looking up to suggest to Mrs. Pichon that perhaps she might put on some coffee or something.

Emily sat very still in her lap where she had stayed since she had noticed the strangely convening visitors and come running across the yard from the swing yelling, "Hey! What's going on? Is it a party?" And Ellen had grabbed her up and sat down with her and said, "Emily, we got some very bad news. John-John is dead." And Emily, amazed, said, "*Really?*"

And then somehow they were all back on the sitting porch. Even before she saw him she had felt her Papa's long strong fingers running possessively through her hair, running up from the back and gripping her whole skull. And then his arm encircled her shoulders, briefly, tersely, and he had whispered into her ear only a single disguised command, "Dumpling, why don't you sit down?"

So now she knew what she had somehow known without knowing. His mother on returning from a weekend trip had opened her closed garage to put away her car and had seen his. He was in the front seat, the pistol in his lap, a note to her beside him. The image spun in her mind along with the images of Mr. Sorrel and Mr. Fielding.

At some point Ellen realized she still had his letter in her hand. She handed it to Horris and said, "How about taking care of this for me?" He did not glance at it but folded it with a certain awe or respect and reinserted it in its envelope. And then instead of sticking the letter in his pocket, as he might have, he handed it to Claudette with a nod that suggested she tuck it in her shoulder bag, which she did.

Later, with Emily spraddling her hip, she withdrew and said they were going to lie down for a little while. In her bedroom they lay very close and very still without saying anything for a long time. At last Ellen said, "Emily?" And Emily looked up, and Ellen said, "Emily, John-John loved you." Emily put her head back down on

Ellen's chest and said, "He loved us the best he could, and we loved him, too, the best we could."

Again Percy Ensley had eased her ordeal by flying her to Natchez, and he and Horris stood with her through the rites. No gesture had been made by the mother, no suggestion that she come to the house, no conciliatory word through the intermediary who had been the only person Ellen could reach.

So they went directly to the cemetery, and there Ellen saw again the woman she had seen only once before—that Saturday afternoon in New Orleans, with her son at the exhibit around the square, the art workshop exhibit, where Ellen had glanced over to discover him looking at her in such an embarrassed or shy way. Now the mother of John Eubanks acknowledged her existence with only a minimal nod and glacial silence.

It filled Ellen with pity until suddenly she glanced at the stones marking the graves alongside the one that would receive John Eubanks. One of them said, *Frederick L. Eubanks, Jr., 1919–1938.* On the other she read, *Frederick L. Eubanks, 1891–1953.*

Ellen thought, *His father!* He had not been told of his own father's death. Or had he been told and so contained it that she had got no hint? No, impossible. Now Ellen stared at the mother of John Eubanks and felt a bitter detestation, and then, more sharply, a bitter melancholy at the enormity of the gulf that had separated Mr. Eubanks from all of those who might have brought something green to the desert of his life.

It was a short graveside service that had somehow the quality not of a ceremonial with motion and an interplay of meanings but of a tableau. It was strangely static and almost wordlessly mechanical, wordless except for the habituated recitations of the preacher. Somehow, as they stood there, they all seemed to have sprung out of the unreal green of the synthetic carpet of plastic grass that had been laid alongside the grave and about the small tented shelter in which some of them stood and sat.

Attendance was sparse, or so it seemed. There was the mother, and several others of her age, none of them recognizable to Ellen. And there were a few of Eubanks's former teammates from his football years. These all stood together, somehow of an ilk, and one of them seemed familiar to Ellen at a glance but in a way she did not instantly recall. His eyes, instead of acknowledging hers, suddenly turned down, and then his head came up, the head with wavy blond hair that was receding, and he whispered something to the woman beside him, presumably his wife, she a woman who had once been pretty, probably, but who was letting her pudginess run steadily to obesity: probably a college cheerleader now barely recognizable within her layers of folded flesh. Then she remembered: *Billy Brism.* The moment of his boisterously drunk entrance into the dining room at Doubloon's Inn came back to her, and Mimi with her purplish hair and bright angry face, Mimi vehemently denouncing the son of a bitch for ditching her. Ellen wondered if Brism was like Mr. Eubanks, so frequently remembering little or nothing of what was said or done while he was drinking. On their first anniversary he had begun crying and said that he knew he had been a failure as a husband except on their honeymoon and declared his determination to make it different; next day he had not remembered that they had decided to drive up to Carterville for the anniversary dinner at which he had said it.

The casket was suspended on straps. Now, to the accompaniment of a small electrical whirring, it began to sink from view. Ellen flinched—at herself—as her mind suddenly entertained an aphorism for the tombstone: *This child delivered from cradle to the grave untouched by human hands.* She thought it and then flinched and then was filled with bitterness at the truth of it.

But then suddenly the bitterness was transformed into guilt and self-reproach. Suddenly in the vast skein of her life's connections and peregrinations she could see only that her fateful linkage to the life of John Eubanks had led him inevitably to this death. Now the scathing scorn and detestation she had felt toward his mother fell upon herself, but more: Suddenly she wondered if she had secretly hoped for this death, for this liberation, for this in the interest of her own convenience so that—

She could not bear to articulate what she now distinctly felt. A wave of horror at these phantasmal implications swept through her, and she was not quite aware of the astounded expressions that leaped to the faces of all the others as she burst into tears and sobs and convulsive shaking. She was only barely aware of the hands of Horris and Percy encircling her arms on either side.

Now after an interim of seemingly no time they were in the air again, and Horris kept shouting at her, she sitting beside Percy in the little four-seater plane and Horris sitting behind but leaning forward and shouting, as though she had committed some crime in just telling them finally what she had felt. At first she could not quite hear him even with his voice raised at her for the first time she could ever remember, and then, still trembling, she began to hear, and now he was going on as though he would never stop.

"Goddamit, Ellen, you're playing God is what you're doing, and I'll be goddamed if I'm going to sit here and let you do it to yourself. I wouldn't even pay two cents for this shit about your being responsible for his death, not any of it, none of it. You neither began his life, goddamit, nor ended it, and when you even begin to imagine that you did you deprive the poor wretch of the only shred of dignity and humanity he had left, which was precisely and just exactly enough to allow him to see that he had failed of both dignity and humanity all the way along, and the only real pity is that he couldn't also see that it was no fault of his own, and that having seen what he had seen he probably could have come out of it all and started over again. But you didn't do it, you didn't cause it, you didn't precipitate it, you are not responsible for it even in the tiniest way. And, as a matter of goddam fact, when the last of the story is written, you in all likelihood by your very existence and qualities probably put off the time of his death, which is maybe even what he meant in that letter. He himself says you and Emily were the best things ever to happen to him, merely being in proximity was the best thing in his life. So I'm just not going to have you get it fixed in your mind that this was your doing in any way. Good God, look at it in any one of a million ways and what do you see? What the hell if he hadn't done this, where the hell would he have been sitting if he had gone to the protest like he was supposed to, wouldn't he have gotten exactly what Grindell got? So what's your next step in this line of thinking? Do you go on to see that you're also responsible for Grindell's death? Goddamit, Ellen, now stop it, and listen to me—"

"Horris, don't shout at me any more. Please. I can't stand any more. I'm listening. You don't have to shout."

"Well, I'm sorry I shouted, but goddamit, Ellen, I love you and I want you to root out that kind of pernicious thinking right now, that's why I shouted. I mean right now, before you repeat it to yourself two or three times and then begin to believe it's really true. Now that's why I was shouting. Maybe still am. But you just listen for a minute, and listen carefully. You and I don't even know what finally tipped the scales and caused this man to go as he did. But we do know it wasn't you. Hell, he may have been on the way already that day after Cecil Drum came to see him in his office, because that's when they jerked his whole public identity effectively out from under him. So maybe he had had it even before he came back down and saw Henry and Henri. But what if he hadn't? Whenever he snapped, when did it actually begin? Hell, Ellen, it began long before you ever saw this poor man. It was happening right there on the street of New Orleans when you first saw him. And, for God's sake, Ellen, what the hell could you have in mind by seeing some connection between your wish for Henry and this event?

"Now, that's what I really mean by playing God. Do you think you *willed* Henry to come back at just this moment? If you could have, don't you think you'd have done it a lot sooner? Why, you couldn't will him back any more than you could have willed him away. Don't you see? I know you see. But, yes, by God, even if you do see I want to rub it in so damn hard you *never* forget it. I'm just not going to have you going around with some stupid pointless goddam albatross hanging around your neck. Why, as for you merely wishing for Henry to come back at the moment of this thing, well, there's no more connection there than between your wish that the sun will shine tomorrow and the fact that it will. The goddam sun's a gift beyond your power and so is Henry Rust's return.

"If indeed the wandering scoundrel has yet returned. At the airport, incidentally, when I called my office, Aaron Hatch had left a message saying he had asked that the hearing be put off until tomorrow. No telling what that means. But it does mean the case isn't closed yet. So—now, Ellen, do me one favor. Please."

Ellen reached up and took Horris's hand over her shoulder. She said, weakly, "Okay."

"Forgive me for shouting."

She squeezed his hand.

Suddenly Percy sighed at the controls. Then he tensed again, his thin face darting about, looking for—what? He was nursing the plane through a buffeting updraft.

Below them lay the green rolling countryside that was the approach to McClung's tiny airport.

Thursday there was nothing to do but wait. After she had gotten Emily off to her first full day's schedule at school, Ellen thought she would try to do it by catching up on her sleep. But it was useless. After half an hour she was up, sitting for a bit with Aunt Margaret, who was shelling peas, then going to her third floor workroom with the decrepit old briefcase of cracked leather, the bag full of materials she still had not glimpsed since packing them before the trip to New York and Vermont.

Now again, as she had many times, she felt a temptation to take down the clay head of Henry that looked crookedly out upon the room from its impalement on the wallhook. But it had long since taken on some of the sacred aspect of a talisman. To disturb it now might mean—what? She left it.

Downstairs she slumped down on the creaking leather arm of her Papa's chair and chatted for awhile. He greeted her solicitously and with a dawning look on his face.

"Oh, Dumpling, there's something I wanted to tell you," he said.

"What is it?" she said.

The creases of his long leathery face knitted for a moment before he spoke.

"Son of a bitch if I know," he said. "Ask Cliff. He'll remember."

Cliff was out back, mending the wire of the pen in which she saw the new beagles strewn all over the overturned body of Tina Beagle, whose liquid brown eyes rolled up in an attitude of heroic resignation and forebearance.

"That would have been about Gene Earley," Cliff said. "Aaron Hatch thought it wouldn't do any harm to show 'em a congressman down there, so—Well, when he asked Gene to make his presence felt, all he got was excuses, so he got Papa to call him."

"That means it's really bad, doesn't it?"

"Now, don't leap to that," Cliff said. "Anything like that's bad trouble if things don't go right. But don't you imagine when the congressman pays a call on them things will tend to go about as well as you can expect them?"

"Cliff, would Gene Earley do just anything Papa asked him?"

"Well—maybe there would be a limit. But I don't think Papa has ever carried him close to it."

"Well, will he just go down to St. Teresa's and fix the case? So to speak?"

"No, no, no, it won't work like that with this outfit. The law won't let him make direct representations before a federal body, and this hearing officer amounts to that. What Gene'll do is just drop in on the immigration and customs people *before* the hearing even begins. You know, just enough to see and be seen. He'll manage to remind them that he's on the subcommittee that happens to look after appropriations for their agency, and such as that. Then he'll go on his way. Then, later, when the hearing starts, there'll be Aaron Hatch, who's pretty impressive all by himself. Only today he took with him as an associate counsel Gene Earley's law partner."

"Does this mean it's all sewed up, you think?"

"No, frankly, I don't, but I don't want to make you worry any more than you are now. Now, I suspect it *would* be sewed up except for certain things—that you're aware of. Of course, it's because of that—this is why Aaron got Gene brought into it."

"Cliff, do you know something I don't?"

"Ellen, that may just be the case. Nobody's wanted to talk to you about all this, considering everything you've had on your mind. But I don't see why you can't face the facts as cool as me. They aren't fatal, anyhow. You see, this whole damn thing would be brushed off as a silly misunderstanding except for some of the things Henry's been up to the last few years. That is, as you know, he's been kind of close to a lot of people Washington just doesn't look kindly on at the moment.

"Now, I don't personally know any more about all that than you do, maybe not as much. But what's happened is that the government has gotten wind of some of these associations, and you know the temper of the times. Hell, that's why Gene Earley tried to dodge the thing when Aaron first asked him. And of course Henry's switch of citizenship, if he really legally switched, won't help him. And it's lousing this up, whether it was legal or not. Still, if the question were only one of illegal entry, well, they'd just almost routinely order him out. You know, no criminal charge at all, actually, but what if some of the flag-wrapped vipers in Washington or somewhere get the idea of making a case against Henry under some of these damn espionage laws. Sounds silly, doesn't it? Still, there's been some whispering about it at least. That's why Aaron asked for the postponement of the hearing in the first place."

Cliff began hammering a staple to fix another piece of wire, but stopped. He regarded her closely and said, "Ellen, you've been through a lot here lately. Don't you think you could sleep a little? Not a damn thing for you to do but wait it out, anyhow. It's most likely going to go all right."

"But as you just said, it might not. He could wind up in prison on some stupid—Cliff, don't you think people ought to be able to go anywhere on earth they want to without a damn passport?"

"Ellen, I've felt that all my life. Every time I used to get to a port and saw some gimlet-eyed official coming to ask to see my papers I'd feel like saying, go to hell, who I am is my damn business. And, of course, once or twice I forgot and said it. And wound up in trouble myself. But, Ellen, the vipers and sons of bitches are in charge of the world from America to Zanzibar."

"Does that include Gene Earley?"

"No, no, it doesn't. Gene's good of heart. He's merely venal, and what the hell's especially wrong with being venal in a country whose religion is venality? The only thing really wrong with it is that it destroys a man. All he really wants is more, so he never gets a chance to enjoy what he's got. But, no, Gene's not one of the vipers. They're the ones with the real power, you know. They're the ones who invented passports. They're so goddam gluttonous for power they don't want any of their subjects to leave without permission. Hell, Ellen, you know the vipers and sons of bitches. You've pointed a few out to me. They're the ones who keep you as a hostage but so want you to love them they wrap themselves in a flag you're supposed to love. And they're the ones you can't ever beat. You've got to outsmart 'em. The best way is to salute their goddam flags with an invisible thumb on your nose, and do your best to enjoy life. Now, that really gets 'em. Yes, as soon as the vipers in Washington or Koppalouka get wind of anybody really enjoying life they immediately sit down to dream up a law against it, and, of course, this is good business, too, because then they can hire all of their two-headed cousins and moronic uncles to enforce the new law. Those they can spare from checking passports."

Suddenly Ellen found that alongside Cliff's atrabilious view of the order of things her own scorn and bitterness toward the authors of Henry's difficulties seemed perhaps tame, possibly even bearable.

"Cliff," she said, "nobody ever called you a company man, did they?"

"Well, some of my men may have from time to time, but they were mistaken. I'll tell you this. The companies I worked for never called me a company man. I always said that if I ever ran across a company that had any goddam soul I might let it have a piece of mine. But until then, I said, all I had to sell was some seamanship. I tried to keep my ships afloat, but as for the companies, I have yet to see one that I could care whether it sinks or swims."

"Do you think there's a chance they'll actually order Henry out of the country?"

"Sure, they could. But, actually, Ellen, what if they did? Now you could go to him."

"But Emily's in school."

Cliff rapped the top of a fence post with his hammer as though calling court to order.

"Ellen, listen here. If you even thought of letting Emily's being in school keep you from getting back to this fellow, you sure better think again. Why, goddam, she's already smarter than most of her teachers are ever apt to be, and she would learn more in one week of seeing you with a man you love than she could learn if she went to school for the next sixty years." He rapped on the post again and began digging something out of a back tooth with his tongue. He said, "Case closed."

There had still been no word when from the front steps she heard a faint distant thud that said Emily had just hopped out of Florence's car. Soon she heard the crunch and scattering of pea-gravel in the drive, the sounds of steps that alternately and erratically ran, walked, skipped, left the gravel for the ground under the plumes of oleanders.

Then Emily was crossing the near yard at a weird spinning run. When she got to the steps she was reeling drunk, her pale blue eyes crazily grasping for focus. When she had sobered up four or five seconds later Ellen said, "How was it?"

Emily warped her own symmetry with an exaggerated one-shoulder shrug and scrootched her face and said, "Oh, I don't know. *Comme ci, comme ça.* Have you been sitting here all *day?*"

Ellen scrootched her face in mimicry and said, "Oh, now yes, now no."

Emily tossed a stack of books and tablets to the seat of a rocker on the porch and sat down on a step above and directly behind Ellen, straddling her waist with legs as lean and springy as ligaments, straddling and leaning her body against her mother's back as she let her chin fall forward onto Ellen's shoulder.

Thus they gossiped for awhile, and after that grew thoughtful, silently communicant until at a certain instant when Emily was asking, "Is summer over?" and Ellen was saying, "Well, summer's almost over," and they were saying these things at exactly the same instant—then they laughed. And Emily said, "RSVP," and Ellen said, "Maybe you mean ESP," and Emily said, "Maybe, why don't we go swimming while we still can?"

"Now why didn't I think of that?" Ellen said.

Emily tapped her finger two or three times against Ellen's temple and said, "No RSVP, that's why."

Barefooted and in their suits but with enormous yellow towels falling behind them like capes they walked across the grounds, Emily's dark hair now falling in a braid to her shoulders and Ellen's perhaps darker hair a great cloud of tousled curls.

"There's Mr. Ensley," Ellen said, pointing.

They looked up and saw him wigwagging the wings of his blue

and white plane as he habitually did when he flew over his house and thus necessarily theirs on his going and coming from frequent flights around the state to the mills and offices of the lumber company that was his legacy. Now he seemed almost to be directing the signal right to them, so they waved, and Emily turned her face up to the sky and with her hands cupped about her mouth she yelled:

"Hel-loooooo, Mis-terrrrrr Ens-leeeeeeeeee!"

"I know he heard you," Ellen said.

"Sure he did," Emily said, "didn't you hear him yell back? He said, 'Hel-loooooo, Em-i-leeeeeeeeee!' "

"Goose," Ellen said.

As they reached the trees, the grove, the tall old pines arising from ground that sloped gently down toward the big spring, they fell into a hastening pace, Ellen trotting, Emily hopping, skipping, the pace wordlessly growing faster as they approached the spring with its constantly flowing icy water giving off its illusion of stillness.

Both were sprinting as their feet touched the cedar plank jetty. Without pause, each dropped behind the towels that furled down into yellow crumples as they sailed to the water in flat racing dives. Without stroking they glided almost a quarter of the way across the surface. Then they flipped to their backs and stroked on across, veering and turning in the way they had done a thousand times. Back at the very center they treaded, dived, surfaced, dived, surfaced, talking in gasps and spewings of the clear cold water. Their voices eerily carried over into the adjacent pines and there mingled with the eternal squawking of the jays.

After awhile they began treading water with minimal motion, resting, breathing deeply and evenly.

"Let's do four minutes," Ellen said. "You feel like it?"

Underneath Ellen moved with slow measured motions, conserving, while Emily darted about like a minnow. Emily couldn't resist trying to touch the fish—cat, bream, perch, trout—and tended to lose breath in impulsively squirting bubbles at them.

Ellen waved to catch Emily's eyes. And a slight emission of bubbles escaped her own mouth as, in enormously exaggerated pantomime, she framed the words: *Take it easy.* Ellen saw Emily reaching her limit by the time her mysterious inner timer told her two and a half minutes had gone by. With an upward jerk of her thumb she commanded an ascent. They rose slowly through the icy encasement, through that soundless world wherein once again all terrestrial anguish and strain had seemed simply to seep or flow out of her.

They surfaced with enormous gaspings, as always. At the jetty

Ellen grasped Emily and hoisted her up and then scrambled herself onto the warm faintly fragrant planks. Lost in the sounds of their own breathing, they sprawled on their stomachs, Ellen resting her cheek on pillowing hands with her elbows extended like wings, Emily lying vertically with her arms somehow doubled and vanished beneath her chest and her chin resting on the incleft flesh right at the bend of her mother's elbow. They closed their eyes and could see as well as feel their racing pulses, could see the pulse in the darkening red/black glow underneath the lids. Above them the jays fussed, then stopped, giving them the ululant hum of the pines, and then fussed again.

Even the oblique sun of the ending summer felt very good, as did the warm planks underneath them. Ellen realized she had dozed away, perhaps fallen into a deep sleep, when she heard a sudden excited whisper.

"Mama! Look!"

At first she saw Emily's face. It was not alarmed, but agape, fascinated, wide-eyed now. And its narrow cleft chin was dropping, its eyes leaping far off somewhere above Ellen's ear, fixing on something behind her head. Not in haste, somehow not yet knowing, not in this instant of all instants quite expectant, Ellen raised and then turned her head.

At first she saw nothing, because at that instant they had passed behind some of the pines.

Then she saw them.

They were walking toward them through the trees, walking down the gradually sloping ground, walking not in haste but not slowly either. She saw their forms, their figures, before she saw their features. In silhouette she saw the dishevelment of hair on each head.

Henry was walking with that easy swinging but leashed grace that she had seen a million times and imagined ten million, coming on now, and the boy, Henri, was at his side but almost falling behind, and now skipping a step to catch up, coming closer, coming on as for some reason the cedar planking beneath her began losing its substance, turning not fluid but simply plastic or tilty and uncertain so that she wondered if it could support her weight if she tried to get up, or whether it might capsize like a boat.

They were coming out of the trees now and onto the treeless bank. And both of them had on those easy smiles as though, for God's sake, they had just dropped by for a chat the way they might have done every Thursday about this time for the last ten or twelve thousand years.

She glanced at Emily and saw that she was grinning and holding up a mute hand of greeting and somehow managing to get a footing on the quaking evaporating cedar planks of the jetty.

Only even Emily was not risking standing but was just hunkering there, and grinning, and, oh, for God's sake, he was right there, they were right there, and why did her heart have to start beating behind her eyes like that just when the jetty was collapsing. And was he going to stand there like that forever just searching her eyes and face with his, with those blue rays that were already spearing into her and gathering her up like some eerie vapor? Yes, it was not the jetty that was dissolving, she was dissolving, already had dissolved, and—

"Mama, aren't you going to get up?"

So she did, somehow, and even tried to speak, thought of saying something, only now it was not only beating behind her eyes and making them hot, it was filling up her throat, and it was going to suffocate her if it didn't stop. But she knew that her mouth had moved, even if it had not said anything, and he would just have to understand that she had tried to say something, had wanted to say something, had said something, in fact, only it couldn't be heard.

And, anyway, why didn't he say something? Was he just going to stand there for another million years with his damned eyes racing all over her face and making his mouth quiver like that, making hers quiver, too? Why didn't he smile the way she was smiling, could he see she was smiling even if her mouth wouldn't do it, even if her lips kept flying back between her teeth? Was he just going to stand there forever with his stupid hands in his hip pockets while she was trying to reach out to him, at least trying, even if she couldn't make the damned arms do anything, was he?

The damn arms now like the damn throat and the damn mouth and the damn eyes, pounding and about to shake apart with the damn beating that was running up and down her like a tornado from feet to head and back. So maybe, yes, they would just stand this way forever, five or six feet apart, and let the jaybirds do all the talking, or maybe just leave it to the children, because at least Emily said something, and Henri at least said:

"I'm Henri."

But, no, he would have to stand there smiling and letting it vanish, the smile, into all those quivering little muscles, and then smiling again, recovering again and again, maybe just so she could see how controlled it was, his damned weathered face with all the damn hard sculpted little creases that he could make come back and then go away.

"Henri, this is my mama," Emily was saying.

"I know, this is my papa," Henri was saying.

"Mama says they're old friends," Emily was saying.

"Papa told me," Henri was saying.

"Do old friends always do this?" Emily was saying.

"Je ne sais pas," Henri was saying.

"Sometimes people just can't think of anything to say," Emily was saying.

"Papa sometimes goes for a long time without talking at all," Henri was saying.

"Wouldn't you think they would at least say hello?" Emily was saying.

"I would think so, but to each his own," Henri was saying.

"Are you going to visit us for supper?" Emily was saying.

"I don't know what the plan is, if there is a plan," Henri was saying.

"Are you staying with the Ensleys again?"

"We went there, but I don't know how long. Mr. Ensley flew us back here in his plane."

"Oh, you were in the plane when it went over?"

"Oui."

"Did you hear me yell?"

"Mr. Ensley said he could hear you yelling, but I did not hear. I don't know how he heard you. He called out your name. Em-i-leeeeeeee."

"Mama, I told you, I told you. Mama? Henri, can you get your Papa to talk to you?"

"I don't know. I will try. Papa? Papa?"

"Well, Henri, will you be here for a long time now?"

"No, no, I do not know how long but only a short time. The authority said we must leave the country."

"Forever?"

"No, I do not understand it. Papa told me it was what is called a compromise. We must leave, but we will be permitted to come back if we apply in the usual way."

"Will you take the boat?"

"Oh, yes. We must take the boat. Papa said that we must report outbound at the immigration checkpoint within forty-eight hours from midnight."

"Oh, you won't be here but a little. Mama? Mama?"

"There is nothing we can do if they do not wish to talk," Henri said.

"Henri, would you like to see our beagles? We have some new beagles."

"Papa, may I go see the beagles? Well, I guess it is all right. He does not say no."

Now Ellen was sure she saw him nod, and then thought she nodded herself when Emily asked that they be excused. And then she saw them scampering up the slope through the trees. And then his eyes were still racing from one of hers to the other, to her hair, her ears, her cheeks, her neck, back to her eyes.

And now the pounding had become almost a singular thing. Suddenly she was shaken by a tremulous chill, and then she saw him move, oh God, he was falling, no, bending, he was reaching down and now he came up with the enormous yellow towel, and he was putting it about her shoulders, and how did he manage to do that without actually touching her? Now he was back there right in front of her and her hands were going, yes, going up to clutch the upper corners of the towel to pull it about her, but he seemed so close there now she could see the cells of the eyes into which, yes, she was being poured, was disappearing, and—

Then it happened like the flight of lightning between sky and earth.

They were one.

Without words.

Needing none.

After a time that seemed both an eternity and a tick he withdrew his face from the nest of her hair. And looked again long and searchingly into her face as though examining some astonishing curiosity. And now smiled, without quivering, smiled. And was actually making a sound, was actually saying something.

"Goddam," he said, "I think I love you."

"Dumpling," her Papa had said at a moment when Emily had briefly vanished from where they were packing, "didn't I tell you there was no need to worry? Didn't I tell you that boy wasn't stupid enough to forsake you?"

And then at the tie-up her Papa had opened his arms so that Emily could leap up into them again, and had looked into the child's face and said, "Now, Ellen, dammit, you take care of yourself." And Emily had said, "Papa, I'm not Ellen, I'm Emily." And he had said, "Well, what's the difference, Dumpling?"

Then he had hugged Ellen, and got to coughing, and then overcome it, and after that had taken her face between his big bony hands and said, "Now, dammit, Charlotte, don't you forget to write. And remember I love you." So for a moment she had become his first-born again. This time she merely enjoyed his lapse, feeling not alone at all, and hugged him once again, after which he looked at her closely and said, "Son of a bitch, you're not Charlotte, you're Ellen." And Ellen said, "Well, what's the difference, Papa?" And Emily from below them said, "Well, I'm Emily." To which her Papa gruffly rejoined, "Nonsense, you're Ellen, and I know it."

Now from the tie-up he was waving his big stick like a triumphant sword at the command of all the others who were waving and calling out: Cliff and Aunt Margaret and Mrs. Pichon, who would wave and then cover her mouth and titter, and then wave again. And Horris, tugging at the eternally soggy rim of his collarless shirt and chopping the air with his other hand, while Claudette, slouching with her elbow propped on Horris's shoulder, kept making a slow lanquid circle in the air and smiling a special secret woman smile at Ellen. *"Cheri,"* she had whispered, "if you will only take me aboard while Horris is not looking—and you will find that the menage is not so bad when there is someone who knows how to cook." And there were Florence and her children, and their father, Percy, who had seen to it that a few iced bottles of champagne were on hand for a *bon voyage* only hours in the planning and preparation.

Emily stood just in front of her, waving and shouting, too, and Henri was alternately stowing the lines and popping his head up at the little crowd. Percy aimed another champagne bottle toward them, and they could see the spewing fizzle and the flying cork but couldn't hear the pop over the sputtering engines. Henry addressed himself intently to bringing the boat about and into the main channel, and only then, only when he was on course, running the exact line he sought, only then, and not before he had pushed the throttle hard and sent the not pretty but sound old fishing boat surging along with the current, then he looked back, briefly. He examined them all with a single steady glance, and raised his arm, and smiled, and then turned away, and looked back no more.

Henri joined him at the wheel, but Ellen and Emily watched and waved until they had swung around the next bend and the tie-up could be seen no more, only the muddy swirling wake of the boat in the ancient Bulomkubee.

"Mama!" Emily suddenly said. She bent her head backwards and peered upside down upward across Ellen's breasts to her now downturned face. "I completely forgot! What about *school?*"

"Well," Ellen said, with a satirical smile, "maybe we'll send them a postcard."